Praise for Sharon Sala

"Sharon Sala is a consummate storyteller. Her skills shine in her Blessings, Georgia series. If you can stop reading then you're a better woman than me."
—Debbie Macomber, #1 *New York Times* bestselling author

"Sharon Sala's Blessings, Georgia series is filled with unforgettable charm and delight!"
—Robyn Carr, #1 *New York Times* bestselling author

"I love returning to Blessings... If you enjoy pure romance, wonderful characters, great couples, and a small-town atmosphere, then you should be reading this series."
—*The Reading Café*

"[Sala's] Blessings, Georgia series is full of heartfelt emotions and laughter."
—*Fresh Fiction*

"With plenty of danger and passion, Sala will have readers flipping the pages to see if these two will finally get to be together."
—*RT Book Reviews* for *The Color of Love*

"A strong and positive second-chance romance that fans of Robyn Carr and Susan Wiggs will enjoy."
—*Booklist* for *Come Back to Me*

"For those who like gently-paced, touching small-town romance... This town and its people welcome me with true Southern hospitality."
—*Delighted Reader* for *Saving Jake*

"Sala's fans will enjoy returning to a picture-perfect Southern town with wholesome American values."

—*Kirkus Reviews* for *A Piece of My Heart*

Also by Sharon Sala

The Christmas Wish

SHARON SALA

sourcebooks
casablanca

Published by Sourcebooks Casablanca, an imprint of Sourcebooks
P.O. Box 4410, Naperville, Illinois 60567-4410
(630) 961-3900
sourcebooks.com

Printed and bound in the United States of America.
OPM 10 9 8 7 6 5 4 3 2 1

PROLOGUE

From the day Wade Montgomery bought the house Bridgette Knox grew up in, he had dreams of one day bringing her back to it as his wife. But over time, it was beginning to dawn on him that her dreams and his dreams did not coincide.

Wade had never considered himself a player, but he'd never thought of himself as a loser, either. And yet in the past six months, Bridgette had laid waste to his ego, his hopes of ever having a relationship with her, and his decision to come back to Blessings. If he had not promised his uncle Dub to manage Truesdale's Feed and Seed store, he might have already thrown up his hands and called it quits.

─────────

On this morning, he'd just finished shaving and paused to look at himself in the mirror. His aunt Nola called him a dark-haired version of Thor. He knew she was referring to some Australian actor named Hemsworth, but Wade didn't see it. He just saw himself. A guy with blue eyes and a dimple in one cheek. Still, he wondered what it was about him that turned Bridgette Knox into an ice princess. He'd gotten the cold shoulder from her so many times he was beginning to get a complex. He just considered himself a normal single guy in a small southern town, trying to get the attention of the only girl he cared about, and he wasn't so sure she would throw water on him if he was on fire.

Bridgette—sweet Bridgette—had become his waterloo. She had an excuse every time he asked her out, so he quit asking.

He was trying to come to terms with the fact that maybe it was because he just wasn't her type. She was the biggest failure of his adult life, and it was killing him.

He left home in a mood, and it stayed with him all the way to the feed store. When he saw her car parked in her usual place, his gut knotted, but there was still a tiny seed of hope that had yet to die.

Maybe today is the day she sees me.

Bridgette Knox, a.k.a. Birdie to the people who knew her longest, had a dilemma.

She had a major crush on her boss, but it was complicated. They'd grown up together, but then he'd moved away when they were still in high school, only to show back up in Blessings six months ago to manage the feed and seed store where she worked.

She'd been the bookkeeper there since graduating from high school. She loved her job, and she would always have a soft spot for Dub Truesdale for hiring a nervous teenager with a head for numbers and a glowing letter of recommendation from her business teacher.

But Dub's retirement took them all by surprise, and the guy who haunted Bridgette's dreams, and made her heart flutter just from a simple look, was now her boss.

It made everything weird.

Sometimes she thought Wade felt the same way about her, because he seemed so friendly, and then she'd talk herself out of it because he was friendly to everyone.

So she admired him from afar and kept her feelings locked up tight. The only man she'd been attracted to in years was now the man she answered to at work, and the dilemma remained.

Bridgette was feeling sorry for herself this morning as she pulled up into her parking spot at work. Her steps were dragging as she went in the side door and into her office. She stowed her things and went up front to say hello to the crew and see what, if anything, was new on the day's docket.

It didn't take long for her to get caught up in the customers coming and going, and fending off the teasing she got from being the only female employee on the place.

She was leaning on the counter, listening to one of the old farmers relating a story about his wife and a mean rooster and, like everyone there, waiting to see how the story ended.

"She didn't put up with all that spurrin' and floggin' long," the old man said. "She went after him like a heat-seeking missile, wrung his dang neck, and *bam!* Chicken and dumplings for Sunday dinner."

Bridgette was still laughing when she saw Wade walk in the store.

Wade came in with car keys in one hand and his coffee in the other. The first person he saw was Bridgette. She was standing behind the counter among a half-dozen men, her black wavy hair framing that pretty heart-shaped face, and something inside of him snapped.

"Bridgette, when you are finished with what you're doing, please come to my office," he announced, and moved past her with long, steady strides.

She blinked, said her goodbyes to the customer, and headed down the hall, wondering what was wrong.

The door was open.

She walked in.

"Close the door, please," he said.

Bridgette's heart skipped a beat as she pushed it shut.

"What's wrong?" she asked.

"I don't know!" Wade said. "You tell me!"

She was stunned. Wade was never mad at her.

"I don't understand what you're getting at," she said.

Wade dropped down in the chair behind his desk and then looked up at her.

"Neither do I. You're friendly and funny and engaging with every person in Blessings except me. Are you mad because I bought the house where you grew up, or do you just dislike me? I really need to know."

Bridgette was in shock. "Of course I don't dislike anything about you. I am not mad, and no, I do not hate you. That's ridiculous."

Wade shoved his hands through his hair in frustration.

"Then, do you just want me to quit asking you out? To just leave you alone? I need to know so I can turn loose of this dream I had, or find out what the hell is wrong and fix it."

Birdie was shaking inside. She had to ask, but was afraid to hope.

"What dream?"

Wade stood. This was where it could get messy. "The one where you and I go on dates, and fall in love, and live happy ever after."

Birdie gasped. "I had no idea... You never said..."

Wade threw up his hands in disbelief. "Bullshit, Bridgette. How many times have you rejected my invitations?"

There was a lump in her throat and a knot in her stomach that kept twisting tighter and tighter.

"I thought that was you just being friendly. I didn't want to get hurt...and you're my boss. I never... It didn't seem right to..."

His voice softened, and then he sighed. "Well, I was being friendly because that's how relationships start. And Dub is still everyone's boss here. I'm just the nephew who agreed to be manager. Did working for me put me out of the running? Because if that's all that's holding you back, I'll quit my job."

Her eyes welled.

"I don't know what I'm supposed to say. No, I don't want you to quit. Am I fired?"

"Oh, for the love of God! No, you're not fired. What kind of a monster do you think I am? If you don't want anything to do with me personally, then I get it. But six months of giving you time to grieve the loss of your mother, and the loss of your family home, is all I've got. Your job is fine. I'm fine. You're fine. I guess all I need to know is…am I wasting my time dreaming about you and me ever having a future together?"

Bridgette's hands were wadded into fists and clutched against her stomach. She knew her voice was going to shake. This was like something out of a fairy tale where the prince with the glass slipper finally found the princess it fit.

"No, you're not wasting your time."

Wade sighed, then ended the distance between them when he hugged her.

"Dammit, Bridgette. I did not mean to make you cry. I adore you. I always have…pretty much since first grade. What do I need to do to make it right with you?"

She looked up. "Kiss me?"

So he did.

———————

Two weeks later, they were sitting in Granny's Country Kitchen, waiting for the waitress to bring them their ticket for the meal they'd just eaten. What had taken six months to begin between them had gone into full bloom in two weeks, and it showed.

People in Blessings were starting to talk about Wade and Birdie— Birdie and Wade, but Peanut and Ruby Butterman were the first to ask, when they stopped at their table to say hello.

"Hey! I'm sure seeing a lot of you two together these days. Is there something going on here that I don't know about?" Ruby asked.

Wade grinned. "Now, Ruby…you always know what's going on in Blessings before it happens."

Ruby shrugged. "It's not my fault. Sitting in a chair at a hair salon is almost the same as being in a confessional, but you haven't confessed a thing, and I'm asking… *Are* you two—"

"Girl, let them be," Peanut said, and tried to steer Ruby toward the exit.

"Oh, it's okay," Bridgette said. "We *are* doing our best to become 'something,' but not before Wade dared me to stop pretending I didn't know he existed."

"I was getting desperate," Wade said.

Peanut glanced at his wife, remembering their own journey and the struggle it took to get where they were today.

"I know the feeling. I've been there. And now that Ruby has satisfied her curiosity, we're getting out of your hair," Peanut said.

Ruby winked, and then they were gone.

Wade eyed the rosy flush on Bridgette's cheeks.

"So we're working on something, are we?"

"That's how I see it," Bridgette said.

"Then what else can I do to make that something become our thing?" he asked.

"Make love to me."

Wade felt like he'd been punched in the gut. He pulled a handful of bills out of his pocket, tossed them down onto the table, and got up.

Bridgette grasped his hand, holding on tight as he pulled her through the dining room and out into the night.

"My place or yours?" he asked, as Bridgette reached for her seatbelt.

"Mine is closer," she said.

Wade drove out of the parking lot and headed across town. He'd been dreaming of this for so long he had the scenario down pat, and then Bridgette up and knocked him off his feet.

When he pulled up into the parking lot at the Cherrystone Apartments, he was seriously glad hers was on the first floor, because his legs were shaking too much to climb stairs.

She got out of the car holding the key and, with his hand on her back, unlocked the door into the foyer.

A long hallway ran the lower length of the building, and a set of stairs beside it led to the second floor. Her apartment was the last one on the left at the end of the hall.

Wade glanced down at her as they walked, marveling at the calm on her face. He felt like a lit fuse.

Once inside her place, they abandoned their coats on the sofa and moved toward her bedroom. It was the calmest approach to coming undone that Wade had ever experienced, and it felt right.

But once inside, the bed might as well have had flashing red lights, because it was the only thing he saw—until Bridgette began taking off her clothes, and then all he could see was the beautiful woman who'd stolen his heart.

He stripped as she turned back the bed, and then they were lying on their sides, face-to-face. He slid his hand over her belly, up across the mounds of her breasts to the curve of her cheek, then leaned over and kissed her.

"I don't have words for how much I love you," he said.

Bridgette sighed. "Then show me. I ache from the want of you. Make love to me, Wade."

And so he did, tracing the shape of her with his hands, and then his lips, finding the places on her body that made her breath catch and feeling the rapid rising of her pulse beneath his fingertips. And then, with all the grace and restraint he could muster, sliding inside her as she wrapped her legs around his waist—keeping time with the rise and fall of her body as she met him thrust for thrust, until all of their restraint was gone.

Wade went deeper, faster, winding her up so tight she finally broke, leaving him one step behind as he shattered within her embrace.

The next level of "them" had just happened, and it was perfect.

CHAPTER 1

Six months later
Jacksonville, Florida

SIXTEEN-YEAR-OLD DUFF MARTIN WAS MISSING, AND HIS OLDER brother, Allen, and his mother, Candi, were in a panic. His bed hadn't been slept in, Allen's car was gone, and it appeared some of Duff's clothes might be missing.

Candi was hysterical.

"Oh my God! What happened? Is this because of last night? We have to call the police!"

"And tell them what, Mom? He took my car and ran away? So do you want him reported as a car thief? Dad's already in prison. We don't need to send Duff down that road, too," Allen said.

Candi sat down on Duff's bed, her shoulders slumped, tears running down her face.

"It's all my fault. Last night, when we began talking about your daddy going to prison, Duff freaked out. I still don't know what I said that set him off."

"He was just six when Dad was sentenced. How much of all that did you ever tell him?" Allen asked.

Candi shrugged and wiped her face. "At the time? Not much. He was too little to understand. And then over the years, he never asked for details. He just knew it was for theft."

Allen sat down beside her and gave her a quick hug. "What exactly were you saying right before he blew up? Do you remember?"

Candi sighed. "Lord...I don't know. I mentioned seeing Selma Garrett's obituary, and he asked who she was, and I think I said... she was the woman who accused Zack of stealing her jewelry.

And then Duff got this funny look on his face and asked, 'What jewelry?'"

"Oh yeah," Allen said. "And I added they were family heirlooms, valued at over a quarter of a million dollars, that went missing while Dad was painting at her house."

Candi nodded. "Something about that set Duff off. When he jumped up from the table all pale and shaking, then started hitting himself on the head and crying, I knew something was wrong. I should have talked to him last night, but he wouldn't let me in. And now this!"

"But why would that have upset him? After all this time? And what about all that would have made him run away?" Allen asked.

"I don't know, but he's gone, and I'm scared of what might happen to him," Candi said.

"Does he have access to money?"

Candi gasped. "His college fund!"

"Quick, Mom…check his bank account," Allen said.

Candi pulled up their joint account, checked it, and groaned.

"There's a thousand dollars missing."

Allen nodded. "Okay, then he's not about to go robbing some Quick Stop for money. Call him to see if he answers."

"Yes, yes," Candi said, and quickly sent Duff a text.

Allen gave her a hug. "Okay. We've reached out. Now we need to wait and see if he responds. The bottom line here is that he's sixteen, so he's a minor. He wasn't abducted, so the cops will call him a runaway. And the only way the police will get involved is if we press charges for him taking the car, and I'm not going to do that. Something is going on with Duff. He's a good kid, and I'm not going to fly off the handle here and make a bad thing worse."

"You're right," Candi said, and then broke into tears again. "But he's just a kid, and we just put up the Christmas tree, and now he's gone."

"So pray, Mama. Pray for a miracle that we get him home."

Duff Martin didn't run away from home, but he was on a mission. Something his mother said last night had triggered a long-forgotten memory. All he could think afterward was *what if it was my fault?* And the only way he could know for sure was to go back to the place where it all began.

So he packed up a bag and headed north, driving out of Florida into Georgia, going back to Blessings, the little Georgia town where he'd spent the first six years of his life. He didn't tell anyone where he was going, because in his sixteen-year-old mind, this was his problem to solve.

He'd snuck out of the house just after 2:00 a.m., arrived in Blessings about 5:00 a.m., and immediately got a room at the only motel. It wasn't the cleanest, but he didn't have money to waste on the nicer bed-and-breakfast he'd seen online, and this place was a roof over his head.

He stretched out on the bed, so tired he ached, but this wasn't the time to sleep. Now that he was here, he was uncertain where to start. He had memories, but they were vague, and he wasn't sure how much of them was real.

He couldn't remember the house they'd lived in.

He couldn't remember the name of the lady his dad had been working for. He'd heard his mother say it, but he was so freaked out about the rest of the story that it didn't soak in. The only things he could remember for sure were being in first grade at the elementary school and the lady who babysat him after school. Miss Margie. He'd called her Miss Margie.

His first instinct was to start driving the streets of Blessings and see what rang true. He wasn't on a schedule, but as soon as the town began opening up, he took off down Main, oblivious to the holiday atmosphere and decorations, and started his first loop through the residential areas, looking for houses and faces he might remember.

When his phone signaled a text, and he saw who it was from, he sighed.

They knew he was gone.

―――――――――

Even without snow, Christmas spirit was alive and well in Blessings. The little town was in full-on holiday mode.

Decorations were hanging from every streetlight on Main.

There was an ongoing storefront-decorating contest and a trophy to be won for the business that had the best Christmas theme, and the upcoming Christmas parade on Saturday with more trophies to win.

Because snow in this part of Georgia was almost always a no-show, Crown Grocers had brought in its own brand of snow by setting up a snow-cone stand at the north corner of the parking lot, next to the roped-off area where they were selling Christmas trees.

Bridgette could feel the magic of the season all the way to her bones as she drove down Main on the way to work.

In the months since she and Wade had become a couple, the only awkward moment between them had been walking back into the home she'd grown up in and accepting it belonged to him now.

Then as it turned out, it wasn't as hard as she had feared. Her brother Hunt had updated and remodeled it to such a degree before the sale that she soon forgot the old house and saw only the one it was today—the one that belonged to Wade. And the first time they made love in that house, in his bed, memories of the old house were no longer visible to her there.

Making love to Wade was passion at its best, but it was feeling cherished that had put the sparkle in her eyes and the bounce in her step. When she thought about how close she'd come to messing it up, she shuddered. He was now, and would forever be, the best thing to ever happen in her life.

She braked at the stoplight, and while she was waiting for it to turn green, it gave her a few moments to check out the decorations going up in the storefronts. They weren't quite on the level of Bloomingdale's or Saks Fifth Avenue in New York City, but they were Blessings's best, and she couldn't wait to see the finished displays.

The day started out cool—right at fifty degrees, but with a promise to warm up to the mid-eighties around noon—and she had a busy day ahead of her with end-of-month reports.

December marked the beginning of a busy season at the feed store, including the new gift section Wade had created a few months ago. Among the items available for sale there were little packs of dog and cat toys, halters and spurs for the locals who fancied themselves cowboys, and colorful bandannas, along with a whole series of country-style Christmas ornaments, and Made in Georgia specialties like peach jams and jellies.

Bridgette had always enjoyed working here, but the fire that gutted the warehouse last year, resulting in the death of a long-time employee, had taken the heart out of all of them. Then Wade came on as manager and changed the vibe to such a degree that the store barely resembled what it had been.

The stoplight turned green, and she drove through the intersection. Once she reached the feed store, she parked and hurried inside out of the cold.

———————

Wade was on his way to the Crown to pick up an order of Christmas cookies for the break room, but he was thinking about Bridgette.

They'd spent the weekend together at his house. The house where she'd grown up was now the place where they played house. Cooking together. Watching movies together. Making love in his bed, and on the living room sofa, and in the shower, and wherever else they were when the notion struck. But she'd gone home after Sunday dinner to do the chores needed at her own place, and waking up alone this morning made her absence even more pronounced.

He was looking forward to work, knowing he'd be spending the day with her, as he pulled into the Crown parking lot. Then he saw Bridgette's brother Junior on the far side of the parking lot and waved as he got out. Junior saw him and smiled, then returned to unloading and setting up the new shipment of Christmas trees.

Once inside the store, Wade headed straight to the bakery.

"Hey, Sue. I have an order of Christmas cookies to pick up."

"Morning, Wade. I just boxed them up," she said and went to get them. He took them up front to pay before heading on to the store.

Bridgette's car was already in her usual parking spot when he arrived. He parked and hurried into the store with the cookies, greeting customers and workers alike as he went down the hall to the office area, then paused outside her office, peering at her through the wreath dangling over the window of her door. She was laser-focused on the computer screen, her fingers flying across the keyboard.

He knocked and walked in.

"Hey, sweetheart! I missed you this morning," he said, and then stole a quick kiss.

Bridgette cupped the side of his face.

"I missed you, too."

"I brought cookies for the break room, but you get first dibs. Take out all you want now, because they won't last long."

"Ooh, yum," she said as he opened the box. "I love iced sugar cookies."

"There are some gingerbread men on the bottom. Dig through and get what you want," he added.

"I'll get some out for you, too," Bridgette said, then grabbed a handful of napkins, laid out a sugar cookie and a gingerbread man for herself, and then two each for him. "There, you can take the rest to the break room. I'll put yours in your office."

A couple of hours later, her sugar cookie was gone and the

gingerbread man stashed in her desk. She was almost through with the monthly reports when she realized the total between receipts and deposits was off. There was data in the computer showing sales, but the total of monthly deposits didn't balance out, so she went back over her input again, then pulled up the readouts from the front register until she found the exact amount she was off. The transaction was there, but that day's money deposit was short $532.50—the exact amount of a receipt she had for a feed purchase.

Her heart sank.

Either someone pocketed the money, or gave away the feed and hoped no one would catch it. In all the years she'd worked here, this had only happened a couple of times, and both times it had been theft.

Once a clerk pocketed the money, and the other time, a man working in the warehouse did his buddy a favor, loaded up feed, wrote out a ticket for it to balance out the inventory count, and hoped no one would catch the money missing.

She read the transaction again and saw the register code. It belonged to Donny Corrigan. But that didn't always mean he was the one who'd rung it up. If he'd stepped away from the register to help someone else, any employee could have used it to check a customer out, without keying in their own code. It would be an easy way to take money with no expectation of getting caught.

The next thing Bridgette did was check the time cards to see where Donny was that day, and if he was in the store at that time. She found where he'd clocked in, and then three hours later had clocked out and hadn't come back that whole day.

She frowned, trying to remember why, and then she realized that was the day Donny's wife went into labor with their first baby. He had clocked out, but in his panic, it appeared he had not counted out his till, which left his code in the register, which now made everyone else in the store a possible suspect.

She picked up her phone and called Wade.

CHAPTER 2

WADE WAS ON THE LOADING DOCK, TALKING TO A CUSTOMER WHO was waiting for his order, when the call came. When he saw it was Bridgette, he frowned. She never called him like this. She usually came looking for him.

"Excuse me. I need to take this. Good to see you again," he said, and was already talking as he walked away. "Hey, honey, what's up?"

"Can you come to my office?"

"On the way," he said, and hastened his step. The moment he walked in and saw the look on her face, he knew it wasn't going to be good. "What's wrong?"

So she began laying out what she'd found and how she'd found it—explaining Donny's absence during the time of the theft, and that it appeared someone had stolen over five hundred dollars from the till while Donny's employee code was active.

"Well, shit, Bridgette. Does this kind of thing happen often?"

She sighed. "Two times in all the years I've been here, but I had a thought. You put up security cameras when the gift shop area went up. Are any of them pointing toward the front register? And if so, how long do we keep footage?"

Wade jumped up and ran back into the store and eyed the cameras again to remind himself. The one over the front door was aimed straight at checkout. He ran back to her office.

"Good call. Bring your notes and come with me."

Bridgette stood, grabbed her pad and pen, and followed him. He was in his office, standing at the little alcove where the security system was set up.

"So, what was the day of the theft?" he asked.

"It was last Thursday," she said.

Wade checked the calendar, then pulled up the stored files and searched for the date.

"And what time was it when Donny clocked out?" Wade asked.

"11:35 a.m.," Bridgette said.

Wade began fast-forwarding. "Okay, got it! Here he is taking the call. You can see the excitement on his face. Then there you are walking into the store area."

"Yes, he's telling me he needs to go. I wave him on, and that's Josh who comes to stand in for him. Donny clocked out, but he didn't check himself out at the register," Bridgette said. "Now we need to go to 2:17 p.m. That's the time stamp on the receipt that correlates with the exact amount of money missing."

Wade nodded and fast-forwarded again until 2:14. Then they began to watch.

"That's Duke Talbot," Bridgette said, pointing to the customer who came in through the hall from the warehouse. "He's the listed buyer."

Wade points at the footage. "He walks up to the register and hands Josh a credit card. Josh scans it. Duke signs the receipt, gets his copy, and then he's gone. So he didn't pay in cash."

"Wait!" Bridgette said. "Look. Josh just lifted up the cash drawer."

"Son of a bitch," Wade muttered. "He's taking out the bigger bills beneath it. Likely for the same amount. Can you tell if that was a bank debit card or a card from a credit company?"

Bridgette ran back to her computer, did some quick checking, and then came back.

"It was a debit card. That amount showed up the next day in our bank account, so it would not have gone through the store's daily take that day, but it showed up in our account the next day. And it would have all balanced out at the end of the month, if Josh hadn't taken cash from our daily receipts."

Wade was pissed. "My first instinct is to call Josh in and fire his ass. But I'm going to call Uncle Dub first, because he's still the big boss around here. We'll keep this between us for now and wait for Dub to show."

Bridgette started to walk away when Wade stopped her.

"Good job, sweetheart. Good job!"

Bridgette sighed. "I feel bad Josh did this, and right here at Christmas. What's this going to do to his family?"

"He should have thought of that before he stole something that didn't belong to him," Wade said. "Don't feel guilty for someone else's sin."

Bridgette nodded. "You're right. I was just doing my job, and caught him failing at his."

"Yes, ma'am, you sure did. It's almost time for lunch. You take an early one. By the time you get back, this will all be over with."

"Josh is still going to know it was me that found it, because I'm the one who balances the books," Bridgette said.

Wade frowned. "If he didn't want to get caught, he should have paid it back, or packed up and run. Go to lunch."

"I'm going to Granny's. Want me to bring something back for you?" she asked.

"That would be awesome. If it's on the menu today, a chopped brisket sandwich and fries. If not, a burger and fries."

Then he pulled a couple of twenties out of his wallet.

"Lunch is on me today. Leave now and you'll have an hour and a half for lunch, and you have more than earned it."

Bridgette put the money in her pocket. "Thanks for lunch, but I'm sorry you're going to have to do this."

He grimaced. "That's why I get paid the big bucks."

Bridgette went back to her office long enough to save the reports and print out copies, then logged out of her computer, grabbed her coat and purse, and left through the side door.

Wade was in the office, already calling Dub. The phone rang a couple of times, and then his uncle answered.

"Hello."

"Uncle Dub, it's me. We have a problem at the store, and I wanted to talk to you before I acted on it."

"What's wrong?" Dub asked.

"Josh King stole over five hundred dollars out of the till. Bridgette caught the discrepancy when she was doing the end-of-month reports, and we checked security footage and caught him in the act."

"Josh? Son of a gun! I would not have believed he would do something like that."

"If it wasn't for Bridgette checking details, it would have fallen on Donny Corrigan's shoulders. He was logged into the register when he got the call that his wife had gone into labor last week. He clocked himself out, but he forgot to log out on the register, and Josh stepped up and began checking people out without changing the code. I guess he thought we wouldn't know who'd done it, since it was Donny's code but he was gone. Josh obviously forgot about the security cameras. They haven't been up that long. Look, I have no problem firing him, but I want to know if you want me to press charges or—"

"I'm coming down to the store. We'll be doing this together. And I'll decide on the way about having him arrested. Are you okay with me stepping in on this when you're in charge?" Dub asked.

Wade didn't hesitate. "You're still the boss, Uncle Dub. You're the owner. I am your manager, and your decisions will always be the ones I go by."

"Good enough. I'll be there in about ten minutes. What I want you to do is call Josh to your office and then wait there with him. I don't want him taking off for lunch. Don't let on you know. Just tell him I need to talk to him," Dub said.

"Yes, sir," Wade said. "I'll page him right now. See you in a few."

―――――――――

Josh King was in the warehouse loading chicken feed for a customer and wishing he'd worn a lighter-weight shirt. He was already getting too warm and was planning to change shirts when he went home for lunch.

"Okay, buddy," Josh said as he loaded the last sack into the back of the pickup. "There's your twenty bags. Sign here."

The man signed his name, took the customer copy, and got in his truck and drove away.

Josh stepped inside the warehouse office, laid the store copy in a tray on the desk, and was going to wash his hands when the pager squawked, and then he heard Wade's voice.

"Josh King to the main office, please."

Josh's heart skipped a beat, and then he told himself it didn't have to mean anything and walked through the main store and down the hall to the office area with his chin up and a strut in his step. The door was open. He paused on the threshold.

"Hey, Wade, what's up?" he asked.

Wade glanced up. "Come in and shut the door."

A chill washed through Josh, but he didn't let on. Instead, he shut the door and walked to the desk.

Wade pointed at a chair on the other side of his desk.

"Sit."

Josh sat, but he was still playing dumb.

"What's going on, Boss?"

"Dub wants to talk to you. He's on the way."

Josh looked straight at Wade. "About what?"

Wade said nothing and stared him down.

At that point, Josh began to panic. *Shit. Shit. Shit. Say nothing. Play it cool. Donny's employee code is all over the sales. They can't prove a damn thing.*

The next five minutes were the longest five minutes of Josh's life. By the time Dub walked into the office, he was sweating.

"Dammit, Dub. What the hell are y'all playing at?" Josh asked.

Wade stood. "Your seat, sir," he said, and moved aside as Dub eased himself down behind the desk.

"Why?" Dub asked.

Josh frowned. "Why what?"

"Why did you steal from me?" Dub asked.

"I didn't steal shit from you!" Josh shouted, and jumped up, which was a mistake because seconds later Wade's hands were on his shoulders.

"Sit your ass back down in the chair. Being mad you got caught isn't going to change what you did."

Josh felt the grip all the way to his bones and dropped back into the chair with a thud.

"I didn't take your money," Josh muttered.

"Except you did," Dub said. "You're not a smart thief. I don't know why you thought you'd get away with it. We already know Donny Corrigan's employee code is on the sale receipt, but the problem is Donny clocked out hours earlier because his wife went into labor. He just forgot to log out of the register, and you took advantage of his error to steal from me and lay the blame on him."

"I–I… If you have money missing, it could have been anyone. Why are you picking on me?" Josh cried.

Wade was leaning against the wall with his hands in his pockets, watching a man's life coming apart before his eyes.

"I guess you forgot about the security cameras," Wade said. "There's one over the front door aimed straight at the register. We caught the whole thing, from the time Duke Talbot walked out to you lifting the cash drawer and pulling big bills out from beneath."

All the color faded from Josh's face.

"I…uh…well, hell," he said, and then ducked his head.

Dub was disgusted. "I'm gonna ask you one more time. Why? After all these years, why did you think it was suddenly okay to steal from me? I never treated you any way but right."

Josh scrubbed his hands over his face and then swallowed past the knot in his throat and shrugged.

"I owed a debt I couldn't pay. I didn't want to get beat up."

Dub looked up at Wade. "Call the PD for me, Wade."

"Yes, sir," Wade said. He pulled up the number from his contacts and made the call.

Avery Ames, the day dispatcher, answered.

"Blessings PD."

"Avery, this is Wade Montgomery. We caught a thief here at the store, and we're pressing charges. Can you please send an officer to pick him up? We're in the office."

"Yes, sir, dispatching now," he said.

Wade heard the call go out, and then Avery was back on the line.

"They're on the way. Do you need an ambulance?" he asked.

"No. We're all fine…except for the dumbass in here with us," Wade said.

"Yes, sir," Avery said, and disconnected.

Josh moaned. "I'll pay it back. Don't press charges. I can't go to jail. It's coming up Christmas. What's my wife gonna think? And my kids. Please."

"You should have thought of all that before you stole money from the place where you work," Wade said.

"Out of curiosity, how did you get in that kind of debt?" Dub asked.

Wade frowned. "Did it have anything to do with poker?"

Josh slumped without answering.

Dub looked at Wade in shock. "How did you know that?"

"Josh brags when he wins and comes to work hungover when he loses. I never said anything because he's never come to work drunk, and what a man does on his own time is his business, but after knowing he stole the money I guessed the rest," Wade said.

"So, your wife and kids are really far down on your list of important things to care for," Dub said.

"I'm sorry," Josh said.

"Tell that to your family," Dub said.

Wade glanced out the window and saw a patrol car pulling up to the store.

"They're here," he said.

A few moments later they heard footsteps coming up the hall, and then two officers walked in.

Dub pointed at Josh. "This man stole over five hundred dollars from me, which makes it a felony in the State of Georgia. I'm pressing charges, and I'll follow you to the station to fill out the paperwork."

One officer pulled Josh out of the chair and began cuffing him as the other one read him his rights.

Josh's head was down, his steps dragging as they marched him up the hall, then out through the store and into their car.

"Thanks," Dub said, and gave Wade a quick thump on the shoulder. "You did good, Wade, and you tell Birdie this makes three thieves she's found out since she came to work for me. She hasn't had a raise in years, and I think she's due. Tell her to add four hundred dollars a month to her salary."

"Yes, sir," Wade said. "I'm sure she'll be very appreciative."

"As am I," Dub said. "I'm going by the station now, before I go home."

Wade watched Dub as he left by the side door, his steps dragging as he walked, and then he got in his car and drove away.

———

Duff had driven up and down streets to the point he felt like he was making people nervous. Blessings was small. A stranger was easy to spot. Only he wasn't really a stranger. Just someone who'd been gone a very long time.

By the time noon came around he was hungry, so he headed straight for Granny's Country Kitchen because it was the only real café in town and because he remembered it from before. Once he was seated and had ordered his food, he began watching faces, looking for anyone who looked familiar, but it soon became obvious that he'd been too young, and too many years had passed. Without knowing their names, he couldn't identify anyone. So he sat and watched, and when his food finally came, he transferred his attention to that.

He was almost through eating when a young, dark-haired woman walked in. Something about her seemed familiar, and after she was seated and studying the menu, he blatantly stared.

She was someone from before. Someone he'd known.

━━━━━━━━

Bridgette was still struggling with the revelations of the theft when she got to Granny's, but the delightful aromas that met her at the door shifted her focus.

Sully Raines was manning the register for his mother, Lovie, who owned Granny's. He looked up at Bridgette as she entered.

"Hello, Birdie. Are you dining alone or meeting someone?"

"I'm alone," she said. "A small table anywhere is fine."

"Gotcha," Sully said. "Follow me," he added, and led her through the dining room to a table for two near the front windows. "Your waitress will be here shortly. The special is baked ham and two sides." He left a menu and hurried back to the lobby.

Bridgette was still trying to decide what she wanted when Lovie showed up with a glass of water, a basket of Mercy's famous biscuits, and an apology.

"Hi, Birdie. Sorry for the delay. I'm short a waitress today, and I'm way out of practice. What do you want to drink?"

"Oh, sweet tea, for sure. And I think I'll have the baked ham, with fried okra and mashed potatoes and gravy. I'll also need a brisket sandwich and an order of fries to go."

"Got it," Lovie said. "I'll turn in the to-go order in a bit. Enjoy the biscuits."

Bridgette didn't have to be prompted twice. Mercy Pittman was the baker at Granny's. Her baking skills were famous now, but it was her biscuits that had put her on the map.

Bridgette broke one of the biscuits in half, buttered both pieces, and then took her first bite. Light as a feather, dripping in melted butter—delicious.

Lovey came back with her drink, and while Bridgette was waiting for her food, she noticed a young teenage boy—a stranger to Blessings—staring at her from across the room.

She thought nothing of it and looked away.

When her food came, she ate without looking up, and when Lovey brought the ticket and her to-go order, she left a tip and got up to leave. Even without glancing his way, she knew he was still watching her, but then forgot about it as she headed back to work, wondering what had happened while she was gone.

She didn't have long to wonder. The moment she walked in, it was obvious the confrontation had occurred. Employees were bunched together talking, and there was an instant hush when the door opened, until they saw it was her.

One employee, a man named Roger Brown, started talking so fast he ran out of breath and had to stop in the middle of a sentence and inhale so he could finish.

"Whoa, Birdie! You missed all the excitement! The cops came and hauled Josh King off in handcuffs and… Wade said Josh stole money and Wade caught it on that camera over the door."

Joe Trainor, who worked in the warehouse, punched Roger on the shoulder.

"Dang it, Roger. Who do you think discovered the money was missing? Birdie does end-of-the-month reports every month. And when things don't balance, she goes looking for why. You can't put nothin' over on this girl. I've been here a long time, and this isn't the first time she's found a…a…"

"Discrepancy?" Bridgette said.

"Yeah! That!" Joe said.

Bridgette nodded. "I did know there was money missing, but Wade is the one who discovered who did it. I'm just sorry it happened."

Roger shook his head. "Josh is the one who's gonna be sorry. Him and his stupid poker games. He's addicted, that's what."

Bridgette didn't want to be in the middle of their gossip and used Wade's lunch as an excuse to move on.

"Gotta take the boss his lunch and get back to work," she said, and went down the hall to Wade's office.

The door was open. He was on the phone. He waved her in, gave her a thumbs-up for the food. She tiptoed in, left the sack and his change on the desk, blew him a kiss, and went back to work.

About a half hour later, Wade came in and kissed the back of her neck as she was sitting at the computer, and then sat down in the chair on the other side of her desk.

"Thank you for bringing my lunch."

She shivered. "You're welcome."

"Uncle Dub says to tell you good job! And he's giving you a raise. The next time you make out your own paycheck, add four hundred dollars a month to it."

Bridgette's eyes widened. "Are you serious?"

Wade smiled. "Yes, ma'am. That's what he said."

"Oh wow! That's a wonderful Christmas present to me. Please tell him thank you."

Wade nodded. "I will. I've got to go make some calls. The company we buy salt blocks from lost our shipment."

———————

Dub had filled out all of the paperwork and signed the complaint against Josh King. He didn't have to, but he felt it was his duty to tell Josh's wife what had happened and left the police station with a heavy heart.

Josh and his family lived a couple of blocks from the elementary school, in a pretty white house with blue shutters. Dub knew the kids would be at school today, and he also knew Josh's wife, LaJune, was a stay-at-home mom. At least he could talk to her without the children present.

He pulled up in the drive, eyed the cheery little Santa Claus hanging on their door, and got out, anxious to get this over with.

He knocked, and a few moments later, the door swung inward.

LaJune King recognized Dub and frowned. In all the years that Josh had worked at the store, his boss had never come calling.

"What's wrong?" she asked.

"May I come in?" Dub asked.

She sighed and stepped aside as Dub entered.

"Take a seat," she said, indicating the sofa just to Dub's right. Then she sat in a nearby chair beside their Christmas tree, her face turning paler by the minute as her hands fisted in her lap. "Just spit it out. You wouldn't be here if Josh hadn't done something wrong."

"I'm sorry to have to tell you this, but Josh stole something over five hundred dollars from me. We caught it on the security camera."

She moaned, but her gaze never wavered. "He gambles," she said.

"Yes, ma'am, so I found out. He admitted it and said it was to pay a gambling debt. He showed no remorse whatsoever. I had him arrested."

LaJune reeled where she sat, clutching the arms of the chair she was in. Her voice was shaking.

"I'd like to say I am surprised, but I'm not. One wrong road always leads to another. I couldn't stop him. Maybe jail will. I am so sorry. I'm afraid I don't have the money to pay you back."

Dub hurt for her situation. "I do not expect you to, LaJune. It is not your debt. And I'm sorry, too. Are you going to be able to manage here on your own?"

"No, but my parents have a little farm on the other side of Savannah." She sighed and wiped the tears running down her cheeks. "This is pretty much the last straw for me. The kids and I can go there until I figure out what to do."

Dub nodded. "I don't know what your situation is here, and I know paychecks went out yesterday, but considering Josh gambled, you might be short for the month. I want you to have this, too," he said, and pulled a check out of his shirt pocket. "This is from my personal account."

He got up and laid it in her lap, then briefly patted her shoulder. "Do me a favor and don't bail him out of jail with this. I'm sorry as I can be to give you this news. I wish you and your children well."

LaJune was crying openly now. "Thank you for your generosity. You didn't have to do this."

Dub sighed. "Well, if I ever hope to sleep again, then yes, ma'am, I do. I'll see myself out."

He walked out, quietly closing the door behind him, and could hear her sobbing as he walked off the porch.

"Sorry-ass man," Dub muttered, then got in his car and drove home. He had to tell Nola what had happened, and that he'd just given a good sum of money away today. There were no secrets between him and his girl, ever, and forty something years into a marriage, he wasn't going to start.

CHAPTER 3

JOSH KING WAS FINALLY BOOKED INTO JAIL AND BEGGING Deputy Ralph Herman to let him make a phone call.

"I need to call my wife and tell her to get me a lawyer!" Josh said.

Chief Lon Pittman had been at lunch when he got the call about the arrest and immediately returned to the station. He walked into the jail area just as Josh was making his demands.

The deputy glanced up as Lon walked in.

"Afternoon, Chief. Josh wants to make a phone call."

"I heard," Lon said. "I've got this."

Ralph nodded. "Yes, sir. I'll be going back on patrol," he said, and left the building.

Lon pulled out his cell phone. "What's your number?"

Josh told him, and when the call began to ring, Lon slipped his phone between the bars.

"Don't screw with me, Josh, or you'll regret it," Lon warned.

Josh nodded and put the phone up to his ear, waiting for the call to be answered. It rang, and rang, and rang, and he was about to panic when he finally heard LaJune's voice.

"Hello."

"Hey, baby, it's me. Listen, I'm in jail, and I need you to get me a lawyer. I'll explain everything later, but—"

"You don't need to explain anything," she snapped. "Mr. Truesdale already paid me a visit. You are a sorry sonofabitch, and I am not going to take the food out of my babies' mouths to pay a lawyer anything. You can get a free lawyer assigned by the court, and I hope you rot in jail for what you've done to us."

Josh blinked. The line went dead. She'd hung up on him!

He handed the phone back to Lon through the bars.

"I'm gonna be needing one of them court-appointed lawyers," he mumbled.

Lon nodded. "I'll let the proper authorities know. They'll assign one to you. Meanwhile, enjoy."

Josh dropped onto the cot, his hands clasped between his knees. He'd never planned on spending Christmas in jail, and he had a strong feeling that when he got out, there wouldn't be anyone to go home to.

———

As soon as LaJune hung up the phone, she got her jacket and the extra set of car keys and left the house. It was about a fifteen-minute walk to get to the feed store. The truck in the driveway hadn't worked in months, and Josh damn sure wasn't going to be needing the car. The air was still a little chilly, so she walked faster to warm up.

As she was nearing Main Street, her cell phone rang. She glanced at caller ID and then rolled her eyes. What were the odds? Then she answered.

"Hey, Mom."

"Hi, baby. Daddy and I were talking about the upcoming holidays and wanted to check in with you. I just got word from your brother that he and his family will be here for dinner on Christmas day. Are y'all still planning on coming, too? It would be wonderful if I could have both my babies home for Christmas."

LaJune swallowed past the lump in her throat.

"The kids and I will be there, but Josh just got arrested and is sitting in jail as we speak. I'm walking to the feed store to get our car."

"Oh my God! What did he do?" her mother asked.

"Stole money from his job and got caught on video doing it, and all because of his damn gambling. He had a debt he couldn't pay, and now here we are. I'm leaving him, Mom. This is the last straw."

"I'm so sorry, LaJune. You and the kids come home. We've got the whole upstairs in this house just begging for little footsteps on the floors again."

"Oh, Mom…thank you. I don't want to be a burden, and it won't be forever. But I need a place to be so I can regroup. I'll need to get a job and save up some money to get a place," LaJune said.

"We'll figure it out together," her mother said. "Do you want us to come get your things?"

"I'm not taking anything but ourselves, the car, and our clothes. Our old truck won't run, so if Josh wants a ride, he'll finally have to fix it."

"If you're going to do this, don't wait until he bonds out of jail. I'm afraid he'll hurt you when he finds out you're leaving."

"He would never hurt me physically, but this broke my heart. The kids are in school right now. I'll have everything loaded up by the time they get home. Leaving this abruptly will be hard, but going to see Grandma and Grandpa will make them happy. I'll start them in school there when the semester begins after the first of the year, and Josh can figure out the mess he made of our lives on his own."

LaJune heard her mother sigh.

"I love you, baby. It's going to be okay," her mother said.

"I love you, too, Mom, and thank you for always being there for us."

LaJune hung up, then cried all the way to the feed store, got their car, and drove home.

One hurdle crossed.

About a thousand more to go.

———

It was quitting time, and Bridgette was shutting down her office when Wade appeared in the doorway.

"Hey, darlin'. Wanna go with me to get a Christmas tree for the store? I'll throw in a snow cone for your trouble."

"Oooh, yes!" Bridgette said.

"Do you want to take your car home first, or leave it here and I bring you back to get it later?"

"Are you going to bring the tree back here to the store?"

He nodded.

"Then I'll leave it here."

She grabbed her jacket and purse and followed him through the store as he locked up access doors and made sure the security cameras were working. Wade noticed the pensive look on her face and stopped long enough to give her a quick hug.

"This was a weird day, wasn't it, honey? Are you okay about everything that happened?"

She sighed. "Yes. Just sorry for Josh's family. I know LaJune and the kids well enough to visit with them when I see them around. This makes me sad for them."

Wade pushed a curl from her forehead, then brushed a kiss across her lips.

"I think Uncle Dub was feeling the same. He called me a couple of hours ago to let me know that he went by Josh's house. He thinks they were having a hard time of it because of Josh's gambling."

Bridgette gasped. "Gambling? Is that why he did it?"

Wade nodded. "Dub thinks this will likely end their marriage. He said she has family up around Savannah. However, that means a family is leaving Blessings."

Bridgette sighed. "People come and people go, and life goes on." Then she gave Wade a quick hug. "I'm just glad you came back to Blessings."

He wrapped his arms around her. "And I'm glad you were still here, even if it did take half a year and me throwing something of a fit to get you to notice me."

Bridgette shook her head. "You are never going to let that go, are you?"

"Maybe, one day," Wade said, and then kissed her. "Now, let's get the rest of this place locked up and go get a Christmas tree. I want to display those ornaments we have for sale, and the best way to do that is decorate a tree with them."

"Oh…I want to help," she said.

Wade grinned. "Oh! You are officially in charge of decorating."

They left the feed store arm in arm, got in the store truck they used for in-town deliveries, and then went straight to the Crown.

"What do you want to do first…snow cone or tree?" Wade asked as he parked.

"Let's do both. Get snow cones to eat while we look at trees. Just let me get my jacket. Eating that shaved ice is going to make me cold, but it will put me in the Christmas mood for sure."

The snow-cone stand looked like a little brown cuckooclock with snow on the roof. The steep slope of the pointed roof had ornate gingerbread trim, and the place where the cuckoo would have come out was the window where the orders were taken.

The workers inside the stand were dressed like elves, with green suits and pointed hats, and the menu of available flavors posted on the wooden sign beside it was straight out of the North Pole.

- Rudolph's Nose—cherry flavor
- Christmas Tree—lime flavor
- Candlelight Bright—lemon-pineapple flavor
- Heavenly Blue—raspberry flavor
- Starlight White—coconut flavor
- Santa Wrecked the Sleigh—combo of all flavors

There were small tables with folding chairs set up around the stand where people sat and visited and a short line at the window.

"What's your poison?" Wade asked as they approached the stand.

"Candlelight Bright!" Bridgette said.

Wade grinned. "Go say hi to your brother. I'll get in line to order."

Bridgette took off across the lot toward the Christmas trees and noticed Junior loading up a tree for Jack Talbot. It would be Jack and Hope's first Christmas as parents. Bridgette shivered longingly. Wade and babies sounded wonderful to her.

As she waited for Junior to finish the transaction, she couldn't help but notice the confidence he had about him now—a drastic change from the way he'd been before. It was a tragedy their mama had to die before the secret that had devastated the family was finally revealed and resolved. But after it all came about, it was as if someone had freed Junior from an emotional prison. He had a steady job now, had finished his GED, and had resurrected his personal life, as well. He'd been dating a sweet little woman named Barrie Lemons who lived in the Bottoms, and had finally moved in with her about five months ago. Barrie had two small children—Lucy who was school age, and Freddy who was still a toddler—and Junior was smitten by all three of them.

And then Junior saw Bridgette and came running to give her a quick hug.

"Hi, Birdie!"

"Hi, Junior. How's it going?" she asked.

"Goin' good, honey, goin' good, but we heard there was some kind of commotion at the feed store today. Cops showed up and everything. What happened? Were you in any danger?"

"No. Someone just stole some money and got caught," Bridgette said.

"Ooh, that was stupid," Junior said, and then changed the subject. "I see you're here with your sweetie. I bet I know what kind of snow cone you're getting."

Bridgette grinned. "And that would be what?"

"That lemon one," he said.

Bridgette laughed. "How would you know that?"

"Even as a kid, you were always sucking on a lemon. Made my jaws hurt just looking at you, but you sure did love 'em."

"Guilty," she said. "And here it comes, delivered by my one and only."

Junior smiled. "It's good to see you happy, Sis."

Bridgette patted the side of his cheek. "I'm glad you're happy, too. Are you and Barrie taking the kids to the Christmas parade this Saturday?"

"We have to. That's all Lucy has talked about for a week."

"Then I'll see you there. The guys at the store are making some kind of a float, and I have been informed I will be riding on it. Lord only knows what it will be."

At that point, Wade walked up beside her.

"Evening, Junior. Here's your snow cone, sugar, and you'll hear all about the float tomorrow. Right now, we're gonna buy a Christmas tree for the store."

"We have sizes from four to eight feet tall. What size would you be wanting?" Junior asked.

Wade pointed at Bridgette, who was nose deep in her snow cone.

"This is the lady in charge of that. As soon as she gets over the brain freeze from that monstrous bite, I'll let her tell you."

Bridgette would have laughed, but she was too busy riding out the pain in her head from the bite she'd just taken.

"Ooh, my bad," she said. "The snow cone is so good, but I did not allow for that. What kind did you get?"

Wade showed her. "I couldn't decide, so I got Santa Wrecked the Sleigh. It has some of all of them. Want a bite?"

Bridgette eyed the conglomeration of colors and wrinkled her nose. "I'll pass."

Both men laughed, then Wade began eating his as they started through the lot, looking at shapes and sizes of the trees, trying to decide between pines or firs, with Bridgette ignoring most of what they were saying. She was envisioning the ornaments they had at the store and wanted the perfect tree to use for display.

They had circled the lot and were working their way inward when she spotted a tall, sturdy one with a solid shape.

"That one," she said, pointing. "It will be perfect in that corner by the gift area."

"Load her up," Wade said, and Bridgette followed along behind them.

She took a last bite of the cone, and then dropped what was left in the trash bin near the stand as they walked away. As she turned to catch up, she saw the stranger from Granny's again. This time, he was leaning against a car, his arms folded across his chest, staring at her.

She stopped and stared back until he was the one to break his gaze and walk away.

It bothered her that this was happening, and that he was still in Blessings, even though he had made no advances or threatened her in any way. And once again, she shook off concern, and hurried to catch up.

They took the tree back to the store, left it propped up in the corner, then locked up and walked to the parking lot.

"That was fun. Thanks for taking me along, but tomorrow I fully expect to find out what the big secret is about me and that float," Bridgette said.

Wade grinned. "You're going to be the hit of the parade."

Bridgette shook her head. "No. Santa is going to be the hit."

"Who does Santa?" Wade asked.

"Peanut is Santa again this year, and Ruby is Mrs. Claus, or so I heard."

"Awesome. Ever since my parents passed, I've been kind of lost as to what to do about holidays. Uncle Dub and Aunt Nola are the only blood relatives I have left, and I'm excited about all of this and making memories with you," Wade said.

Bridgette felt the pang of knowing this would be her family's first Christmas without their mother, Marjorie, too.

"It doesn't matter how old you are when you lose both parents... You feel like an orphan, don't you? But we have each other now and new memories to make."

Wade hugged her. "I love you, Bridgette. So much. And if we weren't standing here in front of God and everybody, I'd kiss you senseless."

She laughed. "Propriety is boring, but I guess we can't be scandalous right here before Christmas and get on Santa's bad side. I'll see you tomorrow, and you *will* tell me about the float."

He grinned. "I'll see you tomorrow, for sure."

She shook her head, then got in her car and drove away.

Wade sighed. He had to go by the cleaners and then stop off at the hardware store, then head back to the warehouse behind the store where they were building the float. His day was far from over.

Duff Martin was rattled. That lady at the Crown had called his bluff and stared him down, but she looked so familiar, and it was driving him crazy. Why couldn't he remember?

He was beginning to realize he couldn't do this on his own. He should have told his mom and Allen what he was doing, but he still wasn't sure that what he remembered had anything to do with why his dad was in prison.

It was getting late and chilly, so he went into the Crown and got some food from the deli, then took it back to his motel. He needed to let his mom know he was okay. He wasn't going to tell her what he was doing, but he didn't want her thinking he was dead. So as soon as he got back to his room, he put his groceries on the table and sat down on the side of the bed and called.

Candi was too upset and too rattled to focus on work and had called in sick, letting Allen take her car to work instead. And now every time her phone rang and it wasn't Duff, the knot in her belly grew tighter.

It was almost sundown when her cell phone rang, and when she saw Duff's number pop up, she couldn't answer fast enough.

"Hello! Duff? Honey?"

"Hi, Mom."

"Oh my God…where are you? Why did you run away? Was it something I said? If it was, I'm so sorry. Just come home. We'll figure it out."

"No, Mom, no. You didn't do anything wrong and I'm not in trouble. But there's something I have to do. I can't say more now, but I'm not doing anything illegal. I promise I'm not in trouble."

Candi was crying now. "Where are you, Duffy?"

"I'll call you again in a day or two," Duff said. "Just don't worry."

In a last ditch effort to get him back, Candi threw out the obvious. "You're missing school."

"Tell them it was a family emergency. I'll make up my classes, I promise."

Candi sighed. "I don't like this. I don't like lying to people."

"I'm not lying about anything," Duff said. "Just trust me on this. If I'm right, it may be the best thing that has happened to us in a really long time. Tell Allen I'm sorry I took his car without asking, but I'm taking good care of it. I love you. Bye."

And then he was gone.

Candi looked at the dark screen on her phone and then clutched it to her breast.

At least she'd finally heard from him. At least now she knew he wasn't in trouble. And he'd given her no choice but to trust him.

But Duff was feeling a lot of what his mother was feeling. Sad, worried, unsettled, and guilt. More guilt than he'd ever known existed.

Tomorrow he would go to the local library. If they had back issues of the local paper, the story of his dad's arrest and incarceration should be in it. He needed to know the whole truth before he took the next step.

─────────

Wade went home long enough to change into old clothes and then headed to the empty warehouse where they were building the float.

"Did you bring your hammer? We're building a fence here," Roger yelled as Wade walked in.

Wade just grinned. "Just remember to build it in sections, like short sideboards, so we can slide them into place on the flatbed Saturday morning before the parade."

"If the guy doesn't show up with your critter, what are we gonna do?" Roger asked.

"The guy will send a crew with the critter, as you call it, and load it on our trailer. The man who owns the company is a college friend. He guaranteed they would be here by 7:00 a.m. Saturday, and I'll be waiting. They will stay for the parade, then load it up and take it back. I just have to get power to it. I have a generator that will do the job, and we can hide it with some hay bales."

"Birdie is so going to be the hit of this parade," Roger said.

Wade knew Bridgette. She was going to love everything about this. Tomorrow was Friday. The parade was Saturday. There was no time to waste.

━━━━━━

Bridgette went to sleep thinking about Wade, but when she dreamed, she dreamed of the stranger who was following her, and when she woke up the next morning, he was still on her mind. He reminded her of someone. If only she knew his name, maybe that would trigger a memory. If she saw him again, she was going to confront him, because this was beginning to get creepy.

She thought about telling Wade, and then didn't. If it was totally innocent, she didn't want to get the kid in trouble. Maybe he was just here visiting family for the holidays and bored. Maybe they just happened to be in the same place at the same time twice. So what. Blessings was a small town, and strangers were noticeable. That had to be it.

Now that she'd talked herself out of being concerned, she went to get ready. She was anxious to find out what the float was about and what she was supposed to wear. Probably overalls, or jeans, or maybe a red plaid shirt and a Santa hat. Something farm-related, for sure.

She ate a bowl of cereal, checked the weather, and headed to the car. Office work was on hold. Today she got to decorate the Christmas tree.

She drove slowly up Main, eyeing the window fronts with delight. The contest was getting serious. There were some awesome displays.

When she saw the display at the Curl Up and Dye, she laughed out loud. Ruby had a store mannequin in the window and had dressed it in an old-fashioned, jade-green prom dress—the strapless kind with a long, poofy skirt covered in ruffles. The skirt billowed out from the waist like a dainty little bell, thanks to an old hoop underskirt. Ruby, being Ruby, had spray-painted an old wig forest-green and put it on the mannequin, added a gold tiara, then draped it from head to toe with flashing multicolored Christmas lights, as if the mannequin had become the Christmas tree. And she'd surrounded her with boxes elaborately wrapped to look like gifts, sprayed artificial snow around the outer edges of the window as a frame, and had silver icicles dangling from the eaves outside of the storefront.

Driving further, the window of the flower shop was a mass of poinsettias in every color, displayed on tables and stools of different heights. And there was an oversize Elf on the Shelf sitting beneath the spreading leaves of a white poinsettia, waving.

The hardware store was Bridgette's favorite. They'd created a Santa's workshop with little mechanical elves looking like they were making toys, and so it went all the way down the street. Whoever had thought about the storefront contest had really put the zip in Christmas this year. Blessings didn't need snow to get in the spirit. It was everywhere. Even the police cruisers were sporting Christmas wreaths on the grills.

By the time she got to the feed store, Bridgette had an idea of how she wanted the tree to look. And when she pulled up and parked, and saw the big green wreath with a huge red bow hanging on the door, she grinned.

In all the years she'd worked for Dub, he'd never done anything like this. Wade was good for Dub, good for business, and so good for her it made her ache.

She jumped out and went in the side door to stow her things in her office. The first thing she saw when she walked in was the long box on top of her desk. Curious, she opened it, and began pulling out the different items—red jeans, a red-and-white-plaid shirt, a black bandanna, and a pair of black boots. She opened a big square box beside it and grinned. A red cowboy hat. She'd definitely be noticeable, no matter what the float looked like.

Still grinning, she put everything back in the box, set it aside, booted up the computer, and then headed into the store.

Wade already had the tree in a stand, and when he saw her, he waved her over.

"Morning, darlin'. You're just in time. Do you want these clear lights on the tree so that all it does is twinkle, or do you want the colored lights?"

"Oooh, the clear ones. That way nothing will be competing with the ornaments," Bridgette said.

Two of the men came in from the warehouse, both of them grinning.

"Did you tell her yet?" they asked.

Wade shook his head. "No. She just got here."

Bridgette grinned. "Tell me what? I just saw the clothes you want me to wear. Are you talking about the float?"

"Yes, they're talking about the float. So what do you think of the outfit?"

"I think it's cute, and definitely fit for a feed-and-seed-store float. So tell me what it's going to look like."

Wade took a deep breath. "How does riding a mechanical bull down Main Street strike you?"

Bridgette's jaw dropped. "For real?"

"Yes, please," Wade said. "It's a big red bull named Rudolph, and we're going to have it on the slowest, safest speed. Basically, you'll just be hanging on and waving that hat and being cute."

Bridgette blinked. At that point, every man on the premises was standing in the store, waiting for her answer.

"Holy cow," she mumbled.

"Ummm, no, it's a bull," Wade said.

Bridgette burst out laughing. "I'm in."

Wade clapped his hands and then swung her off her feet.

"We're gonna win the trophy for best float, I guarantee…and we're going to put it on the shelf right there behind the register, between the dewormer meds and the ointment for sore teats."

The men whooped and started clapping and laughing.

"Outstanding," Bridgette said. "But it's gonna cost you."

Wade grinned. "Name it and it's yours. Now let's decorate a tree. The rest of you guys, back to work."

They were still laughing and talking as they dispersed to their regular jobs, leaving Donny up front to man the register, while Wade began stringing the lights and Bridgette started gathering up two of every ornament they had for sale to put on the tree.

CHAPTER 4

DUFF DIDN'T GET MUCH SLEEP.

His mattress was lumpy, and the couple in the room next door fought off and on all night. He missed home. He missed his mom, and waking up to the smell of bacon and coffee, and he even missed Allen's gentle nagging.

He showered, got dressed, then ate a honey bun, drank a pint-size carton of milk, and called it breakfast before he left the motel.

When he got in the car, he immediately noticed he was low on fuel, so his first stop was at the gas station to fill up.

"Twenty dollars on pump four, please," he said as he went up to the counter to pay.

The clerk rang up the sale and turned on the pump as Duff walked out.

Lovie Cooper had just pulled up on the other side of Duff's pump and smiled at him as he passed.

"Morning," she said.

"Morning," he said, and ducked his head.

Lovie knew everyone in town, and she didn't recognize him. And she was nosy.

"It's a bit cool this morning, isn't it?" she said.

"Yes, ma'am," Duff said, watching the numbers rolling over on the pump.

"I own Granny's Country Kitchen, and I think I saw you in there the other day."

Duff nodded. "I was there. Food's good."

Lovie smiled. "Music to my ears. Are you here visiting family for the holidays?"

"No, ma'am. We used to live here, but we're in Florida now."

"Well, I'll say. Who are your people?" Lovie asked.

"Zack and Candi Martin."

"Names are familiar, but I can't place them. Have y'all been gone long?"

Duff sighed. There was no need to hide his truth.

"About ten years. I was just a little kid when we moved, so I don't remember hardly anyone."

"So, are you here for the festivities? There's a big Christmas parade tomorrow. It starts at 10:00 a.m. If you're still here, you won't want to miss that."

Duff nodded, and then his pump kicked off.

"I guess I'm done here," he said. "Nice talking to you." Then he replaced the nozzle and put the gas cap back on the car.

"See you at the parade!" Lovie said.

Duff waved, then got in the car and drove away.

Lovie watched, still trying to remember why that name was familiar. The kid was clean-cut and polite. A little skinny, but he had pretty brown hair with a tendency to curl. And she knew those names from somewhere. It would come to her later.

Her pump kicked off. She finished up and headed to Granny's. She was still standing in for one of the waitresses who'd come down with the flu, and there was no time to waste.

———

Duff had driven by the library yesterday, and Blessings was too small to get lost in, so he found his way back with no problem. His phone dinged as he was about to get out. This time, it was a text from Allen.

> Thanks for checking in. Whatever is going on, be a man about it. Don't wind up like Dad. And bring my car back in one piece. Love you.

Duff's eyes welled. Men admitted their mistakes. Men told the truth. He was working on both of those, but before he went to the police for help, he needed to make sure he knew what he was talking about. He got out of the car with purpose, went inside, and then straight up to the lady at the desk.

Gina Green looked up, surprised anyone was here this early, and even more surprised to see a face she didn't know.

"Good morning," she said as the boy stopped at her desk.

"Morning, ma'am. Do you have back issues of the local newspaper on file?"

"Yes, we do. Are you looking for a particular story, or researching?"

"A particular story."

"Do you have a date?" Gina asked.

"Not a specific date, but I know it was ten years ago...and it was in the summer, so June or July because school was out."

"Okay...what's the story about?" Gina asked.

"Zack Martin being arrested for stealing jewelry from a woman, and any supporting stories afterward."

Gina nodded, opened up the link to the local paper, typed in *Zack Martin, arrest, jewelry*, and made some notes.

"This is on microfiche. If you'll follow me," Gina said, and led him to a back corner of the room and their only microfiche reader. "Just have a seat and I'll pull the film."

Duff's heart was pounding. His stomach was in knots. If that old woman hadn't passed away, then his mama would never have mentioned that name and he wouldn't have heard her and Allen talking about the details of what sent his dad to prison, and he wouldn't be here trying to right a wrong. It seemed sad that a lady had to die for him to know he'd done something wrong.

Gina came back with two small tin cylinders. "The stories regarding this arrest and the ensuing trial are in both of these. I'll load the first one for you. When you've finished, I can either load the next for you, or you're free to do it yourself. Just replace the first one in the same tin you took it out of before you remove the next."

"Yes, ma'am," Duff said, watching carefully as she loaded the film then showed him how to use the reader.

It was awkward at first, but he soon got the hang of it and began searching.

He found the first story right off, and the photo of his dad in handcuffs and being escorted into the courthouse for arraignment was horrifying. According to the article, his dad kept proclaiming his innocence. They couldn't prove he'd stolen the jewels, but he'd been the only member outside of the family in the house, and they discovered the jewels were missing after he left. And as Duff read, he saw his dad even had some prior offenses that weighed against him. He read it all with tears in his eyes.

He switched to the second roll of microfiche and started looking for follow-up stories. There were two. One was a story about the trial, and the second was the story about the verdict. Bottom line…his dad was in jail for something he didn't do, and Duff hoped he could prove it.

He got up with the tins of microfiche and took them up to the desk.

"Thank you for your help," he said.

Gina smiled. "Of course. Did you find everything you were looking for?"

Duff sighed. "Yes, ma'am," and then left the library and went back to the car and got in.

The air-conditioning in the library hadn't been all that cold, but he was shivering. It felt like he was coming undone. A part of him regretted even hearing what his mom and brother were talking about, and at the same time, he was horrified that they'd never told him.

His stomach was protesting from the meager breakfast he'd had. Maybe if he got some food in his belly, the shaking would stop. So he started the car and drove back to Granny's. He wanted to be inside, eating real food, not premade stuff from the grocery store deli.

He couldn't help but think of the pretty woman he kept seeing as he pulled in and parked. It still felt like she was part of his story here, but he couldn't make the connection. He got out and went inside.

As soon as he was seated, he ordered coffee. Maybe that would stop the shaking. It came with a basket of biscuits. He ordered beef stew and cornbread, and then while he was waiting for his order, he began buttering biscuits and downing them like popcorn. He didn't stop until they were gone.

The hot coffee and warm food stopped the shaking, but they did nothing to ease the knot in his belly. When his food came, he buttered the cornbread, too, and then ate slowly, savoring the thick, hot stew, rife with bite-size chunks of beef, tender coins of carrots, perfectly cubed potatoes, and small slivers of onion. And as he ate, a calm came over him. Whatever happened now just had to happen, because this was what it meant to do the right thing.

Lovie didn't wait on his table, but she saw him and came to say hello.

"Hello again, young man. How about a piece of pie on the house?"

Duff blinked. "Uh…yes, ma'am. That would be awesome."

"We have chocolate, lemon, and coconut cream pies. We also have apple and cherry pie, and peach cobbler. What's your pleasure?"

He smiled shyly. "I think I'd like some of that peach cobbler."

"Awesome choice! Do you want it à la mode, or straight?"

"I never turn down ice cream," Duff said. "I'll take it à la mode."

Lovie gave him a quick pat on the shoulder.

"Coming right up," she said, and headed for the kitchen.

Duff was still smiling when the same pretty dark-haired woman walked into the dining room, only this time she wasn't alone. She was with another woman, and they were talking and laughing as they were being seated. All he could think was this was meant to be. He wanted to talk to her, and here she was.

And then Lovie returned with dessert, and he finished off his meal, devouring the peach cobbler à la mode.

Bridgette had just hung the last ornament on the Christmas tree when her sister, Emma, walked into the store. She saw Birdie and headed straight toward her.

"I didn't know y'all had Christmas ornaments! For that matter, I didn't know there was a gift shop here!" Emma said.

Bridgette nodded. "It was Wade's idea. The gift shop has been here for several months, but the ornaments are special for Christmas. What better way to advertise they are here than to see them on a tree?"

"Oh my word! You even have those cute little cast-iron pans that make sticks of cornbread look like ears of corn! I always wanted one of those. And look at the potholders and aprons! And the jars of jams and jellies. Oh my lord! Cute little dog sweaters. They have Santa Claus on them. Makes me want a dog just so I could dress it up!" Emma said.

Bridgette rolled her eyes. "About the third time you had to get up at night and let it out to pee, you'd be tired of that dog and its cute clothes."

Emma giggled. "You know me so well. Still, there are some really nice things here. I'm going to have to come back to do a little Christmas shopping. Right now, I'm here to invite you to lunch. Can you go?"

"Yes, sure. Just let me tell Wade," Bridgette said, and left Emma poking about the gift shop as she went to look for him.

He wasn't in the office, which meant he was likely somewhere in the warehouse working on the float. She sent him a text, grabbed her purse, and went back to find Emma at the register.

"I just couldn't resist this salt and pepper shaker set," Emma said. "Look, the rooster is the pepper shaker, and the hen holds the salt."

Bridgette grinned. "Awesome."

A few minutes later, they were in Emma's car and on their way to Granny's. The parking lot was filling up, and the dining room was already getting busy. Bridgette didn't see the boy again until she and Emma had already ordered, and then all of a sudden he was standing at their table.

"Ladies, I apologize for interrupting your meal, but could I talk to you for a minute?"

Emma was startled, but Bridgette was intrigued.

"Yes, if you'll explain why you've been staring at me every time we happened to cross paths," Bridgette said.

Emma frowned. "If my sister says okay, then sit, but this better be good."

"Thank you," he said, and sat in one of the empty chairs at their table. "I won't bother you but a minute. My family was from Blessings, but we moved away when I was six, so I don't remember many names."

"What's your name?" Bridgette asked.

"Duff Martin. What's yours?"

"Bridgette Knox."

"Most everyone calls her Birdie," Emma said. "I'm Emma, her older sister."

Duff's eyes widened. "Oh my gosh! Yes. Birdie. You're Miss Margie's girl! She babysat me after school! I knew you looked familiar."

Bridgette sighed. "And you're Duffy! I remember you. I think you were probably the last one she kept, and you were such a little guy."

Duff nodded. "Yes, ma'am. Would it be possible to talk to Miss Margie? She might be able to answer some questions for me."

Both Emma and Bridgette shook their heads.

"No. I'm sorry. Mama died last New Year's Day," Bridgette said.

Duff's shoulders slumped. "Aw, man…I'm sorry."

But Emma was frowning now, remembering. "Your parents were Candi and Zack, right?"

Duff nodded. "Yes, ma'am. And yes, Dad's in prison. That's part of why I'm here. There's very little I remember about that time, and I was hoping your mother would be able to fill in some blanks."

"So ask us," Bridgette said. "Emma and I always knew the children Mama kept, and they knew us."

"What do you remember about me?" he asked.

Emma thought a few moments. "You had curly hair, and you liked jigsaw puzzles. I remember seeing you and Mama working them together at the kitchen table."

Duff's eyes widened. "I'd forgotten all about jigsaw puzzles. I was obsessed with them for the longest time."

"Oh, I remember one thing," Bridgette said. "You dug holes all over the place. Mama was always having Ray or Junior, those are our brothers, filling them back up again."

Duff frowned. "I dug holes? Why was I digging holes?"

"You liked to play pirates," Emma said. "You were always begging Mama to let you watch the DVD she had of *Pirates of the Caribbean*. And then you would stomp all through the house, saying 'Argh' and 'Ahoy, matey.' You were so cute."

Bridgette nodded. "That's why you kept digging the holes. You were looking for buried treasure. I remember one day your dad was working for a lady, and he called Mom, asking if she could come get you because he was trying to finish up this job. I was home. Mom was busy, so she sent me. When I got there, you were head down in some hole the gardener had just dug, and he was trying to plant some new rosebushes. I got you out of the hole, brushed you off, and we left. We went through the drive-through at Broyles Dairy Freeze to get ice cream before I took you to Mom's. Do you remember that?"

Duff was in shock. "Oh my God."

Bridgette frowned. "What's wrong?"

Duff just shook his head. "It's a long story, but I can't thank you enough for talking to me. I've got to go."

"Wait!" Bridgette said. "Is your family here for a visit, or by any chance are you moving back?"

"No, ma'am. We're not moving back, and thank you both again. You'll never know how much this meant to me, and it's really nice seeing you again."

He got up and hurried out.

"What in the world was that all about?" Emma asked.

Bridgette shrugged. "I don't know. I have been seeing him around, and every time he would just stare at me. Now I know why."

"I wonder what he's doing here," Emma said.

"I have no idea," Bridgette said.

Emma shrugged it off. "Oh well, here comes our food, and what's this I've been hearing about you being on one of the floats in the Christmas parade? I heard the guys at the feed store talking about it."

"It's just advertisement for the feed store. Wade asked if I would and of course I agreed."

"What fun!" Emma said. "I wish I was going to be in the parade."

Bridgette grinned, thinking about the mechanical bull.

"I'll wave at you," she said, popped a french fry in her mouth, then reached for the salt.

Duff was dumbstruck at what he'd just learned. It validated the vague memories he had, but he was afraid to go straight to the police. In the stories he'd just read at the library, a local lawyer named Butterman had represented his dad pro bono. If he still lived here, Duff wanted to talk to him. Maybe the lawyer would be the go-between Duff needed to approach the police with this outlandish story.

He started to google the info on his phone, and then stopped and went back into Granny's.

Sully glanced up. The kid had just walked out, and now he was back.

"Hi. Did you forget something?"

"No, sir. I have a question. Is there a lawyer in Blessings by the name of Butterman?"

"Yes. His office is across the street from the courthouse. You can't miss it. Got a big sign out front," Sully said.

"Thanks," Duff said, and headed back downtown.

The courthouse was a block off Main and the largest building in town.

Duff was thinking it shouldn't be hard to find the lawyer's office, but the name was a little startling. P. Nutt Butterman? Who had a name like that? Still, it was the same name from the newspaper, so before he could talk himself out of it, Duff got out and went inside.

———————

Betty Purejoy had just returned from lunch and was checking voicemail when the door opened. She paused as the young man approached.

"Ma'am, my name is Duffy Martin. Would it be possible to speak to Mr. Butterman?"

Betty glanced at Peanut's calendar. He didn't have an appointment for another two hours.

"He's not back from lunch yet, but if you want to have a seat and wait, he shouldn't be long."

"Yes, ma'am. Thank you," Duff said.

Betty smiled at him, then went back to what she was doing.

Duff checked his phone for messages. There was one from his mom that made his heart hurt.

You are in my heart and in my prayers. I love you, Duffy. Please be careful and come home soon.

He sighed, then pulled up his Snapchat account and began scanning through his friends' most recent posts, thinking how simple and shallow his life had been before this revelation.

He was still scrolling through social media when the office door opened. A tall, lanky man strode in like he owned the place, and then Duff realized he probably did. It appeared this man was the lawyer he'd come to see.

Peanut smiled at Duff.

"Afternoon, young man. I'm Mr. Butterman. Are you waiting for me?"

Duff nodded. "Yes, sir."

"Then let's go into my office," Peanut said. He led the way, then closed the door to his office and pointed to a chair as he sat down behind his desk. "Take a seat."

Duff sat.

"What's your name, and what can I do for you?"

"My name is Duffy Martin. Ten years ago you represented my father, Zack Martin."

Peanut's eyes widened. "I remember you. You were just a little kid."

"I was six."

Peanut nodded. "Why are you here?"

"To pull off a Christmas miracle."

Peanut grinned. "I'm good, but I'm not sure I'm that good. Talk to me."

Duff sighed. "You said you remember me, but I remember almost nothing of that time. One day my dad was at home and our lives were normal, and then he was gone. My mom didn't explain much then. All I knew at the time was that he took something that didn't belong to him and went to prison."

"Must have been hard for you," Peanut said.

"What's really hard is that I barely remember Dad even being with us now. I have an older brother, Allen, who's become the father figure I didn't have…and Mom, of course. Over the years, I was just the kid whose dad was in prison. And nobody talked about any of it at home, until the other night."

"What happened?" Peanut asked.

"Mom mentioned during supper about seeing an obituary for a woman from Blessings. It was Selma Garrett. I didn't know who she was, but Mom and Allen started talking about her, and how Dad had gone to prison for stealing her jewelry." Duff's hands were shaking as he took a deep breath.

"When I heard that, I nearly fell out of my chair. I had not known the details of my father's crime, and the mention of jewelry triggered a memory. I freaked, and after everyone went to bed, I took my brother's car and came to Blessings to see if what I remembered was true and maybe fix a horrible mistake."

"Wait. Where do you live now?" Peanut asked.

"Jacksonville, Florida. I've been here a couple of days, trying to remember, and wondering if the memory I have is real or just something I made up as a kid."

Now the kid had Peanut's full attention.

"Does your family know where you are?"

"They don't know where I am, or what I'm doing, but I have been in contact with both of them. They know I'm okay."

"So what *are* you doing here?" Peanut asked.

"Trying to get my father out of prison and clear his name."

Peanut sighed. "I know your father swore he never took the jewelry, but he was the only stranger on the property, and working in the upstairs of the house at the time it went missing."

Duff leaned forward, his demeanor shifting from shy to forceful and intent.

"No, he wasn't. I was there, too. School was out. It was summer. He took me to work with him that day. What I remembered was confusing to me, until today when I spoke with Birdie and Emma Knox. I used to go to their mother's house every day after school and stay until my parents got off work. Miss Margie babysat me anytime there was a need. Birdie and Emma told me that she'd passed away, so I asked them what they remembered about me from that time."

"What did they say?" Peanut asked.

"That I was obsessed with pirates. I used to beg to watch *Pirates of the Caribbean* all the time, and I dug holes all over their yard that their brothers had to refill. And when I heard that, I knew what I remembered of that day was true. Mr. Butterman, Dad didn't take that lady's jewelry. I did. I'd been outside playing. I came in the house to get a drink, then went upstairs to ask Dad how long it would be before we went home. He told me he was going to have to work longer, and he'd call someone to come get me, and told me to go back outside and play. As I was walking back toward the stairs, I passed an open door. It was a bedroom, and there was a little chest on a table. It looked like a pirate chest. I went in to look, and when I opened the chest, I saw treasure. So much treasure. And I took it outside to bury it."

"Oh holy shit, boy! Are you kidding me?" Peanut asked.

Duff's eyes welled. "No, sir. I'm pretty much devastated that my dad has spent the last ten years of his life in prison for something I did. I didn't know. I was just a little kid. It was a game. Obviously one that I was obsessed with."

"Where did you bury it, and how in hell did you find something to dig with?"

Duff's shoulders slumped. "As it turned out, I didn't have to dig anything. There was a man out in the rose garden. He was planting stuff. He had a great big hole already dug and was down by the garden shed, so I put the chest in that hole. I didn't have a shovel, so I was dragging loose dirt from the pile back down in the hole to cover it when Birdie came to pick me up and take me to Miss Margie's house. Birdie said I was belly down in the dirt when she arrived. And as she was brushing me off, I watched the gardener take a new rosebush out of a pot and put it down in the hole. He planted it right on top of my treasure."

"Oh shit. Oh shit. Oh shit," Peanut muttered. "Why didn't you say something?"

Duff was crying. "I don't know. It was a game, and I didn't know it was Birdie who was coming to get me. But Miss Margie sent Birdie, and she took me away, and I guess in my six-year-old mind, the game was over. The next morning the police were at the door and everyone was hysterical, and I didn't know why, and no one would tell me anything because I was just so little."

Peanut jumped to his feet. "I wish to God that Selma Garrett was still alive, but her daughter and family are at the house. They're going through everything, getting ready for an auction. I need to let Chief Pittman know. He wasn't the police chief then, but he was an officer here. He'll remember. If we took you back out to the garden, would you remember where it was?"

Duff nodded. "I think so, unless they've changed things. Birdie might remember better than me. She's the one who came and got me."

Peanut shook his head. "Selma didn't like her stuff messed with, so I'd lay odds nothing has been changed. And I believe her gardener was still working for her when she passed. He might even remember where the new roses were planted that day. It's sure worth a shot."

"I don't have any money to pay you, but will you help me make this right?" Duff asked.

The hair was standing up on the back of Peanut's neck. "I couldn't keep your dad out of prison, but with your story, and recovering that jewelry, I can damn sure find a way to get him out."

Duff nodded. "Thank you. This will be a real Christmas miracle for Mom and Dad if I can make this right."

"Sit tight," Peanut said, and reached for his phone and called the police station.

A few moments later, Lon Pittman answered.

"Chief Pittman."

"Lon, this is Peanut. Are you free right now to come to my office?"

"Uh…yeah, sure. I can be. Is something wrong? Do I need to bring backup?"

"We don't need backup. I'll explain everything when you get here," Peanut said.

"On the way," Lon said, and disconnected.

CHAPTER 5

LON PITTMAN ARRIVED AT PEANUT'S OFFICE WITHIN A FEW minutes. Betty waved him in.

"He's expecting you," she said.

Lon knocked once, then entered.

Peanut stood. "Lon, thanks for coming. Have a seat."

Lon sat down beside Duff as Peanut introduced them.

"Chief, this young man is Duffy Martin. Duffy, this is Chief Pittman. He wasn't chief when Zack was arrested, but he worked here."

Lon frowned. "Martin? Zack Martin?"

Duff nodded. "Yes, sir."

"So why am I here?" Lon asked, and Peanut began to explain. When he was finished, Lon was as stunned by the revelation as Peanut had been. And then something occurred to him, and he asked Duff point-blank. "You came by yourself?"

Duff was trembling. "Yes, sir. I'm so sorry. I didn't realize. I didn't know what I'd done. I didn't take anything. I was just playing, and the game got interrupted, and I was so little, I guess I forgot. Then I heard my mom and brother talking a couple of days ago and couldn't get here fast enough to try and make things right."

Lon just kept shaking his head. "Lord have mercy, son."

"If we find the jewelry, is it possible to get my daddy out of prison?" Duff asked.

"Let's see if we can find the jewelry first," Lon said. "And you said it was Birdie who came and got you?"

Duff nodded. "That's what she said."

"Did you tell them what you'd done, or why you're here?"

"I haven't said a word to anyone except you and Mr. Butterman."

"Okay, so here's what we're going to do," Lon said. "I'm going to contact Selma Garrett's daughter and tell her what you just told me. Then I'm going to ask Birdie Knox and Selma's gardener, Woody Rice, to meet us at the house. Peanut, can you bring Duff?"

Peanut nodded. "I have an appointment later, but that is about to get rescheduled. I wouldn't miss this for the world. I need to notify the photographer at the local paper. I want this all on video."

"Good idea," Lon said. "I'll get one of my officers to film it, too. Okay, Duffy Martin, I hope to God you're telling the truth. Let's go dig up a treasure."

―――――――

Bridgette was posting invoices when Wade came into her office.

"Hey, honey. Chief Pittman is on the phone. He wants to talk to you. He's on line two."

She frowned, stopped what she was doing, and picked up the call. "Hello?"

"Birdie, sorry to bother you at work, but I need your presence at Selma Garrett's house. Do you know where she lived?"

Bridgette's frown deepened. "Yes, but why—"

"It has to do with the conversation you and Emma had with Duffy Martin at lunch. It's important."

"Oh. Okay…yes, I'll be right there," she said, and hung up.

"Is anything wrong?" Wade asked.

"I don't think so, but I have to meet the chief at Selma Garrett's house. It's up near the country club."

Wade frowned. "Do you want me to go with you?"

"I might need a ride," Bridgette said. "I think I have a slow leak on my right rear tire. I noticed it when Emma brought me back from lunch. I was going to get it fixed after work, but now I don't want to drive all the way up to the country club and have it go flat on me."

"Get whatever you need and meet me outside. I'll go tell Donny we're leaving."

Bridgette hit Save on the work she'd been doing and logged out. She went to wash up, then grabbed her purse.

Wade was waiting for her by his car and opened the door for her as she approached.

"You'll have to tell me how to get there," Wade said. "I don't remember that lady."

Bridgette told him the street to take as they left the parking lot.

"So what's going on?" Wade asked as he turned off Main and headed west.

"I'm not sure. The chief said it has to do with a boy named Duffy Martin. He and his family used to live here. Mama used to babysit him after school. They moved away years ago, and I forgot about them. Today, he was at Granny's when Emma and I were there and he came to our table, asking if he could talk to us. He began asking all of these questions about himself as a child and what did we remember about him. Stuff like that. We were talking, and then something I said set him off, and he thanked us and left. And now I get this call from the chief."

"I guess we'll find out soon enough," Wade said, and then pointed at the fork in the street up ahead. "Which direction do I go?" he asked.

Bridgette pointed. "Oh…take the street on the left," she said, and then glanced at him, thinking how absolutely gorgeous he was, then had to make herself focus. "That's the house…the one with the patrol car parked in the drive. Looks like Chief Pittman is already here."

Wade glanced in the rearview mirror as he pulled up into the drive. "Isn't that Peanut's car behind us?"

Bridgette turned to look. Not only was Peanut parking behind them, but another car was pulling in behind him.

"Yes, and that's Duffy Martin in the seat beside him. I wonder what's going on?"

As they exited their vehicles, Lon came out of the house to meet them and signaled to the officer sitting in his patrol car. The officer got out carrying a camera and a tripod.

"Everyone is here except for Woody Rice, and he's on the way," Lon said, then glanced at Duffy. The boy was visibly shaking and so pale he looked like he might pass out at any moment. "Are you okay, Duffy?"

The boy nodded. "A little overwhelmed, but I'll be okay."

Peanut gave him a quick pat on the back. "You're doing great, Duffy, and you're not alone. We're all here for you." Then he pointed at the man getting out of the other car. "Everyone, this is Anthony Roland, the new photographer for the *Blessings Tribune*. He's going to film this for me."

"Just call me Ant," the man said.

Bridgette was intrigued with the height of Ant's Mohawk and the single earring he was wearing. It looked like a scorpion, and as Ant began gathering up his gear, she realized she'd been right. It was a scorpion—a very detailed metallic scorpion, which in her mind would have been the kind to have if someone was of a mind to wear one in their ear.

And then she looked past the photographer and saw Duffy standing off to one side, tears rolling down his face. She immediately ran to him.

"Honey, what's wrong?"

He just shook his head.

Hoping to shift his focus, she introduced him to Wade.

"Duffy, this is my boss, Wade Montgomery."

Duff's chin went up as he shook Wade's hand.

"Nice to meet you, sir."

Wade saw the tears in his eyes and, like Bridgette, was immediately sympathetic.

"Nice to meet you, too. Bridgette was telling me that Marjorie used to babysit you."

Duff sniffed and swiped at the tears on his face. "Was that her name? All I remembered was Miss Margie."

"That's what all of her kids called her," Bridgette said.

And then Lon brought the lull to an end.

"There comes Woody," he said. "If you'll all follow me, we'll be going around back to the formal gardens. I have permission from Selma's daughter, Rita, to be on the property."

"What's going on? Why am I here?" Bridgette asked.

"We're on a treasure hunt," Lon said, and led the way.

———————

Duff's heart was pounding as he circled the stately home and, within seconds of seeing the grounds behind it, remembered running through the gardens on that winding flagstone path. But it wasn't the masonry that drew his attention. It was the perfectly manicured rose gardens, and in particular the one closest to the house.

He guessed the couple looking at them from the veranda must be the lady's daughter and husband, but he couldn't worry about what they were thinking about him. His whole focus was on what he'd done.

Lon stopped. Both his officer and the photographer from the paper were already filming, and he wanted everything recorded as they proceeded, including Duffy's comments.

"Duffy, do you see anything familiar?" Lon asked.

Duffy pointed toward a large window at the back of the house. "Yes. I'm pretty sure it's that rose garden closest to that big window."

Lon spoke to Birdie next. "Ma'am, would you please state your name for the camera."

"Yes, sir. I'm Bridgette Knox."

Lon nodded. "Duffy told me you once came and picked him up here. Is that true?"

"Yes," Bridgette said. "His dad took Duffy to work with him one day, and then late in the afternoon he called my mother and asked if she could pick Duffy up because his dad planned to work late to finish the job. My mother, Marjorie, was Duffy's regular babysitter when the need arose. But Mom was busy at the house that day and asked me to go get him and bring him to her. So I did. Duffy was really little… maybe six or so." Then she pointed toward the house. "He was out here in the gardens when I arrived."

"Can you remember where Duffy was, and in particular, what he was doing?"

Bridgette smiled. "He was over in that rose garden beneath that big window, belly down on the ground pulling dirt into a hole."

At that point, Woody piped up. "I remember that! One of Miss Selma's rosebushes died, and I'd dug it up about a week earlier. That day the new rosebush to replace it had arrived, and I cleaned out the hole again, then went to the shed to get the new planting. On the way back, I see Birdie coming across the grounds. Then I noticed the kid dragging dirt back into the hole I had just cleaned out."

Duff was silent, but wide-eyed. What he remembered and what they were saying was verification for so many things.

Wade was listening intently to the story unfolding and, like everyone else, still wondering what one thing had to do with another.

"So, Woody, what did you do after Birdie got the boy?" Lon asked.

The old man frowned. "Well, as I recall, I popped the rosebush out of the pot, dropped it in the hole, and began filling in the dirt as they left. I finished and went home. That's all I know. And 'scuse my language…but what the hell are we all doing here?"

"I need you to dig up that rosebush you planted," Lon said.

Woody's eyes widened in horror.

"Oh, I can't do that! It was one of Miss Selma's favorites. And it's huge."

"I know," Lon said. "But Rita has given her permission. We're going to cut it down at the ground and then dig up the roots."

"But why?" Woody asked.

Lon looked at Duff. "That's your story to tell, son."

Duff took a deep breath and then turned to face the people behind him, and in doing so gave both photographers a clear view of his face.

"Because I was playing pirates that day, just like I did every day. I found a treasure chest in the house and I put it in the hole. It was just a game to me. And then Birdie came and got me and said it was time to go home, and I forgot. And when the jewelry went missing, they put my dad in prison for it. I was so little, I didn't understand what was going on, and my family never told me details until just the other day. It triggered the memory of me doing this, and when I realized what it meant, I came back to dig up my treasure, which was actually Mrs. Garrett's missing jewelry, and clear my dad's name."

Bridgette gasped. "Oh my God! I was standing right beside you and never looked into that hole."

Woody was in shock. "Well, I looked in the hole, but I didn't see anything but dirt. I reckon he had pulled enough back into the hole to cover it up."

"So, let's get busy," Lon said. "We need to cut down the rosebush first."

"I have Uncle Dub's chainsaw in my car," Wade said. "We've been building a float for the parade tomorrow."

"Go get it," Lon said.

"I'll get shovels," Woody said, and headed for the garden shed out back, while the rest of them went to the veranda.

Selma's daughter, Rita, met them at the steps, well aware she was being filmed as well.

"This is exciting and, at the same time, a tragedy. My mother isn't alive to witness this, and this boy's father has spent ten years in prison for something he didn't do." Then she put her hand on Duff's shoulder. "As for you, all I'm going to say is that you are possibly the bravest young man I have ever known. This is an honorable thing you are doing. Your family must be so proud of you."

"His family doesn't know where he is," Peanut said. "They just know he's gone, but they do know he's okay. He wouldn't share any of this with them for fear he was remembering something that wasn't actually real."

Rita shook her head. "Amazing. How old were you, anyway?" she asked.

"I was six," Duff said, and then Wade came back with the chainsaw, and Woody came back carrying two shovels, and their conversation ended.

"I don't have any gloves, but I'll cut it down for you," Wade said.

"I've got gloves," Woody said.

"Do you have an extra pair?" Peanut asked.

"There are some in the house," Rita said, and ran in to get them.

Peanut took off his suit coat and put on the gloves, and he and Woody went through the path to the bush nearest the house.

"It's this one right here," Woody said. "It was done bloomin' for the year, and now I guess it's done bloomin' forever."

Wade started up the motor on the chainsaw, then got between the house and the bush.

"Okay, guys, hold back the branches and let's do this," he said.

"Well, hell, there went my shirt," Peanut said as a row of thorns on one limb tore through his sleeve. Then he laughed. "But what's a shirt when you're digging up treasure, right, Duffy?"

Duff couldn't see the humor in anything. He was mortified that he'd caused all this, and it was beginning to dawn on him that he still had to confess all this to his family, including his dad. He was convinced they were going to hate him.

Bridgette saw the tense set of Duff's jaw and put her arm around his waist. After a few moments, Duff gave in to her empathy and put his arm around her shoulders.

Within moments, Wad had the rosebush down. Woody tied a piece of nylon rope around the trunk and quickly dragged it away from the house. Once it was out of the way, they began digging.

Wade took one of the shovels and Woody took the other, and they began cutting into the tiny feeder roots with their shovels, trying to get under the main root ball.

"Originally, how deep was that hole?" Lon asked.

"At least two feet down, maybe a little more, and about that big in circumference to let the roots spread. But they have been growing for a long time now. Lord only knows how deep they are," Woody said.

Rita was leaning over the railing of the veranda, watching.

Lon glanced up at her.

"What was that jewelry box made of?" he asked.

"Mahogany, like the furniture in Mama's bedroom. I know it's been in the dirt for ten years, but Mom always said that wood was as durable as God."

"You heard her, boys," Lon said. "When you get to that depth, you might want to give up the shovels and start using your hands."

"Let me," Duff begged. "I'm the one who made this mess. Let me be the one to end it."

"When they get the hole dug down that far, it's all yours," Lon said.

Duff glanced at Bridgette, then walked away, moving closer to where they were digging, then closer still until he was standing nearly toe to toe with Wade and Woody as they dug.

Bridgette sat down on the steps, and Peanut sat down beside her.

"What do you think about all this?" he asked.

Bridgette shrugged. "I guess how sad it is. How long was Zack Martin's sentence, anyway?"

"Fifteen to twenty," Peanut said.

Bridgette frowned. "Why was it so long just for stolen jewelry?"

"He had priors. Nothing big. Just stupid stuff from when he was a young man. But the value of the missing jewelry was what did it. It was insured for over a quarter of a million dollars, mostly because of the family heirlooms. That stuff was irreplaceable."

Bridgette gasped. "Why would Selma Garrett even leave valuable jewelry out like that?"

He shrugged. "I have no idea. Here I was thinking the biggest excitement I would have this week was putting on the Santa suit, and now we're doing this. And speaking of Santa, are you ready for the parade tomorrow?"

She thought about the costume back in her office and grinned.

"As ready as I'll ever be," she said, and then pointed. "Oh look, they've put up the shovels."

"I don't want to miss this," Peanut said.

"Me either," Bridgette said, then got up and followed him.

———————————

"I think that's far enough," Woody said. "I wouldn't have dug a hole any deeper than this."

Wade glanced up, then took off his gloves and handed them to Duffy.

"Here you go, son, and good luck."

The officer filming hadn't missed a moment of the removal of the bush or the digging, and neither had Ant, and now they were both moving in closer to get footage of the hole and of Duffy digging.

Duff gloved up, and as everyone moved back from the hole, he got down on his knees and looked in, then stretched out on his belly and started digging through the roots, pulling up soil handfuls at a time, and as he did, for a few fleeting seconds he was six again, playing pirates, covering up his treasure. And then the vision segued to the handful of dirt he was pulling out and reality returned.

He scooted closer to the hole, thrusting in both hands, digging and feeling his way through the webbing of roots, praying that jewelry box was intact enough to feel it.

It was slow going, and despite the number of people around him, it was eerily silent until he jammed his finger into something solid. He paused and then began throwing dirt in every direction, like a dog digging up a bone.

"Did you find something?" Lon asked.

"Maybe," Duff said, and shoved his hand into the dirt he had loosened, and felt a corner. "It's here!" he said, and started crying. "I feel it... It's here, it's here."

And then Wade was on his knees beside him, helping him remove dirt from around and beneath the chest, until its top half was clearly visible.

Duff kept mumbling, "I'm sorry, Daddy, I'm so sorry," until Bridgette was in tears.

Then all of a sudden, Duff came up with it in both hands, then rocked back on his heels, holding it close against his chest.

"Oh my God…Miss Rita, I am so sorry. I wish your mama was here so I could apologize to her for what I did. Chief Pittman, I guess this goes to you and Miss Rita now. You'll have to verify everything is there, but I know for a fact I never took anything out. I just shut the lid and carried it out of the house. I never opened it again. I just buried it."

Lon lifted it carefully out of Duff's hands and then carried it up the steps of the veranda, with his officer right behind him, still filming.

"Set it here," Rita said, pointing to a glass-top table near a pair of wicker chairs.

"It looks rough, but it held together," Lon said, and lifted the lid.

The contents had not seen the light of day in ten years, but the moment the sunlight hit the diamonds in an antique choker, they began winking fire, as did earrings and bracelets. The silver was tarnished, but everything gold was pristine.

"Wow," Lon said, and then looked back at Duffy. He was leaning against the house with his head down on his knees. "Duffy, do you want to see this?"

Duff got up, brushing dirt off his clothes as he went, and then walked up the steps and stared down into the chest.

"I don't know how I'm ever going to explain this to my family. I don't know how my daddy will ever forgive me." His voice was shaking as he looked at Lon. "Am I under arrest or anything?"

"Lord no, son," Lon said.

"Absolutely not," Peanut added.

"So how do we go about getting my daddy out of jail?" Duff asked.

Peanut frowned. "That's going to be up to the DA who pressed charges, and then the courts, but once I present the evidence and your statement, and with affidavits from Woody and Birdie to back your story, this should be smooth sailing."

"And I will do whatever needs to be done on the family's behalf to make sure the court knows we are satisfied and wish to withdraw the charges," Rita added.

Peanut glanced up at Ant.

"Did you get all of what went down?" he asked.

"I sure did," Ant said. "If they're going to itemize the jewelry, I'll stay for that, too."

"Make sure I get a digital copy ASAP, and send me the bill. I'm going to need to be sharing it with a number of sources."

"My boss, Mavis, is going to want to see this," Ant said.

"Let her watch. She can write her story from it. There's nothing here to hide. We need the truth out. We need to get an innocent man out of prison."

"You got it," Ant said.

Duff looked down at his clothes, grimy from digging, and stood a little straighter.

"Mr. Butterman, I need a ride back to get my car, and I need to call my family," he said.

"Now's the time to tell them where you are," Peanut said. "You're going to have to give your statement, but this is Friday and I won't be in the office tomorrow because of the parade. We can do all this in my office Monday morning. My secretary will type it up for you, and then I'll need you to sign it before you go home. We'll stay in touch by phone and email."

"Yes, sir," Duff said, then added, "I want people here in Blessings to know what happened. I want my dad's name cleared. Even if it takes the courts longer, there's no reason to keep any of this a secret."

Lon grinned. "Oh, it won't stay secret long in Blessings. Nothing does. And if you want it told, then Peanut can drop by the Curl Up and Dye and tell his wife. Once news passes through the beauty shop, it's a done deal."

Duff nodded. "That's what I want. And don't sugarcoat my part in this. I'm the one who was guilty."

Bridgette hugged him. "No, Duffy. A little boy just got caught up in a game. A man made it right."

CHAPTER 6

Everyone dispersed from the Garrett property but Lon and Woody and the two men still filming the recovery.

Rita took every piece of jewelry from the box, then stated for the camera that all the missing pieces had been recovered. At that point, Ant packed up and left, and Lon sent his officer back to the station. Woody was filling up the hole and getting ready to haul off the rosebush as they left.

Rita and her husband went straight to the bank and put all the jewelry in her mother's safety deposit box.

Wade and Birdie went back to work, while Peanut took Duff to get his car, then headed to the Curl Up and Dye.

Ruby was curling LilyAnn Dalton's hair when Peanut walked in. He looked disheveled and somewhat guilty, which always meant he had something to confess.

Twin stylists Vesta and Vera Conklin had clients in their chairs, too, and when Peanut saw who they were, he grinned.

"I never saw so many pretty ladies in one place in my life. And if I'm not mistaken, you are all past Peachy Keen queens. By any chance will you be in the parade tomorrow?"

LilyAnn Dalton, who was sitting in Ruby's chair, gave him a thumbs-up. "You guessed it, Peanut. We are riding on the City of Blessings float."

Peanut winked. "Good. You're all way prettier than the mayor and the council members."

But Ruby wasn't buying the impromptu visit.

"What's going on?" she asked.

"You will not believe what I've been doing," he said.

And all of a sudden, the salon was silent. Even Mabel Jean

Doolittle, who was cleaning up her manicure station, stopped and turned to listen.

"Well…spill it," Ruby said.

"I just helped dig up Selma Garrett's missing jewelry."

They gasped.

"The jewelry that Zack Martin stole?" Vera said.

Peanut paused for effect. "Oh, but that's just it! Zack Martin did not take the jewelry after all," he said, and then he began to explain.

By the time he was finished, every woman in the place was in tears.

"Poor man. And poor little boy," Vera said.

"He's not a little boy anymore. He's a teenage kid who is completely shattered by what he just learned he'd done. But it took guts to come all this way on his own to make it right, and I'm going to do everything I know how to get this info to the proper authorities and get Zack Martin out of prison."

Ruby threw her arms around Peanut's neck.

"What a wonderful Christmas that would be for them. What are you waiting for?" she said.

Peanut hugged her. "I guess I was just waiting for that hug, and to confess that I tore the heck out of this shirt helping dig up a rosebush."

Ruby shrugged. "I think it's worth losing a shirt to get a man out of prison."

"I think you're right," Peanut said. "Oh…and by the way, the lights on the boobs of your Christmas tree lady are the only thing flashing."

Ruby gasped. "What? Oh lord! They weren't supposed to be flashing in the first place, they were supposed to be winking, and not just her boobs."

"Well, nothing is lit up except the lights across her boobs, so…"

"Crap. Probably a loose bulb. Oh well, I'll deal with that later. I've got to finish LilyAnn's hair so she can get home."

"And I need to get Betty started on some paperwork," Peanut said. "See you at home later."

"Oh wait!" Ruby said. "Are we allowed to talk about the jewelry?"

Peanut nodded. "Yes. Duffy specifically wanted everyone in Blessings to know that it was him, and not his dad, who took the jewelry. And he has both Birdie Knox and Woody Rice to back up his story. So talk away. The more people know his dad was innocent all along, the happier he's going to be."

As soon as Wade got Bridgette back to the store, it became obvious the tire on her car was even flatter than before. Wade ran in to get the boxes with her costume and loaded them into her car.

"If I come by later, will you model the costume for me?" Wade asked.

Bridgette got into the car, then rolled down the window.

"I'll put it on for you if you'll help me take it off," she said.

Wade leaned in the window, brushed his finger down the side of her cheek, then kissed her. "Count on it, darlin'. Now, from the looks of that tire, you better head to the station. Call me if you need help."

Bridgette gave him a thumbs-up and spun out of the parking lot.

Wade just shook his head as he watched her speed away—as if driving fast would get her there before the tire went flat. She was such a hotshot. He couldn't help but wonder if he was creating his own little monster by putting her on that mechanical bull. Every single guy in town was going to be chasing after her now. What the hell made him think this was going to be a good idea?

Duff got back to his motel, stripped and showered until the hot water ran cold, then dried off and put on clean clothes. He had accomplished a lot today, but confessing to his family was going to be even harder than to the lawyer and the police.

He crawled up on the bed, then glanced at the time. The school where his mom taught should be out by now, and he needed to hear her voice.

Candi Martin felt like she was a thousand years old. Having to focus on teaching first graders when her own baby was in some kind of trouble made her heart hurt. Every breath she took exacerbated the knot in her stomach, and she was constantly blinking back tears. It was all she could do to get through the day, and then the drive home was its own brand of hell.

Traffic in Jacksonville was never smooth, and at this time of day it was a nightmare. But she loved teaching, and the job kept a roof over their heads.

By the time she pulled into the driveway of their little bungalow and got out, her steps were dragging. Once inside, she began turning on lights, opening curtains, adjusting the air-conditioning, and letting light into her world.

She put her things in her room, changed out of her work clothes, and headed into the kitchen for something cold to drink. She had just plopped down on the living room sofa and taken her first sip of ginger ale when her cell phone rang. She glanced at caller ID and then quickly set her drink aside to answer.

"Hello! Duffy?"

"Hi, Mom."

Candi heard exhaustion, and something else in her son's voice that almost sounded like fear. The knot in her stomach grew tighter.

"Honey…are you okay? What's wrong?"

Duff started crying. "I'm okay, Mom…but I have something to tell you."

And then he began—from relating his shock upon learning why his dad had gone to prison, to his journey to Blessings, to the trip to the library and meeting up with Birdie and Emma, and then going to the lawyer, and the police. And all through the story, he kept saying, "I'm sorry, I'm so sorry," over and over and over until the story came to an end.

And all the while, Candi had listened in utter horror, unable to believe what he was telling her, blaming herself for all the years she thought she was protecting him. But it wasn't until he said the words "We found the treasure I buried. We found the jewelry" that she gasped in disbelief.

"Oh my God! Duffy! This means they have to release your dad, right?"

Duff wiped his eyes and then grabbed a handful of tissues and blew his nose.

"They couldn't tell me when it would happen because it all has to go back through the courts. But Mr. Butterman said while he couldn't save Dad from going to prison, he would do everything necessary to get him out."

Now Candi was weeping. "Oh, Duffy…I don't know what to say. You must have been horrified, but I'm so proud of you. Oh my God! I can't believe what you just did. And all on your own."

Duff was silent a moment, then his voice was shaking when he spoke.

"So, you aren't mad at me?"

Candi groaned. "No! Sweetheart! Why would I be mad? You were six years old. It was just a game to you. And we told you nothing. If I hadn't tried to protect you from what was happening, this might never have gone this far. All of us did that. Even your dad didn't want you involved in the ugly side of it. You were never in the courtroom. You never heard any of the details. We made sure of that."

"But Dad went to prison for something I did," Duff said, and then broke into tears all over again.

"And you're also the one who went the extra mile to clear his name and get him out. Are you still in Blessings?"

"Yes. I have to be here until at least Monday to sign my statement for Mr. Butterman and for the police chief."

"Then Allen and I are coming to you."

Duff wiped tears off his face again and took a deep breath.

"This motel is pretty crummy, Mom. I don't think—"

"Is there another place to stay?" Candi asked.

"The Blessings B and B, but I didn't want to spend the money."

"You don't worry about anything else. Just tell me where you are and we'll come to you. We'll figure the rest out after we get there."

"I'm at the only motel. My room number is five. You'll see Allen's car parked in front of the door. The motel is on the far end of Main, across the street from the Blue Ivy Bar, and there's a big Christmas parade in town tomorrow."

"Then we'll come tonight," Candi said. "As soon as Allen gets home, we'll leave. How long did it take you to make the trip?"

"About two and a half hours, I guess," Duff said.

"Okay. Go get something to eat, and just breathe. The hard stuff is over. I love you. I'm proud of you. And we'll see you soon."

"Love you too. Drive safe," Duff said.

He disconnected, then got up and went to wash his face. One look in the mirror, and he was wishing he'd brought his sunglasses. His eyes were red-rimmed and swollen from crying. But he didn't have to go inside anywhere. He could do the drive-through at Broyles Dairy Freeze, and maybe go to the park to eat.

While Duff was getting a grip on his emotions, Candi was on her laptop, looking up Blessings Bed and Breakfast. As soon as she got a number, she made the call.

"Blessings B and B. Merry Christmas. This is Rachel."

"Rachel, do you have a couple of rooms available for this weekend?"

"Yes. How many per room?" Rachel asked.

"I'd need one room with a couple of beds for my sons. They're not children, they're men. And one room for me. Bed size is immaterial there. We're driving in from Jacksonville, Florida, this evening."

"Yes, we have those available," Rachel said. "I'll need a credit card to hold them."

"Yes, of course," Candi said, and a few minutes later, she had a confirmation email.

She'd been so scared something bad was happening with Duffy, when all the while he was doing something heroic. She just wanted to see his face and hold him in her arms.

She sent a text to Allen, telling him to get home as soon as he could, that she knew where Duffy was and that he needed them, and then she went to pack.

Allen was in an Uber and on the way home when he got the text. About thirty minutes later, he came running into the house. When he saw his mom in the living room and a suitcase by the door, his heart dropped.

"What's going on? Is he hurt? Where is he?" Allen cried.

"He's not hurt. He's in Blessings. You know the other night when we were talking about Selma Garrett passing away, and that it was her jewelry your dad went to jail for stealing?"

"Yes, but what's that have to do with—"

"Do you remember the day your dad went there to paint, and he took Duffy with him because I was at the dentist getting a wisdom tooth pulled?"

Allen nodded.

"Well, Duffy spent the day at Selma Garrett's house playing pirates while your dad was working."

Allen grinned. "He was always playing pirate when he was a kid."

Candi sighed. "Yes, well, while he was upstairs, he saw Selma Garrett's jewelry box sitting open on a table in her bedroom, thought it was pirate treasure, and took it outside and dropped it in a hole the gardener had just dug."

"Oh my God," Allen mumbled. "He didn't!"

"Yes, he did. And then Birdie Knox came to get Duff and take him to Marjory's house, and Duffy forgot about the game, and the gardener planted a rosebush on top of the treasure. And your daddy went to jail. That's where Duffy went. Back to Blessings. And long story short…he went to the police. They found the jewelry, and your dad's lawyer from before is going to do all the paperwork to get your dad released and clear his name."

"Oh man! Mom! That's the most amazing thing ever," Allen said. "Do we know where Duffy is staying?"

"Yes. And he can't leave Blessings until he signs all the paperwork for his statements, which can't happen until Monday, and I'm not leaving him there another night on his own. I have rooms reserved for us at a B and B. Go pack."

Allen picked his mother up and swung her off her feet. He was laughing and crying all at once.

"Oh man! What if Dad gets home before Christmas? Talk about a miracle."

Candi was laughing with him. "I know. We can't count on the timing, but we are getting him back! Now go! Pack. The sooner we get to Blessings, the sooner I will see Duffy. I'm getting my guys back, even if it's one at a time."

━━━━━━

LaJune King left Blessings in shame and in tears. Her mother and dad took the kids and their clothes and toys with them when they left, leaving LaJune to lock up and follow.

She'd packed up her own clothes and left everything else.

She took half of their money from the bank, and their car, leaving Josh with the truck that didn't run and a note.

I am going to file for divorce, and I don't ever want to see your face again. When the children are old enough, if they want to come find you, they can. But at this point in your life, you are not a fit parent. You are a liar, a gambler, and a thief, and as far as I'm concerned, you have abdicated your parental rights.

As for what's missing in this house, it is nothing more than what you threw away. We didn't matter enough for you to do the right thing, so I did it for you.

You are not the man a father should be.

You gambled and you lost...us included.

Then she laid the truck keys and her key to the house on top of the note, picked up her purse, and headed out of the house. She paused at the door to turn the lock, then pulled it shut behind her.

Everyone in Blessings now knew why Josh King had been arrested, and a good number of them, including some of Josh's gambling buddies, also knew he'd been arraigned and bail had been set, but Josh was still in jail. So they posted his bail and were waiting outside the police station when Josh emerged.

He had been curious as to who had put up the money to get him out, but when he saw the Linley brothers leaning against their truck, his heart dropped.

Shit. Now he was indebted to them again.

"Mack! Arnie! Are you the ones who posted my bail?"

They nodded, grinning as they slapped him on the back.

"Us and a couple of the other guys. That's what friends are for," they said. "We thought we'd wait around to give you a ride home."

"I appreciate it!" Josh said. "My wife is pissed, so I was guessing I would be in jail until my court date."

They all piled into Mack Linley's pickup, still talking as they drove away.

"This is your first offense, right?" Arnie said.

Josh nodded.

"Shoot, then you got this beat," Arnie added. "You might have to do a couple of months at the most, but if your lawyer is any good, he'll likely get you paroled and into some weekly Gamblers Anonymous meetings."

Josh nodded, but he was also aware that he was going to need a job. His last paycheck wasn't going to last long, and after what he'd done, no one in Blessings was going to want to hire him.

"Uh…turn right up at the next street," Josh said. "It's the white house with blue shutters."

"Nice," Mack said as they saw it up ahead. He pulled into the drive long enough for Josh to get out. "See you around, buddy," the Linley brothers said.

"You bet, and thanks again."

"Just show up in court or we'll take it out of your hide," they said, and then threw back their heads and laughed.

Josh grinned, but he wasn't laughing inside. The Linley boys were no one to mess with. They were why he'd stolen the money to begin with. They were the enforcers for the man in Savannah who'd held his IOU.

They drove away as Josh was going up the steps. He'd already noticed the only vehicle under the carport was his truck. That was not a good sign. He unlocked the door, and the moment sultry heat hit him in the face, he knew they were gone. The air-conditioning was off, and there wasn't a sound within the walls.

His heart sank as he headed for the kitchen, and then he saw the keys and the note. Shock, then sadness grew with every word he read; then he ran through the house, unable to believe this was happening.

Everything was still there, except them.

The pain that shot through him nearly sent him to his knees. He thought about his son's laugh, and reading his daughter stories every night before she went to sleep. He thought about how good LaJune smelled when she came to bed at night, all fresh from her shower and warm as she cuddled up next to him.

This was the biggest fuckup of his life.

He took his cell phone out of his pocket and put it on the charger, turned on the air-conditioning, then went back to the kitchen to find something to eat.

He grabbed a can of beer from the back of the fridge and popped the tab, took a long drink, then chose a container of leftover fried chicken and ate until there was nothing left but bones.

By that time, he was two beers in and his belly was full. He was hurt and trying to move into defiant, but the truth was he had a roof over his head for the rest of this month, money in the bank, and time to figure out what to do next. And, like the Linley boys said, to make sure he didn't miss his damn court date.

But the moment he thought about money in the bank, he wondered if she'd taken that, too, and ran to get his phone to check their balance. His heart sank when he saw half of it was missing, but he couldn't fault her. She'd left him half when she could have taken it all.

———————

Bridgette was standing in front of the full-length mirror, grinning. All of the red, white, and black was reminiscent of Santa's clothes, but the style was certainly farm-related.

The red jeans cupped her backside just enough. The red-and-white-plaid shirt fit a little snug across her breasts, but not too tight. She put on the black belt, then tied the little black bandanna around her neck, slapped that red cowboy hat on her head, and stepped back to view the full effect.

Thirty-four double-C boobs. Check.

She got a hand mirror so she could see what she looked like from behind.

Tight pants. Firm butt. Check.

All girl. Double check.

And then her doorbell rang. Wade's timing was perfect.

She left the mirror on the counter and strutted with every step. Flung the door open, and then stood there with her hands on her hips.

"Is this what you were going for?"

Wade was dumbstruck at how utterly sexy she looked.

"Not to that degree," he muttered and quickly walked in, shutting the door behind him.

"Well, there's no way to change any of this now, and I'm fine with it."

"Oh…I'm fine with it, and every male over the age of ten who sees you on that bull will be fine with it, too," Wade said. He picked her up in his arms and carried her back to her bedroom, then began peeling her out of the clothes, one item at a time.

He had the overwhelming male instinct to mark her so that other people would know who she belonged to, but the ring he planned to give her for Christmas was at his house, and he was too deep in want to do anything but sink into her sweet, hot depths.

They made love not once but twice, with a red cowboy hat hanging on a bedpost and her bra on the floor beside her boots. And they didn't stop until their hearts were pounding and their muscles were trembling—satisfied and satiated from the gluttony of their lust.

"You make me crazy," Wade whispered as he nuzzled the soft spot beneath her ear.

Bridgette rolled over on top of him and wrapped her arms around his neck, then tucked her head beneath his chin.

"Believe me, it is my pleasure."

CHAPTER 7

It was almost nine o'clock when Allen and Candi drove into Blessings.

"Oh, honey, look how pretty it all looks," Candi said. "Christmas is everywhere."

"It feels weird coming back like this," Allen said.

"I don't feel anything but relief Duffy is okay and awe of what he did."

Allen nodded. "I know, Mom. I always knew he was a good kid, but facing all this on his own is amazing. That would be hard for a grown man to do."

"I can't wait to put my arms around him," Candi said. "Just keep driving up Main like you're going out of town. The motel is at the southern end of Main."

"I kind of remember it," Allen said.

"It's been there forever," Candi said. "But we're not staying there. We're going to a bed-and-breakfast. I have the address. As soon as we get Duffy checked out, we'll head that way."

A couple of minutes later, Candi pointed. "There it is!"

Allen saw his car almost immediately and parked beside it.

Before they could get out, the door to room five opened and Duffy emerged.

Candi gasped. Backlit by the light coming out of his room, Duff looked like an old man. His shoulders were slightly stooped and his clothes were disheveled. It was yet to be seen how this would affect the rest of his life. Was he going to view it as a disaster, or overcoming all odds to do the right thing?

She dropped her purse in the floorboard and jumped out running.

Duff threw his arms around her, too overwhelmed to talk.

And then Allen appeared and began hugging the both of them. He was at peace. The two people he loved most, the ones he was responsible for, were happy and safe again.

"Man, it is good to see your face, Little Bro. Are you packed?" Allen asked.

Duff nodded. "All of my stuff is in the car. I was just waiting for you guys to get here."

"Then I'll go with you to check out. Mom, you get back in the car and wait for us," Allen said.

Candi didn't hesitate, and once inside, she quickly locked the doors. The motel was creepy and old and she was horrified her son had been here at all.

As she waited, she couldn't help but think of all the years Zack had missed with his family, but he was still the only man she'd ever loved and she couldn't wait to give him the good news.

Then she saw her boys returning and unlocked the car as Allen got in.

"We're going to follow Duff. He knows the way," Allen said.

And once more they were on the move. This time across town to the Blessings B and B.

There were two cars in the parking lot when they arrived. The shrubbery around the building was wrapped with multicolored Christmas lights. There was a large green wreath with a red bow hanging on the front entrance, and a tall and brightly decorated Christmas tree was visible through the windows.

"This is wonderful," Candi said.

"You go on in, Mom. Duff and I will get the bags."

Candi grabbed her purse and got out, pausing as she stood to absorb the relative quiet of a small-town Friday night. She'd long since forgotten the good times they'd had here and wondered what their lives would have been like now, had all of this never happened.

Then she shook off the thought. *What if* and *if only* were not phrases in her vocabulary anymore. She took a deep breath of the still night air, glanced behind her to make sure all was well with her boys, then hurried inside.

There was a woman behind the desk and a man coming down the stairs as Candi approached.

"Welcome to Blessings. I'm Rachel Goodhope, and this is my husband, Bud. Are you the Martin family?"

Candi nodded. "Yes, I'm Candi Martin. My sons are on their way in with the bags."

"I'll help them," Bud said, and ran to hold the door as Rachel began checking them in.

Allen and Duff entered, then stopped at the front desk with the bags.

"These are my sons, Allen and Duffy," Candi said.

Rachel's eyes widened as she looked at the family again.

"Oh wait! Martin. Duffy Martin! Are you the Duffy Martin everyone in town is talking about? The one who found Selma Garrett's missing jewelry?"

Candi tensed, thinking she was going to have to defend him, but Duff spoke up instead.

"Yes, ma'am. That's me."

Rachel's gaze went straight to Candi.

"You must be so proud of him. What an amazing young man you have raised!" Rachel said.

Candi relaxed. "Thank you."

"Since you're here for the weekend, you're in for a treat tomorrow," Rachel said. "Our annual Christmas parade begins at 10:00 a.m. and goes all the way past the nursing home before it disperses. The stores on Main will shut down for a couple of hours and traffic will be detoured, so if you're in the mood for all that, you won't be disappointed. We serve breakfast here from six to ten, and then there are other places in Blessings to have your other meals. Bud will show you to your rooms. And if you're hungry, there are mini-refrigerators in each room with snacks, and fresh-baked cookies. Rest well, and see you in the morning."

Bud had the room keys in hand as he turned to the guests.

"We have a small elevator if you'd rather not take the stairs."

"No, we're fine with stairs," Candi said, and as they followed him, the scent of pine from the garlands on the stair rail went with them.

Bud paused halfway down the hall and unlocked the door on his left.

"This is the room your sons will share. It has two standard-size beds." He led them in, showed them around, and what number to use on the house phone if they needed anything, then turned to Candi. "Your room is next door. If you'll follow me."

"I'll bring your bag, Mom," Allen said, and followed them out the door, leaving Duff momentarily alone.

For the first time since Duff's arrival in Blessings, he felt like he could breathe. This place was so clean and welcoming, and the air-conditioning was cool and silent—the polar opposite of the motel where he'd just spent the last two days.

As he set his bag on the bed, he began wondering if there was a place in Blessings where he could do laundry. He was going to run out of clean clothes before he got home.

Then Allen returned, and his mom walked in behind him with a stack of jeans and shirts and laid them on his bed.

"I was afraid you might be needing some clean stuff," she said.

"Aw, Mom, you are the best," Duff said. "I was just wondering where I could do laundry."

"This should hold you until we get home," Candi said.

Allen shut the door, felt the awkwardness among them, and knew exactly what to do. They'd always communicated best at the table during meals, so he opened the mini-fridge, took out three bottles of pop and a plate of mini-sandwiches, added a couple bags of chips from a basket on top of the fridge, and made a picnic on top of the table.

They all sat down around it, dissecting the contents of the sand-wiches before choosing which ones they wanted. As soon as they were settled and eating, Candi paused.

"Talk to us, Duffy. Tell us what you've done and who has been helping you. And how on earth did Rachel Goodhope already know who you are and what you did?"

Duff quickly swallowed his bite and washed it down with a sip of his pop.

"Because I told Chief Pittman and the lawyer that I wanted everyone in Blessings to know why I came back. I wanted them to know we found the jewelry because I'm the one who knew where to look. I wanted them to know Dad was innocent all along, and that it was my fault he went to jail."

Candi nodded. "News travels fast in small towns, and Blessings is no exception."

Allen kept staring at Duffy. The kid didn't even look like himself anymore. He couldn't think what had changed until Duff looked up and caught him staring, and that's when Allen saw it. It was the look in Duff's eyes—like he'd seen hell and was trying to find his way back.

"I'm proud of you, little brother. Are you going to eat the other half of your chicken salad sandwich?"

The question ended the seriousness, and then to Allen's surprise, Duff laid the half of his sandwich on Allen's napkin.

"That's for taking your car without asking," he said. "Now we're even."

Allen laughed. "Only you would consider half a chicken salad sandwich proper compensation for stealing my car."

"I didn't steal it. I borrowed it…and now you have it back. Do you want the sandwich or not?"

Allen ruffled Duff's hair. "Yes, and now we're even."

———

Wade left Bridgette in bed wearing nothing but a smile. She was too satisfied in her soul to do anything but breathe. Her agenda tomorrow was a different story.

She was to meet Wade at the warehouse by 8:00 a.m., dressed for the parade. They had to be in line by nine, so they had an hour to adjust the speed on the bull and let her practice.

She was excited and a little bit nervous. In her whole life, the only animal she'd ever ridden was a horse on a merry-go-round. So once she rode the bull down Main, she'd be two for two on mechanical animals and zero on real ones.

She finally made herself get up, and began retrieving the pieces of the scattered costume and hanging them back in the closet. She caught a glimpse of herself in the full-length mirror and paused, eyeing her own reflection.

There was something about being loved that lit a woman from within. She'd never thought of herself as anything but a girl with ordinary features. But the woman looking back at her now knew her worth to the man who loved her, and she was beautiful.

She sighed, then headed for the shower. Tomorrow would come all too soon.

But as she was turning on the water, the couple in the apartment above her began another round of their late-night fights. She hoped they were over it by the time she went to bed. She didn't want to listen to that again all night.

As the evening progressed, Josh King's mood continued to darken. He drank all the beer in the refrigerator, but with no vehicle to go get more, he turned up the volume on the TV to hide the silence within the house, then went to the garage to see if there was any stored out there.

He didn't find any beer and went back inside and found himself staring at the Christmas tree in the corner. The lights were off, just like the lights in his life.

All of a sudden, he was hit with an overwhelming sense of despair.

He'd had everything, and now it was gone. He wasn't worth shit. His life wasn't worth living.

He picked up his phone and sent LaJune a text.

> *I'm sorry.*
> *I love you.*
> *Forgive me.*

Then he laid the phone down on the table, grabbed his coat and his wallet, and went out the back door and started walking. There was no destination in mind. He just couldn't face what was left of him.

———————

It had taken LaJune an hour to get the kids settled and finally in bed. They were beginning to realize this wasn't just a visit and that they weren't going home, and they were upset.

She was sad and heartsick and second-guessing her decision when she finally got to her room. But at the same time, she couldn't go home to nothing. Josh was going to jail, and even if she had a job, she wouldn't make enough to keep a roof over their heads, let alone pay childcare for the time she was away from home.

When her phone signaled a text and she saw it was from Josh, she frowned. Obviously he was out of jail or he wouldn't have use of a phone.

She opened the message, expecting some big explanation and a plea for her to come home, but as she started reading it, the hair stood up on the back of her neck. He wasn't begging her to come back. It read like he was saying goodbye!

Now, she didn't know if it was just an acceptance of the harshness of the letter she left or something else. She didn't think he would ever do anything to himself. But this made her uneasy. She started to call him, and then stopped.

This was her first test, and so far she had no reason to go back.

Peanut went home satisfied beyond measure. Never in all his years of practicing law had he ever had the opportunity to get an innocent man out of prison, and he was determined not to mess it up.

He and Betty had worked tirelessly all afternoon, preparing the necessary steps to start this.

He'd been on the phone with Lon, requesting a copy of the police report regarding the recovery of the missing items. Peanut already knew the justice system was not predisposed to releasing anyone once they'd been tried and convicted. Even when evidence was discovered later that proved their innocence, it was often a battle. It was a true flaw in the justice system, but one he intended to overcome.

And the more he thought about it, the more certain he was that a big sway of public opinion might go a long way in convincing a judge to vacate the sentence. He wanted an open-and-shut airtight case of wrongful conviction. He not only wanted Zack Martin freed, he also wanted the sentence vacated. That was what Peanut wanted for Christmas.

That and nothing more.

Wade drove home still thinking of Bridgette. He climbed out of the shower still thinking of her, and as he was getting ready to go to bed, he was still thinking of her.

There were no words for how much she meant to him. He'd bought an engagement ring over two months ago and had come so close to giving it to her a dozen times since, but he had this dream of putting it on her finger at Christmas. But that dream was beginning to feel unrealistic. Life was unpredictable, and far too short, and he was tired of waiting. The next time they made love, that ring would be on her finger.

Elliot Graham's day had been purposeful.

He'd started out by wearing his favorite Christmas shirt—a long-sleeved blue T-shirt with a little red cardinal perched on the outer limb of a snow-covered pine tree. It made him feel festive.

Then he drove to the Crown to get iced Christmas cookies. As he went down Main, he took the time to check out the decorated storefronts.

After he picked up the cookies, he drove to the Curl Up and Dye to get his hair cut. It was so long that it had begun curling at the back of his neck.

Within thirty minutes, his hair was back to the way he liked it. He paid and passed Ruby as he was leaving.

She was in the window, trying to get the lights on her mannequin to start blinking again. The only ones working were the ones over the mannequin's breasts. Ruby's face was as red as her hair, and she was muttering beneath her breath as he walked out the door.

But then he stopped, turned around, and walked back into the salon.

"Miss Ruby, if I may suggest…"

Ruby stopped. "Yes, you may," she said, and swiped at a curl on her forehead.

Elliot moved closer, eyeing the multitude of lights, then moved around behind the mannequin. He stood for a moment, then reached down and tightened a single bulb.

"Voilà!" Elliot said.

Ruby gasped. "You did it! They're all on again. How on earth did you… Oh, never mind. I know better than to ask you that, but you are a sweetheart. I could just hug your neck!"

Elliot blinked. "No, no need for all that. Happy to help," he said, and hurried back out the door.

Still unwilling to go home, he meandered through the stores, picking out a gift apiece for his neighbors across the street. Dan and Alice Amos and their two children, Charlie and Patty, had become the family he never had.

He put his things in the car and then drove up the street to Granny's. He got out, expecting to eat alone, and then Sully's wife, Melissa, came in behind him, and before he knew it, he was sitting at a table and having the meat-loaf special with her, listening to her discuss the headache of having one of their steam machines break down at the cleaners and trying to get a repairman out of Savannah before the end of the day.

"If I had the part, I'd fix the dang thing myself," Melissa muttered, and poked a french fry in her mouth.

Elliot nodded, remembering when she'd inherited the cleaners and what a good businesswoman she'd turned out to be. She just needed to vent her frustration, and he was good at listening.

When the meal came to an end, Elliot picked up her ticket to pay for her lunch as well, and when she began to demur, he frowned.

"No. I insist. Your company was a pleasure," he said.

"Then, thank you, Elliot. You're a dear," she said, and kissed his forehead as she got up to leave.

"Hey, hey, don't get too friendly with my wife," Sully said as he passed by their table.

"He's being a gentleman, as always," Melissa said. "And I was just thanking him for my lunch. I have to go. We have an issue at the cleaners."

She blew Sully a kiss and left.

Elliot followed Sully back up to the register, paid for their meals, and meandered back out to his car. He'd turned down dessert, but he had a hankering for a snow cone. This was the month of Christmas. There should be snow but there was not, and the snow cone would suffice, so he drove to the Crown.

A few minutes later he was sitting at one of the tables, shivering ever so slightly as he ate his way through a Heavenly Blue. Finally, the snow cone was gone, and even though the temp was in the eighties, Elliot was chilled and ready to go home.

As he was driving through town, he got one of those feelings. Something was amiss in Blessings. He didn't know what, but he would. Sooner or later, trouble always showed its face to him.

After he got home, he sat down in his easy chair, pulled an afghan over his legs, and read until he dozed off. When he awoke, it was long after sundown, too late to eat a meal but still early enough for a bedtime snack. He went to the kitchen and began making himself a cup of tea to go with one of his Christmas cookies. He was debating between a hibiscus-flavored tea or a plain Earl Grey when the room he was standing in began to fade away.

Suddenly, he was standing outside his house, watching a man walking beneath the streetlights, his head down, his shoulders slumped, his feet dragging.

Elliot felt the man's hopelessness and despair like a physical pain and knew if he said nothing—did nothing—the man was going to die. He turned off the fire under the teakettle and grabbed a jacket on his way out the door.

Within moments of clearing his porch, Elliott saw the man from his vision coming toward him down the street. He took a deep breath and then headed for the curb.

―――――――――

Josh hadn't looked up once since he left his house. He just kept walking from one puddle of light to the next, waiting for the other shoe to fall. Waiting for fate to take him out of this world. He wasn't sure he had the guts to do it himself, but he was ready to quit. All he needed was one more stroke of bad luck and it would be over, and he didn't care how it happened as long as he didn't have to face tomorrow.

So when a man suddenly appeared in front of him, forcing him to stop, he frowned. With the streetlight behind the man, he couldn't see much of his features, but he knew by the white hair that he was old. And then the old man spoke.

"That is not the answer," Elliot said.

The hair stood up on the back of Josh's neck. "Who are you? What are you talking about?"

"My name is Elliot. Will you come inside with me? I have hot tea and cookies."

Josh laughed, and the sound was awful—like a scream of rage and unbearable pain.

"Tea and cookies won't solve my problems. Let me pass, old man."

"I have a message for you," Elliot said.

Josh threw up his hands, trying to shoo the old man away.

"No, you don't. You don't know me. I don't know you or what your game is, but there's not one soul in this town who gives a shit about me."

But Elliot wouldn't quit. "Your name is Joshua. You were born in Louisville, Kentucky, and your parents died when you were ten. You were raised in foster homes until you aged out of the system. You have been trying to prove your worth to the world since the age of eighteen, and failing miserably."

"How the hell do you know that? No one knows that," Josh whispered.

"Who is Lydia?" Elliot asked.

Josh froze. "That was my mother's name."

"That's who told me you were out here. She sent me to get you, to stop you. She says it's not your time."

Josh staggered backward. "What are you?"

"I'm an artist. I paint pictures," Elliot said. "Come inside and sit with me. I have a message to deliver, and I am too old to stand out in the cold."

Josh followed because he had nothing else to do, and because he wanted this old man to be the real deal.

The moment he walked inside, he felt enveloped within the peace.

"Let's go back to the kitchen," Elliot said. "I have the kettle on."

Josh trailed the old man, admiring the elegance of the old mansion and its furnishings, and now that he was seeing Elliot in full light, he recognized his face. He'd just never known his name.

"Sit here, get a cookie, and make yourself comfortable," Elliot said, and took the cover off the cookies.

He made cups of tea, opting for the Earl Grey, and carried them to the table, then gave Josh a long, intent look.

"Your mother is sorry you were left behind, but their time here was over. They knew your path would not be easy, but they have always been with you."

Josh glared. "No, they haven't. If they had, my life would have been different."

"After the age of eighteen, your life is what it is because of the free will of your choices. We all have options. Always. Whether you choose something in the heat of the moment, or study it thoroughly before you make that choice, it's still your free will."

Josh broke off a piece of cookie and crammed it in his mouth. He wanted to be angry. He wanted someone besides him to be wrong.

"Your mother says when things get hard, you quit. Is this true?"

Josh sighed. "I don't know."

"Do you love your family?" Elliot asked.

Josh's eyes welled. "Yes, but they're gone. My wife took our children and left me."

"And you know why," Elliot said. "It was not your first mistake, was it?"

Josh shook his head.

"You chose gambling over them. You stole money from a man who trusted you. And you're mad at everyone but yourself for doing it. Am I right?" Elliot asked.

Josh shrugged.

Elliot could feel the war within the young man. He felt his despair like a physical pain.

"Your mother says the people you hang out with are the ones who bailed you out of jail. She says they did it to pull you back into their circle. She says they're poison."

Josh sighed. "I'm kind of afraid of them."

"Then use your free will and stay away from them," Elliot said.

Josh leaned forward, pinning Elliot with a teary stare.

"I don't have a job. I'm going to run out of money. I will not have a place to live. My family left me. I will likely go to jail. I am tired of life kicking me every time I'm down."

Elliot tilted his head slightly, as if he was listening, and then nodded.

"Your mother says stop feeling sorry for yourself. You had a good job. You had a great family and a home and money, and you chose what happened. Even though you didn't expect the consequences, you chose it."

Josh started crying, and once he did he couldn't stop.

"If I could go back, I would never pick up a deck of cards again, but there aren't second chances for people like me."

Elliot felt the stir of energy around him. It was like standing in a whirlwind only he could feel. He listened, and then reached across the table and laid his hand on Josh's arm.

"I will help you. Tomorrow morning I will come to your home, and we will go to Dub Truesdale and give him the money you stole."

"I don't have it," Josh said. "I used it to pay a gambling debt."

"I do," Elliot said. "So, we will pay what you owe, and after that it will be up to Mr. Truesdale as to how he proceeds. He will not want you working for him again, but I will hire you to work for me."

Josh wiped his eyes, unable to believe what he was hearing.

"You'd do that for me? I'm a stranger to you."

"I do not share tea and cookies with strangers," Elliot said, and then smiled slightly. "And Lydia vouched for you, or I would not have let you in the front door."

"What's the job? I don't have many skills," Josh said.

"Can you drive a forklift?" Elliot asked.

"Yes, sir," Josh said.

"Perfect, and you have a strong back, and that's what I require. After we speak to Dub Truesdale, I will take you to the Crown and introduce you to Wilson Turner, the manager, and then you will work in the back, unloading shipments. You will get paid twice a month, and you will not let anyone down, ever again. Do you understand me?"

"I never thought anyone in Blessings would ever hire me again. But what if the manager says no?"

"Well, it's not common knowledge, and I'd appreciate you keeping it to yourself, but I own the Crown, so the manager works for me," Elliot said.

Josh was in shock. Although it was often the topic of conversation, no one knew who had bought the old Piggly Wiggly store and turned it into the Crown. No one knew this. And this old man just trusted him with the information.

"I'll be honored, sir. But when my court date comes, I'll have to appear, and there's a good chance I'll wind up doing time."

"Why?" Elliot asked.

"Because I stole—" His eyes widened. "Oh. Right. You're paying it back. Are you saying Dub might drop the charges?"

"I do not speak for anyone but myself…and, of course, the endless number of spirits who have plagued me all my life. However, I do know there is the possibility that might happen. We can always hope. And in the meantime, you will be working on regaining the remnants of the man you are meant to be."

"Yes, sir. Thank you, sir. I will never be able to repay you for this kindness."

"Then pay it forward," Elliot said. "Now…it's getting late and you need to go home. Finish your tea. I'm going to get my keys and drive you."

"No, sir, you've done more than enough for me. I can walk," Josh said.

Elliot shook his head. "If you aren't home safe and sound, Lydia will not let me rest."

He stepped out of the room long enough to retrieve his keys, then led Josh out the back, pausing to turn on the floodlights lighting the garage. Then they got in his car. Elliot left the driveway like a race-car driver taking a curve at LeMans, only backward.

Josh grabbed onto his seatbelt to hang on.

"Uh...I live a—"

"Lydia is directing me," Elliot said. "We'll be there in no time." And he was right. He pulled up to the little white house with blue shutters and put the car in park. "I will come pick you up early in the morning, and we will go to Dub Truesdale's house."

"How early?" Josh asked.

"Eight. Don't be late."

"No, sir. I mean, yes, sir. Oh lord...I don't know how to thank you," Josh said.

"Thank your mother, and don't disappoint her again. Oh. I need Dub's phone number, which I assume you have."

"Yes, sir, I do," Josh said.

Elliot handed him pen and paper. Josh wrote it down, then got out, and the moment he shut the car door, Elliot sped away, turning a corner on three wheels, and disappeared.

Josh went inside, so rattled he wasn't sure what to think. But if Elliot was right and God was good, maybe he wouldn't go to jail after all.

As for Elliot, the moment he got home, he called Dub.

It was almost 10:00 p.m., but when Elliot Graham was on a mission, time did not exist. The call rang several times before Dub answered.

"Hello."

"Mr. Truesdale, this is Elliot Graham. I apologize for the late call."

"No, no, that's okay. We were just watching TV. What can I do for you, sir?"

"I need to bring Josh King to your house in the morning at eight. We will be paying back the money he took from you."

Dub was stunned. "Uh…what? We? You mean you're coming with him?"

"Yes. I'm paying his debt, and then he's going to work at the Crown come Monday."

Dub was dumbstruck. "The manager needs to know Josh isn't trustworthy."

"Well, I beg to differ, and the manager will be fine with it," Elliot said. "So, we'll see you in the a.m. and then we'll all be free to enjoy the weekend."

"But, why?" Dub asked.

"Why what?" Elliot countered.

"Why are you doing this?"

"Because it's Christmas, and he's too young to die," Elliot said.

Dub gasped. "What? Josh is dying?"

"Not now," Elliot said. "Not after I convinced him he still had a life worth living."

The hush that followed was telling.

"So, eight o'clock?" Elliot asked.

"Yes. Eight o'clock," Dub said.

———————

Candi Martin had gone to her room around 10:00 p.m., exhausted emotionally and physically from the day, but the comfort of knowing both her boys were together again—and safe in the next room—was a relief.

Once she crawled between the lavender-scented sheets and pulled the covers up over her shoulders, she was out.

It took Allen and Duffy a little longer to settle down. For Duff, being in a room with his brother, and having a soft, clean bed in which to sleep, was the ultimate in luxury. The stress of the past few days was easing, and the relief of knowing his mom and brother didn't hate him was huge. Now the only person he had left to confront was his father, and he was sick to his stomach with dread.

Allen didn't close his eyes until he was certain Duffy was asleep. He was still worried about him. He looked haunted, and the usual sparkle in his eyes was missing, but there was nothing Allen could do to change what had happened, so he kept telling himself that his dad would be as understanding as their mom. Finally, he closed his eyes and fell asleep, only to be awakened in the night to the sound of crying.

He turned on the lamp beside the bed and sat up.

Duff was crying and talking in his sleep.

Allen frowned. The torment was real. He got up, then sat down on the side of Duffy's bed and shook him awake.

"Duffy, wake up, buddy."

Duff stilled, then rolled over and opened his eyes.

"What's going on?" he asked.

"You were having a bad dream," Allen said. "Do you want to talk… or want something cold to drink?"

Duff sat up, then felt the tears on his face and wiped them off.

"No, thanks. I'm okay, but I'm sorry I woke you."

"That's what big brothers are for," Allen said. "Do you want to talk?"

Duff scrubbed his hands over his face. "The only person I need to talk to is our dad."

"Coastal State Prison isn't far from here. We'll talk to Mom. In the meantime, how about we try and get some more sleep? The parade will be something fun to do," Allen said.

Duff slid back down between the sheets and rolled over.

Allen got back in bed, pulled up the covers, and turned out the light.

"Night, Allen."

"Night, Duffy."

And then they closed their eyes.

CHAPTER 8

Saturday morning began as a day of anticipation.

Wade was up by five and at the warehouse by seven. They would be delivering the mechanical bull anytime now, and his crew would be there by eight to finish up the float after the bull was in place. After that, it was a matter of getting Bridgette on board.

A few minutes later, Wade got the call. The delivery crew was already in town and headed for the warehouse, so he got on the tractor and backed out the flatbed so they'd have more room to load the bull. When he saw the truck pulling in, he started grinning. This was going to be the best day.

———

Candi was ready for breakfast at a little after eight and texted Allen.

I'm ready to go down to breakfast. What about you two?

A couple of minutes later, there was a knock on her door. She opened it.

"Didn't think you were ever going to surface. We're starving," Allen said. "Let's go."

Candi laughed, grabbed her purse, and pulled the door shut behind her. The enticing aromas of fresh baked breads, hot coffee, and bacon frying met them at the top of the stairs.

"This sure beats a honey bun," Duff said, and galloped down the stairs without waiting.

Allen shook his head and took his mother's elbow as they descended.

They entered the dining area to a small gathering of other guests and a long buffet table laden with all manner of breakfast foods. Even locals who weren't staying here often came to breakfast, so the amount of food cooked belied the number of guests.

Hot biscuits and gravy, fresh pancakes and waffles, a warming tray of sausage links and another of crisp bacon strips hot from the skillet. Scrambled eggs. Omelets cooked to choice. Blueberry muffins, hot cinnamon rolls, an assortment of honey, butter, jellies, and syrups. Orange juice. Coffee. Hot tea. Milk.

Duffy took one look at it all and picked up a plate.

"Stand back, Allen. Let a hungry man eat."

Candi sighed. Duffy could eat both of them under the table and never gain an ounce. Youth had a remarkable metabolism. She'd long since lost that skill.

They chose their food, and as they sat down to eat, Rachel came in with a fresh platter of bacon to add to the buffet, saw them and waved, and went back into the kitchen.

"That lady sure can cook," Duffy said.

"Yes, she can, and don't talk with your mouth full," Candi said.

Allen ate in silence, as always, never taking for granted their freedom of choices, knowing his dad's had long since been taken away. But that was about to come to an end.

———

Elliot was at Josh King's house five minutes before eight.

Josh came out wearing his best clothes, his hair combed, and clean-shaven, and hurried to the car.

"Good morning," Elliot said. "You look very handsome."

Josh grinned, a little embarrassed but pleased.

"Good morning, sir. I was so excited by this, I didn't get much sleep."

Elliot nodded. "Expectations are good," he said, and handed Josh an envelope. "Put that in your pocket. It's the money you're going to give Dub. And I assume you have a proper apology prepared as well."

Josh's hands were shaking as he slipped the envelope in his jacket pocket and swallowed past the lump in his throat.

"I don't know if it's proper, but it's heartfelt," Josh said.

"That will suffice," Elliot said. "And we're off."

This time, Josh was prepared for the launch and rode it out. They sped through the streets, and sooner than Josh would have expected, they were arriving at his former boss's home.

"I'll wait right here," Elliot said. "Just know that Lydia and I have your back."

Josh patted his pocket. He got out and strode straight up to the front door and rang the bell, then took the envelope out of his pocket.

Within moments, the door swung inward and Dub was standing in the opening.

"Good morning, sir," Josh said. "Thank you for agreeing to meet with me. This money is in payment for what I took from you. I cannot get back the respect you had for me, but that's okay. I don't deserve it. I just want you to know I will be profoundly sorry for the rest of my life."

Dub took the envelope, but he heard more than the words. He heard the tremble in Josh King's voice. He was looking at a broken man, and it hurt his heart in a way he would never have imagined.

"Thank you for this," Dub said. "I understand you will be going to work at the Crown?"

"Yes, sir. Driving a forklift, moving grocery shipments back in on the docks. I don't have words for how all this happened. All I know is it did, and I am so grateful. I lost myself. I lost my family. And I will be losing my freedom, but this has given me what I needed to pick up the pieces when it's over."

He turned and was starting to walk away when Dub stopped him with a word.

"Wait!"

Josh turned around.

"Yes, sir?"

"I'll be withdrawing the charges against you," Dub said. "Don't make me sorry."

Josh didn't mean to, but the tears started rolling. He kept trying to say thank you, but all he did was shake.

Dub sighed, then walked out onto the porch and hugged him.

"You can do this, Josh. It's just one day at a time, and merry Christmas."

"Thank you. I won't let you down, and I won't let Elliot down, either. He saved my life last night, and you just gave me a second chance I don't deserve. God bless you, Dub. Merry Christmas to you and Nola."

He turned and hurried back to the car.

"Well?" Elliot asked.

"He's withdrawing the charges against me," Josh said. "I've been given a second chance. I will not let either of you down."

Elliot nodded. "Now then…have you had breakfast?"

"Uh…not yet," Josh said.

"How about we stop in at Granny's before this parade gets underway?"

Josh stared. "You sure you want to be seen in public with me?"

Elliot grinned. "I am absolutely positive."

Josh wiped his eyes. "Then yes, I would like that."

"Buckle up," Elliot said.

Josh didn't have to be told twice, and then they were off.

———

Dub was on the phone to Lon Pittman within seconds of going back into the house, hoping he'd catch him at the office before he got involved with the parade.

The phone rang several times, and Dub was getting ready to leave a message when Lon picked up.

"Chief Pittman speaking."

"Lon, this is Dub. I know you're probably up to your ass in alligators with this parade, but I needed to tell you something."

"I'm listening," Lon said.

"Elliot Graham brought Josh King to my house this morning to pay back the money he stole. There's a long story to go with this, but the bottom line is I'm withdrawing the charges I made against him. It's Christmas, and that's all I'm going to say."

"That's very generous of you," Lon said. "I'll get the paperwork started."

"Thank you. It was very generous of Elliot Graham, too. I'll probably see you at the parade," Dub said. "Be sure to watch for our float. It's a doozy."

Lon chuckled. "I'll keep that in mind. Have a nice day."

———

The day was already sunny. It would turn into steamy later, but right now it felt good. Bridgette was dressed and on her way to the warehouse, excited for the day and glad she'd have a place to park at the feed store, because there would be no parking anywhere on Main until the parade was over, and the side streets were filling up fast.

She wheeled into the parking lot, locked her purse in the trunk, put her keys in her pocket, and carried the cowboy hat as she went to look for Wade.

He was standing in the open door of the warehouse, watching his guys mounting the "corral" onto the trailer, pushing the braces into the slots where sideboards would have gone.

The bull was in place, and so was the air mattress beneath it. The generator was hooked up and already tested to make sure it had power enough to run the bull. They were throwing loose straw all over the air mattress to hide it and waiting for Bridgette to arrive so they could test the speed and make sure the ride would go slowly enough not to throw her off.

"There comes your rider," Roger said, pointing.

Wade turned, then grinned. "And ain't she somethin'."

The men all turned, then burst into a barrage of wolf whistles and cheers.

Wade went to meet her. "Prettiest bull rider I ever saw," he said, and gave her a quick kiss. "Are you ready for all this?"

"Yes. I just need to make sure I can stay on it."

"Then let's get you mounted up and see how it goes. It's already set on the lowest speed. You should be fine, but let me pull the trailer into the warehouse first. We don't want to give away the surprise before we're even in the parade lineup."

Wade climbed up on the wagon tongue to the tractor and pulled the trailer into the warehouse, then helped her climb over the little corral they'd put in place.

But the moment she stepped onto the trailer bed, it felt like the floor beneath her was rolling.

"What's under the hay?" Bridgette asked.

"Basically, a big air mattress. It's part of their safety feature. So even if you do slide off, it's not going to hurt."

"Oh lord," Bridgette said. "So, how do I get up on this thing?"

"Climb up this little step stool. I'll move it after you're mounted, and don't worry, I've got you."

She jammed the hat tight down on her head, walked up the steps, grabbed the leather loop to hold onto, and slung her leg over the bull's back. At that point, Wade pushed her the rest of the way up.

The men clapped and cheered.

"Looking good, Birdie!"

"You did it, girl!"

"Ride, Birdie, ride!"

Bridgette laughed. "I haven't done anything but sit on it. Let's see if I can stay on it before you start cheering."

"Turn it on," Donny said.

"Are you ready?" Wade asked.

Bridgette tightened up her grip and then nodded.

"I'm ready."

Wade turned around and hit Power.

Even though she was expecting it, the motion made Bridgette's heart skip. But it was more like a slow, gentle roll than bucking.

At first, she was only focused on keeping her legs clamped tight around the bull's width and holding tight to the leather. She wasn't thinking about how she looked.

"You're doing great!" Wade said. "Oh man, this is going to be great. See if you can ride it and wave your hat," Wade said.

Bridgette yanked off her hat and waved it over her head as the bull did a little dip and roll, and when she did, Wade laughed out loud and then turned off the power.

"If I didn't already love you to distraction, this would be what did it," Wade said. "You've got this in spades."

Bridgette was grinning from ear to ear. "How long before we have to get in line?"

"Soon. Do you want to ride the float to the lineup, or get on after I get us in line?"

"I like the view from up here. I'll ride," Bridgette said.

Wade gave her a thumbs-up. "Then hang on, sugar. We're going to tie things up here and head out."

Bridgette watched from her perch as the men gave the mini-corral a final safety check, then opened the doors of the warehouse as Wade climbed up on the tractor. He glanced back to make sure she was ready, and when she gave him a thumbs-up, he pulled out of the warehouse.

It was a three-block trip through the streets of Blessings to get to where the parade entries were lining up, but they weren't the only group en route to the starting point.

Truesdale's Feed and Seed float would be the fifth in a lineup of eleven, with different entries between them, including the high school band, some antique cars, an old covered wagon pulled by a team of mules.

Santa Claus would bring the parade to an end.

After they got in place, Bridgette sat, waiting and watching as all of the other entries began arriving and finding their place in line.

Granny's had an entry decorated to look like a cloud. Mercy Pittman was riding on the float dressed as an angel, complete with wings and a sign claiming Granny's Country Kitchen was the home of the famous "heavenly biscuits."

The City of Blessings had a float with past Peachy Keen Queens, as well as the reigning queen sitting on a little throne.

Blessings Elementary had a float with children who had excelled in the past year. A spelling bee champion. A little boy who'd entered and won a state art contest. The twins whose entry won the science fair.

The country club had a float decorated like a mini putting green with two of their star golfers on it.

The dry cleaners had a number of Santa outfits on a rack and one Santa suit hanging on a hanger. One of their employees was dressed as Mrs. Santa and using a leaf blower to clean the suit.

There were so many fun and funny depictions of the holiday on the floats that Bridgette was excited to be a part of it. The entries were representative of their little town and the people they held dear, and Bridgette was suddenly teary, wishing her mother was still alive to see this. Then she heard someone calling her name and saw Dub and Nola coming toward them.

"Lord, girl, make sure you hold on!" Dub said.

"Wade already has that covered," she said. "You'll see."

Dub gave her a thumbs-up and then moved up to where Wade was standing. She saw them talking head to head and then Wade nodding. Whatever it was, they seemed to be in agreement.

Then all of a sudden, there was a loud boom. It was the signal for the parade to begin and for all of the parade goers to get up on the sidewalks and out of the streets.

Wade stepped onto the wagon tongue.

"Are you ready, darlin'?"

She nodded.

"You are the cutest thing. Enjoy the ride," he said. He winked and pressed the power button, then climbed up on the tractor.

Once again, Bridgette was on the move. She threw back her head and laughed as the bull began the slow dip and roll, but her legs were locked around the belly of the beast, and she had a death grip on the leather in her hands.

The convertible carrying the mayor and his wife led off as their driver took off down Main, with the Blessings High School band marching behind them playing their state song, "Georgia on My Mind." Two cheerleaders marched with them, one carrying the American flag and the other carrying the Georgia state flag. Within seconds, the whole of Main Street was awash with voices… "Just an old sweet song…keeps Georgia on my mind."

They were singing so loudly, they drowned out the voice of the parade announcer, and he was forced to give up and join in, slightly off-key, but no less enthusiastic.

After that, the City of Blessings with the Peachy Keen Queens was the first float in the parade. Mike Dalton was in the crowd down by Phillips Pharmacy, holding his little boy and waiting to see his favorite Peachy Keen Queen, his wife, LilyAnn.

When the float came by, Mike pointed. "Look, buddy, there's Mommy. See Mommy?"

LilyAnn waved and waved until she knew her little boy had seen her, and then blew him a kiss.

"Mommy!" he screeched, and then got so excited he forgot how to blow kisses and spat one instead.

———

Granny's float was the next one down Main. People in town were really fond of Mercy's biscuits and pies, and cheered for her loud and long. When Lon Pittman saw his pretty wife, he whooped the police siren on his cruiser as she passed by the station.

Back in line, Truesdale's Feed and Seed float was slowing moving forward, and when they finally rolled onto Main, the crowd went wild. There was Bridgette on the bull, waving her hat, rolling and swaying with the ride, and hanging on for dear life as the parade announcer introduced the float.

"Here comes our own Birdie Knox, riding Rudolph! Yes, you heard me! That big red bull's name is Rudolph, and she's coming straight out of the chute, compliments of Truesdale's Feed and Seed. Ride, Birdie! Ride!" he shouted, and the crowd roared.

Bridgette started out a little overwhelmed with being the momentary center of attention, but she soon got into the spirit of the parade. Then every time someone shouted her name, she'd turn and laugh and wave.

"Hang on, Birdie!" someone shouted. "Ride, Birdie, ride!" And so she did.

Wade was having a ball, waving now and then when he saw a familiar face in the crowd, but his focus was on Bridgette, making sure she was still hanging on as they passed Granny's, and then the Crown, with everyone pointing and squealing and taking picture after picture of Birdie and the bull.

Birdie was so focused on hanging on that she almost missed seeing Josh King, standing at the curb next to Elliot Graham. She'd always thought of Elliot as an odd but endearing little man, and when he smiled at Birdie, she smiled and waved at both of them.

Then to her surprise, she heard Wade shout out Josh's name and lift a hand in greeting, and then they moved past them, then past the hardware store and then the travel agency.

Wade could tell by the people's reactions that Bridgette must be putting on quite a show, and once in a while if they passed a glass storefront, he could see her in the reflection and knew she was playing it to the hilt.

Just when it looked like the bull was going to dump her, she'd right herself. And then the bull would roll another direction and she'd wave her hat and lean back, as if she needed that momentum to hang on. Except for daring her to love him, this had to be the best idea he'd ever had.

As the parade moved farther down Main, Bridgette saw Duffy Martin in the crowd, and when she saw a taller man and an older woman with him and recognized Candi and Allen, she waved. All she could think was thank God he was no longer here alone.

Then she heard little voices shouting "Birdie, Birdie," and searched the faces until she saw Johnny and Dori Pine and their boys, Marshall, Beep, and Luther.

"Hi, guys!" she shouted, and waved at them just as the bull rolled, which made her shriek in pretend horror and sent the crowd into fits of laughter.

They were right in front of the florist when she saw her whole family all bunched together, laughing and pointing and shouting her name. She blew them a kiss, knowing they were never going to let her live this down.

When they finally reached the end of Main Street, it was a relief, but the parade wasn't over until they rolled past the nursing home a few blocks up.

Wade knew Birdie had to be tired, but she had turned into a real trouper. He got a glimpse of her as he made the turn and she was still going strong, and then a couple of blocks up, they began approaching the nursing home.

The residents were in chairs out on the grounds and in wheelchairs up on the porch, all of them wearing little Santa hats. Wade didn't know whose idea this was, but for him it had taken the parade to a whole new level of the holiday spirit.

He could tell when the residents saw Bridgette because of the spreading smiles across their faces. Old men were slapping their knees in pure delight, and the women were laughing and pointing, and bouncing up and down in their seats, mimicking Bridgette's ride.

By now, Bridgette had the bull's rock-and-roll pattern down pat, pretending she was about to slide off at every bounce and then waving her hat when she righted herself, doing it over and over until they moved out of sight.

At that point, she let go, slid off the bull onto the air mattress, and rolled over onto her back.

Her leg muscles were shaking, and her hand was in a cramp from holding on so tight for so long, but she'd done it.

Wade looked back just as she let go, and immediately stopped. He jumped out of the seat, turned the power off on the bull, killed the engine on the generator, and climbed onto the trailer.

"Bridgette! Honey! Are you okay?"

She was flat on her back, arms outstretched, laughing so hard she couldn't talk. She just gave him a thumbs-up and waved him on.

He grinned, climbed back on the tractor, and headed for the warehouse. She'd done it. He couldn't believe she'd stayed on for the entire parade, but she had.

As for Bridgette, the rest of her ride back to the feed store was flat on her back, nestled within the straw and looking up at the sky.

———

Back on Main Street, the last entry in the parade was the one all the children had been waiting for.

Santa Claus and Mrs. Claus had arrived, riding in the back seat of a cherry-red convertible.

They were on their way to the gazebo in the park where they would hold court, listening to the dreams and wishes of Blessings's youngest generation. For two people who could not have children of their own, every year for one day they had a town full.

CHAPTER 9

WADE GOT BACK TO THE WAREHOUSE, HELPED BRIDGETTE OUT OF the trailer, and then swung her up in his arms.

"You were freaking amazing! Are you okay?"

Bridgette was laughing. "I am going to be stiff tomorrow, but that was so much fun."

"You made it fun, pretending you were always about to fall off."

"It wasn't all pretend, but it was easier than I expected. Thank God for the slow speed."

"Everything is better when you take it slow," he said, and kissed the smile right off her face.

The kiss lasted only until they were interrupted by the crew coming to retrieve Bridgette's ride.

"Dammit, the guys are here to load up the bull and I need to get these sideboards off. Here are the keys to the store. Why don't you go get something to drink and rest. Just give me a few minutes, and then I'll take you to lunch." Then he ran a finger down the side of her face. "Bridgette Knox, you are not just my sweetheart. You're also my best friend. I can't even remember what life was like without you in it. Go rest. I'll be in to get you when we're finished."

Bridgette was still reeling from the unexpected tenderness in the middle of so much frivolity. She felt the love in his words, just as she felt loved in his arms. She hurried across the yard and up the steps into the back entrance, turning on lights as she went.

After a quick stop to wash up, she ran out to her car to get her purse, grabbed a cold pop from the mini-fridge in her office, then sat down to wait.

Once the parade ended, Blessings was back in business.

As parade goers began moving and mingling, it was inevitable that Candi Martin would see an old friend. Her hair was grayer, and she looked a little thinner, but Milly Garner had been one of the few who had not judged her and the boys for what Zack had been accused of.

Their eyes met, and the look of surprise on Milly's face was one of pure delight. Then she was coming toward Candi with her arms outstretched.

"Girl! I couldn't believe my eyes," she said, and hugged Candi tight. Then her gaze moved to the boys. "Allen, you have grown into a big, handsome man. You must be, what…twenty-seven…twenty-eight years old?"

Allen grinned. "Yes, ma'am, twenty-seven."

Then Milly looked at Duff and read everything he was feeling just by looking at his face.

"And here's Duffy, the hero of the hour! Of course, you know how Blessings is. We always hear the latest gossip before bedtime, and it is all over town what an amazing young man you are. It's not everyone who gets to clear their father's name and get them out of jail."

Duffy shrugged. "It's not every kid who's responsible for putting them in there, either."

Milly frowned. "I said it then and I'll say it again. The court was wrong in finding him guilty without a shred of evidence. Like everyone else in Blessings, Selma always left her dang house unlocked. They watched Zack leave the house carrying nothing but his paintbrushes in a bucket to take home to clean. He didn't even have a lunch pail, for God's sake."

"You were a good friend then, and you are a good friend now," Candi said. "And thanks to Duffy, Zack will be freed. We don't know when, but it will happen."

"Does Zack know?" Milly asked.

"Not yet, but soon," Candi said.

Milly glanced at the time. "I wish I could stay and talk all day, but

I've got to get back to work. We only closed down for the parade, and I'll wager half the people here are already in the Crown buying groceries."

"What happened to the Piggly Wiggly?" Candi asked.

Milly shrugged. "It went out of business. Someone bought it. It's the Crown now. Where are you living now?" Milly asked.

"Jacksonville, Florida," Candi said.

"Well, stay in touch. I miss you," Milly said. She hugged Candi once more, waved at the boys, and then took off up the street.

"She's a nice lady," Allen said.

Candi nodded. "Yes, she is, and she's right. They never should have found your father guilty. There was no evidence against him other than opportunity. Now, what do you guys want to do next?"

"Let's go to Broyles Dairy Freeze and get burgers and hot dogs, and go to the park like we used to," Allen said.

"Santa Claus is at the park," Duff said.

"Broyles it is. Watching the kids visiting Santa will be fun," Candi said.

━━━━━━━━

Josh King's parade experience wasn't as joyful as everyone else's. He was grateful for Elliot Graham's presence because it kept other people and their opinions about him at bay.

And he guessed Dub must have told Wade about dropping the charges because Wade had given him a thumbs-up during the parade. But he missed his wife and kids. If he hadn't been such a dumbass, they would all be at the park right now, standing in line to see Santa Claus and getting pictures of them sitting on Santa's lap. He was missing it and everything else because of what he'd done.

Still, he'd been given a second chance to make something of his life and he wasn't going to blow it. He needed to get his old truck running so he could get back and forth to his new job, and since he was already downtown, he headed for the auto parts store to pick up a carburetor and a fan belt.

———

The crew from Savannah took the mechanical bull down Main Street one last time, but no one knew it. It was safely within the truck trailer and on its way home.

The town of Blessings was open for business, and Wade had just found a parking place at Granny's.

"Wow, it's filling up fast today," he said. "A lot more people in town than on a normal Saturday."

"And about half of them are likely still at the park waiting to see Santa," Bridgette said.

"I remember going when I was a kid, do you?"

Bridgette smiled. "Absolutely. Mom always took us. Even when the others got too old to believe, we all still went together because of me."

"You were the baby of the family, and I was the only child. We should both be spoiled rotten," Wade said.

"But we're not, and we can thank our parents for not doing that," she said.

"Do you want a family?" Wade asked.

Bridgette reached for his hand. "I want your babies. Does that count?"

He had a lump in his throat as her words wrapped around his heart.

"Yes, ma'am, it does."

———

Lovey had prepared in advance for the influx of added customers by adding three more waitresses to the shift and opening the banquet room for extra seating space.

She was perched on her stool at the register, decked out in jeans and a Christmas shirt and wearing a reindeer antlers headband in her white, curly hair.

Her son, Sully, was seating customers.

When Wade and Bridgette walked in, Lovey stood up and clapped.

"Girl! We might have the best biscuits in town, but y'all had the best float, by far, and I'm betting money you're gonna pay for that ride. Do you need a pillow to sit on?"

Wade laughed. "She's already complaining."

"I'm a little sore, but I think I'll make it," Bridgette said.

Sully came back and grabbed a couple of menus.

"Table for two, or are you meeting someone?"

"It's just us," Wade said.

Within seconds of entering the dining room, someone yelled out "Wahoo!" and another shouted "Ride, Birdie, Ride!"

Bridgette blushed, but she was laughing. She would have been surprised if the reactions had been any different.

Sully seated them at a table for two. "The special is hush puppies and gumbo."

"Ooh, that sounds good," Bridgette said. "That's what I'm having."

"Me too," Wade said. "And before I forget, I have an update on Josh King."

"I saw you give him a thumbs-up," she said.

"Uncle Dub told me this morning that Elliot Graham kind of rescued Josh. We don't know the details, but he hinted at Josh being suicidal. Elliot gave him the money to pay Uncle Dub back, then took him to the house this morning to deliver it. Josh is going to work at the Crown, driving a forklift moving pallets of grocery shipments."

Bridgette's eyes welled. "Poor Josh. That breaks my heart."

"Yes, he messed up royally, but Dub also dropped the charges against him. Josh is a free man. It cost him his family, but Elliot and Uncle Dub are giving him a second chance. I hope he doesn't waste it."

Bridgette nodded.

"You know, if I was the kind of person looking for miracles, then I'd say that was the second one we've had here in Blessings in less than a week. First Duffy Martin, and now Josh King. They have both had their own kind of miracles. I wonder who's next."

Wade smiled. "What makes you think there will be more? Maybe that was our quota for this holiday."

She just shook her head. "Nope. Good things and bad things always run in threes. That was two bad things that turned into two good things. There will be one more."

Wade smiled, then leaned over and gave her a quick kiss on the lips.

"What's that for?" she asked.

"For being you," he said. "And here comes our waitress with the biscuits."

They ordered, and then took a biscuit apiece, buttered lavishly, and dug in.

They were still waiting for their order when Wade got a text. He glanced at his phone, then broke out in a big grin.

"What?" Bridgette asked.

"That was the parade coordinator. Our float won first place! They'll come to the store Monday morning to present the trophy and take pictures for the newspaper."

Bridgette laughed. "Oh my lord! You called it. What fun!"

About that time, Lovey came into the dining room carrying her phone.

"Hey, y'all! Granny's float won second place in the parade!"

Everyone clapped and cheered, but Lovey wasn't through. She headed straight for Wade and Bridgette with a big smile on her face. "And I can tell by the look on Wade Montgomery's face that he already knows Truesdale's Feed and Seed got first prize, and I think they have Miss Birdie to thank for it. That was one heck of a ride."

The diners broke into cheers and shouts as Bridgette flushed a rosy pink.

"Don't be shy now," Wade said. "Take a bow. You earned it."

Bridgette stood up and waved.

"Who got third place?" someone asked.

Lovey laughed again, this time pointing at Sully. "Melissa and the crew at the dry cleaners got third. I think that was Sully's leaf blower cleaning the Santa suits… Oh, and Bloomer's Hardware got the trophy for best storefront with their Santa's workshop theme."

Sully laughed. "It is my leaf blower, but I can't take any credit for that. It was all Melissa's idea. She and her team at the cleaners did that while I was here washing your dirty dishes."

Lovey swatted him on the arm.

"You don't wash dishes here, and I hear you don't wash them at home, either."

Sully laughed and hugged his mom. "I know better than to argue with the women in my life. I'm going back to work."

The waitress arrived with Wade and Bridgette's food, and the diners returned to their meals, while Santa and Mrs. Claus were still at the gazebo taking pictures and handing out candy.

The snow-cone stand was running out of ice to make snow cones when a last-minute delivery from Savannah saved the day.

Junior Knox had to ask for help loading Christmas trees to keep up with the customers' demands.

The bakery in the Crown ran out of gingerbread men, and the flower shop ran out of potted poinsettias.

The parade was over, but Christmas in Blessings was just beginning.

═══════════

Josh King wasn't in a celebratory mood as he walked home with his truck parts, and as soon as got there, he changed into work clothes. He wasn't the best mechanic in the world, but he knew enough to change out a carburetor and replace a fan belt, and was hard at it when a truck pulled up into his drive. He looked up and then frowned. What the hell were the Linley brothers doing here?

They waved as they got out and then walked up the driveway to the carport where he was working.

"Hey, Josh! What's up, man?"

"Working on my truck," he said. "What do you want?"

Mack Linley grinned. "We just came by to see how you were doing. Thought you might need a ride to the poker game tonight."

"I'm not going to any more poker games," Josh muttered.

"Aw, hey…don't be that way. If you're short on cash, we'll front you," Arnie said.

Josh gripped the wrench he was holding a little tighter.

"I got in trouble playing poker. I'm not doing that anymore."

"But you're out now and it—"

"A friend gave me the money to pay back my old boss. He dropped the charges against me. You guys will be getting your bail money back. I'm with gambling."

Mack Linley frowned. "So you're dropping your buddies just like that?"

"You guys aren't *buddies*. You threatened to beat the hell out of me because I owed the man. Now I don't owe the man, and I don't owe my old boss. I'm gonna keep it that way."

Arnie doubled up his fists.

"That's a fine way to treat us after we bailed you out and all."

"I didn't ask you to. I didn't know you were going to do it, and you're getting it back," Josh said, and then stepped out from behind the truck with the wrench held tight in his fist. "I don't expect I'll be seeing you again, so you guys have yourselves a real merry Christmas. Okay?"

Mack eyed the wrench, and Arnie saw a look in Josh's eyes that made him take a step back.

"Yeah, yeah, sure. It's no big deal. We were just trying to do you a favor," he said.

Josh didn't respond. He was holding his breath, waiting for them to come at him.

They stood there for a few moments, and then Mack suddenly laughed and punched his brother lightly on the shoulder.

"Come on, Arnie. We got things we need to be doin', and Josh is trying to get his truck running. We took up enough of his time."

Glad to have a reason to leave, Arnie nodded.

"Yeah, right. We got things to do."

They walked back down the driveway to their truck and drove away.

It wasn't until they were out of sight that Josh took a breath. For a few seconds, he'd been certain he was going to have to fight them. He didn't trust them any farther than he could throw them, but they were gone, and hopefully they got the message.

———

Wade pulled up beside Bridgette's car to let her out.

"Are you going to be too tired to do anything tonight?" Wade asked.

"I have all afternoon to recoup," Bridgette said. "What do you have in mind?"

"A riverboat dinner cruise in Savannah."

Bridgette gasped. "Are you serious? Oh, Wade! How wonderful! I've never done that."

He grinned. "Awesome. I'll pick you up about five. We start boarding around six thirty or so. The riverboat leaves the dock at seven, and the cruise lasts a couple of hours before it docks back in Savannah."

"Do I dress up?" Bridgette asked.

"It's not formal wear, but it's dressy. You'll be perfect no matter what you wear, but bring a jacket. I'm going to assume it could be a little chilly on the water at night."

"I can't wait! This is the best day ever," Bridgette said.

Wade leaned across the console and kissed her.

"You ain't seen nothin' yet."

———————————

The streets along the riverwalk were teeming with shoppers and diners heading into and coming out of businesses, restaurants, and bars.

The riverboat down at the shore was dressed from prow to stern in holiday lights sparkling from the windows of all three decks and all along the open deck atop it.

Bridgette was shivering with excitement, holding tightly to Wade's hand as they walked the street to where the boat was docked. She felt pretty, and special, and loved, and it showed—from the sparkle in her dark eyes to the smile that lit up her face.

She kept looking at Wade—at the strong cut of his jaw and the tiny crinkles at the corners of his eyes that deepened when he smiled.

Everything about him was so familiar, and yet dressed as he was tonight, in dark slacks, a gray sports coat, and a snow-white dress shirt with an open collar, there was an air of delightful secrecy about him—like he knew something she did not.

———————————

The energy of the waterfront and the people on it were feeding Wade's excitement. Watching the changing expressions on Bridgette's face was pure adrenaline. He'd never seen her in the little black dress she was wearing. He didn't know if it was old or new, but it fit her body like skin, accentuating the woman she was, while the hem of the straight skirt ended inches above her knees.

The jacket he had suggested she wear was as red as her open-toed shoes. She was so beautiful in his eyes, and she loved him. How lucky could one man get?

By the time they reached the *Savannah Queen*, people were already boarding. All Bridgette and Wade had to do was step in line. Within minutes they were onboard and being ushered up to the top deck where drinks and appetizers were being served.

As soon as they had drinks in hand, they moved to the railing. The great paddlewheels were beginning to turn, backing the elegant lady out of the dock and then out onto the Savannah River.

Standing within the shelter of Wade's arms, Bridgette leaned her head against his shoulder, watching the kaleidoscope sky as the sun began to set, awash in an array of pinks and purples, silhouetting seabirds heading to roost against a rapidly fading light.

The paddlewheels that had been in reverse to back them out were now turning forward, cutting through the dark water as the boat headed upstream.

"I can't believe I've never done this. What made you think about it?" she asked.

"I've been on them a couple of times, but just for fun. Never with someone special," he said, and brushed a kiss across her lips, then lifted his glass of champagne. "A toast to us…and to a long and happy life together."

"To us," Bridgette echoed.

Their glasses clinked. The bubbles of champagne exploded on their tongues as they took another sip and then a second kiss, this time tasting the champagne on their lips.

While they were still standing on the upper deck, the *Savannah Queen* moved toward the setting sun. Wind lifted the hair from Bridgette's neck as the last rays of sunlight caught in her eyes.

Wade reached into his pocket, his fingers curling around the tiny velvet box there, then took it out and opened it up before her. When sunlight set a fire in the stone, she gasped.

Wade dropped to one knee.

"My darling Bridgette, I can no longer remember what life was like before you, and I don't want to think of a future without you in it. I love you to the point of distraction. Will you marry me please, before I lose my ever-lovin' mind?"

"Yes, yes, a thousand times, yes," Bridgette cried.

He stood, took the ring out of the box and slipped it on her finger, then wrapped his arms around her. The taste of champagne was still on her lips when he kissed her, and then she was laughing and crying and looking at the ring on her finger, then laughing some more.

It didn't take long for the people around them to realize what was happening, and then everyone lifted a glass.

"To a long and happy union!" someone shouted.

"To love!" another said.

And just like that, the sun was gone, leaving the moon and stars as their guide. The evening was just beginning as they moved down to the second deck for their meal, and the moment they entered, Bridgette had to look at her ring again in the lights above them.

"Oh, Wade, it's so beautiful."

He whispered against her ear, "Just like you. Now let's go find a table."

They followed the other diners into the room, eyeing the holiday decor with anticipation of the dinner and the evening yet to come.

A Christmas tree sparkling with white lights and gold ornaments held court in the center of the room. Buffets loaded with lavish assortments of foods ran the length of it.

Massive steam tables and chafing dishes filled with French and Cajun cuisine sat alongside mountains of cold shrimp on ice, tureens of hot soups, cold salads, and desserts that were true works of art.

Live music from a quartet at one end of the room kept the energy high, and before long, people were getting their food and finding a seat at the banquet-style tables.

Christmas lights from the homes on the riverbanks were sometimes visible through the trees, blinking like fairy lights in the dark.

For Bridgette, the whole night was magic. From the ring on her finger to the man at her side. He was the promise of all her tomorrows, and she didn't want to forget one moment of this night.

When the meal was over, some took to the dance floor while others went back up top. The *Savannah Queen* had made a turn while they were dining and was now headed back downstream toward the city. Wade danced Bridgette out of the dining room and then walked her back up the stairs to the top deck.

"Are you cold, baby?" he asked as he wrapped her up in his arms and pulled her back against him.

"Not a bit. Everything is perfect."

Resting his chin on the top of her head, he smiled. "I'll agree with that."

There were a few moments of silence between them, and then he asked the second most important question of the night.

"When do you want to start wedding planning? No pressure from me, but if anyone asked me, my answer would be tomorrow. However, this is your call to make," he said.

"Tomorrow," Bridgette said, and then turned in his arms and laughed.

"God, how I love you," he said, and swung her up into his arms. "Stay with me tonight. I want to wake up beside you tomorrow."

"Yes," Bridgette said.

And then his mouth was on her lips.

They stood together, watching as Savannah came back into view, and climbed down from the top deck only after the riverboat docked.

They walked back to the car and drove to Blessings, still wrapped in the euphoria of the night and the vows that they'd made.

The big city they'd left behind was still in motion when they drove into the quiet, sleepy little town of Blessings.

The streetlights lit the way toward home, and the porch light on Wade's home lit the way inside.

After that, it was a short walk to the bedroom.

When Bridgette crawled into Wade's bed, the only thing she was wearing was the ring.

CHAPTER 10

SUNLIGHT WAS STREAMING THROUGH A WINDOW WHEN Bridgette opened her eyes, only to find Wade had been watching her sleep. In that moment, she remembered, and smiled.

"Good morning, sweetheart," she said.

Wade lifted her hand and kissed it.

"Good morning to you, too, pretty girl."

Bridgette slid her fingers through his hair, then raised up on one elbow.

"I have an ache," she said.

He frowned. "From the bull ride?"

She shook her head.

A slow smile spread across his face as he slid his hand across her backside and pulled her closer.

"Poor baby. Show me where it hurts."

━━━━━━━━━

An hour and a shower later, they were sitting at the kitchen table having breakfast. Toasted waffles and syrup for Wade. Cereal and coffee for Bridgette. In between bites, they were still talking and planning.

"I have to call my family before they find out from anyone else," Bridgette said.

Wade nodded. "And I have to tell Uncle Dub and Aunt Nola, or I'll never hear the end of it. Are we going to church this morning?"

"I'll have to wear the same dress I wore last night."

"Works for me," Wade said.

"Then yes." She finished her cereal, then took her bowl to the sink, rinsed it, and put it in the dishwasher. "I'm going to call the family, and then I'll get dressed."

Wade stuffed the last bite of waffle in his mouth, gave her a thumbs-up, and grabbed his phone, too, chewing and swallowing as he made the call. His aunt Nola answered.

"Hello."

"Morning, Aunt Nola, is Uncle Dub nearby?"

"Yes, he's sitting right here."

"Put the phone on speaker. I have something to tell the both of you."

"Okay…we're on," she said.

"What's going on?" Dub asked.

"Nothing much. I just wanted you two to be the first people I told."

"Told what?" Dub asked.

"I asked Bridgette to marry me last night and she said yes!"

Nola squealed. Dub laughed. And then both of them were talking at once.

Wade was grinning. "Whoa, whoa. One at a time."

"When's the wedding?" Nola asked.

"Soon enough," Wade said.

"Come to dinner after church," Dub said.

"Let me check with Bridgette and I'll get back to you," he said.

"Congratulations!" Nola said, then started crying. "Your dad and mom would be so happy for you."

Wade sighed. "I know, Aunt Nola, but I am forever grateful I have you and Uncle Dub."

"And we're blessed to have you," Nola said. "Dub and I couldn't have babies, but don't forget twins run in our family. Your dad and I were twins, and our grandfather was a twin. So be prepared."

"Oh, I haven't forgotten a thing. Give me a sec to check with Bridgette about dinner," he said, and took off down the hall to the bedroom.

Bridgette was just about to make a call when Wade appeared in the doorway.

"We are invited to dinner after church. Is that okay?"

She grinned. "Tell Nola it is always okay. I love to eat someone else's cooking."

Wade gave her a thumbs-up and went back to the kitchen, talking as he walked.

"We accept, and with thanks," Wade said.

"Awesome. See you later."

Wade was still smiling as he began cleaning up his breakfast dishes, while Bridgette was making three calls—her first one to Emma.

Emma was at the breakfast table reading the Sunday paper and finishing her coffee. Gordon was in the garage, cleaning out their car. She was debating with herself about having one more cup of coffee when her phone rang. A quick glance at caller ID, and she answered.

"Morning, little sister. How does your garden grow?"

Bridgette beamed. "With silver bells and cockle shells and pretty maids all in a row."

Emma chuckled. "Remember all those old nursery rhymes Mama read to us back in the day?"

"I remember that one," Bridgette said. "And I have news to share."

"Oh…I heard. Your float won first prize, and I am not the least bit surprised. Giiirrlll! What a ride! How did Wade talk you into doing that?"

"The same way he just talked me into marrying him last night."

Emma screamed. "Oh my God! Birdie! Congratulations! I am so happy for you. When's the wedding? And I better get to be matron of honor."

Bridgette burst out laughing.

"Well, of course. I don't have but one sister, you know, and we're in the early planning stage."

"Have you told the boys?" Emma asked.

"Not yet. I called you first."

"Okay, then I won't say anything to them. I'm so happy for you both."

"Thanks," Bridgette said. "I'm calling Junior next, and then Ray.

I'll wait to call Hunt because of the time difference in Houston. I don't want to wake them up. Talk to you later."

And so she did. Junior was awake and getting ready to go to work.

"Hey, little sister. What's on your mind so early in the morning?"

"Wade proposed to me last night, and of course I said yes. I wanted family to know first before it hit the gossip wheel in town."

"Aw, that's great, honey. I'm so happy for you. You deserve a good man and I think he's great."

"Thanks, Junior. What are you doing today?"

"I'm on the way to work. We have another small shipment of trees coming in. We already sold so many. I didn't know there were this many people in Blessings."

Bridgette laughed. "Have a good day, and love to Barrie and the kids."

"I'll tell them," Junior said.

Bridgette was still smiling as she made a call to Ray. Since he and Susie now lived in Savannah, she didn't see them much. The call rang and rang, and just as she was about to leave a message, Susie picked up.

"Hello? Birdie, it's me. Ray is in the shower."

"Hi, Susie. I just called to share some good news."

And then she repeated what she'd told Emma and Junior, and got the same reaction—total delight.

By now, it was just after eight in Houston. Hunt and Ava's working hours were so erratic that she didn't want to take a chance of waking them if they were getting to sleep in. She'd make that call this afternoon. For now, it was time to get ready for church.

As it turned out, the preacher's sermon took second place to their news. Ruby was the first to spy the ring on Bridgette's finger, and after that the news spread through the congregation.

Wade and Birdie were engaged.

Josh King had his old truck running and was in the kitchen frying bacon and making toast when his cell phone rang.

The Crown grocery's name came up on caller ID. He'd already filled out all the paperwork to go to work tomorrow and had instructions to contact Wilson Turner, the manager, and now suddenly he was afraid the job was about to disappear.

"Hello, Josh speaking."

"Josh, this is Wilson Turner. I know this is a horrible imposition, but we just got two semiloads of grocery pallets in this morning that weren't due to arrive until tomorrow, and the dumbass driver left it all on the dock before I even got to work. We have something of a traffic jam back in the warehouse area as it is from losing our other forklift driver, and now this. We need what's already in the warehouse straightened up before we can move any more product in. And it all needs to be inside and checked off the invoices so we can start shelving stuff. By any chance, could you possibly come in this morning?"

Josh blinked. "Yes, sir. Give me about fifteen minutes to get dressed, and I'll be right there. I park in the back and clock in back there, right?"

"Yes. I'll be waiting for you on the loading dock, and I can't thank you enough. You're saving the day."

Josh couldn't believe it. Not only was his job still good, but it was starting today. Thank goodness he'd gotten his truck running yesterday or he'd be hotfooting it to work.

He made a sandwich out of his toast and bacon, downed it in four bites, washed it down with the rest of his coffee, and ran down the hall to change. Heading out the door with the truck keys in his hand, he felt whole—like he was Josh again, only better.

He was uneasy about his reception when he got to work, but he didn't care whether people were going to welcome him or not. He needed this job to send money to his family. He knew LaJune didn't expect it, but he wasn't going to let them down again.

When he pulled into the back and parked, the manager was waiting for him as promised.

"Thank you again," Wilson said, and showed Josh where to clock in.

Then Wilson and two more employees began showing Josh what needed to be moved and where to move it.

Josh knew how to drive a forklift. That was the easy part. But the rest of it would come. Under Wilson's direction, he began moving what they said and putting it where they wanted it, and slowly the floor began to take shape, and everything had been moved inside.

After that, he spent the rest of the morning removing the mountains of shrink wrap from the pallets, then loading flats of cans onto carts so they could restock the shelves.

By the time noon came around, he was moving through the back like a pro. He'd figured out their system and had it pretty much memorized. There was a fresh produce truck due in first thing tomorrow morning, and after a quick lesson in organizing the cooler where produce was kept, he began sorting out what had turned bad. The warehouse was comfortable, but working in the cooler required a jacket. He'd deal with that tomorrow. For today, he was fine.

———

Dub and Nola had hurried home from church so Nola could put the finishing touches on their meal. Dub had the table set when the oven timer went off.

"Oh, that's the dinner rolls. If they're brown enough, honey, would you please take them out?" Nola said.

Dub grabbed a potholder and opened the oven and inhaled. The aroma of freshly baked yeast bread had to be one of the best smells ever.

"They look good to me," he said, and took them out, then turned off the oven.

The doorbell rang.

"That'll be the kids," Nola said.

Dub grinned to himself as he headed to the front door.

The kids weren't kids anymore.

"Just in time," Dub said, as he swung the door inward.

Wade and Bridgette walked in. Dub shook hands with Wade and then gave Bridgette a quick kiss on the cheek. "You're about to be family. I'm allowed. Now let me see that ring."

Bridgette beamed and held out her hand.

Dub nodded. "You did good, boy. You two know what to do with your things. When you get yourself situated, follow your nose. Dinner is just about ready."

"Yes, sir," Wade said.

Bridgette took off her jacket, revealing the rounded neckline and the three-quarter-length sleeves of her little black dress.

"Let me have your purse and jacket," Wade said. "I'm putting them on the spare bed." Then he hurried away with their things.

He came back in the same rush and escorted her past the dining room table just waiting for company and into the kitchen where the action was.

Nola stopped what she was doing and turned and hugged them.

"I am so happy for you two. Let me see that ring."

Again, Bridgette held out her hand, soaking up the compliments, but ever aware of Wade's hand at the small of her back.

"Is there anything I can do to help?" she asked.

"No, darling, but thank you. Dub's a good sous-chef," Nola said. "Dub, if you'll get the platter with the roast, I'll bring the rolls. Everything else is at the table, except for us."

Wade took the rolls out of his aunt's hands and carried them for her, then seated Bridgette before taking the chair beside her.

It took a couple of minutes to get everyone settled, and then Dub bowed his head, blessed the food and the woman who'd prepared it, and the meal began.

Bridgette had few memories of being at a table like this with her family. Her dad died before she hit her teens, and her brothers and sister had all moved away from home. Even when they came home for holiday meals, they weren't celebratory. Just silent disapproval that she never understood until after Marjorie was gone.

This past year had been a year for the Knox siblings to rebuild their relationships. The bond that should have been there was still in the progress of healing. Becoming part of Wade's family, and making their own, made Bridgette hopeful for everything about their future.

But then the conversation at the table shifted to the parade and Bridgette's ride.

"You can't say it didn't pay off," Wade said. "If you want in on the photo op, come to the store tomorrow morning. They're supposed to present the trophy and take pictures for the paper."

Dub shook his head. "Oh, I didn't have anything to do with it."

"It's still your store," Bridgette said. "You have everything to do with it."

"She's right," Wade said. "You should come."

"Maybe," Dub said. "But make sure you get Birdie in the picture. She's the reason we won."

Wade winked at Bridgette. "Oh, we know. We all know that," he said.

"Happy to oblige. Just don't ask me to do it again," Bridgette said.

Laughter rolled around the table. Nola passed the dinner rolls. Wade got a second helping of mashed potatoes and gravy, and Bridgette just kept eating and smiling and listening to the foolishness that only a family who loved each other could dish out.

———

Candi Martin and her boys had eaten breakfast early at the B and B because they were going to Coastal State Prison to visit Zack.

Normally, it was a process to get permission to visit a prisoner, but she'd been there on a regular basis for the past ten years, and after a call to the warden, they'd received special dispensation to come.

It had been a while since her last visit on Labor Day weekend. She tried to come every time there was a long school holiday, but she hadn't been able to make it on Thanksgiving. Only rarely did her sons come with her, and never had both of them come at once.

She knew Zack was going to be surprised, but she was scared for Duffy. She honestly didn't know how Zack would react, but if it was in anger, she knew it would break Duffy's heart.

Because Candi knew the way, she drove, leaving Allen riding shotgun and Duffy in the back seat, which was just as well. There was nothing more they could say to him until this visit was over. And she wasn't sure what she'd do to Zack if he broke Duffy's heart.

And so they drove north from Blessings toward Savannah, then took a highway leading slightly northwest to Garden City and straight to the prison.

The steps it took to get inside were as lengthy and tedious as the steps it usually took to get online permission to even come, so today she wasn't complaining.

When they were finally inside the visitation area, she led the boys over to an empty table and sat down.

"Now we wait. And remember, you don't get to hug him or touch him. We just talk."

"God, Mom. I don't know how you do this all the time," Allen muttered.

"Because I love him. Because I never believed he was guilty. Just because the law decided to punish him didn't mean I had to, too."

Duffy choked on a sob.

Candi reached for his hand.

"No. You are not six years old anymore. You are a man. And what you have done in the past three days has proven that. Your father is not a monster. Your fear is the monster. Stop being afraid of someone who loves you. Understand?"

Duff looked at his mother as if he'd never seen her before. When she handed him a handful of tissues, he wiped his eyes and straightened his shoulders.

"Yes, ma'am. I understand."

"Good. Because we are going to present this as good news. As a blessing. Not the disaster you see. Okay?"

Duff nodded.

Then Candi looked up, and a bright smile spread across her face.

"There comes your daddy. Both of you, try not to look like you're at a fucking funeral."

They were both so startled she cursed that they grinned, which was exactly what she'd intended.

And then she was smiling and waving, ignoring the handcuffs and shackles. Zack's hair was grayer at the temples, and he was a little thinner, but in her eyes he was still the handsome boy she'd fallen in love with so many years ago.

———————————

Zack Martin was surprised with the message that he had visitors. It was a little too early for Candi's school to be out for Christmas vacation, but her faithful visitations were what kept him sane and he wasn't going to question the reason she was here.

As soon as he was cuffed and shackled, the guards led him through the halls, locking one cell block after another behind them as they went, until they emerged into the common room.

Zach immediately began looking for a woman sitting alone, but when he saw her with both of his sons at her side, his heart nearly stopped.

Overcome with emotion, he stumbled, and one of the guards caught him by the elbow to steady him. But by then his gaze was locked. They were here. They were men. And he couldn't even touch them.

The guards seated him, then backed a few yards away to give them privacy to talk.

Zack's voice was shaking and he couldn't quit looking at his sons. "Candi, girl. You brought me the best surprise ever."

Candi smiled. "I miss you, darling. You look good. Are you well?"

Zack nodded. "I'm fine. Same as always."

"You look good, Dad," Allen said.

Zack eyed his elder son with pride. "So do you, son. Are you still working at the same place?"

"Yes, still working at Lowe's in the lumber area."

Zack looked at Duffy and immediately knew something was wrong. His younger son's face was almost bloodless and he looked like he was going to pass out.

"Duffy, are you okay, son? Did you get carsick on the ride up? We can get you some water or something."

"I'm not carsick, Daddy, but thank you," he said.

Candi leaned forward.

"We're here with news, Zack. Good news. The best news you could ever imagine hearing."

Zack's eyes widened.

"What's going on?"

"I'll tell him, Mom. I can do it," Duff said.

Zack looked from one to the other now, confused.

Duff took a deep breath. "I didn't know until a few days ago why you went to prison. At least, not the details."

Zack glanced at Candi, then sighed. "At the time, your mother and I thought it best. You were so little."

Duff nodded. "I understand, but I sure wish you hadn't done that, because you went to prison for something I did. Something I did in innocence. Something I did playing a game."

Zack's eyes widened. He wasn't moving. He was holding his breath, afraid to go there in his head.

Candi picked up the story.

"Selma Garrett recently passed away. I mentioned it to Allen while we were all at the supper table, and during the conversation I guess something was said about the jewelry, and Duffy... Well, it took him by surprise."

"No," Duff said. "It stopped my heart. And then it triggered a memory of something I'd long since forgotten. Remember the day you took me to that lady's house while you were painting?"

Zack frowned. "Yes, but—"

Duff held up his hand. "Remember how I was always playing pirate and digging holes and burying Mom's cups and spoons and anything else I could use for treasure?"

Zack nodded. "Sort of."

"Well, that day, I came up to ask you when we were going home, and you told me you'd call someone to come get me because you wanted to stay late to finish the job. You told me to go back outside and play. So I did. But I saw a pirate treasure in a bedroom, and I picked it up and took it outside to bury. I took the jewelry, Daddy. It was me. I'm so sorry. I didn't know. It was just a game. There was a big hole in the rose garden, and I put the treasure chest in the hole and I was covering it up with dirt when Birdie Knox came to get me. Then the gardener put a rosebush on top of my treasure and planted it, and Birdie took me home and I forgot. The game was over, and I didn't think about it again."

Zach was shaking. His face was sheet-white and there was sweat rolling out of his hair and down the sides of his temples, and Duffy kept on talking.

"The next morning they arrested you, and I didn't know why, and no one would tell me anything, and then you were gone. All I knew was you weren't coming back, and that people accused you of taking something that didn't belong to you."

"Oh Jesus, sweet Jesus," Zach said.

"I'm sorry, Daddy. Don't hate me. I am so sorry."

Zach kept shaking his head.

"I don't hate you. How could I hate you? You are my baby boy. Your mother and I made that decision. We hid the truth from you, and that's on us."

Duff swiped at his tears.

Allen patted his little brother on the back and began talking.

"Oh, but that's not the best part, Dad. That same night Duffy found out the truth of why you were here, he took off with my car, and when we woke up the next morning he was gone. We didn't know where he was for two days, then found out he went back to Blessings. And he got the lawyer you had, and the police chief, and he told them what he'd done, and he took them straight to the house, and they dug up Duffy's buried treasure and gave it back to the family."

Candi nodded and continued the story.

"And the lawyer, Mr. Butterman, is already working on getting you released. He's going to petition the court to have your sentence vacated. It will be as if it never happened."

Zack shook his head, unable to absorb the enormity of what he was hearing, and kept looking at Duffy.

"You went all the way back to Blessings and did this on your own? Weren't you scared?" Zack asked.

"Yes, but not of being found out. I was scared of it not still being there. Then I was afraid you would hate me for what I'd done," Duff said.

Zack grunted like he'd just been punched.

"Hate you? For setting me free? For proving my innocence? For clearing my name? Oh sweet lord!" he said, and then threw back his head and laughed, and then clapped his hands on his knees and laughed some more.

It wasn't a sound often heard in this room, and it drew the attention of everyone, including his guards. But there were no rules against laughing. Only touching.

The guards frowned.

Zack looked at them and grinned, then put a finger to his mouth as if he was shushing himself. There were tears in his eyes when he looked at Duffy, but he was still grinning.

"This is the best Christmas present ever. You gave me back my life, son. I will never be able to fully thank you for that."

Duff shuddered as the last of the fear and the pain and the horror of the past few days slid away.

It was going to be okay.

CHAPTER 11

SUNDAY DINNER AT THE TRUESDALE HOME WAS OVER. THE FOOD had been eaten, the kitchen cleaned up, and the dishes washed and put away. Then after another hour of visiting, Wade and Bridgette said their goodbyes.

"Everything was wonderful. Thank you for dinner," Bridgette said, and Dub and Nola walked them to the door.

"It was totally our pleasure, and welcome to the family," Nola said.

Dub smiled and patted her on the shoulder. "Life is just full of surprises. When I hired you straight out of high school, I knew you were going to be good at your job. But I had no idea we'd ever wind up as family. Might be the smartest hire I ever made."

Wade laughed. "You do not get to take credit for this. I have had a crush on Bridgette most of my life, and if Mom and Dad hadn't moved, this might have already happened years ago."

They left the house, and Dub was still at the door as Wade backed out of the drive.

"I assume you want to go home," Wade said as he braked for a stop sign.

"Yes, but want and need are two different things," Bridgette said. "I want out of this dress. I need to do laundry and run errands. So I have to go home to do all of that."

He grinned. "Message received. And I'm right there with you, but I will not lie. I will be glad when home means both of us in the same place."

Bridgette sighed. "Me too, sweetheart. Me too."

A few minutes later, Wade dropped her off at her apartment, waited until she was safely inside, and went home.

As for Bridgette, she still had one more phone call to make about getting engaged, and as soon as she got into her apartment she called Hunt, and Ava answered with delight in her voice.

"Birdie! Hi, sweetheart!"

"Hi, Ava. Is Hunt home?"

"Yes. He's in the kitchen. Hang on a second and I'll go get him."

"Well, don't go anywhere. Put the phone on speaker when you give it to him. I have something to tell you both."

"Oooh, I love secrets," Ava said. "Just a sec." She got up, running, and skidded to a halt in the kitchen. "Birdie is on the phone. I have it on speaker. She has something she wants to tell us."

Hunt wiped his hands and turned around to listen.

"Hey, baby sister. What's going on?"

"I am engaged. Wade proposed last night."

"Oh wow. That's wonderful news! Congratulations!" Hunt said.

"When's the wedding?" Ava asked.

"At a date yet to be determined," Bridgette said. "I just wanted you to know."

"Best news ever," they said in unison. "We'll be there with bells on when it happens."

Bridgette hesitated, and then blurted it out. "Um…Hunt?"

"What, honey?"

Her voice was trembling just the tiniest bit. "Would you give me away?"

"I would be honored," Hunt said.

Ava suddenly laughed. "I just realized. You're going home! You'll be living back in the home you all sold."

"I know, but I'm already enjoying it. Hunt made it so much better and so beautiful that sometimes I forget I ever lived there because it's nothing like what it looked like when we grew up."

"Thanks. But I was only doing what Mama asked us to do," Hunt said.

"I know," Bridgette said. "But I think of all the hard work you put into it to make it what it is today. It's special to me that you did that to the place where I will be living. Anyway…I won't keep you any longer. I have a lot of stuff to do today, but I waited until after church to call because of the time difference. I love you both."

"We love you, too," Hunt said. "Take care, and tell Wade I said good job!"

She smiled. "I'll do that."

LaJune King wasn't having a good day. Her children had cried twice to go home and see Daddy, and they were upset that they'd missed the Blessings parade.

It had been fun to visit their grandparents, but they wanted to go home—back to their friends at school, and back to their own rooms. They didn't like staying upstairs. The floors creaked, and Grandpa snored. They'd spent the last two nights in bed with LaJune because of all the strange noises.

And she wasn't happy, either. She loved Josh. But he'd changed so much in the past year that she hardly knew him. Stealing money was the last straw. She kept telling herself this was just a crossroad. It wasn't the end of the world. Even though it felt like it.

Dub was sitting outside on the back porch with a beer, studying the lay of the yard and debating with himself about planting more crape myrtles. Nola loved them, and the darker purple ones they'd had died after the hurricane. Their home had been high enough to escape the flood, but the back end of the property had not, and a lot of their landscaping had suffered.

He was still thinking about the possibilities when Nola opened the back door.

"Hey, honey, I'm going to the Crown to pick up a few things. Is there anything in particular you need?"

"If they have any Christmas candy, like peanut brittle, I'd take some," Dub said.

"Duly noted," Nola said.

"Be careful," Dub added.

"I will," she said, and went back in the house.

A couple of minutes later, he heard the garage door go up. Nola was on the move.

He took another sip of his beer and then set it aside. There was something on his mind that he needed to attend to, and he wasn't going to be satisfied until he'd done it.

He'd been the one who'd given LaJune King the bad news about Josh's arrest, and the look on her face still haunted him. He knew she was gone, and that made him sorry for the whole family. It wasn't his business to meddle in what they decided to do, but since he'd been the one to file charges against her husband, he thought it only right to let her know Josh had paid him back and he'd dropped the charges. Whatever happened after that was on them. So he picked up his phone, pulled up his contact list, and called her.

———————

LaJune was in the house doing laundry. Her parents had taken the kids down the road to look at the neighbor's horses, giving her some time alone. They knew she was struggling, but all they could do was offer help without advice.

When her cell phone rang, she hoped it was Josh. His cryptic message was still bothering her. But when she saw caller ID, she frowned as she answered.

"Hello."

"LaJune, this is Dub. Do you have a minute?"

"Yes," she said, and walked into the kitchen and sat down at the table. If it was going to be more bad news, she needed to hear it sitting down.

"The last time we spoke, I had to give you some pretty bad news. I'm not in the habit of doing that to anyone, and it's bothered me a good deal. So I felt it only fair to give you a quick update on the situation. Do you know Elliot Graham?"

She frowned. "Are you speaking of the older man who lives in that big house across the street from Dan Amos? The man who is an artist?"

"Yes, that's him. I got a call from him late Friday night telling me that he was going to bring Josh over to my house the next morning to pay back the money he took from me. He also told me that Josh would be going to work at the Crown, moving pallets. It seems their forklift driver had moved away."

LaJune was stunned. "Why would he do something like that? We don't even know the man."

"That's part of why I called," Dub said. "Elliot didn't come right out and say it, but he alluded to the fact that Josh wanted to end his life."

LaJune gasped. "No. Oh my God. I got a strange text from Josh Friday night. I thought then that it sounded like he was saying good-bye, but I never would have believed he'd think like that."

"I can't speak for Josh…or for Elliot. I'm only passing on what I know because you two share children, and when they are involved, the whole truth should be known. I also want you to know that I have dropped the charges against Josh. Chief Pittman will have the paperwork in the system by Monday to verify that."

"Are you saying that Josh is free? That he's no longer in trouble?"

"He's free, and he's not in trouble with me, and I thought you should know. Merry Christmas to you and yours."

LaJune was still holding the phone to her ear after he'd hung up. Her head was spinning. This was the first glimmer of hope that she'd had since this whole mess began, but she wasn't sure what, if anything, she should do about it. If Josh was still wrapped up with his gambling buddies, this wouldn't solve a thing.

Bridgette woke up the next morning excited about life. She wanted to run all over town showing everyone her ring, but what she had to do was get dressed and get to the store. The mayor would present parade trophies, and there would be someone from the paper taking pictures—likely Ant Roland. She couldn't wait to see how the guys at the store reacted to Ant's Mohawk and the metal scorpion dangling from his ear.

The temperature was already rising, which meant the day was likely to get steamy by midafternoon. There weren't enough Christmas wreaths on earth to turn southern Georgia into a winter wonderland, but locals knew how to keep the holiday in their hearts.

She chose a lightweight cotton blouse in her favorite shade of pink, gray slacks instead of jeans, and pulled all of her long, curly hair to the top of her head, letting the curls fall at will.

She had tax reports to file and needed to send out past-due notices for unpaid bills, so she decided to make her lunch and work through the noon hour. As soon as she had everything together, she left her apartment and drove uptown.

Wade was already at work when she arrived, and when she walked into her office and saw a dozen red roses in a vase on her desk, she dropped her stuff in her chair and headed to his office.

He was at the computer ordering products when she walked in, and when she plopped down in his lap and put her arms around his neck, he pulled her close.

"Good morning, my love," he said, brushing kisses on her lips and down her neck to the base of her throat. "God…you smell so good."

Bridgette sighed. "Lilac bubble bath. And speaking of flowers, the roses are beautiful. You're amazing. I love you madly."

He hugged her. "I love you more."

"I doubt that," she said. Then she got out of his lap, blew him a kiss, and sauntered back to her office.

She stowed her lunch in the mini-fridge, booted up the computer, and then went up front to say hello to the crew, wondering how long it would take for them to notice her ring.

The first thing they did when they saw her was tease her about the ride.

"Are you sore, Birdie?" Donny asked.

"I think she is. She's walking a little bowlegged," Roger said, and then winked.

"You did good, girl," Joe added.

"No, I'm not sore. I am certainly not bowlegged, and thank you for the compliment, Joe."

Their laughter was good-natured, and the conversation immediately turned to winning the trophy. Donny was moving things around on the shelf behind the register to make a place for it when Joe spotted the diamond solitaire on her finger.

"Holy smokes, Birdie! Is that what I think it is?" he asked, pointing at her ring.

"What? You mean this?" Birdie said, and held out her hand.

"You went and got engaged!" Joe crowed.

"I sure did," she said.

"Who to?" Roger asked, and then burst out laughing at the look on her face. "Oh heck, honey. We all know it's Wade. I was just kidding you."

She poked him on the arm and then laughed with them.

Wade appeared and put his arm around Bridgette and pulled her close.

"Yes, I know I am a lucky man, and yes, you'll all be invited to the wedding, whenever we get around to it," he said.

At that point, Dub walked into the store, followed by the mayor, the parade coordinator who was carrying the trophy, and Ant Roland with his camera.

"Who's he?" Joe asked.

"The new photographer for the paper," Bridgette whispered. "And be nice."

But men being men, they bunched up together and stared at Ant like he was an animal in a zoo.

Bridgette could see this might not end well, so she assumed the responsibility of introductions.

"Everyone, this is Anthony Roland. He's the new photographer for the *Blessings Tribune* but you can call him Ant. Ant, from right to left are Joe, Roger, and Donny, employees of the store."

Ant nodded cordially, and when the six-inch Mohawk held the nod without even a bounce, they stared in disbelief.

"What'cha got in your ear?" Roger asked.

"Oh, you mean Pedro? I bought him in Guadalajara about eight years ago after I got stung by a real one. Made me so damn sick I nearly died. So I bought old Pedro here as a reminder to scorpions everywhere that this is what will happen to them if they mess with me again."

The three men nodded, impressed with the story and the significance of hanging an enemy from your ear.

Wade grinned. Ant was to Blessings what a time traveler was to the past. He brought a little of the present world into a town that was proud of being quaint, that had refused to become passé.

"I don't have a scorpion in my ear, but we do have a trophy to accept, so let's get this done," Dub said. "Ant, where do you suggest we stand?"

Bridgette pointed at the gift shop area. "Why don't we go stand by the Christmas tree? That way we get the trophy presentation and a little free PR of the gift shop in the background."

Wade beamed. "And yet another reason why I put a ring on her finger. Smart is sexy, too."

"Gentlemen…shall we?" Bridgette asked, and led the way to the gift shop.

The parade coordinator stood next to the mayor. The mayor stood next to Dub, holding the trophy. Wade put Bridgette between him and his uncle.

"Look at me! Ready…smile!" Ant said and snapped several pictures in succession.

"I guess that does it," the mayor said. "Congratulations. It was a great float, and Miss Birdie all dressed in holiday red made it a fine representation of the holiday and your business. And I haven't even mentioned that memorable ride down Main Street on Rudolph. That was genius."

"That was all Wade," Dub said. "And if you haven't yet taken notice of that ring on Birdie's finger, she and Wade are engaged. The next generation of Truesdale's is in good hands."

Ant snapped another round of candid shots as the mayor congratulated Wade and Bridgette. It would make a nice sidepiece to the story.

The photo shoot ended with the arrival of two customers, and then their day at the feed store began.

The Martin family's day began with a final breakfast at the B and B. Duffy had a nine o'clock appointment at Butterman's Law Office to record and sign his statement, and then they were checking out and going home.

After yesterday's visit with Zack at Coastal State Prison, Duffy's whole demeanor had changed. He was almost back to his old self. He'd actually laughed during breakfast, and he smiled at his mom as they loaded up in the car and headed downtown to Peanut Butterman's office.

"I'm going to miss the low-key aspect of Blessings," Candi said as they drove down Main. "When we lived here, Blessings was just Blessings, but coming back, I see the beauty of staying small and quaint."

"Except for the times when people make horrible mistakes and send innocent people to jail, it's fine," Duff said. "I screwed up, but so did that jury."

Candi frowned. "Honey…first of all, the jury was composed of people from Chatham County, and the trial was in Savannah, not here. People make horrible mistakes everywhere, and innocent people go to jail somewhere every day. We just happened to be part of that statistic. It wasn't a witch hunt. And your dad would be the first one to tell you that his past record played a part in them believing it was possible for him to do that.

"His past should not have been a part of that trial, but somehow it happened, and the jury heard it, and that's where they went with the information. Yes, it was all when he was a kid…like you are now. He didn't have anyone riding herd on him then, and he ran with the wrong crowd. He had a less-than-threatening rap sheet, but it was there, nonetheless. The way for this kind of thing to never happen is to have the kind of sterling reputation that precludes everyone from believing it's even possible."

"Even then, that isn't foolproof," Allen said. "But it helps to always be one of the good guys, and you've already proven yourself there, in spades."

Duff sighed. "Okay. Message received with thanks…and there's the office."

Allen parked, then stared at the sign with Peanut's name on it. "Who in the hell names a baby a name like that?"

Candi grinned. "I remember the day we met, when he agreed to represent your dad pro bono, he apologized for the name and said he had better sense than his parents, who had surely been smoking weed the day they named him. The fact that he is, once again, helping without pay speaks for itself. Now let's go get this over with. I'm ready to go home."

———

When Josh King showed up for work that morning, he was already viewed as part of the crew. He had been given high marks by the employees for coming in yesterday to help sort out the shipments that had piled up.

He clocked in, stowed his lunch box, and went right to work, following all the orders he was given, doing everything that was asked of him without comment or complaint, and speaking only when he needed to ask a question.

He was grieving the loss of his family as surely as if they'd all died.

───────────

LaJune King was still grappling with Dub Truesdale's phone call. She'd had nightmares all night about Josh drowning while she stood on shore, watching without trying to help and then watched him go under. She woke up crying and gasping for breath as if she were the one who'd just drowned.

Her kids were quiet at breakfast, just picking at their food.

"What's wrong?" she asked. "You always like that kind of cereal."

"I'm gonna get behind in school," her son said.

"We were supposed to make Christmas ornaments in art today," her daughter said, and then burst into tears. "I want to go home."

"I do, too," her son said. He laid his head down on the table and wouldn't look up.

"They'll get over it," LaJune's mother said.

"They might, but I don't think I will," she answered.

"What do you mean?" her father asked.

LaJune got up and hugged her kids.

"I'm sorry you're both sad. So am I. Will you please go to your rooms for a while? You can play on your iPads. I want to talk to Granny and Grampa."

It was the word *iPads* that got them out of the room, and as soon as they were upstairs, LaJune sat back down with her parents.

"I got a phone call from Josh's old boss yesterday. He said Josh paid him back the money he'd taken. Apologized profusely, and that he has a new job already at the Crown, driving a forklift."

Her dad frowned. "That's all well and good, but where did he get *that* money? More gambling?"

"No. A nice man in town gave him the money and took him to Dub's house to pay off his debt. Dub told Josh he was withdrawing the charges against him. Josh is a free man."

Her mother leaned forward, reaching for LaJune's hand, but LaJune pulled back and put her hands in her lap.

"Dub also said that the man who gave Josh the money alluded to the fact that Josh was suicidal when he found him. He wanted to give Josh a second chance. And I need to give Josh a second chance, too. If he's trying to get his life back together, then he needs a reason to care, and we're it. I was ashamed and embarrassed when all that happened. I never even gave him a chance to talk to me about any of it. All I know is until he got messed up with the gambling, he was a good man, a good husband, and a good father. And I took a vow when I married him that it was for better or worse. So if this is the worst, then I think we can do better. I'm going to pack up the kids and go home."

Her mother was in tears. "I'm proud of you, baby. We stand behind any decision you make. You're our daughter and we love you. And we won't judge Josh. We won't make him feel unwelcome. Family is family. I still expect you all here for Christmas day, if you can."

LaJune looked at her dad.

He shrugged. "I stand by your mother. And I stand by you. If this is what you want, then we'll help. When do you want to do this?"

"Now," LaJune said.

He nodded. "Then pack up your things. We'll get you all home."

She got up and hugged them, then ran upstairs to start packing. The urgency to get home was strong.

CHAPTER 12

It was nearly noon when Candi and her sons went down to check out of the B and B. Rachel was at the front desk and looked up as they came down carrying suitcases.

"Hello, Martin family. Getting ready to leave us?" she asked.

Candi approached the front desk. "Yes. Our business here is done, at least for the time being, and we need to get home. Your place is wonderful. It was a welcome respite for all of us."

"I'm so happy to hear that," Rachel said.

"You sure can cook," Duffy added.

Allen grinned. "Food matters a lot to Duffy," he said.

"Food matters to me, too, Duffy. It's why we began this business. I love to cook," Rachel said.

"Yes, ma'am," Duff said. "And I love to eat."

Rachel leaned down and pulled out a beautifully wrapped gift basket from a shelf beneath the desk.

"Then this will not go amiss. Merry Christmas to all of you, and thank you for staying with us," she said.

"Oh my goodness! That's so generous of you," Candi said, eyeing all of the baked goods through the clear cellophane wrap.

"It's Christmastime in Blessings, which means there's always a little magic and a lot of love," Rachel said.

"Thank you for everything," Candi said. "Merry Christmas to you and your family."

Rachel smiled and nodded, but as she was watching them load up their car and then drive away, she thought about what Candi had said. *Her family.*

Rachel's family consisted of her and Bud…and friends. They had good friends and a good business here. And they had their health and each other. She'd gone the greedy route when she was younger and nearly destroyed herself. What she didn't have in life was far less important than what she did have, and that was enough.

———

Peanut was on a roll. He had signed statements from all three of the Martins, a digital version of the video Ant Roland took of the jewel recovery, and the proper petition papers to file to vacate the sentence.

"This is still something of a miracle to me," Betty said as she began gathering up her things to go to lunch.

"It's a miracle all around," Peanut said.

"Want me to bring you anything, or are you leaving, too?" Betty asked.

"I'm leaving. I have an appointment in Savannah with the DA who tried the case," Peanut said, "but I need to have Birdie and Woody's signatures on their statements before I leave."

"We could always call and have them come in," Betty said.

"But that means I'd have to wait on them to show up, and I'm not missing my appointment in Savannah."

"What about the story in the paper?" Betty asked.

"I heard Mavis was running one. She will get her info from the video Ant took."

Betty shivered. "This is exciting. We don't often get to do happy stuff here."

"You're right," Peanut said. "The law rarely deals with happiness. Now, off with you. Have a nice lunch. I'll see you later."

Betty left as Peanut grabbed his keys and a manila folder, and locked up the office.

The first place he went was the feed store, hoping he'd catch Birdie before she left for lunch. He grabbed the file folder and headed inside. The first person he saw was Wade.

"Wade, is Birdie here?"

"Yes, back in her office. Do you want me to get her?"

"Just take me back long enough for her to sign her statement about Duffy Martin."

"Will do. Follow me," Wade said.

Bridgette was eating at her desk and finishing up a report to the state tax commission when Wade knocked at her door.

She looked up, surprised to see Peanut behind him.

"Hi, guys. If I'd known I was having company at noon, I would have made more than one sandwich," she said.

Peanut eyed the roses. "Is it your birthday?"

She wiggled the fingers on her ring hand. "No. They're from my fiancé."

"Awesome," Peanut said, and then slapped Wade on the back. "Congratulations to the both of you! The first thing out of Ruby's mouth will be *I told you so*. But enough about my darling snoop. I apologize for barging in, but I need you to read over your statement, and if it suits you, then sign it. Betty transcribed it from the video of what you said at the recovery site."

"Oh, sure thing," Bridgette said. She took the papers he handed her and paused to read them. Then she picked up a pen, signed the statement, and handed it to him. "Thank you for doing this for Duffy."

"It's a good feeling, that's for sure," Peanut said. "Now I've got to go find Woody Rice and get a signature on his statement, and I'll be good to go."

Wade showed him out the side door and then came back in where Bridgette was working.

"Hey, honey, I'm going to the Crown. We're out of coffee in the break room. Do you need anything?"

"Can you get snow cones to go?" she asked.

He laughed. "I'll bet I can, and let me guess. You want the lemon-pineapple one again."

"Yes. It's Candlelight Bright, and thank you. I've been craving one ever since I had the last one."

"All you have to do is say the word and I'll bring you one anytime you want it," Wade said, and leaned over and kissed her. "Mmm, chicken salad?"

She grinned. "Not only are you a good kisser but you're a good taste tester. There has to be a way to make money from that."

Wade burst out laughing, and was still grinning as he walked out the door.

Peanut drove straight to Woody's house. His wife redirected him to an address near the country club and off he went, finally running him down at the mayor's residence.

He got out of the car with his file folder and walked out across the yard to wait for Woody to come back around on the riding lawn mower.

Woody rode right up to Peanut, then killed the engine on the mower.

"What's going on?" he asked.

"I need you to sign your statement about Duffy Martin. Betty transcribed it from what you said at the recovery site. Read it over, and if you agree with the statement, sign it."

Woody pulled a pair of reading glasses out of the pocket of his overalls, read the two pages of text, and then nodded.

"Yep. I said and did all this," he said.

"Then sign it down on the line above your name," Peanut said.

Woody used the steering wheel of the mower for a table, scribbled his name, and handed the statement back to Peanut.

"Thanks, Woody. Have a nice day," Peanut said, and loped back to his car.

He got back to the office, finished up all the paperwork, and sent a text to Ruby.

Going to Savannah. Appt with DA regarding petition for Zack Martin's release. Love you.

He was in the car and buckling his seat belt when he got a response.

Drive safe. Short ribs for supper.

"Yum," Peanut said, then started up the car and headed to Savannah.

He had fifteen minutes to spare when he got to the Chatham County District Attorney's office. He'd already filled Carl Perry in on why he was coming and that he was filing a petition to vacate the sentence, but he wanted to hand deliver the evidence.

DA Perry had agreed to the meeting, with reservations. Peanut was shown into his office.

"Butterman! It's been a while since I've seen you in court."

"Oh, I get around, sir," Peanut said. "I know you hear all kinds of stories about freeing prisoners, but this isn't just a story. We got the whole thing on video, complete with two witnesses from before who didn't even know at the time what they were seeing, and the daughter of the woman who was robbed witnessing the entire recovery and reclaiming her mother's things."

"Well, I must say, I am interested. So lay it out, and then we'll talk."

Peanut pulled out a laptop, a file folder with the petition papers, and another file folder with all of the signed statements.

"I already told you about Duffy Martin, Zack Martin's youngest son. He was only six years old when all this happened, so he had no background info about why his father was gone other than that his dad was in jail for theft. It wasn't until the family saw Selma Garrett's obituary and were talking about it that something was said about stolen jewelry. Apparently, Duffy, who is now sixteen, jumped up from the table, crying and upset, and went to his room. They didn't know what the hell was happening, and when they woke up the next morning and he was gone, they nearly lost their minds.

"He'd taken his brother's car and went back to Blessings on his own. But he didn't remember where anyone lived, and he didn't remember any people, and so he looked up the name of his father's lawyer and came to me. After I heard the story, I was flabbergasted. I called Lon Pittman, our chief of police, who came and also heard Duffy out. Bridgette Knox, the daughter of Duffy's old babysitter, inadvertently witnessed him putting dirt in a hole and thought nothing of it. Woody Rice, Selma Garrett's gardener, had just dug a hole to plant a new rosebush in her rose garden and caught Duffy refilling the hole he'd just dug.

"So Bridgette Knox takes Duffy away. The gardener goes about his business and plants the rosebush. The little kid forgets about the game, because it's the same game he plays every day...at his babysitter's house, and at his home. He's a pirate finding buried treasure or he's a pirate burying treasure."

The DA was shaking his head. "This is like something out of a Hollywood movie."

"Except an innocent man went to prison for something his child did. A child so little he didn't even realize what he'd done. And when they arrested his father the next day, there was total chaos in the home, and no one told him anything. What you're going to see on this video is the recovery crew going to the Garrett property and... Well, it speaks for itself."

Then Peanut pulled up the video, turned up the volume, and hit Play.

He sat, watching the changing expressions on Carl Perry's face and knew it was getting to him. And when Duffy was digging up the box with his hands and crying "I'm sorry, Daddy" over and over, and then finding the jewelry box and falling back against the house with the box clutched against his chest, Peanut knew it was all going to be good.

"Holy shit!" Perry said. "You can't make stuff like this up."

"As you can see," Peanut said, "Mrs. Garrett's daughter, Rita, is thanking him profusely, bragging on him for being brave enough to do this, and verified the jewelry was all there."

The video ended.

"I'll want you to send me a copy of this," the DA said.

"Already in your email, sir," Peanut said, and then slid the file folders across the desk. "Petition to vacate the sentence in this file. Signed, notarized statements from the witnesses and from Duffy Martin himself. Honestly, this boy has put Christmas back in my heart, and it would mean the world to all of us in Blessings to give a little back to them and to get Zack Martin home for Christmas. There was no real evidence against the man other than he had opportunity. I still believe his prior record was part of why he was convicted. People knew he had a rap sheet and assumed the worst, even though all of those offenses were years before when he was a good deal younger."

Perry frowned. He didn't like to think they'd railroaded anyone, and if he hadn't seen all this, he still would not have been inclined to believe it. But this was pretty much irrefutable.

"So, what do you think?" Peanut asked.

Perry picked up the files. "I see no reason to reject the petition. I'm going to proceed with the paperwork to vacate, and I'll let you know when it's done."

"Just so you know, Zack Martin knows about the recovery. His family visited him this past Sunday and told him what had happened. Do you have any kind of timeline for when he might be released? And will they notify his family so they can come get him or what?"

"As the lawyer of record, you will be notified of his release date. You will then let your clients know. After that, it's up to them to get him home after the hearing."

"Awesome," Peanut said. "I'll be awaiting your call, and thank you, sir. Thank you and merry Christmas."

"Merry Christmas to you, too, Butterman. You have one hell of a name, but you also have one damn fine reputation to go with it."

Peanut grinned. "Yes, sir. Thank you, sir."

He left the DA's office on a high, and thought about Ruby's short ribs all the way home.

———————

Josh King sat down in the employee break room at noon and opened his lunch box. It was Millie Garner's time to break for lunch, too, and when she saw Josh sitting there alone, she turned around and walked out.

Josh sighed. Her rejection was silent, and it hurt, but that was on him, so he took a bite of his sandwich and let it go.

He was still chewing when Millie came back carrying two cold bottles of pop and a plastic container from the deli. She sat across from him at the table and then pushed one of the bottles toward him.

"It's thirsty business moving product. How's it going?" she asked, and opened her container of pasta salad.

"Just fine, and thank you for this," he said, and took a big drink.

Millie grinned. "You're welcome."

He ate in silence, while listening to her chatter. She was trying hard to be kind, and he appreciated it, but he still felt awkward and guilty.

Finally, he laid down his sandwich and looked up.

"I paid Dub back the money. He dropped the charges against me. I'm just trying to do the right thing."

"We know," Millie said. "Wilson told us before you came to work. He doesn't hire anyone who might be a problem. We all thought it was a good idea to give you a second chance."

Blinking back tears, Josh nodded.

"Thank you for the pop. Next one's on me," he said.

Millie grinned. "I like Mountain Dew."

"Yeah, so do I," Josh said. "I'm going back to work now."

"Take your drink with you, and when you're on break and wanting a snack, come to my register. I'll get you checked out real quick."

"Thanks," Josh said.

"Sure thing," Millie said, and then added, "Hey, Josh…"

"Yeah?"

"Hold your head up. Be the man your mama meant you to be," Millie said, and then got up and went back to work.

At that point, two more people were coming into the break room to eat, and Josh passed them on his way out. He couldn't bring himself to speak for fear he'd start crying, but his head was up and his shoulders were back.

━━━━━━━━

Wade was standing in line at the snow-cone stand when Junior Knox saw him and waved.

"Hey, brother," he shouted.

Wade grinned. It just dawned on him that he did have brothers now. Three of them to be exact. And a sister. There were all kinds of perks to being engaged to Bridgette besides the obvious—like being so besotted with her that he was standing in the midday sun in line with a bunch of kids, waiting to get her a lemon snow-cone.

By the time he finally got up to the window to order, he was so hot he also ordered one for himself. Even though the to-go cones had little plastic lids, they were beginning to melt by the time he returned. He ran in the side door and went straight to Bridgette's office.

"It's melted some, but there are straws," he said, and set it on her desk.

She pushed back from the computer and blew him a kiss.

"Thank you, Wade. Thank you so much," she said, then removed the lid, took a sip of the melting juice, and then took a big bite.

"Not too big, honey, or—" He winced as he watched her grimace from the brain freeze, then chuckled. "Too late."

"It's that first bite. I guess I'll never learn," she said. "What kind did you get?"

"Christmas Tree. It's lime. Citrus always hits the spot on a hot day. Enjoy. I've got to get the coffee into the break room before I have a mutiny," he said, and left on the run.

———————————

LaJune King pulled into the driveway and parked. The little white house with blue shutters had always been her anchor, and now she felt grounded again. This was where she belonged. Her parents and the kids weren't far behind, but she felt the need to go in alone—to make peace with abandoning the little house as readily as she'd abandoned her marriage.

She grabbed her suitcases, carried them to the porch, and then got the extra key they kept under the door mat, and carried them in.

"Hello! I'm back," she said.

All the response she got was a rush of cool air as the central air kicked in. She didn't know what she expected, but it wasn't this.

The floors where shining. Everything was dusted. There weren't any dirty dishes in the sink, and the bed was made. This wasn't the Josh she'd been living with. Something about him had certainly changed, and this was a good first sign.

She walked through the house, imprinting herself once more within the space of these walls, opening the doors to the kids' rooms to air out, and then turning on the lights. As the vow stated—for better or for worse—she was home.

She was carrying her bags back to the bedroom when she heard a car pulling up the drive. That would be her parents with the kids. It was time to put their world back in order, too.

———————————

The men were unloading a new shipment of cattle cubes, which left Bridgette to man the register until they were finished.

She was dusting off the shelves behind the counter when Dori Pine came in with her three boys.

"Hi, Birdie. Johnny's been promising the boys he'd bring them here for days, but he's gotten so busy, the task fell to me. The boys want to pick out an ornament apiece to hang on our tree."

Bridgette came out from behind the counter and joined them in the gift shop.

"Hi, guys!"

Beep was looking up at her in awe. "We saw you riding that bull," he said. "He 'bout bucked you off!"

Bridgette nodded, her expression as serious as Beep's.

"Yes, it did about buck me off, but I held on tight."

Marshall shoved his hands in his pockets, trying to look unimpressed, but it wasn't working.

"Did you have to practice a long time to get that good?" he asked.

Bridgette thought of the five minutes of practice and then nodded. "Yes, a long time."

"I might like to be a real bull rider when I'm older," Marshall said.

Bridgette shuddered. "Oooh, not me. That mechanical bull was wild enough for me."

Marshall grinned, satisfied that he'd one-upped her with his manly prowess, and turned around and started looking at the tree.

Luther, Dori's toddler, was wiggling, wanting to be put down, but it was obvious Dori didn't want him down and taking everything apart like he did at home.

"Let me hold him," Bridgette said, and Dori gladly handed him over.

Luther immediately gave her a *Do I know you?* look, and then decided it didn't matter and poked her nose with the tip of his finger.

Bridgette laughed, shifted him to her hip, then picked up a little John Deere tractor ornament and handed it to him.

"Look, Luther. It's a tractor. Can you say 'tractor'?"

"Sonofagitch," Luther warbled.

Dori turned thirty shades of pink. "Oh my lord! I'm so sorry! He's at the stage of repeating everything he hears Johnny say, and unfortunately he overheard Johnny's comment when he mashed his finger the other day. Of course the minute Luther said it, the boys laughed, and now it's stuck in his brain."

Bridgette grinned. "Oh, honey, I am the only female employed here. I've heard much worse, and in several different languages." Then she held the tractor up in front of Luther again.

"Want it!" Luther crowed.

"You want this tractor?" Bridgette asked.

The toddler nodded.

"Tell me what it is," she said.

"Trakker," Luther said.

"Bingo!" Bridgette said.

"Bingo!" Luther crowed.

Bridgette put him down and then set the tractor in front of him. Luther plopped down on his butt, grabbed the tractor, and started rolling it back and forth across the floor.

"Bingo! Bingo!" he said as he rolled the tractor across his legs, and then cackled at his own daring.

Dori laughed.

"I think you have just put a new word in his head, and one much better than the last."

Bridgette was still grinning when she looked up and saw Wade watching them from across the room. The look on his face said it all. He had babies on the brain, and she'd just been holding one.

"Come join the party!" she said. "Luther just learned a new word."

"I heard!" Wade said.

"Hey!" Beep said. "I saw you driving that tractor in the parade."

Wade grinned. Beep Pine was a charmer. "I sure did. I saw you guys, too," he said and then shifted his focus to Marshall. "Dang, boy! You sure are getting tall. I think you might outgrow Johnny."

Marshall's eyes widened. Johnny wasn't just his big brother. He was also the father figure they'd never had, and they idolized him. Being bigger than Johnny would be a feat.

"You think so?" Marshall asked.

Wade shrugged. "I wouldn't be at all surprised."

Marshall stood up straighter and then went back to looking at the ornaments.

"When Johnny's not around, Marshall is my second-in-command. I don't know what I'd do without him...without any of them. Johnny and the boys are my heart," Dori said.

"I choose this windmill!" Beep said.

"I choose this bull," Marshall said.

"That's a longhorn. I know I'm not riding one of those," Bridgette said.

Marshall grinned.

Dori picked Luther up from the floor.

"So, baby boy! What one do you want?"

"Bingo!" Luther crowed, and held up the tractor.

They burst out laughing.

"I have created a monster," Bridgette said.

"No, he came this way," Dori said. "Come on, boys, let's go pay," she said, and headed for the register with Luther driving his Bingo up and down her shoulder.

"Oh lord," Dori said. "Marshall, will you please hold this toot long enough for me to pay?"

"I'll hold him," Wade said, and held out his hands.

Luther was used to big men with deep voices. He went from Dori to Wade without looking back, and then spent the entire time in Wade's arms trying to unbutton his shirt.

By the time they left, Wade was smitten.

"Those kids are really something. Dori doesn't look very old, and I know Johnny's not nearly as old as we are. They have a big family to be so young."

"Oh. Marshall and Beep are Johnny's younger brothers. And

Luther is Dori's baby. They have quite a love story. Johnny was trying to raise his little brothers on his own, and Dori had just had a baby and was living with her grandfather when he died in a fire. Johnny took her and the baby in, purely out of human kindness. They got married to keep Social Services from taking their babies away, and now they're living happy ever after."

Wade was riveted by the story.

"You never really know how good you have it until you hear a story like that and meet the people who lived it. I don't say this enough, but you bless me every day."

Bridgette looked up. "Oh, honey, thank you. Believe me, I do not take you or us for granted. Ever."

He hugged her and then shifted the mood with a question.

"Do you want to do something tonight?"

"If you want to come over, I'll make supper," Bridgette said. "Spaghetti and meatballs are on the menu. And I'll show you the chair I bought at a yard sale the other day. I'm going to reupholster it for my bedroom."

"I'd love to," Wade said. "How about I bring dessert from Granny's?"

"Yes, and surprise me," Bridgette said. "Gotta get back to the register. Customers are pulling in," she said.

"I'll do it. You're officially released to go back to your office."

"Good. I was entering invoices and I want to finish before quitting time. Oh...did you see the weather report at noon today?" she asked.

"No. What's happening?" Wade asked.

"Big cold front sweeping through your old stomping grounds. It should hit the Boston area sometime in the next couple of days, with fifteen inches of snow predicted."

Wade shuddered. "Ugh. I've endured a few of those. Can't say as how I'll miss them. I like Blessings's weather, even if there's no Christmas snow."

"Cold weather up there sometimes means we get stormy weather down here, though. You surely haven't forgotten that. Remember our sophomore year when the tornado warnings went off just before Christmas break, and they made us all sit down out in the halls with our heads on our knees?"

Wade frowned. "Now that you mention it, I do remember that. We called that the bend-over-and-kiss-your-ass goodbye formation."

"Let's hope all we get are some thunderstorms, and we aren't called upon to assume the position again," she said, and left the store-front as new customers were coming in the door.

Bridgette worked all through the rest of the afternoon, and when quitting time came, waved goodbye to Wade and took her roses home with her. She wanted to put them on the table tonight for decoration.

CHAPTER 13

JOSH KING FINISHED UP HIS FIRST OFFICIAL DAY ON THE JOB with a feeling of satisfaction, but after clocking out, he had to face going home to that empty house. He stopped by the Dairy Freeze to get a chocolate malt and then set it in the console and headed home.

He had already turned the corner and was on his way down the street when he saw the car in the drive. He thought he was dreaming, and still didn't believe it until he got all the way up beneath the carport and parked beside the car. He didn't know what this meant and was almost afraid to go inside.

He got his chocolate malt and his lunch box and was all the way on the porch when the door opened and his kids came barreling out.

"Daddy! Daddy! We're home! We missed you!" they cried, and then they saw the malt. "Did you bring that for us?"

He looked up, saw LaJune standing in the doorway, and started crying.

"Son, take the malt into the kitchen and divide it with your sister," LaJune said.

They took the malt out of his hands, but he never knew it. All he could do was stand and stare.

"Well, are you coming in or not?" she said.

He stumbled over the threshold and fell into her arms.

"I'm sorry, I'm so sorry. You were right. I hurt the people I loved most, and I don't know why."

LaJune wrapped her arms around him as he cried. He was shaking and sobbing so hard he could barely breathe, and her heart was breaking. Her instincts had been right.

"It's okay, Josh. It's okay. We'll talk about it. We'll figure it out. I shouldn't have walked out without talking to you. I won't ever do that again. For better or worse, remember?"

He just kept shaking his head and kissing her face and then hugging her, then kissing her again, unable to believe this was real.

It was the giggle and then peals of laughter coming from the kitchen that settled his last fear. He would never, for as long as he lived, do anything that might cause him to lose this.

"I better go see what's going on in the kitchen," she said.

But Josh couldn't bring himself to turn her loose.

"You're here to stay?" he asked.

She put her arms around his neck and then pulled him close.

"Yes, sweetheart. I am here to stay."

Bridgette made a quick stop at Bloomer's Hardware before she went home. She already had the fabric and new padding she intended to use on the chair, but she wanted to get a can of upholstery adhesive and some decorative tacks so she'd have everything she needed before she started.

Fred was at the front counter checking out customers when she came in.

"Evening, Birdie. I'll be right with you," he said.

"Don't bother. I know what I need and where to find it," she said, and headed to a back wall on the far side of the store.

After a quick search, she got the upholstery adhesive and the tacks she wanted and went up front and got in line to pay.

Myra Franklin, who owned the florist shop, was in front of her, and when she saw Birdie, she started talking.

"Well, I'll say…I hear y'all won the trophy for best float. It was impossible to compete with that. I don't know how you got the nerve to do it, but I'll say you did a great job."

"Thank you, Myra. I was a bit taken aback when they asked me if I would, and then I thought what the heck. You only live once, right?"

Myra grinned. "That's what they say." Out of curiosity, she glanced down at what Bridgette was buying, and then saw the engagement ring and gasped. "Are you engaged?"

Bridgette smiled. "Yes, as of this past Saturday evening."

"Congratulations," Myra said, and then sidled up a little closer. "Are you having a big wedding?"

"Not a big one, but a nice one," Bridgette said. "We have to decide on a date and all kinds of things."

"Well, I'll be proud to do your flowers," Myra said.

"Thanks…and I think Fred's waiting on you," Bridgette said.

"Oh my goodness! Sorry, Fred!" Myra said, dumped her purchases on the counter, and as soon as she paid, left on the run.

"Did you find everything?" Fred Bloomer asked as Bridgette put her things on the counter.

"Yes, I did. Thank you."

A few minutes later, she was out the door and on her way back to her apartment. She had meatballs to get in the oven so she could add them later to the sauce, and the spaghetti noodles would be the last thing she cooked.

She carried in her roses and put them on her dining table, then ran back to her bedroom to change. She set the can of upholstery spray on the little table and left everything else in the sack. She was getting out of her work clothes when she saw a spider scurry across the floor and run into her closet. She screamed. Of all the critters in the world, Bridgette hated spiders the most. She made a mad dash to her utility room, grabbed a can of bug spray, and then ran back into her bedroom.

She turned on the lights in the closet and began moving shoeboxes and spraying every inch of the closet as she went. She didn't see the spider again, but it didn't matter. After that much poison, it wasn't going to survive, and unless she aired out her bedroom, she might not, either. So she opened her bedroom window a couple of inches to let in some fresh air and made a mental note to close it again before bedtime.

As soon as she was dressed, she headed to the kitchen, turned on the oven, and started making meatballs—keeping them small so that they would cook faster. She browned them off, then put them in a pan to finish cooking in the oven before starting on the sauce.

She poured the jar of spaghetti sauce she'd bought into a saucepan and began adding her own seasonings to it, including one tablespoon of sugar. It was something her mama had taught her years ago to take the edge off the acidity of tomatoes. As soon as the sauce tasted like she wanted, she put a lid on the pan and turned the fire down to simmer.

The Martin family was home.

It felt surreal to walk back into the house when they'd spent the last few days in their past. Some say you can't go home again, but you can when home doesn't change. When home was exactly as you left it. And when it was the only place to find the one thing missing and needed to make the present right.

Candi began doing laundry the moment she got there. Duff had almost a week's worth of dirty clothes, and he was going to need clean ones for school tomorrow.

Allen took his car to be washed and vacuumed, even though it didn't really need it. It was just his way of getting back into their normal routine.

Duffy had righted a wrong and no one was mad at him. They kept calling him a hero, but he felt like a fake. He didn't feel like a hero. His heart hurt for what had happened to all of them. And now he had to go back to school. To the same place and the same classes and the same friends. But he wasn't the same. Would never be the same. And he didn't know if it would show.

Candi made meatloaf and mashed potatoes for their supper

because it was Duffy's favorite meal. When he first disappeared, she wasn't sure she'd ever see him again, let alone do his laundry and cook for him, and doing it now was a gift.

When they all sat down at the table and started passing bowls and filling their plates, she watched Duffy's expressions and knew he was still bothered. This had forever changed the man he would have been to this solemn, quiet, thoughtful person.

She was sad. She wanted her old Duffy back, but that wasn't going to happen. The trade-off was getting Zack back, and learning to give Duffy room to be who he needed to be.

And then Duffy caught her watching him and smiled.

"Good dinner, Mom," he said.

She smiled. "Thank you, Duffy. Are you looking forward to going back to school?"

He shrugged. "I guess. I'll have a lot of work to catch up on before semester break. What did you tell the principal?"

"That we had a family emergency and would be out of town for a few days."

He nodded. "Well, that wasn't a lie. We did, and we were, and now we're home. I'll need a note."

"I know. I'll write it later. Eat your food and quit worrying. We're having some of Rachel Goodhope's cinnamon rolls for dessert."

"Yum," Duffy said, and began scooping the last of his mashed potatoes into his mouth.

Allen rolled his eyes and looked at his mom.

"Well, there's proof the old Duffy is still in there somewhere," he said, and they laughed.

Wade knocked on the door to Bridgette's apartment at straight-up seven, listened for the sound of her footsteps, and then grinned when he heard them.

She was running.

That's exactly how she made him feel. Like he couldn't get to her fast enough.

The door swung inward. Her face was pink. There were curls falling down from the clasp she'd used to keep them away from her face, and she was in sandals, shorts, and a T-shirt.

"Hi, honey! You look amazing, and I'm in these old things. Come in where it's cool."

She shut the door behind him and then put her arms around his neck.

"Mmm, you smell good, too," she said.

Wade grinned. "So do you."

"You smell supper," she said. "Follow me, mister."

He did what she asked, and then remembered the sack he was holding and gave it to her.

"This is dessert. Two pieces of chocolate pie."

"Perfect. I'm going to put them in the fridge to keep them cold. The food is ready."

"And I'm ready for it," Wade said. "Can I help?"

"Nope. Just sit. I'm putting the spaghetti and meatballs on our plates. The rest of the meal is already on the table."

He sat, admiring her shapely bare legs and how the shorts cupped her backside in all the right places, and then had to refocus when she put his plate down in front of him.

"That is one serious plate of food, and it smells amazing," Wade said.

She smiled, kissed the top of his head, and then got the pitcher of sweet tea and poured it over the ice in their glasses, took garlic bread out of the oven warmer, and sat down with him.

"Honey! This is so good," Wade said, after taking his first bite. "And believe me…I've had good Italian food in Boston. Where did you learn to make this?"

"From Mama. On another note, I noticed when I was doing daily receipts that the gift shop stuff is really selling."

Wade nodded. "We'll change up the products after Christmas is over, but keep the rural theme. I think we'll stick with some standards, like the jams and jellies and the cast-iron wares, and some other things that are pertinent to holidays."

"You're a good manager," she said.

"We make a good team," he added.

"Yes, yes, we do," she said, then lifted her glass. "To us."

"To us," he echoed.

The meal ended with the pie, and then dishes. Once they were finished, Bridgette took him into her bedroom and showed him the chair she was going to redo.

"Look. Isn't this grand? The frame is still sound, and cherry wood is one of my favorites. I can't wait to get started."

"Are you going to work on it tonight?" Wade asked.

She nodded. "I'll undo it, for sure. The trick for me is taking off the upholstery in the pieces it was applied, so I can use them for patterns on the new fabric. It's a process, but I love it."

"Then I'm going to leave you to it," he said, and took her in his arms. "I need to gas up my car before I go home. Thank you for a wonderful meal, and for being so damn cute."

She laughed, and then she groaned when he kissed the laugh right off her face before she let him out the door.

As soon as he was gone, she went back to her project, got out her toolbox, set the upholstery adhesive on the end table by the bug spray, and then remembered her window was up, and closed it and pulled the shades.

She turned on the TV for company as she worked, pushed aside the throw rug in front of her bed, and turned the chair upside down. Then she sat down on the hardwood floor with her tools and started removing the old covering.

She worked for an hour, struggling with rusty staples and upholstery strips, trying to get the fabric off without ripping it to shreds, until finally she had all of it off except for the fabric on the chair back.

She stood to stretch her legs, and was leaning over to pick up the pieces of fabric she'd removed when she heard a rustling, and then a squeak, and before she knew what was happening, a mouse dropped out of the seat padding onto the floor.

Bridgette screamed, grabbed the can of bug spray, and ran after it. She couldn't let it get away. She'd never be able to close her eyes.

The mouse was almost at the closet, and in desperation she lowered the can and pressed the cap, hoping something in the bug spray would kill it. Next to spiders, mice were the worst, and here she'd had both in one day.

The halo of spray hit dead center, dousing the back of the mouse and a good twelve inches of flooring around it. And the moment it did, the mouse stopped in its tracks. Like it had just had a heart attack and died.

It looked so tiny and helpless from where she was standing, and now she was feeling horrible. Her heart was hurting, and her eyes were welling as she put down the can of spray and went to get a cloth to wrap it up in. The least she could do was give it a burial.

But when she knelt down to pick it up and saw its beady little eyes looking at her, she screamed and rocked back on her heels.

It was there. But it wasn't moving. What the hell? Did the bug spray paralyze it? Then she looked up and saw the can of bug spray still sitting on the table.

"What the hell, again," Bridgette said aloud, and then turned and looked for the can she'd just put down and groaned. It wasn't bug spray. It was the upholstery adhesive.

She'd just glued a live mouse to the floor!

She got back down on her knees.

The little mouse was just staring.

"I'm sorry, little guy. I'm so sorry. I'll figure something out," she said, and jumped up and began frantically searching for her phone.

The moment she found it, she called Wade. Her hands were shaking. Her voice was breathless, and she was near tears as it began to ring. And then he answered, and she unloaded.

"I glued a mouse to the floor. I didn't mean to. It was in the chair and it ran and I thought it was bug spray and it was the upholstery adhesive and it's not dead and it's looking at me and I'm so sorry. I don't want it dead, now. I just want it gone. But it's stuck! And I can't go to bed tonight with a mouse stuck to the floor. Help me!"

Wade was dumbfounded.

"There is a live mouse glued to your floor. Is that what you're telling me?"

"Yeessss!" she wailed.

He wanted to laugh, but he had a feeling now was not the time.

"Just take a breath and calm down, Bridgette. I'll be there soon, and don't worry. It's not going anywhere."

"That's not funny!" she wailed, but he'd already disconnected.

She ran back to the mouse, got down on her knees, and looked it in the eyes.

"It's going to be okay. Help is coming. I'm sorry I sprayed you with glue. Don't die. Just, don't die."

In less time than she would have imagined, Wade was knocking at her door.

She jumped up and flew down the hall, yanked open the door, grabbed him by the wrist, and pulled him inside.

"Hurry! He's just sitting there, staring at me."

Wade was grinning from ear to ear. "That's because he doesn't know what the hell just happened."

"Don't laugh!" Bridgette cried.

He hugged her. "Honey, as God is my witness, I can't help it. Now show me."

She led him into the bedroom and pointed.

Wade stared. "You really did glue a mouse to the floor. I don't think I've ever seen anything like that."

She punched him on the arm. "He's scared. I don't want him to have a heart attack and die."

"You mean like when you tried to kill him with bug spray?" Wade said.

Bridgette glared. "You aren't helping."

"I'm sorry, honey. But this is a once-in-a-lifetime chance here. Now…I know there are chemicals to remove glue, but if we use something like that, it will also kill the mouse you wanted dead and now want to save."

Bridgette was pacing the floor and wringing her hands. "Then what else is there?"

"In a pinch, we could try peanut butter," he said.

She stopped. "But that's what Mama always put on a mousetrap for bait. And now you're telling me peanut butter will get this one free?"

He shrugged. "I googled it. It's an organic way to get carpet glue off of hardwood when you're trying to go green. We can try it to see if it will get a stuck mouse off the floor. Got any peanut butter in the house?"

She flew out of the room and came back moments later with a jar of creamy peanut butter.

"I like crunchy better," he said.

"Stop being a smart-ass. We are basically using this for soap."

Wade grinned and took the jar out of her hands, then got down on his hands and knees in front of the little mouse.

"He's got quite a stare, doesn't he?" Wade said. "Unless you want me to use my fingers and ruin your jar of peanut butter, I'm going to need a knife to get some out."

"Use your fingers. I may never eat peanut butter again," she muttered.

Wade thrust a couple of fingers into the jar and pulled out a glob. It occurred to him that it might calm the mouse if there was some close enough for it to eat, so he started off by putting a tiny dollop right beneath its little nose.

"His nose is twitching! It took a bite. Oh my God, how cute is that!" Bridgette cried.

"You do know that you will owe me for life on this," Wade said, and then began rubbing the peanut butter all around the little mouse's body, and then rubbing it into the wood and the mouse's hair to release the oils that supposedly would dissolve the adhesive.

"Why are you rubbing peanut butter all over the mouse, too?" she asked.

"Just because his feet and body might come free doesn't mean everything else won't still stick onto its back. He'd be a prime target for every bird and cat in the neighborhood. Like a fuzzball on the move. Eventually, the peanut butter should dissolve the adhesive off of him, too."

"Oh, right. How awful. I didn't think," she said, and sat down to watch.

"So if this works, the little guy is instinctively gonna run again. Do you have any ideas for how to catch it this time?"

"Oh God. Uh…I'll get a plastic container," she said, and jumped up and ran.

"With a lid!" Wade yelled.

"Right!" she shouted, and kept running.

He shook his head and kept rubbing the peanut butter onto the little mouse and all around him.

Bridgette came back and got down on her knees with the clear plastic box, ready to pounce.

And then as Wade was rubbing, he felt something give. The hair was no longer stuck to the floor. He rubbed gently on the tiny feet until one of them was suddenly free.

"We're getting there," he said, and then finally the only thing still stuck was one tiny foot and the tail.

He picked up the little mouse, gently freed the last two digits, and dropped it into the box and closed the lid.

"Now where to put the little guy so that he's not some night owl's meal?"

Bridgette ran over and pulled the rest of the stuffing out of the chair seat.

"We'll put him back in his home. All we have to do is find a new place for all this."

"Well, as cute as he is, he can't live at the feed store," Wade said.

"And he can't live in the house," Bridgette added.

Wade sighed. "Put the padding in a sack. I'll take him to the park. I'll find a place."

"In the dark?" Bridgette asked.

Wade grinned. "I'm not afraid of the dark, honey. I'm also not afraid of mice."

"You are my hero," she said, and ran to get a sack, while Wade went to wash the mouse and peanut butter off his hands.

Bridgette put the padding in the sack.

Wade put the boxed mouse on top of it, and then pointed at the floor. "You can probably clean all that off the floor by now. I think the peanut butter has been on there long enough for the sticky stuff to come up."

"I will," she said. "And thank you. Thank you a thousand times."

Wade just shook his head. "Honey…I will walk through hell for you. I will slay dragons for you. And if this ever happens again, I will unstick mice from your floor for you. I've always got your back."

She hugged her arms across her breasts.

"I'd hug you, but you're holding the mouse."

Wade burst into laughter, and he was still laughing when she let him out the door.

While Bridgette was on her hands and knees scrubbing mouse hair and peanut butter off the floor, Wade was driving across town.

He stopped at the park, carried the sack across the greens to the gazebo, then got down on his hands and knees and pushed the little bit of padding through the lattice around the base. Then he loosened the lid, turned the box sideways and put it flat against the lattice work, and then slowly, like releasing a trap, pulled the lid up, giving the mouse its first sight of freedom. In less than two seconds flat, it leaped through a hole and disappeared.

"Have a nice life, buddy. You've earned it," he said, then gathered up the sack and the box and dumped them in a garbage can on his way back to the car.

Deputy Ralph was on patrol in his cruiser when he saw Wade Montgomery in the park. Wade was walking toward the car parked beneath the streetlight, so Ralph stopped and rolled down his window.

"Hey, Wade. Are you having car trouble?"

"Naw, just letting a mouse loose in the park," he said.

Ralph grinned. "I'll bet there's a story behind that."

Wade nodded. "Oh, there is, but I'm not revealing it under fear for my life."

The deputy was still laughing as he drove away.

Wade got back in his car and went home.

CHAPTER 14

BRIDGETTE COULDN'T GO TO BED UNTIL SHE HAD THE CHAIR stripped down to the frame, scared to death there might be another mouse or a whole nest of them there. But to her relief, the chair was clean of rodents. The TV was still on as she was getting ready for bed, and she heard the late-night weather come on.

She pulled her nightgown over her head, then sat down on the end of the bed to watch.

That massive front of cold air was getting stronger as it moved down out of Canada into the upper region of the Great Lakes and points north. It was being pushed across a broader swath of the upper states than previously predicted, and she didn't like thinking about what else could ensue. But it was late, and she was going to bed a good two hours later than usual, which meant two hours less sleep, because her alarm still went off at the usual time and Truesdale's still opened at eight.

She ran to make sure everything was locked and the deadbolt and safety chain were on, left the night-light on in the kitchen, and hurried back to bed. It didn't take long to fall asleep, but her dreams were crazy.

She was with Alice in Wonderland, having tea with the Mad Hatter and the Dormouse, who looked suspiciously like the one she'd glued to the floor.

She woke up just as the Queen of Hearts was running amok, carrying a spray can instead of a knife and shouting, "Off with their heads."

Bridgette groaned and shut off the alarm. When she opened her eyes and saw the naked chair frame, she shuddered, then threw back the covers and got up, frowning at the slightly darker spot in the wood.

It was oil. Peanut oil. It might be there a while. Or maybe forever.

But the Dormouse was gone, and she was no longer in Wonderland with Alice.

"Lord, what a night," she muttered, and headed for the shower.

━━━━━━━━━━

When Josh woke up and felt LaJune's warm body curled up against his back, at first he thought he was dreaming. And then he remembered and turned over, wrapped his arms around her and pulled her close.

"Morning, sugar," he said softly.

She stretched, and then hugged him back. "Good morning, sweetheart." And then she jumped. "Oh lord. I forgot to set the alarm. You need breakfast, and the kids will be late to school."

She kissed him on the cheek and flew out of bed and began getting dressed, and then took off out of the room to wake the kids.

Josh got up too, but headed for the shower, moving in a state of gratitude and grace.

━━━━━━━━━━

Mavis Webb was at her desk at the *Blessings Tribune*, reviewing the Duffy Martin video again. As owner, editor, and the only writer on staff, she often felt like she never went home.

But she was pleased with this piece. The story was nothing short of remarkable, and she wanted to do it justice. The poignancy of it, and the heroic effort of a son wanting to free his father from prison, should touch even the hardest hearts of any Christmas Scrooges.

After one last viewing, and then another round of edits on the piece she'd written, Mavis plugged it into the front page on her computer layout as the headline story.

BURIED TREASURE IN BLESSINGS!
MYSTERY OF MISSING JEWELRY SOLVED!

And then she uploaded the piece and the video to her online site as well. When the paper came out tomorrow, this would go live online, and she wouldn't be surprised if the video wound up going viral. It was a tearjerker.

At that point, Ant came sauntering in from the back room, which had become the place where he did his job.

Mavis looked up.

"Oh...I need you to run by the elementary school and take some pictures. Apparently today is Pajama Day at school, and teachers and students came to school in their pjs. We won't run more than three or four photos, but get enough so we'll have some good ones to choose from."

"Assuming that they're in class, am I to go from room to room or what?" Ant asked.

"Oh. No. I'm sorry. I meant at noon, when they're all in the cafeteria. The principal knows you'll be coming. Their lunch period begins at eleven, so check in at the principal's office and do your thing."

"Ooh, lunch. Do you think they'll ask me to eat with them?" Ant asked.

Mavis blinked. "Why would you choose to eat school food with about two hundred kids, half of whom are still lacking in both table and social manners?"

He shrugged. "I'm a kid at heart. I like free food. Besides, kids like me."

Mavis eyed the scorpion earring and the Mohawk and nodded.

"I can see that," she said. "Anyway...that's your assignment for now, and if anything newsy breaks, I'll let you know."

"I'm going to get a snow cone. Want one?" he asked.

Mavis laughed. "You are a kid at heart. I'll pass. Ohhh...now that you mention that. Hang around out there a bit and maybe get some shots of people buying Christmas trees, and the elves at the snow-cone stand."

"Will do," he said, and went to get his camera and bag and left through the back door.

As soon as he was gone, Mavis picked up the phone and called Arlene Winston, the elementary school principal.

Arlene answered abruptly, as if she was in the middle of something, and Mavis was already regretting this call, but it was too late to hang up.

"Hello. Principal Winston speaking."

"This is Mavis Webb, from the newspaper. Am I catching you at a bad time?"

Arlene Winston pinched the bridge of her nose. She already had a headache and it was barely 9:00 a.m.

"No, no, it's fine. What can I do for you?" she said.

"I wanted you to know that my photographer will be at your school at the lunch hour to take pictures for Pajama Day, as you requested."

"Thank you. We look forward to meeting him."

Mavis chuckled. "He's a diamond in the rough. I like to think of him as unique. Be prepared for a remarkable Mohawk and a scorpion earring. Other than that, he's perfectly harmless."

"Oh my," Arlene said. "No one is Blessings wears their hair that way."

"You mean they don't as of yet, but I'm going to predict that will change. All it takes is someone willing to step out of a rut. I adore him. I hope you enjoy his sweet spirit as much as I do."

"Yes, of course, and it's just hair. Better than the drama I had this morning when a sixth-grade girl came to school in her mother's negligee. How she got out of the house like that I will never know, but the boys in her class will never be the same, and she has gone home to change."

Mavis laughed out loud. "Oh, the joys of puberty."

"Indeed," Arlene muttered. "And…we'll take good care of your photographer. Have no fear. If he's not afraid of school food, we'll feed him as well."

"Music to his ears, and thanks," Mavis said.

Wade left home early and stopped at the Crown and ran inside. He went straight to the dog and cat food aisle, looking for cat toys, and within seconds found exactly what he wanted. Then he stopped by the bakery for an assortment of doughnuts and went up front to pay. It never occurred to him that he might see Josh King, but he got a glimpse of him pushing a cart of produce up an aisle and whistled.

Josh heard it and looked up, saw Wade giving him a thumbs-up, and smiled.

Wade took off to the feed store. It was about time to open up, and it would be just like some farmer to be sitting there waiting on him, but to his relief there was not.

He got out on the run, juggling door keys, the box of doughnuts, and his purchase, and went in the front door, turning off the security alarm as he entered.

He ran down the hall, took a doughnut out of the box and left it on a napkin on Bridgette's desk, then pulled a little gray rubber mouse with raggedy whiskers out of the sack, removed the price tag, and set its nose to the doughnut like it was eating it.

He grinned, then took the doughnuts back to the break room, started coffee brewing, snagged a doughnut for himself, and went to open the register.

He was licking the sugar off his fingers when Donny and Joe arrived, with Roger right behind them.

"Doughnuts in the break room. There'll be a delivery of chicken feed and salt blocks sometime this morning. And there may be another shipment of jelly and jam for the gift shop. Donny, you're up front until further notice today," Wade said.

"Then I better get me a doughnut before the hogs all get to the trough," Donny said.

"Hey!" Joe said.

But Roger grinned. "You got us pegged. I can't say no to sweets."

"Okay, there comes our first customer. Hop to it," Wade said, and went to plug in the lights on the Christmas tree and straighten up the merchandise.

They all scattered to their respective jobs, opening the doors at the loading dock area and turning on lights as they went.

Bridgette arrived a few minutes later, and the moment Wade saw her going in the side door, he waved at everybody up front, put a finger to his lips to be quiet, and pointed down the hall.

Curious as to what was going on, they stopped, listening.

When an ear-piercing shriek split the silence, they jumped, and before they could react, something came flying up the hall and hit the wall.

Wade collapsed laughing, and when Bridgette came stomping up the hall and saw him doubled over, she whacked him on the shoulder.

"You are so bad!"

"I couldn't help it," Wade said.

"To quote you, Wade Montgomery…I call bullshit. You could help it. You just didn't want to."

Wade was still laughing when he wrapped his arms around her to keep her from whacking him again and held on until Bridgette was laughing, too.

"Okay. This is all entertaining, but what the heck is going on?" Roger asked.

"It's just a rubber mouse," Joe said as he picked it up.

"Come on, guys… Let us in on the joke," Donny said.

"Let me go," Bridgette said.

"Are you gonna hit me again?" Wade asked.

"No. Once was sufficient," she said, and then walked over to Joe and held out her hand. "May I have my mouse back, please?"

Joe dropped it in her hands, and then they all stood watching her, waiting.

"It's no big deal," Bridgette said. "Wade had to come over to my apartment last night to dispatch a mouse."

"How do you dispatch a mouse? Was it in a trap or running loose?"

"Oh, it wasn't going anywhere," Wade said, grinning.

Bridgette led with her chin. "It was running. I sprayed it with bug spray, okay?"

Wade gently brushed a curl away from her forehead. "But it wasn't really bug spray, was it, honey?"

Bridgette sniffed. "And here I thought you loved me."

He frowned. "And here I thought rescuing the mouse you glued to the floor is the ultimate proof of my love."

All three men turned and stared at Bridgette in disbelief.

"Damn, Birdie. Why would you want to glue a mouse to the floor?"

She sighed. "I did not *mean* to do it. I thought I was using bug spray, but it turned out to be upholstery adhesive. I'm redoing a chair. The mouse jumped out of it…and oh well…it's a long story. I wanted it dead, and then it was so teeny…and stuck…and I freaked and didn't want it dead anymore. And Wade got it loose and took it to a new home. I don't want to know where. I am going back to work now. Thank you for my mouse, Wade. I am going to name it Peanut Butter."

She turned on one heel, strode back down the hall with the rubber mouse, and went into her office.

Wade had his hands in his pockets, watching her go. He was grinning.

"I am so going to pay for that," he said.

They nodded solemnly, eyeing him with new respect.

Roger frowned. "Uh…Wade?"

"Yeah?"

"How *do* you unstick a mouse glued to the floor?" he asked.

"Without killing it," Joe added.

"Peanut butter. Google it. It works."

Ruby opened the Curl Up and Dye, and then as soon as the girls showed up, she headed to Savannah. She didn't have an appointment until afternoon, and she was on a mission. There were still families in the Bottoms who were struggling, and she and Peanut had decided that instead of getting each other expensive Christmas gifts, they wanted to get something for someone else. He'd left the choice of the gift and the recipients to her.

It was rare that she went anywhere alone these days, and even more unusual to leave town, because she was always at work. But not this morning.

The sky was full of white, puffy clouds, but the sun was shining, Christmas music was on her favorite radio station, and she was making good time.

Within an hour, she reached the outskirts of Savannah and turned on her GPS to get her to her destination. She'd been looking online for days. Her problem had quickly become obvious early on, that the only place within reason that carried what she wanted was in Atlanta, which was hours and hours away. But then last night she'd spotted a possibility on an online site in Savannah. She'd made a phone call, then asked for an address and an appointment time to view, and now she was here.

She pulled up into the parking lot of a Methodist church and called the man she was meeting to let him know she was here. Then she got out and slung her purse over her shoulder, waiting for him to emerge from the church.

Within a couple of minutes, a short, stocky man wearing a yellow Hawaiian shirt and khaki pants came out to meet her.

"Good morning, Mrs. Butterman. I'm Sean Patrick, the pastor here."

"Good morning to you, too, and please call me Ruby."

He smiled. "Yes, ma'am. So you're interested in the shuttle van we have for sale?"

"Yes."

"Then follow me," he said, talking as they walked around to the parking lot at the back of the church. "We bought the van new in 2010, so it's going on eleven years old. It has over a hundred and fifty thousand miles on it. It's never been wrecked. And we've taken good care of it. There it is, parked next to our new van. Our church has actually outgrown it, which is good, but keeping it tagged and insured when we can't transport the number of children we need to anymore isn't, budget-wise. So the board opted to sell it. It runs great. It just doesn't serve our purpose anymore."

Ruby's heart was pounding as she eyed the shuttle van.

"How many does it seat?" she asked.

"Twenty-five, and it has seat belts. The heat and air work, and we put new tires on it less than eight months ago."

"What are you asking for it?" she said.

He paused, eyeing the intent expression on her face.

"If I may ask out of curiosity, what are you going to do with it? I mean…is it going to another church or—"

"No, not a church. I live in Blessings. It's a little town about an hour out of Savannah. It's a very special place to all of us who live there. We have troubles and sometimes bad things happen, but we always manage to find a way to pull together and make things right. Last year, a woman who came into a large sum of money went to the poorest section of our town. It's called the Bottoms. And she proceeded, with her own money, to buy the property from an absentee landlord and fix up every shack and shanty there. She remodeled them, replaced appliances, put in heat and air they didn't have, and even bought new furniture. It put us all to shame that we'd seen their need for many years but hadn't made it our business to do what should have been done.

"They still have needs. A lot of them don't have vehicles, or they only have the one, and that leaves families at home, unable to go get groceries or get to a doctor when the need arises. Which brings me to the reason I'm here. My husband and I want to gift the Bottoms with their own little shuttle bus. Their own Uber, so to speak. Families will have a way to go to the store and the pharmacy and get their hair done if they want to or take their kids to the park to play. This would be our Christmas gift to them. We'll have donations to pay for the insurance for it. But I need to know the asking price. It wasn't in the ad, and I don't want to drive it, fall in love with it, and then realize we can't afford it."

The pastor was touched by the story and her purpose. It was such a loving, giving thing to do.

"The price is negotiable," he said. "Let's go for a ride. You drive. If you're nervous, just drive around the parking lot for a bit. It's nice and empty right now. But if you're good to go, let's hit some city traffic."

"I'm good," Ruby said.

He unlocked the door, got in, sat in the driver's seat, and started the van up so he could show her how to open and close the door and where all of the instruments were that she'd need to use. Then he got up and gave her the seat.

Ruby buckled up, put the van in gear, and drove out of the parking lot and onto the street, then took off with the pastor in the seat behind her, giving her places to turn, instructions on how to watch both of the exterior side-view mirrors, and how much space she needed to make turns.

By the time they headed back to the church, Ruby was sold on it, but she still didn't know if she could buy it. She pulled back up into the parking lot and drove the van back around behind the church, then stopped and turned off the key.

"Well, what do you think?" he asked.

"It's perfect for what they need, but how much?"

"The board has given me discretion to sell it at a reasonable price. What were you planning to spend?"

"Ten thousand dollars is my cutoff point."

Sean Patrick smiled. "How about eight, and I'll throw in a tank of gas to get you home."

Ruby gasped. "Are you serious?"

"Yes, ma'am. And one day, I'd love to come to Blessings and see your little shuttle service at work."

"Oh, thank you!" Ruby cried. "You'd be most welcome anytime. I can write you a check for it this minute, only I don't have a way to get it back to Blessings today. I can arrange to have it picked up tomorrow, though. There are always willing volunteers in Blessings."

"Then come into my office. I have the title in my desk. I can sign it and my secretary can notarize my signature and yours, and then you can file the title in your name when you get home."

"Could I have some kind of bill of sale, too?" Ruby asked. "Since this is a charitable donation?"

"Absolutely. Follow me. Just give my phone number to whomever you send to pick it up, and I'll come out to show them where it's at."

"Yes, yes, I will," Ruby said. She paused to take a couple of pictures of the shuttle and then followed him inside.

About a half hour later, she left Savannah with two sets of car keys, the title, and a bill of sale. Now all she had to do was tell Peanut what she'd done. He probably wasn't expecting this, but he had left it up to her, and she knew her man well enough to know that he was going to be as excited about this as she was.

Now all she had to do was get home and get through the rest of the day without spilling the beans. It was hard for Ruby to keep a secret and the good Lord knew it.

———

While Ruby was on her way back to Blessings, Ant Roland was walking into Blessings Elementary to take pictures. He entered the principal's office and paused at the secretary's desk.

"I'm Ant Roland, the photographer for the newspaper. I think Principal Winston is expecting me."

Reneta Cole, the school secretary, looked up, blinked, and then picked up the phone and buzzed her boss. "Mrs. Winston, the photographer is here," she said, and hung up. "She'll be right out."

"Cool," Ant said.

Moments later, Arlene Winston came out of her office, smiling.

"Mr. Roland. Thank you for coming. The children have just gone into the lunch room, so there will be kids standing in line and some already sitting. I think you should be able to get some good shots for the school page of the paper."

"Yes, ma'am," Ant said. "Lead the way."

Arlene stopped to speak to Reneta. "I'll be back later. You know where to find me if you need me," she told her, and they walked out the door and then down the hall. "The kids are going to be excited to see you. Some will act like monkeys, and some will hide their faces, but that's how kids are, you know. Do you have children?"

"Never been married, and none to my knowledge," Ant said. "But I like kids. I'm gonna have to look into that one of these days. I think I'd be good at it. I didn't have a father around when I was growing up, so I already know what not to do, right?"

He grinned, and Arlene Winston with the stiff upper lip had the strangest urge to hug him.

"Yes, I would say you do, Ant."

"Umm, I already smell lunch. What are they having?" he asked.

"It's hot dog day. Chips or fries, and put on your own toppings. Chocolate chip cookies and fruit. After you've taken all the pictures you need, if you can stomach lunch-room cafeteria food, we would love for you to be our guest."

He beamed. "Oh wow! Yes, ma'am. I'm not picky and I like to eat."

Arlene hadn't eaten in the cafeteria more than once a year since she became principal, but she was going to do it today because Mavis Webb was right. This man had a sweet spirit, and she needed a little spirit lift herself.

And then they entered the cafeteria.

"Go ahead and get your candid shots before they all realize you're here."

"Yes, ma'am," he said. He pulled his camera out of the bag on his shoulder, adjusted a few settings, and began snapping shots, moving around the room as he did, catching two little girls in snowman pajamas who had already deconstructed their hot dogs and were dunking their french fries in their milk.

He caught one little boy in red and white pajamas and red fuzzy house shoes wadding the hot dog into his mouth in huge bites, and another one dressed in blue pjs who was eating a lunch he'd brought from home with all of the social grace the other little boy was missing.

He got photos of two teachers, both in fuzzy slippers and pajamas, opening milk cartons for some of the little ones and riding herd on the older ones with nothing more than a sharp look.

And then he snapped pics of the cooks, and more kids, and called it done and put his camera back in his bag.

It wasn't until he and the principal walked up to the line to get a tray that the raucous chatter in the room suddenly stopped.

"They've just seen you," Arlene muttered under her breath.

"Is it okay if I turn around and wave?" he asked.

"Absolutely," she said.

Ant turned around. "Hi, kids. My name is Ant. I'm a photographer. Is it okay if I eat lunch with you today?"

He got almost two hundred nods and maybe three quiet little voices who said yes.

"Awesome," he said, then got his tray and followed Arlene to the end of a table that was empty.

They sat. And Ant ate and talked to Arlene as if he'd known her for years, while every kid in the room chose to walk behind their table, carrying their trays back to the kitchen on their way outside.

One little boy stepped out of line and walked straight up to Ant.

"Hi. I'm Melvin Lee. Can I touch your hair?"

"If it's okay with Mrs. Winston," he said.

She nodded, waiting to see the reaction.

Melvin Lee touched the flat of his hand to the spikes, then pulled back his hand as if he'd been stung.

"Does that hurt?" Melvin Lee asked.

"Doesn't hurt me. Did it hurt you?" Ant asked.

Melvin Lee shook his head and followed up with another question. "Is that scorpion real?"

"Nope. It's made of metal, like your lunch box."

Arlene frowned. "That's enough, Melvin Lee. Go play."

"Yes, ma'am," Melvin Lee said, and took off running.

"Cool kid," Ant said.

"You have no idea how cool he really is," Arlene said. "Would you like another hot dog?"

"I'd take one to go, if that is okay?"

"It's okay," Arlene said. She got up and went back to the lunch line and came back a couple of minutes later with his hot dog. "It has mustard, but you can go add whatever else you want, and then I'll walk you out," she said.

"Oh, I'll take it just like this," he said. He wrapped it up in the napkin beneath it and followed her back up the hall, and then paused outside her door. "It was a pleasure to meet you, Mrs. Winston, and thank you for lunch. It was good."

"It has been a pleasure meeting you as well, Ant, and please call me Arlene. I'll look forward to seeing the pictures in the paper."

"Yes, ma'am...I mean Arlene. Have a nice day."

"You, too," she said. She watched him go out the door, then headed back to her office.

"Did you eat in the lunch room?" her secretary asked.

"Yes, why?"

"You have a bit of mustard on your blouse. You might want to get that off with some cold water before it sets."

CHAPTER 15

It was almost six o'clock when Ruby locked up the salon and headed home. Peanut's car was in the drive. She pulled up beside it and got out. She was excited, and anxious, because she wanted him to be as thrilled as she was.

She had already started up the steps when the front door opened.

"Hi, sugar!" Peanut said. "I heard you drive up."

"Yes, it's been a day," Ruby said. "And I can't wait to tell you what I did."

He grinned. "Should I be worried?" he asked as he shut the door behind her.

"No, because you told me to make the decision about this, and whatever I chose, you'd be fine with, remember?"

"Oh! Right. The Christmas thing. So what did we do?" he asked.

"Let's sit down. I've been on my feet all afternoon, and I want something cold to drink and the weight off my feet," she said.

"Then sit, honey. What do you want, pop or tea?"

"Maybe a Coke, if we have any?"

"Done," he said, and hustled off to the kitchen.

Ruby plopped down on the sofa, and then took the title and the bill of sale out of her purse and held them in her lap.

God, please don't let him freak out over the money.

He came back, handed her the glass, watching as she took a good drink and then she set it aside.

"A couple of months ago, you said something that got me to think-ing," Ruby said.

Peanut sighed. "Lord. Should I already be kicking myself for talking?"

She frowned. "No. And don't you dare be negative about this, because it's for the people who live in the Bottoms."

"Okay. I'm all about making their lives easier. So what did we do?"

"I'm getting to that," she said. "I've been looking online for weeks and weeks, and finally saw something like what I had in mind. I drove to Savannah this morning to check it out."

"You went to Savannah?"

Ruby rolled her eyes. "Are you not listening to me? Did I not just say that?"

"Well, yes, but I didn't know."

"You were in court, and now you do," she said.

He grinned, resisting the urge to pat her on the head.

"Touché," he said. "So what did you look at in Savannah?"

"A used church shuttle bus. It seats twenty-five and is in really good condition."

Peanut's eyes widened. "A shuttle bus."

"Yes, because most of the people in the Bottoms do not have daily transportation to get food or to get to a doctor. Cathy Talbot gave them a new way of life, and I thought it would be awesome if we gave them their own little Uber service."

He was in shock, and it showed.

"Who would drive that?" he asked.

"Anyone willing to be the driver that day. I drove it all over Savannah. Then the pastor asked me why I was looking for something like this, and I told him about the Bottoms and what Cathy had done and how this would go even farther in enriching their way of life."

Peanut nodded, but he was still locked into what she'd been doing while he was in court with a client who was disputing a neighbor's claim to some of his land.

"You drove a shuttle bus all over Savannah this morning?"

She sighed, got out her phone, and showed him the photos.

"This is what it looks like."

Now she had his attention. "Oh my God, Ruby. That looks brand new."

"It's not. It's ten years old. It has over a hundred and fifty thousand miles. But it has new tires, and it runs great."

"But those cost in the thirty-thousand-dollar range," he said.

"Really? Maybe when they're new, but if that's the case, then I think I got a deal." She handed him the papers in her lap.

It took about five seconds for it to register that she'd already bought it, and then he saw the bill of sale.

He stared, and then looked up at her in disbelief. "Eight thousand dollars? You bought that for eight thousand dollars?"

"Yes, and I'm not sorry," she said.

He whooped, put the papers aside, and pulled her into his lap.

"Girl! I'm not sorry, either! That's not a deal, that's a steal! The next time we trade cars, I'm letting you do all the talking." Then he kissed her soundly. "So, where is it? I want to see it."

"It's still at the Methodist church parking lot. The preacher's name is Sean Patrick. I told him I'd find someone to go get it tomorrow. He said to give them his number, and when they arrive, he'll show them where it is. The church just bought a new one, a much bigger one than this, and they don't need it anymore."

"Oh man! I'll go get it! I'll get someone to drive me. I can't wait to drive that home."

"Thank you, darling," Ruby said. "You're the best. And now that I found it, it's going to be up to you to figure out the legal aspects of how it's insured having multiple drivers, without having it belong to the City of Blessings, because it's for the residents of the Bottoms to use. If the city wants one for the rest of the town, then they can buy one and run it with their fleet of city vehicles."

"I'll make it work," Peanut said. "I told myself all I wanted for Christmas was to get Zack Martin out of prison, and it's happening. And now this. Merry Christmas to us, my darling girl. This is awesome."

━━━━━━━

Bridgette was getting ready to leave work when Wade appeared in the doorway.

"Hey, honey, I know you're getting ready to leave, but can you come out to the gift shop area for a sec? We have a customer asking questions about cooking that I can't answer."

"Absolutely," she said, and followed him up the hall and then into the front of the store. "I've got this," she said, and headed toward the gift shop. "Good evening, Mr. Ruth. Wade said you had a question about cooking?"

"Oh, hi, Birdie. About this big cast-iron pan."

"Ah, that's called a Dutch oven. It's the original slow cooker from before there was such a thing. What do you want to know?"

"I know what they are. But you have two sizes. Which one would be best for just me and the wife?"

"Then I have a question for you. Is she at a point where lifting heavy things is becoming an issue for her?"

He nodded. "Yes. She has arthritis in her hands, and neither one of us is as strong as we were."

Bridgette patted him on the arm. "Oh, we're all headed that way, if we're blessed enough to live a good long life. I would suggest you pick the smaller one. It's a four-quart size. Just about right to make a good pot of oven stew or simmer something on a back burner and still be able to move it around."

"Thank you, Birdie. That's just what I needed to know."

"You're welcome. Do you want to shop around a little more, or is this it?"

"Maybe I'll look a little more," he said.

"Then I'll take this to the register for you, and you can check out when you've finished shopping."

"Thank you," he said, and then he grinned. "You're sure something, riding that mechanical bull all the way down Main without falling off. Me and the wife got a kick of it."

"That was the purpose," Bridgette said. "And just between you and me, it was set on the slowest speed. If it had been even one notch higher, I would have been in the hay."

He laughed, and was still laughing as she took the Dutch oven to the counter.

"Mr. Ruth will pay for this later. He's still shopping," she said.

Donny nodded. "Wade's in the warehouse. He said he'd call you later, and thanks for helping."

"Of course," Bridgette said. "I'm leaving now. See you tomorrow."

She went back to her office, got her things, and left.

She had a grocery list to fill and a poinsettia to pick up at the florist. Her apartment was too small for Christmas trees, but she had a wreath on her door and she wanted a little something to represent the holiday inside.

She felt a slight shift in the wind as she was walking to her car and glanced up at the sky. It was clouding up. Looked like rain later. Maybe after sundown. But she'd be home by then, and the rain would cool things off a bit.

Still, she decided not to dawdle and headed for the Crown. Unfortunately, all the working people were of the same mind. There were a lot of cars coming and going as she pulled into the parking lot.

As she parked and got out, she saw Junior with Barrie and the kids. They were walking through the Christmas tree lot hand in hand, while the kids were playing hide-and-seek among the trees.

She glanced wistfully at the snow-cone stand and then hurried into the store, grabbed a shopping cart, and headed down the baking aisle.

Forty-five minutes later, she emerged on the run. She'd been delayed by a half-dozen people remarking about her bull ride, and even more who'd noticed she was now engaged.

And the sky was even cloudier than it had been before. She put her groceries in the car and headed for the florist.

It was almost closing time when she rushed inside.

Myra Franklin was dusting shelves and looked up when the bell rang over the door.

"Oh, hello, Birdie."

"Hi, Myra. It looks like rain, so I'm kind of in a hurry. I came to get a poinsettia. I see you have different sizes and colors, but I think I want a traditional red one, and not too large."

"Oh sure, honey. Let's look over here."

Bridgette followed her to a display shelf on the opposite wall and quickly pointed.

"That one! It's just the right size. How much is it?"

"Let me check," Myra said and pulled it down, then looked at the price on the backside. "It's thirty dollars."

"I can do that. I'll take it," Bridgette said.

Myra carried it to the register, rang it up, and then opened the door for Bridgette as she left.

"Enjoy!" Myra said.

"I will," Bridgette said. She put the poinsettia in the front seat beside her, shoved her purse against it to keep it from toppling over, and jumped in.

She drove home with one hand on the wheel and the other on the pot, making sure it didn't fall over, and it was the first thing she carried inside. She set it on the kitchen counter, then ran back to her car to get the groceries and was about to shut the trunk when Wade pulled up behind her.

He jumped out on the run and grabbed the sacks out of her hands.

"I've got them, baby. You get the door. We're about to get rained on."

She ran back to the apartment building and held the door open for him to come inside.

"Thank you so much," she said, and led the way down the hall to her apartment, where she held that door open for him as well.

"In the kitchen?" he asked.

"Yes, it's all groceries."

Wade saw the poinsettia as he set the bags on the counter.

"Nice," he said.

"I never put up a tree. No need because Emma does a big one and we always have dinner there. I have the wreath on my door, but I never see it unless I'm coming or going. I wanted something Christmas in here as well."

"We could put up a tree at my…at our house and host a dinner for all our families."

Bridgette's eyes widened. "Oh! Oh, I would love that. I would have to talk to Emma. I don't want to ruin plans she's already making."

"And I'd have to talk to Uncle Dub and Aunt Nola for the same reason."

Bridgette hugged him. "Then we'll see. But if not this year, then next year for sure."

Lightning cracked somewhere nearby, followed by a loud clap of thunder that rattled the kitchen window over her sink.

"Yikes. I think the storm is here. Would you turn on the television? I want to make sure there aren't any tornado warnings with this."

The kitchen was open to the living room, giving her full view of the TV. She began emptying the grocery bags as Wade flipped to the local news. There was a scroll running at the bottom of the screen, announcing the counties involved and a flash flood warning for low-lying areas in a nearby county.

"I think we're good," Wade said.

"Yay," Bridgette said. "I wanted to make some fudge tonight."

"Am I allowed to stay long enough to taste test?" Wade asked.

"You're allowed to stay as long as you want, and you know it," Bridgette said.

"After the mouse thing this morning, I wasn't sure."

She grinned. "Looking back, that was funny. But it did give me a momentary heart attack. That *is* a feed store, and it wouldn't have been the first time I found a mouse in the office."

He laughed. "I'm sorry I missed that."

"No, you're not. The first time it happened, I wouldn't go back in my office until Dub set about a half-dozen traps. The next time it happened, I set my own."

"So...no mercy for those mice?"

"Well, those had a chance to run away. I took that option away from this little guy. It didn't seem fair."

Wade shook his head. "I just love you, and that is all."

She smiled. "Ditto. Give me a few minutes to get out of these work clothes and wash up, and then I'll see what we have to eat. There's left-over spaghetti and some roast beef from the deli to make sandwiches."

"Roast beef sandwiches sound good," Wade said.

"You scrounge to see what else is in the fridge, and bread and chips are in the pantry. I'll be right back."

She hurried to her bedroom, stripped out of her work clothes, and ran to wash up.

She was reaching for a towel to dry her hands when there was a loud thump above her head and then shouting from the couple who lived above her.

"Oh, lord. Not again," she muttered, and then grabbed clean shorts and a T-shirt and put her hair up in a ponytail.

The shouting was louder, and all of a sudden Wade was standing in the doorway, frowning.

"What the hell is all that?" he asked.

She rolled her eyes. "The neighbors above me."

"Does that happen often?" he asked.

"Enough," she said. "Eventually, they'll quit. They always do."

He frowned, but said nothing more as they went back to the kitchen together.

A few minutes later, they had meat and bread on the counter, and Wade was digging through the refrigerator.

"Do you have horseradish sauce?" he asked.

"Um...I think so. Look in the door of the fridge."

"Oh. Right! And there it is. Awesome."

Bridgette had just purchased a container of deli potato salad and got that out, along with a jar of dill pickles and a little container of French onion dip to go with the chips.

By now, the rain was blowing against the kitchen window.

"I didn't know this rain was predicted, but I'm sure glad it waited until we got off work," Bridgette said.

"I have that big carport I added this past June. You'll be able to go in and out the back door without dealing with weather when we're together."

"Yet another reason I said yes," she said, and then laughed at the look on his face. "Oh please. When you put this ring on my finger, the last thing on my mind was carports."

He grinned. "So, what was on your mind?"

"You, always you," she said. "Do you want pickles on your sandwich, or on the side?"

"Side, please."

They worked in tandem until their food was ready, then carried it to the table. As they ate, their conversation shifted to wedding dates.

"What kind of a timeline do you need?" Wade asked.

"Um, long enough to find a wedding dress, but I don't want a Christmas wedding. In the years to come, we'll wind up combining holiday celebrations, and I want to celebrate us on our own day."

"I promise to celebrate us every day, but I agree," he said.

Bridgette smiled. "You win for best answer of the day."

Once they had finished eating and had their plates loaded into the dishwasher, she began pulling out the ingredients she'd bought to make fudge.

"Ummm, the best dessert is always chocolate," Wade said.

"Or lemon," she said.

"Oh hell yes. What was I thinking?" he drawled.

She poked him playfully. "Don't bash my lemon. I acknowledge chocolate is amazing, and I love fudge. This recipe doesn't take long. I'm making what they call Fantasy Fudge. The kind with Marshmallow Fluff and chocolate chips and a butt-load of butter and sugar."

"I remember that," Wade said.

"Well, you're about to get a crash course," she said. "Oh…are we doing this with pecans or plain?"

"I say pecans, but—"

"Right answer," she said, and leaned over and kissed him.

"What do I get for helping you stir?" he asked.

She pulled a big, deep cast-iron skillet out of the cabinet and paused.

"I'd say whatever you want, sir."

"Then I want you," he said.

She kissed him again, but this time slower, lingering longer.

"And...back to the fudge," she said. "We can continue this while it's cooling."

Within a few minutes, they had a pan of butter and sugar bubbling on the stove. She had the timer set, and everything else in little bowls, ready to add when the timer went off.

When it did, there was a whirlwind of adding chocolate chips and vanilla and the Marshmallow Fluff into the hot, bubbling syrup.

They stirred madly, added the nuts, and poured it up in a buttered baking dish to cool, and then stood over the big skillet, eating the scrapings from the bottom of the pan.

"Lord, this is good," Wade said.

She nodded, scooped a last bite, and then set the pan aside until it was cool enough to clean.

"Are you ready for dessert?" she asked.

"I thought you said the fudge needed to cool."

"I am dessert," Bridgette said. "If you want any, follow me."

———————

Two hours later, Wade walked into his house with a container of fudge and a smile on his face. He ate two pieces, then went to bed with the hammer of rain on the roof and the sound of Bridgette's laughter in his ears.

It had taken him a long time to get her in his corner, but every long, miserable moment he'd feared she wouldn't love him was worth what they had now.

―――――――

Bridgette was in her kitchen without a stitch of clothes, her elbows on the counter, eating one last piece of fudge. She had to get this out of the house or she would make herself sick, so she decided she'd take the rest of the fudge to work tomorrow. It wouldn't take long for the guys to devour it, and she wouldn't be tempted. Besides, she could always make more if the need arose.

She swallowed the last bite, covered up the dish, and licked her fingers on the way back to her bedroom, then shook her head at the sight of her bed.

"Looks like someone had a good time in here," she said, and then laughed at her own joke. "Oh, that would have been me."

She tucked the sheets back in at the foot, pulled the fitted sheet over the corner it had come off of, straightened the covers, and then turned out the lights and crawled in.

She could hear the rain against the window by her bed, but it wasn't storming, so she pulled the covers up over her shoulders and closed her eyes.

She dreamed of storms, then of mice in the fudge, and then Wade standing between her and danger.

She woke abruptly, her heart pounding, then blamed the crazy dreams on too much sugar and rolled over and went back to sleep.

The next time she woke, her alarm was going off, and it was, as her mother used to say, "another day, another dollar."

―――――――

The newspaper with Duffy Martin's story and the video attached to the paper's online site was all the gossip in Blessings the next morning. Everyone was talking about it, remarking upon the story and the whole aspect of their own little miracle.

Within hours of the online story and video going live on the newspaper's website, it went viral across the nation.

Duffy was at school when it happened, and by lunchtime, people who hadn't even acknowledged his existence before were following him around, trying to get him to talk about it.

He wanted to go home and hide until the world forgot about what he'd done, but he couldn't. His anonymity was over. But the cost was worth it just to get his dad home again.

―――――――

Candi Martin was at her school, grading papers during her planning period, when her principal, Shirley Watkins, suddenly walked into her room.

"Candi! Did you know your family and Duffy are all over the news?"

Candi looked up. "No, but we were expecting it."

"Well, I'll say. I don't guess I knew anything about this. I mean… about your husband being in prison."

Candi frowned. "The school board knew years ago when they hired me. I don't believe you were living here then. You came here four years ago from Miami, isn't that so?"

"Yes, yes, I did. Well, I'm taking up time from your planning period. I'm sure you're all very excited to get your husband home."

"Yes, we are," Candi said, and then sat with a fake smile on her face until the woman was gone. The moment the door closed, Candi rolled her eyes. "Busybody," she muttered, and went back to work.

―――――――

Rain had ended before morning, but it still looked like it was threatening more, so Bridgette dressed for cooler weather and took a raincoat and umbrella to work with her, along with the fudge. She left a small container of fudge on Wade's desk and took the rest to the break room.

About an hour later, she went up front to look for a missing sales receipt, and Roger stopped her.

"Hey, Birdie, thanks for the fudge. It was awesome."

"You're welcome," she said.

"Do you know how to make peanut brittle?" he asked.

"Are you fishing for more candy?" she asked.

He blushed and grinned, then right on his heels, Joe came into the front from the warehouse and saw her.

"Birdie! Thanks for the fudge. Lord, that was good. My favorite Christmas candy is those pretzels dipped in white chocolate. I like salty and sweet together. Do you?"

She laughed. "You two are less than subtle, but if I make more candy, rest assured I will bring you some."

"Awesome! Thanks, Birdie. Oops, there's the bell ringing back on the dock. Gotta go load up an order."

They both went back to work, leaving Bridgette still searching for the missing sales receipt.

A few minutes later, Wade came walking in from the warehouse with a handful of papers.

"Hey, honey, are you missing any receipts? One of these is two days old. It had fallen onto the floor and got kicked under the desk back in the loading zone."

"Yes! Thank you! You are the best! I've been looking all over for it. I had too much money and not enough receipts to account for it. I knew it had to be somewhere."

"But better than not having enough money, right?"

She rolled her eyes. "Oh lord, don't even go there. I don't ever want that to happen again."

"The guys loved your fudge," he added.

"Yes, I know. And have politely mentioned they also like peanut brittle and candy-coated pretzels."

He laughed. "Now that they mention it, so do I."

She just shook her head, took the receipts, and went back to work.

After a phone call to Dan Amos last night, Peanut had his ride to Savannah. Dan picked him up just after 9:00 a.m., and they headed out of Blessings.

With both of them being lawyers, they bounced ideas off each other on how to make the shuttle service work for the Bottoms without any of them having to take ownership.

And then Dan asked a question that made everything suddenly fall into place.

"The land and the homes all belong to Cathy Talbot, right? So why don't you get her in on this, have her add the liability of the vehicle to the property already in her name. You know it's all insured. Maybe there's a way to insure it under a fleet of cars policy…even though there will only be one. She might have further ideas to go with it."

"Yes, yes, if she's willing, that should work perfectly," Peanut said. "I'll call her later."

"Call her now. I'm driving, so what are you waiting for?" Dan said. "Put it on speaker, tell her I'm listening, and call it a conference call."

Peanut laughed. "You miss this, don't you?"

Dan frowned. "What? Being a lawyer? Oh hell no. And I was a criminal attorney, which made it worse. I'm perfectly happy being a landlord and a family man."

"Okay, point taken," Peanut said. "I'm going to call Cathy now. We can talk while you drive."

By the time they got to Savannah, Cathy Talbot was not only on board with the idea but already planning to add a small, enclosed garage where the van could be parked. And she knew exactly which two men to use as drivers. Both were unemployed and with no vehicles to get to work.

"How perfect is this?" Cathy said. "I can pay them salaries to be the drivers. They'll have income, and if they are my employees, then I have deductions against my income. It's a win-win for both sides. As for donating the shuttle, you and Ruby are to be commended for such a generous and thoughtful donation. My renters are going to be so excited. Their very own Uber service…free of charge to them."

"Awesome," Peanut said. "And if any other legal issues arise, just let me know."

"I know a contractor. I think I can get him right on building the garage. And when you get it home, let me know. I'd love to come see it. We'll have to set up a public press conference to officially donate the shuttle van to the Bottoms, okay?"

"Sure thing. And just so you know, I was all for doing something charitable for Christmas, but it was Ruby who thought of this and went to the trouble of finding it and buying it. She came home with the title and bill of sale last night and laid them in my lap."

Cathy laughed. "We all love Ruby, and this is only one of the reasons why. She knows how to get things organized and get things done, and she has a heart of gold. What a wonderful Christmas present!"

"Thanks. I'll pass on the compliment to her tonight. And, it looks like we're pulling into Savannah. Thank you again for helping us."

"Any time, and merry Christmas to the both of you. Dan…my love to Alice and the kids, too."

"Thanks, I'll tell her," Dan said.

They disconnected, and then Peanut plugged the address of the church into the GPS of his phone, and they began winding their way through the streets of Savannah until they found it.

"This is it!" Peanut said, pointing to a stately, two-story redbrick church with three white spires atop the apex of the gabled roofline, pointing the way to heaven.

They pulled into the parking lot and called the pastor's number. A couple of minutes later, a short, stocky man emerged, wearing a blue-and-white Hawaiian shirt and white slacks.

"He's certainly a Methodist," Peanut said.

Dan laughed. "What does that mean?"

"That he's obviously not quite as uptight as us Baptists, but after the deal he gave Ruby, he sure has a heart of gold."

They got out and went to meet him.

"Pastor Patrick, I'm Peanut Butterman, Ruby's husband. And this is my friend, Dan Amos."

"Call me Sean," he said. "And it is a pleasure to meet the man married to that fine lady. Your Ruby is truly a gem, and I don't mean that facetiously."

"I won't disagree," Peanut said. "We're anxious to see the shuttle van she bought."

"Then follow me," Sean said, and led them around the church to the back parking lot. "You have the keys, I presume?"

Peanut nodded and took them out of his pocket.

"You'll need to unlock the door. Have you ever driven a vehicle like this?" Sean asked.

Peanut had the door unlocked and was already crawling into the driver's seat.

"I worked my way through college doing all kinds of jobs, one of which was driving a van like this for a senior citizens' center for almost a year. I've got this!"

Sean laughed. "I have no doubt."

Peanut started it up, and Dan climbed in to look.

"This is absolutely awesome!" Dan said. "I'll follow you home, just in case."

"Okay. Hang on and I'll drive you back to your car." Then he waved at the preacher. "Thanks again, Sean! Your generosity did not go unnoticed."

Sean smiled, gave them a thumbs-up, and then stepped back and waved as they drove away.

Peanut stopped to let Dan off, then waited for him to get in his car and start it up before he took off. There was a tiny part of him wishing he was retired, because driving this van for the Bottoms would be the best. But Cathy's idea about hiring two men to be full-time drivers was even better and would give them much-needed employment.

He kept an eye on the rearview mirror, checking to make sure Dan was still behind him, and then enjoyed the drive.

The little van drove like a dream. The seat was comfortable, and the air-conditioning kept him and the bus cool.

Bless my little Ruby. She is a genius for thinking of this.

When they finally got back to Blessings, Dan went one way and Peanut another. He parked the van up in their carport and locked it up, then got in his car. He sent Ruby a text to let her know he was home and the van was an amazing buy, and then headed to the office. The drive had been a brief but welcome respite from his routine, and he couldn't wait to tell his secretary, Betty, what they'd done.

———

It was just afternoon when Johnny Pine arrived at the Bottoms where Duke and Cathy Talbot were waiting. He had one of his dozers on a trailer and unloaded it in the empty lot that he and Cathy had talked about.

After a short discussion with Duke, Johnny began leveling off the lot to build a pad for the shuttle garage.

Residents began hearing the dozer, but when they saw Duke and Cathy, they came out in droves, curious as to what was going on.

Barrie Lemons and her kids walked up the street to see Cathy, and the moment Cathy saw them coming, she went to meet them and took Freddie out of Barrie's arms.

"Hi, Lucy. There's my pretty girl! And, oh my goodness! Look at how big this boy is getting!" Cathy said.

"Kaki," Freddie said, and then patted Cathy's face and laid his head on her shoulder.

"He sure does love you," Barrie said.

Cathy smiled. "I love him, too. He was such a little guy when we all started this project last year, and now look at him."

Barrie nodded.

"What's that man doing?" Lucy asked.

"He's cleaning off a place where we can build a garage."

"What will it be for?" Barrie asked.

"Someone has donated a shuttle van to the Bottoms. And we're building a garage to keep it in. There are so many of you without a second vehicle, and it leaves you kind of stranded during the day if someone needs a ride to the store or to the doctor. There will be a couple of designated drivers, and it will be like your own private Uber."

Barrie gasped. "Oh, Cathy! That's going to make a world of difference for all of us. I have the luxury of Junior working at the store, so he always picks up what we need before he comes home, but almost everyone here either has to wait for their husbands to come home or walk. And if you remember, that's how we met. I had walked to the grocery store with the kids, and it was cold, and you took me home. This has been a mild winter, but it's far from over. And carrying groceries and babies all that way is exhausting. Is this a secret? Can I tell?"

"It's not a secret that it's happening, but we're going to have a special ceremony when the garage is built and the shuttle is delivered. The people who donated it will be here then, and you can all thank them personally."

Barrie couldn't quit smiling. "This is wonderful. Thank you so much."

"Oh…none of this was my idea. I'm just helping the donors," Cathy said.

About that time, Freddie wiggled to be put down, and Barrie took her kids and walked home.

People knew something was stirring when they saw Cathy, their Christmas angel, on-site. She'd worked miracles last year. They couldn't wait to see what was happening now.

Bridgette's instinct to bring a raincoat and an umbrella to work had been on point. It began raining again about midafternoon. Not a downpour, but a slow, steady rain that soon had rivulets running in the streets and dampened everyone's desire for shopping.

Only the farmers who were completely out of feed were willing to come to town in this weather, and when they did, they had weatherproof tarps to cover their purchases on the way home.

The only place in town that was rarely affected by weather was Granny's. People gathered there for meetings, to eat, and to share a little gossip between friends.

The jewelry recovery and Duffy Martin's confession were still all anyone talked about. Everyone who'd had access had watched the video of the recovery at Selma Garrett's property, and no one could talk about it without getting a lump in their throats. The horror of what he'd caused was there on his face, and then being the one to find it again had been a full-circle moment for Duffy that they could all empathize with.

"Do you think they'll let Zack Martin out of jail?" someone asked.

"Well, they kind of have to now, don't they? Since this proves Zack's innocence," another said.

Comments abounded, while Lovey sat on her stool at the front register. Every time someone opened the door to come in or go out, she got a glimpse of the rain. It was really coming down, and it gave her the creeps. After being trapped in her own home during the hurricane and nearly drowning from the rain coming in a broken window, even the sound of rain on a roof made her anxious.

Sully came up from the dining room, saw his mother staring pensively out the window, and stopped. Something told him she was having a bad moment so he walked up behind the front register and hugged her.

She looked up at him and smiled.

"What's that for?" she asked.

"Because I wanted to, and because you looked a little sad."

She leaned her head against his chest.

"I'm fine, just thinking," she said.

"Okay, but whatever is making you sad, don't forget I love you."

She turned around on the stool and wrapped her arms around him.

"Thank you, Son. I love you, too."

At the other end of Main, the Curl Up and Dye was doing business as usual. Women with hair appointments did not cancel due to rain. The only thing that halted business there was a power outage, and so far the afternoon rain had not produced even one clap of thunder.

Ruby was about to burst from the secret of what she and Peanut had done, but she wasn't going to tell. Eventually, someone was bound to see the shuttle van in their carport, but they would have no idea of its purpose and likely assume they just had guests.

Bridgette was caught up on bookkeeping. She'd cleaned her office, and then she'd cleaned Wade's just for something to do. She was in the employee break room and cleaning it when Wade walked in.

"There you are, and what the heck are you doing? We have a cleaning crew for this."

"I know, but I'm caught up on everything and I can't just sit and do nothing."

"Then go home, honey. The day is almost over, and it's too wet for our kind of customers."

"But—"

"No buts. Even if we get busy in the next couple hours before we close, you can do what you need to do tomorrow."

She sighed.

"Okay, but I wouldn't be doing this if Dub was still here."

He grinned. "Well, you're engaged to the manager, so there should be a perk or two to go along with that."

"Oh, there are already perks," she said, and then hugged him. "So I guess I'm going home."

He tilted her chin and brushed a quick kiss across her lips.

"This is good sleeping weather, sugar. Take a nap. Watch a movie. Do something for you."

"Will you call me later?" she asked.

"You know I will. I don't suppose you're making candy again tonight?"

She shook her head. "Not tonight. I'd be trapped in my apartment with a whole batch of it, which would surely lead to gluttony."

He grinned. "You're something else. So, go home and chill out. Call me if you need something. I can always drop it off on my way home."

"Okay, and thank you," she said.

"Always."

A few minutes later, Bridgette exited the store and made a run for her car, thankful for the raincoat she was wearing and the umbrella over her head.

When she finally got home, she shook off her umbrella and then headed down the hall to her apartment.

It felt strange to be here in the middle of the afternoon on a work-day. She left the raincoat to drip in her utility room and went back to her bedroom to change.

She had a load of laundry she could do, but the urge to crawl into bed was strong, so she stripped, crawled between the sheets, rolled over onto her side, and pulled the covers up beneath her chin.

The sheets were cool, the pillow soft beneath her cheek. She thought of Wade and closed her eyes, and then she fell asleep.

About two hours later, her phone rang, waking her. She picked it up and answered without looking to see who it was.

"Hello?"

"Hi, Birdie, it's me, Emma. Did I wake you? You sound sleepy."

"I'm just resting," she said. "What's up?"

"Friday is our anniversary, and Gordon has made a reservation for us at the Olde Harbour Inn in Savannah. We'll be there from Friday night to checkout time on Sunday, and I'm so excited."

Bridgette sat up. "That's wonderful, honey. You'll have so much fun. That's right on the river, too. I'll bet there will be all kinds of special stuff going on because of Christmas."

"I know. The reason I'm calling is to ask you if you'd take me to Savannah sometime Friday afternoon. Gordon works there, so he would already be in the city. And I thought it would save him a drive home if I caught a ride into the city and just met him at the hotel later."

"Of course," Bridgette said. "I'll work through my lunch hour and take off an hour early. I can pick you up at four and get you into Savannah around five. Would that work?"

"It would be perfect. Gordon doesn't get off until seven. They're all working later hours because of the holiday. I sure appreciate this, Sister. Thank you."

"You're so welcome," Bridgette said, and then hung up and glanced at the clock.

She'd slept almost two hours, and it sounded as if the rain was letting up. She got up, dressed in a pair of sweats and a T-shirt, and went into the kitchen to see what she had to eat.

There was still that leftover spaghetti, and she didn't want to cook, so she set it out on the counter. If she didn't think of anything better in the next thirty minutes, then spaghetti it was.

She turned on the television in the living room and then poured herself something to drink and curled up on the sofa to watch the evening news.

She watched all the way through the news and weather, and then looked for movies to watch before settling on the Hallmark Channel.

Whatever was showing would be about Christmas, and she was in the mood for a happy-ever-after in the snow.

―――――――――

Wade sent the crew home thirty minutes early and then waited until closing time at 5:00 p.m. before locking up, bringing a dreary afternoon to a close.

He thought about calling Bridgette but was afraid he'd wake her up, so he drove by the bank to drop off the night deposit and then headed home.

There was a stray cat under the carport when he parked—obviously looking for a place out of the rain. It scurried behind the garbage can as he got out, and when he walked into his house, he knew how the cat felt. This was his personal place of shelter and safety after long days on the job. What he wished was to see Bridgette in this house every day. It wouldn't be much longer. Neither one of them had a reason for wanting to wait.

He changed out of his work clothes, showered, and then got a pair of sweatpants and a T-shirt and headed to the kitchen to see what he had in the way of leftovers, unaware he and Bridgette were on the same wavelength tonight with clothes and food. While she was heating up spaghetti and meatballs, he was heating up a can of soup and making a sandwich.

It was a heat-up and hole-up kind of night.

―――――――――

Bridgette ate in front of the TV, still watching the movie, and then cleaned up and started the dishwasher before going back to the sofa. She laid her phone on the end table, pulled an afghan over herself, and curled up, waiting for the hero to tell the girl he loved her. And while she was waiting for the movie to end she fell asleep, only to be rudely awakened later by loud voices and a lot of stomping in the apartment above her.

"Not again," she moaned, and lay there a moment, listening.

But something about it was different tonight—more volatile than usual. She heard what sounded like furniture being shoved and glass breaking. The man was shouting and cursing, and then all of a sudden, the woman started to scream.

Bridgette was reaching for her phone to call the police when she began hearing gunshots. And then to her horror, a mirror hanging on the wall behind where she was lying suddenly shattered, and she realized a bullet had come through the floor from above and hit her wall, missing her head by inches.

She grabbed her phone and her afghan and ran out her door and then out of the building in a panic. The woman was still screaming, but the gunshots had ended. Bridgette was still wrapped in her afghan, shaking from head to foot, as she stood beneath a streetlight to call the police.

Larry Bemis was on duty, and the night had been still until he answered her call.

"Blessings PD."

"Larry, this is Bridgette Knox at the Cherrystone Apartments. There were shots fired in the apartment above me, and a bullet came through the ceiling of my apartment and broke a mirror on the wall. They were having a terrible fight just before the shooting began."

"Hang on a sec. Dispatching officers to the scene," he said. She heard him on the police band, sending out the call, and then he was back on the line. "Were you hurt?"

"No, but I ran outside, and now I'm afraid to go back in."

"Just stay there. Officers are on the way."

"Yes, I will. I hear sirens and I see flashing lights."

"Just stay with me until they arrive," Larry said. "Do you know the names of the neighbors above you?"

"Only their first names. Brad and Tisha. They've lived here about six months. The police are pulling up now. Can I hang up?"

"Yes, but don't go back inside until they say you can," he said.

Bridgette hung up as three police cars rolled up to the scene.

The first officer on the scene got out of his car with his weapon drawn and ran up to her. It was Deputy Ralph.

"Birdie! Are you okay?"

"Yes. A bullet came through my ceiling, missed my head, and broke a mirror behind the sofa where I was lying. It's apartment six on the second floor, right above mine. They fight a lot but there was never gunfire before."

A half-dozen other residents were out in the hall when the police entered the building.

"Get back in your apartments and stay there," the officers said, and headed up the stairs with their weapons drawn.

Bridgette was shaking so hard she could barely breathe. Shock was beginning to set in, and her safe place had been violated. All she could think was to call Wade.

———————

Wade was just getting ready to send Bridgette a good-night text when his phone rang and her name popped up on caller ID. He smiled. Now he'd get to talk to her.

"Hey, sugar, I was just getting ready to—"

"Can you come get me? That couple. The ones who live above me. They were fighting again tonight and one of them started shooting. One shot came through my ceiling. It broke the mirror behind my sofa where I was lying. The police are here and—"

His heart stopped, and he was already looking for his shoes and keys.

"Bridgette, honey...are you hurt?"

She started crying. "No, but it scared me so bad, and I can't go back into my apartment."

"I'm on the way, baby. I'll get there as fast as I can."

"Okay," she said, still crying, holding onto the phone even after he'd hung up because she didn't want to lose the connection.

By now, the whole neighborhood had heard the sirens and seen the flashing lights. Some were on their porches watching, while others watched from doorways or standing in the street.

Bridgette was shivering from the cold and from shock when she saw an SUV come flying down the street. She sighed. That would be Wade.

He got out and headed toward her with his arms outstretched, and she ran into them, sobbing.

"It just missed my head. It broke the mirror behind the sofa."

"Can you leave?" he asked.

"I don't know. I'm the one who called it in."

"We'll wait in my car until we know for sure, and then I'm taking you home with me."

They started walking, then when he realized she was barefoot, he picked her up and carried her.

"Is Birdie okay?" someone shouted.

"Yes, just scared," Wade said as he got her inside the car and then got in with her. "I don't want you to go back there."

She burst into sobs. "I don't think I could even if I wanted to. It doesn't feel safe anymore."

"So you can just move in with me a little earlier than planned. Okay?"

"Yes," she said, and then felt something running down the back of her neck. When she reached back to feel it, her fingers came away bloody. She looked at them in disbelief and then held them out. "I'm bleeding."

"Son of a bitch!" Wade said. He slammed the car into drive and took off down the street, heading for the ER.

CHAPTER 16

BY THE TIME WADE GOT TO THE ER, THE WHOLE BACK OF Bridgette's neck was bloody. He pulled in beneath the entrance, then carried her inside.

"We need to see a doctor, now."

The clerk recognized the both of them and saw the blood on Birdie and picked up the phone. Within seconds, a nurse came into the lobby, pushing a wheelchair.

Wade put Bridgette in it. "I'll push. You lead the way," he told the nurse.

Bridgette's heart was pounding. She was feeling light-headed, and the room was beginning to spin. The wheelchair took a sharp left, and she felt like she was going to fall out of it, and then they were in a room, and Wade was lifting her out of the chair.

"I feel dizzy," she mumbled, and passed out in his arms.

"She's unconscious!" Wade cried, and within moments Dr. Quick, the ER doctor, and two more nurses were in the room.

Wade wouldn't lay Bridgette down on her back for fear of glass that might be embedded in her head and quickly explained what had happened.

Dr. Quick nodded in agreement. "Put her on her side," he said.

Wade watched, telling himself that she'd just fainted. That it was shock and not some unseen injury that had caused her to pass out.

Her blood pressure checked as normal. Her heart rate was steady, so they began checking her head for the source of the blood flow.

"Ah...I think I found it!" Quick said. "There's a chunk of glass embedded in her head. Can't tell how deep until we get it out." He motioned to one of the nurses. "The small forceps, please. Okay... just a sec...I lost it...too much blood. I need a swab. Yes. That should do it. Ah! Got it!" he said, and then held it up to the light, unaware that Bridgette was coming to.

She was cognizant enough to see where she was and remember why she was there, and then she heard Dr. Quick's voice and tuned in to what he was saying.

"The sliver was longer than I thought, but it didn't do any lasting damage. We'll get this cleaned up, and I think a little glue will serve the purpose here," Quick said.

Bridgette wailed. "Oh no! You're gluing my hair? This is all happening because I glued that mouse to the floor. It's karma. Wade? Where's Wade?"

Wade was so relieved to hear her sass and know she was conscious again that he went weak with relief.

"I'm here, baby. I'm right behind you. Just lie still. Dr. Quick is going to glue the cut in your scalp. He is not gluing your hair."

But now she had the ER team's attention.

"She glued a mouse to the floor?" Dr. Quick said.

"I didn't mean to," Bridgette said, then winced when he began parting her hair to get to the cut. "Are you going to cut off my hair?"

"I'm only going to clip away the tiniest bit so we don't get glue *in* your hair," he said. "With all your pretty curls, no one will ever know there's any missing."

"Okay. Is there only the one cut?"

"Yes, Birdie, only one cut," Quick said.

"I should not complain at all. It could have been a bullet," she muttered.

"Indeed," Dr. Quick said, frowning.

Wade couldn't laugh about that. He didn't have words for the horror of how close he'd come to losing her tonight.

In a few short minutes, the doctor had the cut glued shut.

"Birdie, do you feel like turning over on your stomach so we can make sure there isn't any more glass in your hair?" he asked.

"I think so," she said, and when she sat up, she saw Wade. The fear on his face was gone. He smiled at her and then winked. Satisfied all was right with her world once again, she let the nurses help roll her over.

Another half hour passed before she was pronounced fit to leave. They sat her back in the wheelchair and rolled her out to the exit. Wade's SUV was still parked at the door, so he loaded her in, then buckled her up.

"Okay, baby?" he asked.

"Okay," she said as he got back in the SUV. "Will you please drive back by my apartment? If the police are still there, I want to go in and get my keys and a change of clothes. I won't be able to get back in without my keys."

"Are you up for that?" he asked.

She nodded, so he drove back across town.

Not only were the police still there, but there was crime-scene tape across the front yard.

"Oh lord, does that mean someone died?" Bridgette asked.

Wade frowned. "It definitely means they are investigating a crime scene. There's Chief Pittman in the doorway. Let me find out if you can go in." He got out and headed toward the building.

Bridgette saw them talking, and then Wade was pointing at the car, and Lon looked startled, and then they both came back to where she was sitting. She rolled down the window as the chief approached.

"Birdie! Nobody told me you were hurt!" Lon said. "We've been in your apartment already and taken pictures of where the bullet came through your ceiling and where it hit the wall over the sofa. Wade said you missed getting shot by inches."

"Yes, and I didn't know I'd been cut. I just grabbed my phone and ran. Can I go in and get my house keys and some clothes? I'm going to spend the night at Wade's."

"Yes. Both parties have been transported. Neither one of them was wounded. You're the only one who suffered an injury. How many gunshots did you hear?"

"Four."

Lon nodded. "That coincides with how many rounds were fired from the weapon. You two can go in and get what you need for tonight. Wade says you're moving out?"

"As soon as possible. I won't ever feel safe here again."

"I'm sorry this happened," Lon said. "We're still going to be here a while, so take all the time you need."

As soon as Bridgette got out of the car, Wade picked her up and carried her over the dirt and gravel to the sidewalk, and then they went inside. When she walked into her apartment, she got a chill.

Wade's gaze went straight to the sofa and the shattered mirror hanging over it, and then he hugged her.

"Let's go get you dressed and a bag packed. We'll deal with the rest of this in a day or two, when you're up to it."

They went back to her bedroom, where Wade helped her out of her bloody clothes. While she was dressing, he tossed them in her washer and started it to washing. He got a suitcase down for her and began carrying the clothes she wanted from the closet to the bed, and then three pairs of shoes.

She tossed in nightclothes and underwear, then packed up her makeup and toiletries and put them in her overnight bag, grabbed all of her charger cords and her laptop, and called it done.

"Oh, wait. I'll throw those clothes in the dryer before we leave," Wade said. "You can get them out of the dryer when we come back to get things later."

They were out of the building in a little over an hour and on their way back to Wade's. It was 1:00 a.m. when they walked inside.

"Is your head hurting, honey? Dr. Quick said over-the-counter pain meds should take care of it, and you know where they are."

Wade carried her bags to his bedroom while she went on into the adjoining bathroom to get the pain meds. She paused, stared at herself in the mirror, and saw reflections of the shock and exhaustion of what had happened. Then she opened the medicine cabinet, got a couple of painkillers, and downed them with a swallow of water.

When she came out, Wade had already pulled out one of her nightgowns and had it lying on the bed.

She sighed, then dropped to the side of the bed to start taking off the clothes she'd just put on, and before she knew it, tears were rolling.

Wade sat down beside her and pulled her into his lap.

"I'm so sorry, sweetheart. I'm so sorry. But you're safe and still in one piece, and I'm so damn grateful I have no words."

She leaned against him, taking comfort in the strength of his embrace, and cried until there were no more tears. Then he helped her into her nightgown and into bed, and then undressed and slipped in behind her and pulled up the covers.

"You're safe," he said, as he pulled her close against the curve of his body. "And you are so loved."

"Love you too," she whispered, and let go.

He knew when she fell asleep because he felt her body go limp. But he wouldn't close his eyes for fear of the dreams that would come.

He'd lost his parents so suddenly, and from another person's mistake, and now he'd come so close to losing Bridgette the same way. All this had done was reawaken old fears, and he'd be a while getting over them again.

———

By morning, news of the shooting was all over town, but at that point, no one knew Birdie had been injured.

When Wade came to work without Birdie, he told the guys what had happened. And they called their wives, and their wives called their friends, and friends called their families, and within a couple of hours, the story was out that Birdie got shot in the head while she was in her own apartment.

She was still asleep in Wade's bed when her phone started ringing. She rolled over to answer.

"Hello?"

"Birdie! Oh my God! What happened to you?"

"Emma?"

Bridgette heard a snort, and then her sister unloaded.

"Yes, this is Emma. Are you okay?"

"Yes," and then Bridgette explained, ending with, "I'm at Wade's and I'll be moving in here and staying. I will never feel safe there again."

"Oh, honey, I am so sorry. I don't know who those people are who lived above you. Did you?"

"Like I told Chief Pittman last night, only by their first names. And I knew nothing about them except that they fought all the time."

"Well, they're both in jail right now. Neither one will admit who fired the gun, but the gunshot residue was on both their hands, so they're probably both guilty."

"Gunshot residue? How do you know all of that?"

Emma sniffed. "I have my sources. At any rate, I want you to know that you are officially released from the request I made about taking me to Savannah on Friday. Ray and Susie volunteered to come get me. So all you have to do is rest and feel better. Do you have stitches in your head?"

"No. Dr. Quick glued the cut."

"Oh, well then. That's good. That stuff kind of dissolves, and you don't have to have anything removed after it's healed. I love you to pieces. I'm so glad you're okay. And just so you know, it's all over town that you were shot in the head."

"Better that than everyone knowing I glued a mouse to the floor," Bridgette muttered.

"What?" Emma cried.

"Oh, it's a long story. I'll tell you about it when my head's not about to explode, okay?"

"I guess," Emma said. "Do you need anything? I can bring you food or go get clothes out of your apartment for you."

"Wade helped me do that last night. I'm good for now. You and Gordon go have fun this weekend, and if I don't still have the headache from hell, Wade and I will do the same."

Emma chuckled. "Okay, darlin'… Oh, I'll call Ray and Junior and make sure they know you don't have a bullet in your head."

"Well, lord, then go ahead and call Hunt and Ava, too, or they'll be put out that no one let them know," Bridgette said.

"I will," Emma said. "You rest. I feel so much better now that I know my baby sister is okay."

"Good. And if you're out and about today, say…like at the Curl Up and Dye or at Granny's, please be sure to let everyone know the bullet missed me, and I got cut by flying debris. They can get truth out faster than CNN."

"I'll make it a point," Emma said. "Go back to sleep." Then she hung up in Bridgette's ear.

Bridgette sighed. She could no more go back to sleep now than she could fly. She got up, took some pain pills, then showered and dressed.

After the pain had dulled, she sent Wade a text to let him know she was awake and fine, and then she went to the kitchen to find something to eat.

Lon Pittman came into the jail with two of his officers. They were carrying handcuffs and shackles and heading toward the cells where Brad and Tish Pennell were being held.

Tish Pennell's eyes were turning black, and her lip was swollen to twice its normal size.

Brad had a broken nose and a knot on his forehead the size of a goose egg.

They had bruises all over their bodies and, as yet, were still unaware that what had happened in their apartment had affected their neighbor below.

"What's happening?" Brad said as he saw the officers approaching his cell.

"You're both being arraigned this morning. You'll see court-appointed lawyers in consultation rooms before your arraignment, and then you will most likely be transported to Chatham County Jail to await charges."

"What the hell?" Brad said. "We had a fight. We have lots of fights. We don't hurt no one but ourselves."

"Yeah," Tish said, and then winced. "Hurts to talk," she mumbled.

"Well, that's no longer the case," Lon said. "Last night you fired four rounds into the walls and floors of your apartment, and one of those bullets went through the floor of your apartment into the ceiling of the apartment below. It just missed the resident living there, shattered a mirror, and she was injured by flying debris. So now, you have all kinds of nasty little charges added to domestic abuse."

They both turned pale. "We didn't mean to—"

"Oh…you were only trying to kill each other, not someone else?" Lon asked.

"I didn't want Tish dead. I love her."

"I love you too," Tish said.

"Look at yourselves. That's not love. And anytime you fire a weapon, the danger of killing someone is always there. Officers, get them ready for transport to the courthouse."

"Yes, Chief," they said, and cuffed and shackled Brad Pennell first, and then his wife, Tish, and took them to the courthouse in separate police cars.

As Lon had predicted, after their arraignments, they were transported to the Chatham County Jail where they would abide until their cases came to trial.

This was not the Christmas they had planned.

It was a little after 11:00 a.m. when there was a knock at the door.

Bridgette set aside the magazine she'd been reading and got up to answer.

It was Junior, holding a to-go snow cone. "It's that lemon kind," he said, then leaned in and kissed her on the cheek. "I'm on a quick break. I can't stay, but I wanted you to know I love you, and I'm sure glad you're okay."

Bridgette took the snow cone and the kiss with tears in her eyes.

"Thank you, Junior. This is the sweetest thing! I love you too."

He beamed, and then he was gone.

She went back into the house with her treat, and then sat down and took her first bite, winced momentarily at the brain freeze, and then settled in to enjoy.

About an hour later, Wade called.

"How's my best girl?" he asked.

"I'm fine. Most of the headache is gone, and I could actually come to work this afternoon if you need me."

"We're fine," Wade said. "I just called to see if I could bring you some lunch…and maybe a snow cone for dessert?"

"Oh, I already had dessert. Junior came by about an hour ago and brought me a lemon snow cone. My tongue is still thawing out from all that ice."

Wade laughed. "Good for him. How about I bring something from the Dairy Freeze?"

"Maybe a chili dog and fries."

"Got it! I'll see you soon," he said, and disconnected.

Bridgette sat there for a moment, smiling, and then got up and went to the kitchen to set the table.

———————————

Johnny Pine finished his dozer work and had the pad ready for the next phase of the shuttle garage.

Cathy was on-site early that morning with the contractor she'd hired, and they were already building the forms to pour concrete. As soon as she was satisfied the project was in good hands, she headed to the Crown to pick up groceries for both Talbot families.

Jack and Duke were in the middle of separating cattle and moving them all to different pastures, while Hope was home with a fussy baby. Gage was teething, and no one was sleeping, so Cathy was shopping for both households today. Her plan was to fill one list, pay for it, and load it into her SUV, then go back and fill the other list, pay for it, and head for home, and that's what she did, adding iced Christmas cookies for both families that weren't on either list.

Peanut was still waiting for a call from the Chatham County DA saying that a court date had been set for Zack Martin to reappear to hear his sentence vacated.

He knew Candi and her family had to be anxious, but he didn't dare jump the gun and assume. There'd already been too much heartache because of a mistake. He didn't want to add to it.

The video of the recovery dig had gone viral after it was posted on the online site, and the last time Peanut looked, it had over a million views. He could not imagine how it must have impacted Duffy Martin's day-to-day life in Jacksonville, but he guessed it had to be different in a thousand ways.

After a slow morning at the office, Peanut drove down to the Bottoms on his lunch hour. Cathy had called to tell him what was happening, and he wanted to see the progress already being made on the garage. When he got there, he could only smile. Cathy and Ruby were two of a kind. When they got a notion in their heads, they didn't hesitate to implement it. The pad had already been built, and there was a crew on-site building forms to pour a concrete slab floor.

He was excited.

Wade came in the back door with their food. Bridgette was at the counter and looked up and smiled when he walked in. He paused a moment to take in the sight.

"What's wrong?" Bridgette said.

"Nothing. It's just that the other day when I came home, I was thinking how wonderful it was going to be when I wouldn't be coming home to an empty house. I'm sorry about what speeded up our plans, but I like seeing you here."

"I like being here, too," she said. "Come sit and talk to me. I missed being at work this morning. I miss the guys and the foolishness, and I miss visiting with the customers now and then."

"They missed you, too, and they all send their best." Wade started pulling food out of the sack and putting it on the plates she set out.

"You do know that Blessings believes I was shot in the head last night?"

He blinked. "Uh, no. We've been kind of busy this morning. Is this also typical of Blessings?"

Bridgette nodded as she put her chili dog on the plate. "Pretty much. Gossip spreads, and the story always gets embroidered to the point of gaudy."

He laughed. "Great analogy."

"I have my moments," Bridgette said, and took a bite, chewed, and swallowed. "This is good. Thank you for coming home to eat with me. When you leave, I want a ride to my apartment to get my car and bring it back here."

"You good to drive? Not dizzy anymore?"

"I'm good. I haven't been dizzy since last night, and I think that was exhaustion and shock."

"Then, consider me your Uber driver, and I will gladly drop you off."

"Awesome. Do you need anything…either from the pharmacy or the grocery…or wherever?" Bridgette asked.

"Are you going shopping?"

"At the Crown."

"For more stuff to make candy?" he asked.

She laughed. "I hadn't thought about it, but I will. Only not just yet. All of my recipes from Mama are still at the apartment. I'm just getting some staples."

"Please don't overdo," he said.

She reached across the table and grasped his hands.

"Wade. I promise I feel fine. If I'd just accidentally cut my hand or my leg, you wouldn't be this panicky. Yes, I dodged a bullet, but it did not hurt me. It was just a piece of glass and it's gone. I'm tougher than that."

He sighed. "Got it. So grab your keys and put some shoes on. We're going to get your car."

"But the dishes will—"

"I'll put them in the dishwasher. Go!"

She got up running.

He shook his head and then quickly rinsed and loaded the dishes and wiped off the table. By the time she came back, he was through.

"Let's go do this," he said, and grabbed her by the hand. They went out the door together. He locked it with the remote, and then they got in the car and drove away.

The crime-scene tape was on the ground at Cherrystone, and the parking lot was almost empty. Everyone who lived here worked.

Bridgette gave him a quick peck on the cheek, grabbed her stuff, and got out. She jumped into her car and started it, and as soon as he knew she was good to go, Wade gave her a thumbs-up and left the parking lot, with Bridgette right behind him. When she turned off Main into the parking lot at the Crown, Wade kept driving up the street toward the feed store.

Bridgette was on her way inside when she noticed a sign on the front door. The Crown was sponsoring a decorating contest for kids, using the prebaked kits of gingerbread houses they were selling in the store. All the kits would be free to the kids who entered, and donations from the community to offset the costs of the kits were appreciated, but not required.

The contest would be for children in three age categories. Six to eight years old, and nine to eleven years old. And a final category for twelve to eighteen years old. Every child who signed up to participate got a free gingerbread house kit, and they would turn in their finished entries at the high school gymnasium a week from this coming Saturday.

The prizes for first, second, and third in every category were laptops for first place, iPads for second place, and Kindles for third place. Bridgette was stunned. Whoever owned the Crown was certainly generous, and this was an event she definitely did not want to miss.

She went inside, expecting to make this a quick trip in and out, and did not take into consideration the fact that quite a few still believed she had a bullet in her head.

Bridgette corrected the story a half-dozen times, and then gossip did the rest. By the time she checked out, everyone in the Crown already had the update. When she finally headed home, it was with relief.

She put up the groceries, put on some lipstick, and got back in the car and drove to work. She got into her office without anyone seeing her, booted up the computer, and then went up front to collect yesterday's sales receipts.

Donny was at the front counter checking out a customer when she appeared.

"Birdie!" he cried, and stopped in the middle of what he was doing and went to hug her. "Girl, what are you doing here?"

"I got bored." She smiled at the customer. "Afternoon, Mr. Wheeler. Have you got that little calf weaned off a bottle yet?"

"Almost," he said. "He's eating hay and sweet feed pretty good now. I think he'll be good to go by Christmas."

"Awesome," Bridgette said. "You are a good shepherd."

The old man beamed, but Donny was not to be deterred.

"I don't think you should be here. You should be resting," he said.

"I had a piece of glass in my head. It gave me a headache. You guys have given me a headache at least once a day since I came to work here. I'm fine," she said.

"You sure are something. I think you could have ridden that mechanical bull on the fastest speed it would go and still not been thrown off," Donny said.

"I don't know about that, but last night obviously wasn't my time to die, and I'm good to go today. And…I am looking for yesterday's receipts."

"I think Wade picked them up."

"Oh, I didn't think to look on his desk," she said, and went back down the hall and into Wade's office.

The receipts she was looking for were in a stack in the middle of his desk. She picked them up and went to her office.

It took exactly four minutes before Wade showed up in the doorway.

"You just couldn't bear to be away from me, right?"

She grinned. "Something like that."

"Is this a sign of how many times you are going to make me crazy in the years to come?"

"Likely, but not intentionally," she said.

CHAPTER 17

DUFF MARTIN WAS IN HIS ROOM DOING HOMEWORK, AND AS USUAL with his headphones on, rocking some Post Malone. "Circles" was the singer's current hit, and that's how Duff felt. Like he was going in circles.

He'd done a bad thing, and then a good thing, but what he'd lost in his life to do the good thing had turned his life into a bad thing. He had no privacy anymore. No anonymity. Good to bad. Full circle.

And, if he thought about it further, the upset in his life was what had happened to his dad through his actions. So in a way, whatever crap Duff had to deal with now was minor compared to going to jail for something you didn't do.

He was working through his last trig problem when he felt a tap on his shoulder. He hit Mute on the music and slipped his headphones around his neck.

"Sorry, Mom. I didn't hear you. I was doing homework."

She grinned. "I know. I just wanted you to know supper is ready."

"Oh! Give me a sec to wash up and I'll be right there," he said.

Candi left the room smiling, wondering how kids these days would function in life without headphones or earbuds. They no longer heard the world around them, only what they chose to let in, and part of her understood that. Her generation had not given them the best of a world into which to be born. So in a way, the kids had created their own by selective choice of what they'd let in to be heard. But at the same time it took a lot of good parenting, and kids willing to listen, to give them the wisdom not to be brainwashed by what was being fed to them.

In many aspects, it was a scary world for all. And after coming back from Blessings and being reminded of what it had been like to live there, Candi was beginning to realize that she, too, had become immune to the ills of the world. There was so much wrong that she'd forgotten to look for what was right.

"Is he coming?" Allen asked as she walked back into the kitchen.

"Yes. He was doing homework and didn't hear me call."

"Damn headphones," Allen said.

Candi rolled her eyes. "Oh please…at least he's doing homework. You were never a fan of headphones or homework."

Allen grinned. "Nailed me, as usual. Sorry, Mom."

Candi gave him a look. "Never try to con the woman who wiped poop off your butt every day for two years."

Allen burst out laughing just as Duff entered the kitchen.

"What did I miss?" he asked, grinning.

"Mom wiping poop off my butt," Allen said.

Duff froze. "What?"

Candi rolled her eyes. "Everyone sit down. Food is on the table, and you're both potty-trained, so that's the end of the poop story."

Duff smiled. "Yes, ma'am," he said, and sat.

They were in the middle of the meal when Candi noticed Duff had lost focus and was staring down at his plate.

"What's wrong, Duffy? Is something wrong with the food?"

He blinked. "Oh! No! I love enchiladas. I was just thinking of all the meals like this Dad missed."

Candi slapped the table with the flat of her hand, which made Duff flinch, and she had the stern-teacher look on her face.

"Look at me, Duffy, and hear me. Your dad never missed a meal. He was not on the streets. He is not dead. What you eat is never as important as having something *to* eat. Understand?"

Duff stared at her for a long, silent moment, and then he nodded.

"I never thought of it that way, and you're right. Sorry, Mom. It's going to take me a while to get over the shock of all this. You guys have had ten years to process. I just found all this out, like, last week."

She nodded. "Understood and noted."

"I wish we'd hear from the lawyer," Allen said.

"As do I, but the courts are slow to correct their mistakes. However, we all know it's going to happen. After the discovery video wound up on YouTube, they cannot deny Zack his freedom."

Duff held out his plate. "Mom, could I have seconds on enchiladas?"

"Sure," she said. "How many?"

"Two?"

Allen frowned. "That just leaves two," he said.

Duff nodded. "I know. I'm not being selfish. One for you. One for Mom."

Allen looked at Candi, and then once again laughter echoed within their house.

Josh King was on his way home from work when he happened to glance up in the rearview mirror. There was a truck coming up fast on his bumper. The Linley brothers were in it, and they were laughing. He sped up, so they sped up. They were right on his tail, so close that if he slowed down for even a second, they would ram him.

His heart was pounding. He was worried about even going home, because then he would be bringing them to his family and he didn't know what might happen afterward. He grabbed his phone and called LaJune.

"Hey, Josh."

"Honey, the Linley brothers are right on my bumper, trying to ram the truck. I think they're just taunting me, but I don't trust them. Just make sure the kids are in the house somewhere safe. I don't want them in the way if the Linleys follow me up the drive."

Her voice sharpened. "You just come home, Josh King. We'll be fine."

"Okay...I'm so sorry," he said.

"You do not apologize for the actions of others."

"I love you," he said.

"Well, I love you too. Now come on home. Supper's ready."

"Yes, ma'am," he said, and turned left. The sight of his house was all the impetus he needed to keep moving.

He took the turn up his drive in a skid and then drove beneath the carport, parked, and jumped out.

As he feared, the Linley brothers came right up the driveway. He thought they were going to ram his truck where it sat, and then at the last instant, they slammed on the brakes. When they finally rolled to a stop, the bumpers were touching.

Mack Linley got out, grinning, and Arnie sidled up beside him.

"There's Josh King…the hard-working man," Mack drawled.

Josh's fingers were curled into fists, braced for the brawl he knew was coming.

"You're standing on my grass, uninvited," he said.

And then all of a sudden, the front screen door flew back against the house and LaJune came out with a string of black prayer beads in one hand and a lit candle in the other.

She came down the steps with the fire of rage in her eyes, and she walked straight past her husband as if he wasn't even there.

Josh was in shock. LaJune was not a Catholic, and to his knowledge she was also not a witch, but she was a born and bred woman of the South and he did not want to mess with whatever mojo she was about to unleash.

The sight of her wiped the smirks right off of Mack and Arnie's faces. And when she began circling them and chanting beneath her breath in words they could not understand, and waving the candle and the beads at them with every other breath, the hair stood up on the backs of their necks.

"What the hell are you doing?" Mack said.

She didn't answer. She just kept chanting and circling, and a couple of times even slung hot wax on their bare arms and then their clothes.

Arnie started to back up, and when he moved LaJune shrieked.

They froze where they stood, and Josh stumbled backwards. He knew LaJune better than they did. He had the good sense to get out of her way.

LaJune pointed the candle at them and then blew out the flame.

"You have intruded upon my family. You have brought disgrace to my husband by the evil within you. From this day forward, you will not seek him out. You will never again speak his name. You will not bring your evil into Blessings for as long as you both shall live. If you break my decree, you will become impotent with women. You will lose all that you value, including your hair and your teeth. You will walk blind in the world, without friends. Without a home. Go now, or the devil you worship will turn on you."

Arnie was bawling and running for the truck.

Mack turned around to run, tripped on his own foot, and screamed, thinking he'd already been struck down.

Arnie stopped, came back, and yanked him up.

"Run, dammit. You got the keys."

They ran for the truck, leaped in, and slammed the doors. Within seconds, the engine fired, the windows went up, and they backed out of the driveway so fast they left rubber on the pavement and disappeared from sight.

As soon as they were gone, LaJune put the beads in her pocket and turned around.

"What did you just do?" Josh asked.

"I just scared them, like they did you. A man's biggest fear, outside of dying, is not being able to get it up."

"But all that stuff you were doing? The chanting. The candle. The prayer beads."

LaJune grinned. "These aren't prayer beads. They're Tori's Mardi Gras beads from last year. And the candle came from the junk drawer. Last time we used it was when the power went out. And I wasn't chanting a curse. I was mumbling the words to 'Yellow Submarine.'

The Beatles and I ran off the Linley brothers and the devil they brought with them. We're having ham and beans, with cornbread and sorghum. Are you hungry?"

Josh walked across the yard and wrapped his arms around her. He didn't speak. He couldn't. He just held her.

"Honey? It's okay," LaJune said.

Finally, he turned her loose. "I know. I'm just in awe of the woman I did not know you were, and I apologize for overlooking the warrior in you."

She took him by the hand. "It's okay. You can load the dishwasher later while I get the kids their baths. How's that?"

"Deal," he said. "And...I'm starving."

―――――――――

The following day, Peanut Butterman was late getting to work, and when he walked in, Betty frowned. "You missed a call from the Chatham County DA. His number is on your desk."

"I also missed breakfast. Ruby's car had a flat. I gave her mine and took hers to get fixed. So now I'm hungry and delinquent," he drawled.

Betty sighed. "Sorry. Didn't mean to sound cranky. I think I just took my disgust with my husband out on you."

They both looked at each other and then burst out laughing.

"Let's start over," Peanut said. "Betty...do I have any messages?"

Betty grinned. "Why, yes sir, you do! The number is on your desk."

"Thank you so much. I'll be in my office," Peanut said, and was still chuckling when he closed the door behind him.

Betty picked up the phone and called her husband.

"Hello?"

"Jack, this is Betty."

He sighed. "I know my own wife's voice, and I'm sorry I was an ass."

"Awesome. And since you have apologized, I need you to do me a favor. Please go to Granny's and get two sausage biscuits and some of those little jelly packets and bring them to the office."

"Uh…okay. When do you want them?" he asked.

"Now," she said, and hung up in his ear.

———————

Peanut poured himself a cup of coffee, then sat down and returned the call.

"Chatham County District Attorney's office. How can I help you?"

"This is Peanut Butterman, returning a call to Mr. Perry."

"Hold, please."

Within a couple of moments, the call was picked up.

"Good morning, Butterman."

"Morning, Carl. Sorry I missed your call."

"Oh, no problem. I'm calling because I promised to let you know when a court date was set for Zack Martin. You can tell his family that he'll be brought to the Chatham County Courthouse on December 22 at 2:00 p.m. to hear his sentence be vacated. After that, he will be a free man."

"I'll tell them, and I'll be there as his attorney of record to stand with him. Is Zack going to be given this information today, too, or do I need to go to Coastal State Prison to officially inform him?"

"No need. My office is notifying the warden and asking him to give Zack this information."

"Thank you. It's not often we get to do something like this, is it?" Peanut said.

"No, we don't, but it's a good feeling, and I'll see you in court."

Their call ended. Peanut clapped his hands together, glanced at the time, and knew Candi Martin would likely be in class, but he guessed this call might be forgiven and made it anyway.

———————

Candi was on her way back to class after taking one of her students to the office. Flu was rampant in school this time of year, and this was the second student to throw up in her room and first period wasn't even over. Her aide was in the room with the kids, as was the janitor, cleaning up the vomit.

She stopped in the teachers' lounge long enough to wash the puke off her shoes and then scrubbed her hands raw. She was getting ready to leave when her cell phone began to vibrate. They weren't supposed to take personal calls at work, but when she saw who was calling, she didn't hesitate to answer.

"Hello. This is Candi!"

"Good morning, Candi, this is Peanut Butterman. I have good news! The Chatham County DA just called to give me Zack's court date. He'll be taken to the Chatham County Courthouse on December 22 and go before the judge at 2:00 p.m. to hear his sentence vacated. You might want to be there for that. He's going to need a ride home."

Candi gasped and then started crying. "Oh my God, oh my God. Hearing these words is such a gift. I can't thank you enough for helping Duffy, and for helping us again to make this happen."

Peanut was beaming from ear to ear.

"You're welcome, and we're all celebrating this right along with you. Of course, as his attorney of record I will be at the hearing, so I guess I'll see you there. And if you have any questions in the meantime, you have my number."

"Bless you, sir! For everything," Candi said, and disconnected.

Peanut hung up and then leaned back in his chair and took a slow sip of his coffee. This was a great way to start the day.

A couple of minutes later, there was a knock at the door, and then Betty came in carrying a bag.

"Zack Martin has his court date. He'll be a free man come December 22," Peanut said.

"Fabulous," she said, and set the sack down in front of him. "I sent Jack to Granny's. Enjoy."

Peanut sat up. "Do I smell sausage biscuits?"

"Your sense of smell is as good as you are," she said, and quietly closed the door on her way out.

Peanut pulled out the first biscuit, unwrapped it, and took a big bite, chewed, and swallowed.

"Heaven in a bite," he mumbled, and finished the biscuit off, and then the second, then trashed the bag and wrappers. "Now, that's the way to start off a day!"

Zack Martin was in the common room when two guards approached.

"Warden wants to see you," one of them said, and handcuffed Zack and started walking him out.

"What, no shackles?" he asked.

"Keep walking," the guard said.

He'd never been to the warden's office before and only had a vague idea of where it was, but he soon found out.

"Zack Martin," they told the warden's secretary as they entered the outer office.

She picked up a phone, spoke a few words, and then nodded.

"You can go in," she said.

The guards walked Zack in, and as they entered, the warden stood.

"Have a seat, Zack. I suspect you know why you're here," he said, smiling.

Zack sat. "Maybe, but I want to hear you say it."

"Understood," the warden said. "I have been asked by the District Attorney of Chatham County in the State of Georgia to inform you that you are to appear before a judge at 2:00 p.m. on December 22 of this year to hear your sentence vacated. At that time, you will leave the courthouse a free man, with no record of this ever happening to you. Congratulations."

"Yes, sir. Thank you, sir," Zack said.

"I'm happy we were able to get to the truth of this," the warden added.

Zack sat a moment, tempering everything he wanted to say, and then swallowed his anger and looked the warden straight in the eyes. "My son got to the truth. My son is the reason I'm going free." He didn't know tears were rolling down his cheeks, and the warden pretended he did not see.

"I've followed the story. He is an amazing young man. I wish you a long and happy life, Zack."

"Thank you, sir," Zack said.

The warden nodded to the guards.

"He's ready to go back."

They got Zack up by both arms, as if he didn't have the presence of mind to stand up by himself, and even though they'd heard the same thing Zack had heard they did not indicate by word or deed that it made a bit of difference in how he was treated. They did that to keep Zack safe, because he had to do another couple of weeks inside before the legal system would set him free.

They walked Zack back to his cell and let him go without comment, but as they were leaving, one guard turned around and gave Zack a quick nod. An acknowledgment of his news.

As soon as they were gone, Zack sat down on his bunk and stared at the floor. Now all he had to do was not piss anyone off for the next two weeks so he'd still be alive to go home.

Truesdale's was having a busy morning.

A feed shipment was being unloaded, and there was a line of customers in the front of the store.

Wade was on the loading dock, and Bridgette was at the register checking people out, when a man stormed in, waving a receipt, and pushed past the other people in line.

"You people cheated me! You charged me too much, and I want my money back."

Bridgette looked up.

"I'll be happy to help you in just a moment. Please get in line."

"By God, I ain't got time for talkin' to no damn woman. Where's the manager?"

Bridgette flinched. In all the years she'd worked here, no one had ever talked down to her like this and she wasn't putting up with it.

"Do you see this ring on my finger?" she said.

He glared. "What about it?"

"It means that you are now screaming at and denigrating the manager's fiancée, who will be, in a couple of months, the manager's wife. And she's busy. And you're being rude. And you will 'by God' move yourself to the back of the line, because if I have to call Wade up here about this, you are not going to be a happy man."

A dark-red flush ran up the man's neck onto his face, and it was only then that he realized the glares he was getting from the other customers ahead of him.

He muttered beneath his breath and stomped to the back of the line without saying another word, and Bridgette continued waiting on customers until it was finally his turn.

By then, his rage had tempered. He put the receipt down in front of her and pointed.

"I asked for twenty-five bags of 15 percent sweet feed, at $9.50 a bag."

She noted his name—Cy Boardman, a name she was not familiar with—and then looked up.

"So, Mr. Boardman, how many bags did you get home with?" she asked.

"Twenty-two," he muttered.

Bridgette did the math in her head and frowned.

"Well, sir, you were only charged for twenty-two, because your total was $209.00 plus tax, which is correct for twenty-two bags of that feed. I would guess that's all we had at the moment. Let me see who loaded this up and we'll find out." She saw Joe Trainor's initials on the order and reached for the intercom. "Joe Trainor, please come to the front of the store."

Boardman was already aghast at his mistake, and when Wade and Joe both suddenly appeared, it didn't make him feel any better.

Wade looked at the man and then went straight behind the counter to Bridgette.

"Is something wrong?"

"Not anymore. This is Mr. Boardman. He just misunderstood his receipt. Joe, it shows you loaded this up for him, and he says he asked for twenty-five bags and only got twenty-two."

"Did we overcharge?" Wade asked.

Bridgette's eyes narrowed, but she said nothing about the fit Mr. Boardman had had.

"He thought we did, but now he knows we didn't. The question now is why didn't he get the amount he asked for?"

Joe eyed the man and then picked up the receipt, read it, and looked up.

"Oh yeah! This was all we had of the kind you wanted. You were on the phone when I came back to tell you, and you nodded and waved me off, so I went back and loaded up what we had."

Now Boardman was both horrified and embarrassed.

"I guess I don't remember that," he said, and then looked back at Bridgette. "But I will remember you. Thank you for helping me straighten this out."

She smiled. "That's what we're here for."

The man ducked his head and started to walk out when Bridgette called him back.

"Mr. Boardman! You forgot your receipt."

"Oh. Yeah. Thanks," he said, then took it and stalked out of the store.

Joe went back to work, but Wade stayed and then put his arm around Bridgette and gave her a quick hug.

"Now, what kind of an ass did he make of himself?" he asked.

Bridgette grinned. "A big one."

"You don't have to deal with that kind of stuff. Why didn't you call me?"

"Any other time, I might have. He made his first mistake coming in here yelling and shoving people in line aside. But then he said he wasn't talkin' to no damn woman, and I thought, 'Oh yes you are,' and lined him out all by myself."

Wade grinned. "Whatever you said seemed to work. Good job, darlin'. You are officially relieved of duty here."

"Thank you. You know where to find me."

The fuss had been settled at Truesdale's, but the news of the kids' decorating contest was spreading.

A notice had been taken to the elementary school and put up on the bulletin board outside the principal's office, and there were several businesses on Main Street with the same notice posted on their doors.

Back at the Crown, Josh King had unloaded so many boxes for the contest that one whole corner in the warehouse was nothing but boxes of prebaked gingerbread kits, and they were going out of the store almost as fast as he could shelve them.

There was a table set up near the display with an employee filling out entries for kids who wanted to compete. As soon as they were signed up, they got a free kit along with a sheet of instructions. It was the first time there'd ever been a decorating contest for kids, and it was proving to be a hit.

CHAPTER 18

AFTER PEANUT BUTTERMAN'S PHONE CALL, CANDI FELT LIKE HER day had gone into slow motion. Everything seemed to take longer. There were more frustrations with parents and students, and more kids in the school dropping out from the flu.

She just wanted to go home—to tell the boys about Peanut's phone call. And now that this was moving toward reality, she was beginning to plan what she needed to do at home to make a place for Zack.

He had never lived in Jacksonville. He had never seen the house they lived in. It was going to take time for him to re-acclimate to being free—to having choices—and to not become depressed. She knew all of those things were possible because she'd been researching all of this since the day Peanut told them he could get Zack free.

And then, school finally ended. She was on her way home when she got caught in traffic. She slapped the steering wheel in frustration. It was as if the world was conspiring against her. Duffy always got home before her, so she called to let him know she'd be late.

He was standing at the counter eating bean dip out of a can with a spoon when his phone rang. He glanced down, then picked up the phone.

"Hey, Mom."

"Hi, honey. I'm going to be late getting home. There was a wreck somewhere up ahead, and now I'm stuck in traffic. Would you please get a package of chicken out of the freezer to thaw? I'll grill it when I get home."

"Will do," Duff said.

By the time she arrived over an hour and a half later, Allen was home, too. Candi walked in, her feet dragging, to find both of her sons waiting for her at the front door.

"What's going on?" she asked.

"We're taking care of you tonight," Allen said, then took her bags and carried them to the office, while Duff walked her back to her bedroom.

"What are you guys up to?" she asked.

"We're cooking. You work all day, then come home and take care of us. Take a long soak in the tub, Mom. It'll be at least an hour more, so don't hurry."

"Oh, honey. I won't tell you no. Please tell Allen thank you, too. This is the best."

Duff smiled, patted her on the head, and closed the door as he left.

Candi grinned. Duffy just patted her on the head. She didn't know whether to laugh or bark.

She headed to the bathroom to start water running in the tub, added bubble bath, then stripped and climbed in.

The warmth of the water soaked into her achy feet and legs as she slid down into the depths, sighed, and leaned back and closed her eyes.

She stayed until the water was getting cold, and then got out, dried off, and put on a caftan, one of her favorite at-home things to wear, then headed to the kitchen. She could smell barbecue sauce, and when she walked in, she saw a big baking pan of drumsticks and chicken thighs in the sauce and warming on the stove, a huge platter of french fries, a bowl of steaming corn on the cob, and Duffy stirring dressing into a bowl of coleslaw. She gasped.

"Are you kidding me?"

Allen waved a spoon. "Hope you're hungry. We got a little carried away."

She laughed and then hugged the both of them.

"I'm starved, and I am so blessed. I have the best sons in the world."

"Sit down, Mom. We're bringing everything to the table," Allen said.

She sat, watching them working together without a hitch, and thought, *I did a damn good job here.*

As soon as they were all at the table, their plates filled and about ready to eat, she paused.

"I have one announcement to make before we begin. This won't affect Duffy, because he'll already be out of school for Christmas break, but you, Allen, will need to take off work on December 22."

"Okay, but why?" he asked.

"Because that's the day your father will be set free, and we will be in court with him in Savannah when the judge officially vacates his sentence."

They whooped. And then they laughed. And then everyone got a little teary, and then they whooped again, overcome with joy.

"Does Dad know?" Duff asked.

"I'm sure he does by now. Mr. Butterman said the warden would notify him today."

"This will be our best Christmas ever, Mom," Duff said.

"Yes, it will. Now, let's eat. I'm starved and this looks so good."

━━━━━━━━

Bridgette thought of Emma as she was driving home from work. Emma should already be at the hotel, and Gordon would be joining her to celebrate their anniversary. Knowing Emma, every moment of their weekend would be planned, and Bridgette would hear all about it when they got home.

She was tired. Dealing with people all morning was exhausting. She didn't know how Donny did it, day after day. She was used to the quiet of her little office, with the freedom to come out and mix with customers when she wanted to. Not all day, every day.

As she drove by her apartment, she thought of what she would take with her and what she would sell.

One of the bedrooms in Wade's house was devoid of furniture, so her bedroom furniture would become guest room furniture. But her living room furniture had no place to be, and she was going to sell it.

There were things in her kitchen she didn't want to part with, and she'd take them with her. She hadn't expected to have to deal with this just yet, but now that the opportunity had arisen, and in such a horrifying manner, she couldn't wait to get it over with.

The Cherrystone Apartments had been her home for a long time, and two drunks with a gun had turned it into something to run away from, rather than something to just move out of.

As she took the turn west leading to Peach Street, the relief of homecoming was already moving through her. Rays from the setting sun momentarily caught in the diamond on her finger, making a rainbow within it, and then it was gone, but Bridgette was enchanted. That had to be a fortuitous sign. Wade would be home soon, and please God, it would just be a calm, normal ending to a rather hectic day.

Which it was.

———————

Saturday turned out to be a chilly day.

The feed store was only open half a day on Saturdays, but Bridgette hardly ever worked on Saturday, and today she was staying home and doing homey stuff.

It was also Wade's day for the housecleaners. Laurel Lorde and her cleaning crew arrived at 9:00 a.m. It wasn't the first time Bridgette had been here when they came, but it was the first time she'd been officially in residence.

Laurel started her girls in the bathrooms, pausing only long enough to check out Bridgette's ring and hear about the shooting incident.

"Of course, it was all over town that I had a bullet in my head," Bridgette said.

"When I heard that, my heart stopped," Laurel said. "I was never so glad to find out it was just another 'first version' of Blessings news."

Bridgette laughed. "I never thought of it like that, but you're right. News gets out quickly in Blessings, but there's the first version, and then the truth, every time."

"Exactly," Laurel said. "And now I need to get to work or we'll be behind all day. Congratulations on your engagement, and just go do your thing. We'll work around you, if need be."

"I'm doing laundry, so we may both be working around each other. Oh…is Bonnie entering the gingerbread house decorating contest?" she asked.

"My daughter is the one who told me about it, so yes. And thank goodness Jake works from home, because she's already roped him into helping her find the decor she wants and sticking the prebaked pieces together until they dry. Once the house is in one piece, all of the decorating is on her. Are you going to the contest?"

"I wouldn't miss it," Bridgette said, and went to gather up a load of towels as Laurel started cleaning.

It was just after 1:00 p.m. The cleaning crew was gone, and the house was shining when Wade came home. Bridgette had a pot of chili simmering on the back burner and a pan of cornbread in the warming oven. Their laundry was done, and she had the whole rest of the afternoon for whatever arose.

"Do I smell chili?" Wade asked.

"You do. Are you hungry?" she asked.

He cupped her face and kissed her.

"I'm hungry for food, and you, and just doing whatever we want for a whole day and a half. Let's eat. I have some things I want to run by you."

They got their food and sat down, and after the first few bites to ease his hunger, Wade started talking.

"Did you ever talk to Emma about coming here for Christmas this year?"

"No, but I'll do that as soon as she and Gordon come back from their anniversary weekend."

"Okay. Second subject. Do we want to put up a Christmas tree?"

Bridgette's eyes widened. "I would love to. I haven't had one in years. The apartment was always too small."

"Then we'll pick one out this afternoon at the Crown and drop it off here, then drive to Savannah to one of the big stores to get decorations."

About an hour later, they were in the midst of the Christmas tree lot again, this time picking one out for themselves.

"How about this one?" Wade asked, pointing to a medium-size tree about six feet tall. It was a perfect little triangle of green, and Bridgette gave it a quick thumbs-up.

After that, they went back by the house to unload the tree from the back of Wade's SUV. He took it inside, leaned it against the wall near the fireplace, and then came running back to the car and they headed for Savannah.

"Where are we going to shop?" Bridgette asked.

"The Walmart Supercenter on Montgomery Crossroad, where else?" he said.

"Yay! I love supercenters."

Traffic was heavier than usual on the highway, but it was the weekend and only a couple of shopping weekends before Christmas. Because of that, it took longer to get to their destination, and when they arrived, the parking lot was nearly full. Wade finally found a place to park, and then they headed into the store, excited for their next adventure.

They shopped for about an hour in the Christmas decor, then cruised through the rest of the store, picking out gifts for their families. Bridgette already had some things put back that she'd ordered online, but they were still at her apartment. Nevertheless, she and Wade were pushing two carts by the time they checked out.

"That was fun, but it was a madhouse," Wade said.

Bridgette nodded. "I can't wait to decorate the tree, though. It's going to be so pretty."

"Not as pretty as you," Wade said.

Bridgette sighed. "You know what? Besides loving you to distraction, you are fun to be with."

His eyes lit up. "Thank you, darling! I love that!"

She laid her hand on his leg, leaned her seat back a little, then closed her eyes. Within minutes she was asleep and didn't wake up until he began slowing down inside Blessings city limits.

"Are we already home?"

"Yes, and just so you know, you even sleep pretty," Wade said.

"No drool running down the corner of my mouth?"

"Only a little," he said.

She laughed.

———————

After they had supper, Wade put the tree into the stand and watered it.

"We'll let the branches relax tonight, and decorate tomorrow."

Bridgette nodded. "I'm not going to argue that. I'm ready to relax."

But she didn't just relax; she was asleep again within minutes.

Wade didn't care. He just pulled her a little closer, pillowed her head on his shoulder, and changed the movie they'd started from a romantic comedy to action/adventure.

———————

The next morning when Bridgette woke up, she knew before she opened her eyes that she didn't feel good. A couple of the customers they'd had in during the week had both been complaining of not feeling well, and there was a good chance she was coming down with whatever they'd had.

She rolled over, then sat up on the side of the bed and groaned.

Wade was awake within seconds.

"Honey, are you okay?"

"I don't feel so good. I think I'm going to skip church this morning. Some kind of bug is going around, and I just hope I'm not catching it."

He was immediately out of bed and sympathetic.

"I'm so sorry, baby. Can I get you something?"

"Not yet. Let me be awake a little bit. I'll get some coffee later, and maybe I'll feel better by then."

"I'll call Aunt Nola and tell her we're skipping dinner at noon. And just for the record, it's no wonder you're not feeling well. The stress of the past few days is probably just catching up with you."

"Maybe, but if I am coming down with something, I don't want to spread it around. Oh…did you talk to Dub and Nola about coming here for Christmas?"

"No, but I will when I call. Don't get up until you feel like it."

She waited until he was dressed and in the kitchen before she got up. It was another chilly morning, so she took a long, hot shower, and by the time she got out she felt better.

Wade left her a note on the table, telling her he'd gone to get some 7Up to settle her stomach and that he'd be right back.

She smiled. Notes on a table. Another perk of having someone who cared where you were or where you'd gone.

She poked around the kitchen and finally made herself a piece of buttered toast. By the time it was ready, Wade was back.

Bridgette ate toast and sipped 7Up, and after getting a little food in her stomach, she felt better.

"I'm still going to skip church, but I am feeling better. Thank you for the 7Up, honey. I think that helped."

Wade hugged her. "We both need a down day. This is going to be it. Oh…Dub and Nola said yes to Christmas here. Aunt Nola said she'd talk to you later about bringing food, but she's excited about the invitation, and Uncle Dub doesn't care where he eats as long as he eats."

Bridgette grinned. "That sounds just like him. This is awesome."

By the time Wade and Bridgette had their tree decorated, Emma was calling to let her know they were back.

Wade had gone to put gas in his car so he wouldn't have to do it in the morning on his way to work, and Bridgette was on the sofa reading a magazine when her phone rang.

When she saw Emma's name pop up, she guessed they were home.

"Hey, Sister. Are you in Blessings?" Bridgette asked.

Emma giggled. "Yes, a little while ago. I just wanted you to know. We had the best time."

"Uh...I have a question to ask you," Bridgette said.

"Then ask away," Emma said.

"I know you always have Christmas at your house, but how would you feel about coming here this year?"

"Oh, Birdie! I would love it!" Emma said. "Of course, I'll help cook, but it would be a treat for me."

Bridgette sighed with relief. "I am so glad. I was afraid it might hurt your feelings, and I would never want to do that."

"Nope. Having someone else cook for me never hurts my feelings," she said. "Are you talking about all of us? Ray and Susie, and Junior and Barrie and the kids?"

"Yes, and Dub and Nola, too."

"Oh, Birdie...you know what this feels like?" Emma asked.

"No, what?"

"Like we're growing our family again. I'll miss seeing Mama's face at the table, but we're all a part of her, and she'll be there with us just the same."

Bridgette's eyes welled.

"That's beautiful, Emma. I love that."

"Me, too, honey. All we need are Hunt and Ava, but they're so far away."

"Will you call the brothers for me? Even Hunt? I have to ask, even if they aren't free to come."

"I sure will," Emma said. "This is so exciting. We'll be back at home for Christmas...but in a whole new way."

The next morning, Bridgette woke up feeling fine and went to work, and the ensuing week was thankfully calm.

Every evening when they came home from work, she would wrap a few presents to put under their tree, and by Friday the wrapping was over.

The topic of conversation all over Blessings the following day was the kids' decorating contest that night. The high school gymnasium was set up for the three different age groups. Judging was to begin at 7:00 p.m., although nobody knew who the judges were going to be. The children were allowed to begin bringing entries at 5:00 p.m., and the athletic booster club was going to be selling hot dogs and drinks.

It was Blessings's version of a supper club. Food and dining on the bleachers. Entertainment on the floor when the judging began.

The day had been sunny, but it already felt cooler as the day was beginning to come to a close.

Bridgette had her clothes laid out on the bed and was in the shower. The steam from the hot water had already fogged over the mirrors and the shower door, and she was reaching for the bath brush to scrub her back when all of a sudden the shower door slid open and Wade stepped in—beautifully naked and ever so perfectly aroused.

His eyes narrowed at the water running off her body, and then when she turned around and saw him, his gaze moved to the water droplets poised to fall from her nipples.

He didn't say anything. He didn't have to.

He just backed her against the shower wall and took her.

The moment he slid inside her, Bridgette grabbed onto the shower bar with one hand and put her other around his neck to keep from falling.

After that, the only thing she remembered was the water pounding down upon her skin, and him—hard and hot and slick inside her.

Wade finally found a place to park at the high school gymnasium.

"I guess we could have gotten closer if we'd been here earlier," Bridgette said.

"And miss that shower? You're worth all the walking it takes to get there, okay?"

She grinned. When they made love, he made her crazy.

"This will be fun, won't it?" she said.

"Yes, and someday we'll be the parents bringing our kids to school events. It's just more of what we have to look forward to."

He grabbed her by the hand, and they started walking toward the gym.

"I smell hot dogs," he said. "Supper is served."

Bridgette smiled. "It'll be just like old times. Hot dogs in the bleachers."

"Only I never got to do that with you," he said.

"Well, you've got me wrapped around your finger now and I love every minute of it. Let's get inside. I can't wait to see what the kids have done."

There were parents and kids everywhere. Some were checking out the competition while others were posing for pictures beside their entries.

Wade and Bridgette began looking at the youngest division, and immediately saw Junior and Barrie.

"Oh look!" Bridgette said. "Barrie's little girl entered. We have to heap praise."

Wade smiled. "That's the perfect phrase for what's needed tonight. Not who wins, but heaping praise on all of the creators."

Lucy saw them and started shouting.

"Aunt Birdie! Aunt Birdie! Come see my house!" Lucy said.

"It's amazing!" Bridgette said. "I love the way you made icing drip off the roof to look like icicles. And the chimney is awesome! What did you use to make those little red bricks?"

"Dentist gum," she said.

Junior grinned. "Dentyne gum, Sissy. Not dentist."

"Oh yes! Dentyne. Papa J helped me cut them. I'm not allowed to use sharp stuff, but I stuck it all on with icing."

"That looks very real," Wade said. "You did such a good job! And what did you use to make your path?"

Lucy was so excited she just kept jumping up and down as she talked. "M&M candies, and the smoke coming out of my chimney is cotton candy. It looks so real, doesn't it?"

"It sure does. I was almost afraid to put my hand up there because it might be hot," he said.

Lucy tugged on Junior's hand. "Papa J, he thought it would be hot!"

Junior nodded. "I heard. You did good."

"Congratulations," Bridgette said.

"Thank you, Aunt Birdie!" Lucy said, and then more people approached, giving them a chance to move on to look at others.

They moved down the tables, praising the little artists and their creations, and then saw Duke and Cathy Talbot standing beside a little boy and his family. He was holding on to Cathy's hand while pointing out all the features on his house, and it was obvious there was a bond.

Cathy saw them and waved them over.

"Birdie! Wade! Come see my friend Melvin Lee's gingerbread house. Melvin Lee, these are my friends Birdie and Wade."

Melvin Lee's eyes got big and then he grinned even bigger.

"I know you! You rode that durn bull!"

"Melvin Lee. You do not say 'durn,'" his mother, Junie, said.

"Yes, ma'am," Melvin Lee said, but he was still enamored with Bridgette. "Wanna see my house?"

"I do," she said.

He eyed Wade. "Hey, guy. You wanna see it, too?"

It was all Wade could do not to laugh. This kid was priceless.

"I do want to see it," he said.

"It's this one right here," Melvin Lee said.

There were tiny pink plastic babies all over it—the kind that were baked in King cakes. One was hanging from a fence. One was buried in the "snow" icing all but the head. One was on the roof, and one was crawling out a partially open door.

"That's a lot of babies," Bridgette said.

Melvin Lee rolled his eyes. "There's a lot of kids in my house, but I don't have to take care of them no more."

Junie Wilson frowned and shifted the baby on her hip to the other side, then gave Bridgette and Wade a weak smile.

Wade grinned. He was now an official Melvin Lee fan.

"There were six kids in my family," Bridgette said. "I'm the youngest."

Melvin Lee frowned. "I'm the oldest. We ain't havin' no more."

"That's enough, Melvin Lee," his mother said.

Melvin Lee nodded. "That's what I said. We got enough!"

Cathy patted the little boy on the back. "If you'll stand beside your house, I'll take your picture."

He was still posing and smiling when they walked away.

"That kid is going to be something special when he's grown," Wade said.

"Why do you say that?" Bridgette asked.

"Because he already knows what he does not want in life, and that's more than some grown men can say."

As they moved to the second age group, they saw Dan and Alice Amos and their daughter, Patty. Her gingerbread house was decorated in everything pink and white. Her big brother, Charlie, was standing next to her with his hand on her back, taking his big brother duties to heart.

"Hi, Charlie. Hi, Patty! I love your house. It's so you."

Patty beamed. "Pink and white are my favorite colors."

"It looks good enough to eat," Wade said.

"Oh, we can't eat it," Patty said. "Booger licked it."

Wade blinked.

Charlie grinned. "Booger is my bloodhound, and she's right. Booger gave it a big lick before we could stop him, so it's just pretty to look at now, right, Patty?"

She sighed wistfully, then nodded. "Yes. We're just looking at it."

"It's going to be the centerpiece on our table at Christmas," Dan added. "Then everyone who comes to dinner will be looking at it, too."

They got a few feet away before Wade just threw back his head and laughed.

"Oh my God. You never know what's going to come out of a kid's mouth, do you?"

Bridgette rolled her eyes. "When Mama kept kids, she always said kids knew more about their family's business than their parents' bankers. She said kids told everything. Even stuff their parents didn't know they knew. She just pretended she never heard it, because she guessed we probably did the same thing at school."

Jake and Laurel Lorde were standing beside their daughter, Bonnie Carol, whose gingerbread house was very obviously not a people house. She'd decorated it as a chicken coop, complete with a roost on the outside of it and little plastic chickens perched on the roost, and one standing at the front door that had been painted to look as if it had black and white feathers. Bonnie had made nests on the ground from broken pieces of shredded-wheat cereal and had little round eggs made from white icing in the nests and a Christmas wreath on the door of the coop.

Wade already knew Bonnie had a pet chicken named Laverne.

"Hi, Bonnie. Is that Laverne?"

"Yes! Laverne is my best friend," she said.

Jake and Laurel smiled.

"As if the whole town of Blessings did not already know that," Jake added.

"Good luck, sugar," Wade said, and then winked at her as they walked away.

When they saw Josh King and his family, they stopped to say hello. Josh was doing his best to stay positive, but some people still looked at him askance, as if he had no right to be among "decent" people.

"Hey, Josh...LaJune. How's it going?" Wade asked.

"Good, real good," Josh said.

Bridgette smiled at LaJune and then moved closer to the table. "Hi, Trey. Hi, Tori. Did you both enter?"

They nodded.

"Oooh, show me," Bridgette said, and they immediately went into action, explaining every detail of what they'd put on their houses and why.

"This pink rock you have on the fireplace is nice, Trey. What is that?"

"Um...I just chewed up a whole bunch of pieces of bubble gum and then stuck them on the gingerbread."

"Well, that's the smartest thing I ever heard," Bridgette said, trying to keep a straight face. And then she pointed to Tori's little house. It was surrounded by trees, with only one tiny path to get to the front door. "Tell me about your house," she said.

"Those trees are pointy ice cream cones," Tori said. "Mama made me some green icing and I covered all the cones, then turned them upside down to look like Christmas trees. And my house is a little cabin in the woods, with a wreath on the front door, and I put a gold star on top of one tree. See?"

"I love it," Bridgette said, and then winked at LaJune. "They did great. Good luck, kids, but remember...no matter who wins the prizes, you're still artists and everyone is getting to see your hard work."

And so Bridgette and Wade went past all the other entries,

looking and talking and bragging on houses and kids until they'd seen them all.

"Let's get some hot dogs and find a place to sit," Wade said. "They'll start the judging in a while and probably send everyone to the bleachers to get them out of the way."

She followed him to the band boosters' stand to get hot dogs and drinks, and then headed for the bleachers.

It didn't take long to eat, and they were just visiting with the people around them when there was a squeal from the sound system as it came on, and then Wilson Turner, the Crown's manager, began speaking.

"It's time for the judging. As soon as everyone takes their seats in the bleachers, we'll begin. And no heckling the judges, please. Your children are already winners, regardless of the names that are announced."

It took a few minutes for the floor to clear, and then three people carrying clipboards walked out to where Wilson was standing.

"You all know Mr. Fraser, the art teacher at Blessings Elementary. Michelle Frame, the cake decorator at the Crown. And our very own world-renowned artist, Elliot Graham. They will pick a first, second, and third place in every division, and then announcements will be made."

CHAPTER 19

THERE WAS AN UNDERCURRENT OF MUMBLING AS THE JUDGES moved to the youngest group. The entries were identified by numbers only, so the judges had no way of knowing who'd entered them.

They began by looking at all of the entries collectively, and then going back and looking at others more intently, then finally picking their individual three choices, and then conferring with each other to get those nine choices down to three—one for first, second, and third.

After that, they moved to the second age group and did the same, and then moved to the last division and repeated the process before carrying their results up to Wilson Turner.

Wilson had the master sheet with the names that corresponded with the winning numbers, and they compiled a final sheet for the announcement.

"And we have the winners," Wilson said. "I'm going to call out the names in the youngest division first, and as I call your name, please come down to the floor to receive your prize. A parent may come with you if you want. In third place, Melvin Lee Wilson."

Melvin Lee let out a whoop from where he was sitting. "I got this, Daddy. Y'all just stay seated," he said, and took off down the bleachers, which made everyone laugh.

"In second place, Audrey Flowers."

They watched a little redheaded girl jump up and then start crying. She wouldn't go down without her daddy.

"And in first place, Bonnie Lorde."

Bonnie stood, then looked back at Jake and reached for his hand. Jake took it without hesitation and walked her down.

Wilson passed out the Kindle for third place, the iPad for second place, and the laptop for first place.

Everyone clapped and cheered, and then they began announcing the winners of the second division.

To Wade and Bridgette's delight, Tori King won first place for her little cabin in the woods.

The oldest division was the last, and after those winners were announced and the prizes handed out, Wilson looked up into the stands.

"And now, I'd like to introduce you to the person who sponsored this contest and the prizes…the owner of the Crown, Mr. Elliot Graham."

It was as if the whole crowd inhaled at once, and then people were on their feet, whistling and clapping. At long last, the elusive owner had been revealed.

Elliot simply smiled and waved, and then stood back with the other judges.

"So that's it for the evening," Wilson said. "Thank you to Blessings High School for allowing us to hold the contest here. Thank you to all the people who helped us set up the tables, and who donated money so that all of the gingerbread kits were free to the children who entered. And most of all, thank you to Mr. Graham for his unending generosity to us, his employees, and to the Township of Blessings, Georgia."

People began filing down out of the bleachers and back down on the floor to retrieve their children's entries, and to their surprise, when they picked up their children's displays, there was a five-dollar bill beneath every gingerbread house.

Tonight, everyone was a winner.

The squeals and cries of elation rang out again, but when they turned to thank Elliot, he was gone.

———————

Wade and Bridgette walked out of the gym, and when they got in the car he just sat there, watching families walking to their cars and seeing the animation on their faces.

"If I ever doubted the wisdom of leaving Boston to come back to Blessings, tonight would have ended that doubt," Wade said. "These are the kind of people I want to be around. This is the kind of community I want to raise our children in one day. There is a kindness here that's missing in big cities. Oh, I know it's there, but on a smaller and often less personal scale. But here…" He stopped, and just shook his head. "Home is where the heart is, and my heart is here forever, with them and with you."

"I guess I take all this for granted because I've never lived anywhere else. Your perspective is good for me," Bridgette said. "It's good for all of us. Sometimes you don't know how good you have it until it's gone. After Mama died, it felt like our family came apart. I never felt so alone in my life, and then there was you. Knowing I was going to see you every day at work, even when I didn't think I had a chance in hell of you seeing me as anything but an employee, gave me something to look forward to. And now this…and you…I don't even know where to begin to say how much you mean to me."

He reached for her hand, gave it a quick squeeze, and then started the car and drove away.

———

There was a notice in the daily paper the following Monday about a special event happening in Blessings that same evening to dedicate a new building and a shuttle van for the residents in the Bottoms. All were welcome to attend.

It was a revelation. The residents of Blessings all began to take notice. They knew Cathy Talbot had been building something else down there, but since they didn't live on that side of town, they kind of forgot it was happening. But now this piqued their curiosity, and when five o'clock rolled around that evening, there was a gathering crowd.

Mavis and Ant from the paper.

Duke and Cathy Talbot.

The residents of the Bottoms.

And a large crowd from the other side of town.

The brand-new metal building was shining, and the new concrete driveway leading to it from the street was pristine.

Duke helped Cathy into the back of their pickup, and then she picked up the mic from their portable sound system.

"Duke and I want to thank all of you for coming out to help us dedicate the brand-new garage for the Bottoms new transit vehicle. When we were notified a couple of weeks ago that a very kind and generous couple here in Blessings was donating a shuttle van specifically for the people in residence here, we were elated. The Bottoms is a community of wonderful people. But they had a need that had not been addressed. Some families have only one vehicle, and some have none. Often, they have no way to get to the store, or the pharmacy, or to a doctor during the day, except to walk…or, on rare occasions, hitch a ride with someone else. This wonderful couple saw their need and wanted to give them an easy access to transportation, just as we enjoy. So Duke and I built the garage to accommodate the shuttle. Two men who live here have already been hired as permanent drivers: Al Carmen and Ted Loomis."

The men took off their hats and waved to the crowd.

And then Cathy pointed over the heads of the people gathered.

"And here come Peanut and Ruby Butterman, driving the shuttle they are so generously donating to you, the residents of the Bottoms. No more walking in the rain. No more waiting for your husband to get home so you can get medicine for your sick babies. No more being afoot."

The crowd was cheering as Peanut and Ruby drove past and then pulled up into the driveway of the brand-new garage and got out.

Peanut handed over both sets of keys to the two men and then shook their hands, while Ant was taking pictures.

Cathy jumped down with the mic and walked over to where Peanut and Ruby were standing.

"I know the story," Cathy said. "But they want to hear it, too," she said, and handed the mic to Peanut.

Peanut turned to the crowd.

"Some time back, Ruby and I decided that our gifts to each other this Christmas were to do something for Blessings. We didn't need more stuff. We have enough stuff, and we have each other. But this was where the fun began. I just handed the reins of the choice over to Ruby. And all you men out there, you know what I mean when I say... here's where a thing can go wrong fast. I said, 'Ruby honey, I'm just going to leave this in your hands. I don't know what to do, so I want you to decide.'"

The crowd roared with laughter, and Ruby was standing there with a little smirk on her face.

"Anyway, this shuttle was her idea, and she found it and she made the deal and bought it outright. If you think you're surprised, you should have seen my reaction when she told me."

The crowd laughed again.

"Anyway," Peanut said, "this turned out way better than I could have imagined, and we are so happy to be able to do this for you. Merry Christmas and God bless."

At that point, they were swarmed, and after the crowd began to disperse and Duke and Cathy were gone, Peanut realized he and Ruby were now afoot.

He turned around and looked at the two drivers.

"Hey, guys. Could one of you give us a ride home?"

It was December 22. The day of Zack Martin's hearing, and Peanut was wearing his next-to-best suit as he left Blessings for the court-house in Savannah. He didn't have opening remarks to prepare. He didn't have anything to do but stand beside Zack Martin and listen to the words that would change Zack's world, so he drove with careful purpose, making sure nothing prevented him from getting where he needed to go.

———————

Candi Martin and her sons had left home early that morning to make sure they were there when 2:00 p.m. rolled around. Candi had on her favorite red dress, and the boys were wearing their best dress clothes.

All the way there, Candi had cautioned them about not asking questions about Zack's years inside and not asking him about plans. The only thing that mattered was going home together and taking it one day at a time.

———————

For the first time in ten years, Zack was in street clothes. Dark-gray pants and a blue cotton shirt, compliments of the State of Georgia. The shoes were black faux leather, and the socks were thin white cotton. The State of Georgia had footed the bill for his release clothes, and as long as they weren't prison orange, he would not complain.

He'd gone to Coastal State Prison on a prison bus, and he left it in the back of a car, handcuffed, with a wire cage between him and the two officers in the front seat. Just because he was about to be set free didn't mean he was free until a judge read the decree.

———————

Peanut was standing on the courthouse steps when he saw Candi Martin and her sons approaching. He waved, and when they saw him, they hurried up the steps.

"I'll walk you in," he said.

They went through the security checkpoint and then into the courthouse and up the stairs to a courtroom on the second floor. It was fifteen minutes to two when they went inside and took their seats on the benches in the gallery, behind the table where Peanut would sit with Zack.

A few minutes later, DA Carl Perry arrived and behind him two guards escorting Zack into the courtroom.

Zack saw his family and his lawyer at the same time, and that's when everything began feeling surreal.

He sat in the chair beside Butterman, but when the guards removed his handcuffs, he went numb. He knew Butterman was talking to him and patting him on the back.

He knew the DA who put him away was at the other table, but he wouldn't look.

He was just waiting for the judge.

And then the bailiff stepped forward.

Zack heard "All rise" and stood, then sat when Peanut pulled him back down.

The judge had carried a file into the courtroom, and now it was on the desk in front of him.

He opened it, then looked up, straight into Zack Martin's gaze.

There was a long, pregnant silence before he began to speak; then when he did, Zack began to shake.

It took less than five minutes for the judge to speak his piece and then read the petition vacating Zack's sentence. But he was waiting... waiting...for the words that would end his exile.

And then they came.

"Zachary John Martin, you are a free man."

The judge banged the gavel, then stood up and walked out of the courtroom.

Candi came off the bench, around the barrier, and threw her arms around her husband's neck. He held her against him so tight it felt like she would break, but she wouldn't let go.

And then their sons were there, hugging and laughing, and Zack was swallowed up within their embrace.

Peanut crossed the aisle to shake Carl Perry's hand.

"Merry Christmas, Carl," Peanut said.

"Merry Christmas to you, too," Carl said, and after one last look at the Martin family, he walked out of the courtroom.

It was done.

"Martin family, I do not want to break up a good thing, but do you want to face the reporters on the steps or go out the back way?" Peanut asked.

"Back way," Allen said, and then they followed Peanut out of the courthouse, pausing long enough for one last goodbye.

"Thank you for helping me put my family back together," Zack said, and shook Peanut's hand.

"It will probably be the best case of my career," Peanut said. "Now all of you go have a merry Christmas and a happy life."

They waved, and then they were gone, moving quickly through the parking lot and then up the sidewalk to where they'd parked. Peanut watched until he saw them driving away, then got in his car and headed home.

———

Nothing felt real for Zack. Not the ride home, or listening to his family's chatter, or the freedom to stop and go into a rest stop or to fuel the car.

Sitting in the back seat with Candi, holding her hand and listening to their sons chatter in the seat in front of them. Feeling the warmth of her body against him, listening to the sound of her laughter.

He'd forgotten how that sounded.

The traffic was nerve-racking. The sounds of semitrucks flying past them made him jump. The sight of Christmas everywhere. He'd forgotten all of that. He didn't know he was crying until Candi gave him a handful of tissues.

The high of being free had been replaced with the uncertainty of what next. And then she'd just reminded him it didn't matter. They were together again. They would figure it out.

The same day Zack Martin walked free, Bridgette was at the Cherrystone Apartments, watching the last of her furniture being loaded into a truck. She'd never gone to college, but her furniture was going, and such was the irony of life.

She pocketed the money they'd just given her and after they drove away, walked through her apartment one last time. The rooms were empty now. The broken mirror and glass had all been cleaned up, but the bullet hole was still in the wall—something the landlord would have to fix. She'd even sold the chair frame she'd been going to reupholster. Gluing the mouse to the floor had kind of taken away the joy and challenge.

Everything she wanted to keep was already at Wade's, and now this phase of her life was ending. She left her door keys on the counter, turned the lock on the door, and walked out.

She glanced down at her ring as she got in the car and thought how significant this piece of jewelry was to a woman and yet it would never matter more than the man who gave it to her.

As she started up the car, she was struck by the urge for another lemon-pineapple snow cone, so instead of driving straight home, she headed for the Crown.

The line at the stand was almost nonexistent as she parked.

"Score for me," she said, got out, and hurried to the window. "I'll have a Candlelight Bright," she said, and then shifted from one foot to the other, anticipating the treat.

As soon as it was in her hands, she took the first big bite, savoring the tart-sweet tang on her tongue and the cold, icy treat melting in her mouth, and sighed. Then winced. Brain freeze again.

She glanced toward the Christmas tree lot, saw Barrie and the kids were with Junior, and walked over to say hello.

The kids saw her as she approached and started smiling.

"How are my two favorite people?" she asked, and looked down at Lucy and Freddie.

"We're great," Junior said. "Aren't we, Barrie?"

Barrie smiled at Junior's wit and shook her head.

"Good one," Bridgette said. "Unfortunately for you guys, I was referring to your two cuties."

"Mama, can we have snow cones?" Lucy asked.

"Maybe another time. It's too close to supper," Barrie said.

Bridgette felt bad. "I'm sorry. I shouldn't have brought the temptation to them. Can I give them a sip of the juice from my straw? I haven't touched it and—"

"You don't know what you're asking," Barrie said. "Freddie has the sucking part down great, but he's still pretty bad at backwash."

Bridgette laughed out loud. "Mama babysat kids for a living. There were always littles at our house begging drinks and bites. If I was going to perish from slobber and backwash, it would have happened years ago."

"It's your funeral," Barrie said, and then cautioned the kids. "Just sip, and remember to swallow it good before you take another."

They both nodded.

"I'll go first," Lucy said, giving Freddie the evil eye.

"See? Even she knows the danger," Junior said.

"Hush. Both of you," Bridgette said, and then knelt down so she was on their level. "It's lemon-pineapple."

"I like that," Lucy said.

"I yike it," Freddie said.

Bridgette grinned. "I'll hold the straw. You take a drink, Lucy, then it will be Freddie's turn."

Lucy leaned over and took a little sip, swallowed, and then smiled. "Yum."

"That was just a little sip. You can have one more," Bridgette said.

Lucy took her second drink. "Good. Thank you, Aunt Birdie."

"You're welcome, sugar. Now it's Freddie's turn."

Bridgette guided the straw into his mouth.

He took a big drink and swallowed. "Good. More?"

"One more," Bridgette said.

He took another drink big enough to make his eyes water, but he was grinning when it went down.

"Good. More?"

"No. Two is enough. Leave some for Aunt Birdie," Barrie said.

Bridgette stood, smiling. "I was on my way home when I made a detour. I've been craving these things ever since the stand went up. Now that's my favorite thing, and I don't know what I'm going to do when Christmas is over."

Barrie nodded. "I know about cravings. It was anything salty when I was carrying Lucy, and oranges when I was carrying Freddie."

Bridgette knew she was still smiling, because she could feel it on her face. But everything they were saying faded, and the only thing she heard was her heartbeat hammering in her ears.

Then Junior took her arm.

"Earth to Birdie…where did you go?"

"Oh, sorry, honey. I was just remembering something I need to do when I get home. Sorry."

"I was just saying we're looking forward to Christmas dinner at your house, but I see a customer approaching. It's December 22. You'd think everyone who wanted a tree would already have them up and decorated, but I guess not. I've got to get back to work. Hang on a bit, Barrie, and then we'll go home."

Bridgette was nodding and smiling as she waved goodbye and then headed straight for her car. She trashed her snow cone as she passed the stand, drove straight to Phillips Pharmacy, and marched in like a soldier going to war.

LilyAnn was checking out a line of customers, but Bridgette didn't need any help finding what she came for. She'd walked past it a thousand times without ever once making a purchase, so today was her first. The choices were varied, but they all reported the same results. So she picked one and headed up front to pay.

LilyAnn was waving goodbye to the last customer when Bridgette plopped the little box down on the counter.

LilyAnn looked up and arched an eyebrow.

"Comments are not requested."

LilyAnn nodded, pretended to zip her lips, and checked her out without saying another word.

Bridgette drove home and, the minute she got inside, went straight to the bathroom.

When she came out, she was in shock and coming to terms with the fact her method of preventing pregnancy was fallible. If it hadn't been for her sudden craving for lemons and Barrie's comment about pregnancy cravings, she would never have thought to do this.

Then she thought of Wade's reaction and knew she was about to blow his mind. He'd given her an engagement ring for Christmas, and other than the new boots she had wrapped up for him under the tree, she was giving him a positive pregnancy test.

Then she heard the back door opening and Wade's footsteps as he came in the house.

"Bridgette! I'm home."

"In the bedroom," she shouted, and quickly hid the test stick in a drawer, then sat down on the side of the bed and began taking off her shoes.

He came in, sat down beside her, and slid his arm around her shoulder.

"Did they come pick up the last of your furniture?" he asked.

"Yes, and I'm two hundred dollars to the good," she said. "Did you get everything straightened with the supplier?"

"Yes. They invoiced us the wrong amount. They're emailing an updated invoice tomorrow, so be on the lookout for it."

"I will."

He tilted her chin up and then looked into her eyes.

"You look beat. We're not cooking tonight. Either I go pick up some food from Granny's or I'll take you there."

Bridgette sighed. "I vote for pick it up."

"Umm, what about fried chicken?" he asked.

"Sounds good," she said.

He gave her a quick peck on the cheek.

"You get into something comfortable and I'll go pick it up. Shouldn't take more than thirty minutes or so."

"I'm fine," Bridgette said. "I shared a snow cone with Lucy and Freddie after work."

"Those kids are so cute," Wade said. "I wonder what our kids will look like some day."

"We'll find out when the time comes," Bridgette said.

"Did I ever tell you twins run in my family?" he asked.

She blinked. "Uh…no, I don't guess you did, but if we get two of you, I'll be fine. If we get two of me, then God help us both."

He grinned. "I'm not scared of anything when we're doing it together."

She put her hands on his cheeks and then leaned over and kissed him.

"And neither am I," she said.

"Love you. I'm going to get chicken…and pie, because ever since you made that fudge, I'm craving chocolate."

Bridgette laughed.

"What?" he asked.

"I'll explain later," she said. "Go get my chicken, please. I'm starving."

He grinned, patted her on the butt, and strode out of the room like a man on a mission.

She threw herself backward onto the bed and then put her hands on her belly and laughed.

This was going to be a meal he'd never forget.

Wade came back with the food as Bridgette was setting the table. She started to sit down, and then backed up and got a handful of napkins from the pantry.

"Good catch," Wade said. "I don't eat my fried chicken with a knife and fork."

"And neither do I," she said, and plopped down in the chair across from him.

She sat, watching the changing expressions on his face. Those beautiful blue eyes, that square jaw and dark hair and brows. And when he smiled, his eyes almost disappeared. She wondered how their child would look with a mix of their features. Or if one of them would have a little mini-me.

Wade transferred the chicken pieces from the box onto the platter, then got out the containers with the sides and biscuits and set the dessert containers aside for later.

"It smells so good. Thank you for this," Bridgette said.

"Absolutely, and thank the Lord for this food. Amen."

"Amen," she echoed, and then forked a chicken thigh onto her plate, added mashed potatoes and gravy and green beans, and then buttered a biscuit and took a bite. "Umm, so good," she said.

"No brain freezes with biscuits," Wade said.

She waved her fork at him. "Don't pick on me. I still have glue in my hair."

He winked, and then they began to eat. When they had finished, he began gathering up the refuse. "Do you want dessert?"

"Yes, but later," Bridgette said. "You go ahead and eat yours now if you want, and then you can help me eat mine later."

He laughed. "No, I'm going to wait, too. I'll load the dishwasher. You go find us something to watch on TV tonight, okay?"

"Sure," Bridgette said, and then made a mad dash to the bedroom, got the pregnancy test out of the drawer, and stuck it in the pocket of her sweatpants. She went back to the living room and was searching for movies to watch when he came in and plopped down beside her.

"What did you find?" he asked.

She pulled the pregnancy test out of her pocket and handed it to him.

She wished later she'd thought to video his reaction, because it went from shock to a thousand watts of light in about two seconds flat.

"Are you serious?" he cried. "This isn't a joke?"

"No joke. My infallible pregnancy protection didn't work. Are you mad?"

All of a sudden, he couldn't talk. He just pulled her into his lap, buried his face against the curve of her neck, and held her.

Bridgette wrapped her arms around his shoulders and sighed. He wasn't mad.

"I know we didn't plan this," she said.

He just shook his head and finally looked up.

"But you're wrong. This was all part of my dream…my plan…from the moment I saw you. I thought, 'Oh my God, that's Bridgette Knox. Please God, don't let her be married, because she's supposed to be mine.' And then I thought you didn't want me, but I loved you enough for the both of us and kept dreaming this dream of having a family again. Of having a family with you, and now you've just handed it to me." His fingers were curled around the test stick. "Can I keep this?"

"Yes, sweetheart, it's yours. I'm yours. You gave me an engagement ring for Christmas, and I'm giving you a baby."

He had tears in his eyes.

"Thank you, forever."

"Always, and let's keep this to ourselves for a while. I'm still rolling with the high from the bull ride, getting engaged, and having a bullet in my head. I want to savor those achievements a little while longer before we make another announcement."

"Agreed. Besides, I like having secrets with you."

That night, and long after Bridgette had fallen asleep in Wade's arms, he still couldn't close his eyes. He kept watching the rise and fall of her chest and the occasional flutter of her eyelashes as dreams invaded her rest, and knew he would remember this night and this moment forever. He was holding the love of his life…and his child.

The responsibilities of loving meant sheltering, and caring, and protecting, and so much more. And now she'd given him more to protect, and care for, and love.

At this moment in his life, he would not ask for one thing more.

———

Christmas dinner for the Martin family was a celebration of renewal. Hearts were healing. Lives were being reborn. And as they all sat down at the table, before they began their meal, each family member said one thing they were grateful for.

"I am grateful the empty chair at this table has been filled," Candi said.

"I am grateful for my little brother's courage," Allen said.

"I am grateful you all forgave me," Duffy said.

"And I am grateful my family never quit on me," Zack said.

There was a moment of silence, and then Duffy pointed at the baked ham, sitting in a place of prominence.

"I'll take two slices of that ham," he said.

Candi glanced at the expression on Zack's face and grinned.

"He has not been full in almost three years. Welcome home."

———

Josh King took LaJune and the kids to his in-laws' farm for Christmas, just as he'd done every year since their marriage. He went unsure of his reception, and then blinked back tears when he was welcomed with open arms.

All the years he'd been there before, his focus had been on what he'd lost growing up. But now his eyes had been opened to what he'd gained as an adult. He couldn't see her, but he felt his mother's presence as he sat down at the dinner table by his wife. He'd been given a second chance to do things right, and he was never going to let himself, or his family, down again.

———————

Christmas in the Montgomery house came with its own version of chaos, as every family came in carrying a dish to be added to the table or to the sideboard with other desserts.

The women were in the kitchen heating gravy, dishing up vegetables, mashing potatoes, uncovering the candied yams and corn-bread dressing already baked to a turn, taking hot rolls from the oven, and filling glasses with drinks.

Wade carried a platter piled high with slices of roasted turkey to the table, and then came the women with the sides, putting them anywhere they could find a place until there wasn't a spot left on the table to put another dish.

"Dinner's ready!" he said, and the men who'd been visiting in the living room didn't have to be told twice.

Junior added a booster seat to one chair at the table for Lucy and scooted a high chair up beside her for Freddie, then he and Barrie took the seats on either side of them.

Wade sat at one end of the table, with Bridgette to his right. His uncle Dub sat at the other end, with Nola to his right, and everyone else filled in between. When they were finally seated, Wade stood.

"We're all here but Hunt and Ava," he said. "Distance can keep us apart, but people we love are always in our hearts. Thank all of you for coming to spend Christmas with Bridgette and me...a tradition we hope to continue."

As he sat, they began by passing the platter of turkey around the table, followed by the myriad bowls of side dishes, and when the plates were filled to overflowing the meal began.

Bridgette looked at the faces around their table, listening to the laughter and the teasing and the stories being told, and then she caught Wade watching her. When he winked, she knew what he was thinking. There was one more at this table than the rest of them knew, and this time next year a whole other person would be born.

"Birdie! Wade! Merry Christmas to the both of you! This is wonderful," Emma said.

"It is wonderful, isn't it?" Bridgette said.

"More than you know," Wade added. "A few weeks ago, Bridgette told me that bad things and good things always happen in threes, and here in Blessings, we'd already had two bad things turn into two good things, and I thought that was it. But she stood firm. No, she said. There will be one more. And I just realized this is it. When that bullet missed her head by inches, that was a bad thing. I came so close to losing her. But today, having our families all together on this beautiful Christmas day, I'd say this is the good thing. Bridgette is my Christmas miracle, and with all of you here at our table, I am blessed by what came with her!"

CHAPTER 20

It was the first of February.

A wedding was in progress at Blessings Baptist Church. There had been bigger weddings in that church, but none quite as lively.

Bridgette Knox was marrying Wade Montgomery.

It wasn't a surprise. They'd been so obviously in love long enough that a good many people were of the opinion it was about time.

The guests were in the church pews.

The pastor was at the pulpit.

Wade was standing at the altar, waiting for Bridgette, with Dub as best man beside him.

The music had just begun, giving the matron of honor and the bridesmaids and groomsmen the signal to move.

They came down the aisle two by two.

Emma and Gordon.

Susie and Ray.

Barrie and Junior.

They took their places at the altar as the flower girl and ring bearer followed behind.

To the delight of the congregation, Lucy Lemons was scattering rose petals with wild abandon.

Some went up in the air. Some went into the congregation. And a few fell into the aisle.

Her little brother, Freddie, walked beside her, carrying a tiny satin pillow with the rings securely fastened.

Freddie was not impressed with anything but the rose petals floating about. He had already chewed and swallowed one and was in the process of stomping another one into the carpet when Lucy realized he wasn't beside her. She turned around, saw what he was doing, and yelled at him loud enough to be heard downtown.

"Freddie! Stop that!" And then she looked at her mother standing at the altar and pointed. "Mama, tell Freddie he can't stomp my flowers!"

The congregation erupted in laughter as Junior bolted up the aisle and grabbed Freddie by the hand.

"I got him, Sissy. Do your thing," he whispered.

Still indignant, Lucy scattered the rest of her flowers by the handful and then took her place in front of her mother, while Junior carried Freddie up to the altar with him.

The music stopped.

And when it began again, they all knew what it meant.

There was a shuffling sound as people turned in their seats, looking back up the aisle to the bride standing in the doorway and her brother at her side.

"You are so beautiful, little sister. Are you ready to do this?" Hunt asked.

Her gaze was already locked on the man waiting for her at the end of the aisle.

"Yes, I'm ready," she said.

She'd been ready for this moment all her life.

Bridgette slid her hand around the bend of Hunt's elbow, and down the aisle they went—with him walking her toward the rest of her life.

EPILOGUE

SHANE AND SHELLY MONTGOMERY CAME INTO THE WORLD screaming their objection at being pushed out of their mother's belly.

Bridgette and Wade had known for months they were having twins, so the shock had long since worn off and delight was setting in.

"Oh my God, just look at them!" Wade said. "They have your dark hair…and both have a dimple in one cheek, just like me."

Bridgette was exhausted, aching, elated, and feeling strangely empty. After all those months, and all that weight and wiggling, she felt like she might float away. She just patted Wade's hand and smiled.

"Are they okay?" she asked.

"They're perfect, just like you," Wade said.

She saw the love in his eyes as well as the awe of witnessing their births.

"I don't feel perfect right now, but I am so happy. I feel just like I did after riding that mechanical bull down Main Street. I did it. I'm glad I did it, but thank God it's over."

Wade laughed, and then he leaned down and kissed her.

"You have rocked my world ever since I laid eyes on you in first grade, but I've got news for you. I don't think 'over' is the best way to describe what just happened. I think it's just beginning."

THE END

Count Your Blessings with this
emotional Southern small-town romance
from bestselling author
Sharon Sala

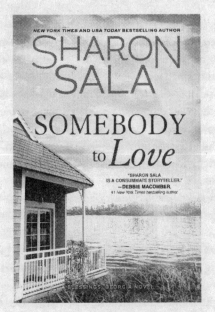

CHAPTER 1

HUNTER KNOX HAD NEVER PLANNED ON COMING BACK TO Blessings, so the fact that he was riding up Main Street in the middle of the night was typical of his life. Nothing had ever gone according to plan.

It was just after midnight when he pulled his Harley up beneath a streetlight, letting it idle as he flipped up the visor on his helmet and glanced up at the Christmas wreath hanging from the pole.

From the sounds going off in town, a lot of people were ringing in the New Year. He could hear fireworks, and church bells, and someone off in the distance shouting "Happy New Year."

He wasn't looking forward to this visit, and he'd planned to get some sleep first, but he couldn't. Too much time had passed already, and there was someone he needed to see before it was too late. So his reservation at Blessings Bed and Breakfast, and the bed with his name on it, were going to have to wait. He flipped the visor back down, put the bike into gear, and rode up Main Street, watching for the turn that would take him to the hospital.

The Knox family had just ushered in the new year in total silence— eyeing each other from their seats in their mother's hospital room— already wondering about the disposition of the family home before their mother, Marjorie, had yet to take her last breath.

It wasn't as if she had a fortune to fight over. Just a little three-bedroom house at the far end of Peach Street that backed up to the city park. The roof was old. It didn't leak, but it wouldn't sell in that condition. The floor in the kitchen had a dip in the middle of it, and the furniture was over thirty years old, but right now, it appeared to be a bigger issue than watching their mother still struggling to breathe.

Marjorie had given birth to six children. The oldest, a little girl named Shelly, died from asthma before she ever started school.

Four of her children—Junior, Emma, Ray, and Bridgette, who they called Birdie—were sitting with Marjorie in her hospital room. Only Hunter, the second child and eldest son, was missing. No one knew where he was now, and all knew better than to mention his name.

Their father, Parnell Knox, had died six years ago of emphysema. Marjorie always said he smoked himself to death, and while she'd never smoked a day in her life, now she was dying of lung cancer from someone else's addiction. The diagnosis had been a shock, then she got angry. She was dying because of secondhand smoke.

———————

Sometimes Marjorie was vaguely aware of a nurse beside the bed, and sometimes she thought she heard her children talking, and then she would drift again. She could see daylight and a doorway just up ahead, and she wanted to go there. She didn't remember why, but she couldn't leave yet. She was waiting for something. She just couldn't remember what.

———————

Ava Ridley was the nurse at Marjorie's bedside. Ava had grown up with the Knox kids because Marjorie had been her babysitter from the time that she was a toddler. Her childhood dream had been to grow up and marry Hunt. But at the time he was a senior in high school, she was a freshman in the same class with his brother, Ray.

She'd spent half her life in their house, making Ray play dolls with her when they were little, and learning how to turn somersaults and outrun the boys just to keep up with them. As they grew older, they hung out together like siblings, but she'd lived for the moments when Hunt was there. At that time, he barely acknowledged her existence, but it didn't matter. She loved enough for two.

And then something big—something horrible that no one ever talked about—happened at their house and Hunt was gone.

After that, no one mentioned his name, so she grieved the loss of a childhood dream, grew up into a woman on a mission to take care of people, and went on to become a nurse. After a couple of years working in a hospital in Savannah, she came home to Blessings, and she'd been here ever since. Ava had cared for many people in her years of nursing, but it was bittersweet to be caring for Marjorie Knox, when she had been the one who'd cared for Ava as a child.

Ava glanced at Emma. She was Emma Lee, now. Married to a nice man named Gordon Lee. Her gaze slid to Junior, and Ray, and Birdie.

Junior was a high-school dropout and divorced.

Ray worked for a roofing company and had a girlfriend named Susie.

Bridgette, who'd been called Birdie all of her life, was the baby, but she was smart and driven to succeed in life where her siblings were not. She was the bookkeeper at Truesdale's Feed and Seed Store, and still waiting for her own Prince Charming.

Ava thought the family looked anxious, which was normal, but they also seemed unhappy with each other, which seemed strange. However, she'd seen many different reactions from families when a loved one was passing, and had learned not to judge or assume. And even though it was no business of hers, she knew the Knox family well enough to know something was going on. Her job was to monitor Marjorie's vitals and nothing else.

The door to Marjorie's room was open, and the sounds out in the hall drifted in as Ava was adjusting the drip in Marjorie's IV. So when the staccato sound of metal-tipped boots drifted inside, they all looked toward the doorway.

The stride was heavy, likely male—steady and measured, like someone who knew where he was going. The sound was growing louder, and they kept watching, curious to see who it was who was passing by at this time of night.

Then all of a sudden there was a man in the doorway, dressed in biker leather and carrying a helmet. He glanced at them without acknowledgment, then went straight to the bed where Marjorie was lying.

Ava's heart began to pound. Hunt Knox had just walked in, and the years since she'd seen him last had been more than kind. His face was leaner, his features sharper. He was taller and more muscular, and his dark hair was longer, hanging over the collar of his leather jacket, but his eyes were still piercing—and unbelievably blue.

She forgot what she was doing and stared as he approached. It took her a few seconds to realize he didn't recognize her.

"Ma'am. I'm Hunt Knox, her oldest son. Is she conscious?"

"Not ma'am, Hunt. It's me, Ava Ridley. And to answer your question, she's in and out of consciousness. You can talk to her if you want."

Hunt's eyes widened. He was trying to see the young girl he remembered in this pretty woman's soft voice and dark eyes.

"Sorry. You grew up some. I wouldn't have recognized you," Hunt said. "Is she in pain?"

"Doctor is managing that for her," Ava said.

When his four siblings finally came out of their shock, Junior stood up.

"Where did you come from? How did you know?" he asked.

Hunt turned, staring until they ducked their heads and looked away, then shifted focus back to his mother. She had wasted away to nothing but skin and bones. Disease did that to a body. He put his helmet aside and reached for her hand.

"Mom...it's me, Hunt. I came home, just like you asked." He waited, and just when he thought she was too far gone to hear, he felt her squeeze his fingers. Relief swept through him. He wasn't too late after all. "I'm sorry it took so long for your message to reach me, but I'm here now."

Her eyes opened. He knew she recognized him. Her lips were moving, but she didn't have enough lung capacity to breathe and talk at the same time.

Finally, she got out one word.

"Sorry," and then, "love."

Everything within him was shattering, but it didn't show. He'd just as soon shoot himself as reveal weakness.

"It's okay, Mom. I love you, too. I made you a promise and I'll keep it. I'm sorry it took me so long to get here. I was out of the state for a while and didn't get your last letter until I got back, but I'm here now and I'll take care of everything you wanted."

Marjorie's eyelids fluttered.

Hunt waited.

His siblings stood and moved around the bed, waiting. They hadn't seen her respond to anything in days, and all of a sudden, she was conscious. Then her lips parted.

They leaned closer, not wanting to miss a moment of her last words.

Then she said, "Hunt."

"I'm here, Mom. I'm right here," Hunt said, and gently squeezed her hand. "I'll do what you asked."

Her lips parted again. "Promise?"

He leaned over and spoke softly, near her ear.

"I promise. I'm here now. You're free to go."

Marjorie exhaled. The light was brighter, and there was no longer a weight on her heart. She let go of her son and let God take her home.

Now all four siblings were staring in disbelief, wondering what the hell just happened. Their mother had been hanging on to life like this for almost a week, and the prodigal son walked in and told her it was okay to go. And she died? Just like that?

Ava was trying to find a pulse, but it was gone.

Marjorie's heartbeat had flatlined on the monitor.

Emma's voice rose an octave. "Is she dead?"

Tears were rolling down Junior's face, and Ray was wiping his eyes.

Birdie, the youngest daughter, covered her face and started to weep.

Moments later an RN came hurrying into the room. She felt for a pulse, then looked up at the clock.

"Time of death, 1:15 a.m."

There were tears on Ava's cheeks.

"I'm so sorry. My sympathies to all of you."

Emma hugged her. "Thank you for taking such good care of Mama," she said.

Hunt had yet to speak to any of his siblings, and was still holding on to his mother's hand. He knew they were gathering up their things and walking out of the room, but he had nothing to say to any of them now. That would come later.

He felt a hand on his shoulder. It was Ava.

"I'm so sorry, Hunt, but grateful you made it. At the last, you were all she talked about."

"Thank you for taking care of her," he said, then let go of his mother's hand, picked up his helmet, and walked out.

Ava had heard pain in the pitch of his voice, but he did not need her concern or her care. Losing a patient was the hardest part of being a nurse, but in this instance, Ava was at peace. Marjorie Knox had suffered a long time. She was no longer sick or in pain, and that was a blessing.

Hunt was on his way back up the hall when he saw his siblings getting in the elevator. He pictured them standing in the lobby downstairs, waiting for him to come down next, and took the stairwell instead.

He was already out in the parking lot and on his Harley as they finally walked out of the building. They watched him ride away without acknowledging any of them.

"Well, dammit, there he goes," Ray said.

"Did any of you ever know where Hunt went when he left town?" Birdie asked.

"I didn't," Emma said.

"Me either," Junior said, while Ray shook his head.

"Mama must have known," Birdie said.

The others looked at each other in silence, finding it hard to believe that the mother they'd taken for granted had kept a secret like that for so long, but the three of them knew why.

"I wonder what Mama asked him to do?" Junior said.

"What do you mean?" Ray asked.

Junior frowned. "You heard him. He told Mama he'd keep his promise and do what she asked him to do."

"Oh yeah," Ray said.

"I wonder where he's going?" Junior asked. "Do you think he's going to stay at Mama's house?"

Emma shrugged. "I don't know. Why don't you drive by the house on your way home and see if he's there. If he thinks he's gonna just move in, he has another think coming. I want to—"

"What you want and what's going to happen are two different things," Junior said. "There are four of us standing here."

"But there are five heirs," Birdie said. "Whatever money comes from selling Mama's house will be divided five ways, not four. The house is old. It's not going to bring anything worth fighting over."

"Nothing is worth fighting over," Ray said.

Emma glared at all of them. "We've already talked about Mama's funeral and stuff, and there's just enough money in Mama's bank account to bury her and nothing more. Let's go home and get some rest."

"Did Mama leave a will?" Birdie asked.

They all stopped.

"I don't know," Emma said.

Junior shrugged. "I don't either."

"How do we find out?" Ray asked.

"Maybe Hunt knows. He already knows something about Mama that we don't know," Birdie said.

"I'm going home. If you want to know where Hunt is at, go look for him yourself," Junior muttered.

Ray got in his car and left, and Junior did the same.

Emma ignored him. "I'm sad Mama is gone, but I'm glad she's not suffering." Then she glanced at Birdie. "I wonder where Hunt's been all these years."

"I don't know, but he sure turned into a good-looking man," Birdie said.

———————————

Hunt rolled up to the bed-and-breakfast as quietly as he could manage on a Harley, cognizant of the other guests who were likely asleep. He locked up his bike, grabbed his bag and helmet, then headed to the door and rang the bell.

Bud Goodhope was still up and waiting for their last guest to arrive, and when he heard the doorbell, he hurried through the hall to answer the door.

"Welcome to Blessings Bed and Breakfast," Bud said.

Hunt nodded. "I'm Hunt Knox. I have a reservation."

"Yes, come in, Mr. Knox. I'll get you registered and show you to your room. You must be exhausted."

A short while later, Hunt was taken upstairs and given a room at the end of the hall.

"It's quieter back here," Bud said. "Breakfast will be served from 6:00 to 10:00 a.m. If you need anything, just press seven on the house phone and either my wife, Rachel, or I will answer."

"Thanks," Hunt said. "Right now, all I want is a shower and a bed."

"Then rest well," Bud said as he put Hunt's bag on the bed. "We'll see you in the morning for breakfast."

Hunt locked the door, put his jacket and helmet on a chair, then sat down and took off his boots. The room was well-appointed and had a warm, homey feel. It had been a long time since he'd been in a place like this.

He poked around and found a basket of individually bagged, homemade chocolate chip cookies, as well as a mini-fridge of cold drinks. He hadn't eaten since noon, and it was already tomorrow, so he chose a cookie and a cold Coke and ate to dull the empty feeling in his belly.

When he was finished, he stripped and walked into the bathroom. The full-length mirror reflected the milestones life had left on his body. The scars of war weren't just within him. Some, like the thin silver ropes left from wounds that had healed, were visible, too.

He turned the water as hot as he could stand it to loosen tired muscles, and then washed his hair before he washed himself. By the time he got out, all he could think about was crawling between clean sheets and sleeping for a week. But there'd be no sleeping in. He'd come a long way to keep a promise, and it wasn't going to be accomplished by staying in bed.

———————

Ava's shift ended at 7:00 a.m.

Normally, she would be looking forward to a little breakfast and then sleep, but Hunt Knox was on her mind as she headed home. She wondered if he was married—if he had children—where he lived—what he did. But it appeared she wasn't the only one in the dark. From the little she'd overheard, his brothers and sisters didn't know, either. Again she wondered what had happened to drive such a rift within their family, and what promise he'd made to his mother before she died.

Ava was still thinking about him as she pulled up beneath the carport. The morning was cold and the sky appeared overcast. But weather wasn't going to affect her day. She let herself in and then went through the house, leaving her coat in the front closet and her purse on the hall table.

Getting out of her uniform was always paramount. It went straight to the laundry, then she went to the bathroom to shower. The ritual of washing all over was both a physical and an emotional cleansing— leaving behind all of the sadness and sickness of the patients she'd cared for last night to the capable hands of the day shift.

She was off for the next two days, and then she would be going back on days. She hadn't minded filling in while one of the nurses had been out of town for a family funeral, but she was ready to go back on her regular shift in the ER.

As soon as she was out and dry, she put on her pj's, switched her laundry to the dryer, ate a bowl of cereal while standing at the sink, then crawled into bed. She was still thinking of Hunt Knox when she fell asleep.

———

Rachel Goodhope met their latest guest when he came down for breakfast. She hadn't seen him in biker gear, but he cut a fine figure in the black Levi's and the gray chambray shirt he was wearing. He hung a black leather coat over the back of a chair, set a biker helmet in the seat of the chair beside him, and then went to the buffet.

"Welcome to Blessings," Rachel said, and added a fresh batch of crisp bacon to a near-empty chafing dish.

"Thank you," Hunt said. "Everything looks good."

"Enjoy," she said. "If you want something to drink other than hot tea or coffee, just let me know."

"This is fine," Hunt said. "Oh…can you tell me where Butterman Law Office is located?"

"Sure. He has an office in a building directly across from the courthouse. There's a sign out front. You can't miss it."

"Thank you," Hunt said, and began filling his plate.

Rachel went back to the kitchen to take a batch of hot biscuits out of the oven. She put them on a counter beneath a heat lamp to keep them warm and was going to bake up some more waffles when her cell phone rang. She wiped her hands and then answered.

"Hello, this is Rachel."

"Good morning, Rachel. This is Ruby. I'm on the church calling committee, so I'm giving you a heads-up about an upcoming funeral."

"Oh no! Who died?" Rachel asked.

"Marjorie Knox finally passed, bless her heart," Ruby said.

"Oh, of course! I heard they'd called in the family," Rachel said, and then gasped. "Oh! Oh my! I didn't put two and two together until now. We had a guest sign in really, really early this morning. His name is Hunter Knox. I'll bet he's family."

Ruby gasped. "Oh my word! That's the oldest son! He disappeared right after high school and never came back."

"Well, he's here now," Rachel said. "And a fine-looking man he is, too."

"I hope he made it in time to see Marjorie," Ruby said.

"He just asked me where Peanut's office is," Rachel said.

"I don't know if Peanut will be in the office or not, since it's a holiday. I guess time will tell how this all plays out," Ruby said. "In the meantime, just giving you a heads-up about a family dinner at church in the near future."

"Noted," Rachel said. "I've got to make some more waffles. I'll talk to you later."

"And I have more people to call," Ruby said. "I'll be in touch."

Hunt ate his fill of eggs, biscuits, and gravy, then went back for waffles. He was making up for having gone so long without real food and had no idea what the day would bring, so eating what was in front of him seemed like a good idea.

He'd reserved the room here for at least a couple of nights, until he had a chance to check out his mother's house. If it was habitable enough to stay in while he repaired it, he'd stay there. Once it was fixed, it would be up to him to see to the auction and pay outstanding bills.

When he'd received her letter, Hunt had been shocked to find out his mother had named him the executor of her estate. Even though they'd stayed in touch, she never mentioned his brothers and sisters, and with good reason. She knew he wouldn't care. By the time the letter caught up with him, the postmark was almost two weeks old, and the date on the letter she'd written was a month before that. When she confessed her days were numbered, he panicked and called her, but never got an answer. The thought that she would die without knowing he would do what she'd asked had sent him on a wild sixteen-hour ride from Houston to Blessings. He knew now she'd been waiting for him to come. She'd trusted him enough to wait. Now it was up to him to do the job.

CHAPTER 2

Hunt went back up to his room after breakfast. He had the lawyer's number in his mother's letter. He didn't think anyone would be at work today, but he sent a text anyway, just in case.

It wasn't long before he got a response.

I'll be in the office until noon. You're welcome to drop in at any time.

Hunt returned the text.

I'll be there soon. Thank you.

At that point, he put on his jacket, grabbed his helmet, and left the B and B. He knew his brothers and sisters were going to be pissed that she'd given the control of her estate to him, but he didn't care. They'd betrayed him years ago. He owed them nothing, and certainly not respect.

He felt the curious stares as he rode down Main Street, and couldn't help but remember the day he left Blessings. Back then, no one even noticed he was leaving, because they would have assumed he would be back. The memory was as vivid now as it was the day it happened.

———————

It was the day he was supposed to leave for college when all hell broke loose. By the time the fight was over, his world and his future had been destroyed—betrayed by his own family.

His mother didn't know he was gone or what had happened until she came back from dropping Birdie off at school and found her family in an uproar. She began begging them all to tell the truth about what happened, but Emma, Junior, and Ray clammed up, and his father, Parnell, told his wife the same thing he'd told Hunt.

"What was done was done, so get over it."

What none of them knew was that Hunt left the house and went straight to Savannah to an army recruitment office and signed up. After testing revealed an aptitude for flying, he went from high school to flight school, and was still in flight school when the United States invaded Iraq.

His first deployment was to Fallujah, flying Apache helicopters, and for the next seven years, he went wherever he was deployed. He was shot at nearly every time he flew out—but somehow always managed to get back. He was fighting a war he didn't fully understand, running from a betrayal he couldn't forget.

And then the inevitable happened. After all those years of taking fire and limping back to base, they were shot down.

His gunner died, and the wounds Hunter suffered sent him stateside. It took eight months to fully heal, and then he mustered out.

It took another six months before he found a job doing the only thing he knew how to do—fly choppers. But now, instead of carrying Hellfire missiles, he ferried oil-field workers back and forth to offshore rigs, and had been doing it ever since. It was what he was doing before he got home to find his mother's letter. And now he was here, carrying out his mother's last wishes.

He found the lawyer's office with ease, parked at the curb in front, then dismounted and went inside.

———————

Betty Purejoy was at her desk when the stranger walked in. When she saw the bike helmet he was carrying, she guessed he must have been the rider on the motorcycle she heard outside.

"Good morning. How can I help you?" Betty asked.

"Morning, ma'am. My name is Hunt Knox. Marjorie Knox was my mother."

Betty thought she remembered him as a teenager, but he'd certainly changed.

"Mr. Butterman is expecting you, and I'm so sorry about your mother. I'll let him know you're here."

"Yes, ma'am. Thank you," Hunt said, and sat down as the secretary picked up the phone.

Within moments, a tall fortysomething man with sandy-brown hair emerged, his hand outstretched.

"Mr. Knox, I'm Peanut Butterman. My sympathies on your loss. Please come into my office."

"Just call me Hunt," he said, and took a seat in front of Peanut's desk.

Peanut waved a hand to his secretary.

"Betty, would you please bring me the file on Marjorie Knox?"

Betty stepped into an adjacent room where hard copies of clients' files were kept and pulled the one for Marjorie Knox, then laid it on his desk before leaving them alone.

Peanut quickly scanned the paperwork, which included a cover letter and the will he'd written for her a few years back.

"Okay... You do know she named you the executor?" Peanut asked.

Hunt nodded. "I didn't until I received her letter. It took a few weeks for it to catch up to me," he said, and took the letter out of his pocket and handed it to Peanut to read.

Peanut read it, then handed it back.

"Of course, I'm not going to pry, but she alludes to hard feelings between you and your siblings. However, the will is straightforward. The property is to be sold and proceeds divided five ways, so that shouldn't be an issue."

"I guess you could call it hard feelings," Hunt said. "One of them, or maybe all three of them—they never would admit any of it—stole money I'd saved to go to college. Over $8,000. It took me over four years of mowing yards, raking leaves, and sacking groceries to save it up. And the morning I'm leaving for school, it was gone. We had one hell of a fight about it. But all of my siblings backed each other, and no one would say who'd done it. My dad told me to forget it and figure something else out. Mom wasn't there. She'd taken my little sister to school, so she came home to me gone and everyone clammed up as to what had happened. Mom and I stayed in touch, but I never came back. Until today."

"Good lord," Peanut said. "That must have been devastating. What did you do?"

"Joined the army. Flew Apache helicopters in Iraq until I was shot down. Now, for the most part, I fly oil-field workers back and forth to offshore drilling rigs."

Peanut leaned back in his chair, eyeing the man before him with new respect.

"I know she wanted the house fixed up before it was sold. Do you intend to do what your mother asked?"

Hunt nodded. "I arrived in time to see her before she passed. I told her I'd keep my promise."

"Well, that explains a part of what's in her will. If your siblings have copies, then they already know it. Do you have a copy?"

"Yes, she sent me one," Hunt said.

"Good. In it, she states that once her property is sold, you are to receive eight thousand dollars off the top, and then what's left is to be divided five ways. So keep the receipts of what you spend as you remodel it, and you will receive that back after the sale, as well as the eight thousand, and then what's left will be divided among the five of you."

"They might not like that she did that," Hunt said. "But they won't fight me about it. Now that they're all grown, I doubt they would want that coming out as public knowledge."

Peanut nodded. "Yes, I understand. And as executor, you are to have access to her checking account, although there's not much in it… probably just enough to bury her. I'll get all of the paperwork started for that. Do you plan to live at the house while you're working on it?"

"Yes," Hunt said.

"Do you have a key?"

"There was one in the letter," Hunt said.

"I would advise changing the locks first thing," Peanut said. "If any of them have keys, and they stole before, they may be tempted to do it again before a sale can be held."

"Already thought of that," Hunt said, and then pulled a business card from his pocket. "This has all of my contact info on it. Just let me know when you hold a reading of the will, and anything else I need to do. I've never been an executor of an estate before, so I'm kind of flying blind on procedure."

"I'll be in touch, don't worry," Peanut said.

"Are we through here?" Hunt asked.

"Yes," Peanut said.

"Pleased to meet you," Hunt said. "Thank you for seeing me on a holiday." He was up and out of the room in seconds.

Peanut followed him out and handed Hunt's card to Betty.

"Hang on to this info. We'll need to contact him again later," he said.

"Yes, sir," Betty said. "He's a nice-looking man, but he seems very stern."

"War and betrayal will do that to a man. As soon as you finish what you're doing, go on home, and thank you for coming in this morning," Peanut said, then went back into his office.

———————————

Hunt rode across town, past the park, and then west down Peach Street to the little house at the end of the block. He'd seen this house a million times in his dreams, but it hadn't looked sad and run-down like this.

A black pickup was parked beneath the carport, so he rolled up and parked beside it. He got the house key out of his pocket, but as he headed toward the back door, the hair stood up on the back of his neck. He didn't believe in ghosts, but this house didn't feel like it wanted him there. That was fair.

He didn't want to be here, either, but a promise was a promise.

He unlocked the door and walked into the utility room just off the kitchen, turning on lights as he went. All of the furnishings were here. If it hadn't been for the faint layer of dust all over everything, he could imagine his mom had just stepped out to run an errand and would be back soon.

There was a low spot in the middle of the kitchen floor—probably floor joist issues. The old hardwood flooring was scarred and worn, and the furniture was threadbare. The sight of this neglect made Hunt angry. How could his brothers and sisters let this happen? They were all right here in the same town together.

The year Hunt began high school, they'd remodeled the attic enough to call it a bedroom, and for the first time in his life, he'd had a room of his own. Curious to see what it looked like now, he went straight up the narrow stairwell at the end of the hall and opened the attic door. The single window was bare of curtains or shades, and the dust motes in the air stirred as he moved through the space now filled with boxes of old memories that should have been laid to rest years ago.

The bed he'd slept in was gone. The closet door was missing, the closet empty. Even the rod where his clothes used to hang was gone. It was as if they'd wiped away all memories of him. If only he'd been able to do the same.

He went back downstairs, glancing in his mother's room and accepting it was the only one decent enough to sleep in, then began eyeing all of the things that needed repair.

He went back to the kitchen to check out the appliances. The burners on the gas stove lit, the oven came on. The dishwasher was clean, and the single glass in the top rack told him it had recently been in use and was likely in working condition—something he'd find out later.

The water pressure was good, and the washer and dryer appeared to be in working condition. The refrigerator was the newest appliance in the house, but nearly everything inside it needed to be thrown away. He didn't know for sure how long his mother had been in the hospital, but the carton of milk was over a month out of date, and the single container of peach yogurt had long since expired.

The ice in the bin beneath the icemaker had all frozen together, which meant the electricity must have been off at one time long enough to melt it. Then when the power returned, it froze back. So he took the bin out and dumped the ice in the sink, then put it back beneath the icemaker to start making fresh ice, then dumped everything that was in the freezer and refrigerator into the garbage.

The central heat and air were still working, and they looked newer than he remembered, which was good. There was a big job ahead of him to do this right, but in the long run, it would make a huge difference in the sale of the house. However, this task was going to take tools as well as supplies, so he went out back to the toolshed to see what, if anything, was left.

The light bulb was burned out in the shed, so he left the door open as he went in to look around, and it was just as he feared. There was nothing left in it but a couple of old hammers, a hand saw, and an old sack of roofing nails. Seeing the nails reminded him he needed to check on the condition of the roof as well. He could rent tools and hire help. It wasn't the end of the world, but it was going to be a pain in the ass coping with his family while it happened.

He found a set of car keys hanging on a hook in the kitchen and guessed it was to the truck. If it ran, it would be handy to use while he was hauling stuff to the house to make repairs, so he went out to check. The insurance verification in the glove box was in Marjorie's name. He turned the key to see if it would start, and the engine turned over immediately. So he locked the house and drove to the bed-and-breakfast to pack up his things and check out.

Bud was scanning Hunt's card to pay for his room when Hunt thought about the locks he needed to change.

"Hey, Bud, is there still a locksmith here in town?"

"Yes, there sure is. Mills Locks, next door to Bloomer's Hardware on Main Street. The owner's name is Cecil, but everything is probably closed today."

"Okay...I remember him," Hunt said. "Thanks, and thank you for your hospitality," he said, then carried his bag out to the truck. Out of curiosity, he drove straight to the locksmith, saw the Open sign on the door, and went inside.

The man at the counter looked up.

"Welcome to Mills Locks. I'm Cecil Mills. How can I help you?"

"I need a couple of new locks put on a house I'll be remodeling. Would you be available to do that today?"

"Yeah, sure. Here in town?" Cecil asked.

"Yes, where Marjorie Knox lived. I'm her oldest son, Hunt. I'm going to fix it up some before it's put up for sale."

"Lived?"

Hunt nodded. "She passed away early this morning."

Cecil frowned. "I hadn't heard. I'm real sorry about that. I'm waiting on a customer who's on the way in from his farm, but I can get away around noon, if you don't mind me coming at your lunch hour."

"I'm not on any schedule. You sure you're okay working on New Year's Day? It could wait until tomorrow," Hunt said.

Cecil shrugged. "I've already been called out twice today for emergencies, and my wife is home and sick with the flu. I'd just as soon be here."

"Then noon is fine. Do you know the address?" Hunt asked.

"It's the last house on the right at the end of Peach Street, right?"

Hunt nodded. "Yeah. My Harley and her black pickup will be under the carport."

"Then I'll see you at noon."

"Right," Hunt said, and left the shop, then stopped by the grocery store. He was surprised to see that it was no longer a Piggly Wiggly, and had a new facade and a new name to go with it. The Crown.

Nobody recognized him, which made shopping easy, until he got up front to pay. The cashier who was checking him out kept looking at him, and when he put his credit card in the reader, she finally spoke.

"You sure do look familiar. Are you from around here?" she asked.

Hunt nodded as he put his card back in his wallet. "I'm Hunt Knox. I used to sack groceries here back when it was still the Piggly Wiggly. You're Millie, aren't you?"

"Yes! I'm Millie Garner! I knew you looked familiar. I just heard about your mother's passing. My sympathies to the family," she said.

"Thanks," he said, and began putting his bags back in the shopping cart.

"Do you plan on staying here?" she asked.

"Only long enough to fix up the family house so it can be sold at auction. I promised her I'd do that," Hunt said, then walked out pushing the shopping cart.

By the time he got back to the house and unloaded the groceries, it was getting close to noon. He took off his jacket, then began emptying the sacks and putting up the things he'd just bought.

By the time he was through, Cecil Mills was knocking on his door. He let Cecil in, and then pointed out the locations where new locks were needed.

"There's just the front door, and then a back door in the kitchen."

Cecil nodded. "I'll get those switched out for you and get both locks synced to open with one key. How many keys are you going to want? It comes two keys to a set, so you'll have four."

"That's plenty. I'll be the only one using one here, but when it sells, then that will be handy for the new owners."

"Then I'll get right to work," Cecil said.

"Call out if you need me," Hunt said, then took a notepad and a pen and started in the kitchen, making a list of the things that needed to be fixed.

========

Emma slept in, but when she finally woke up, she was startled to see her husband, Gordon, sitting on the end of the bed staring at her.

"What on earth are you doing?" she muttered, combing her fingers through her hair.

"You were talking in your sleep," he said.

Her heart skipped a beat.

"I had nightmares all night," she said. "My mama died. I'm sad."

"You were crying in your sleep. You were muttering something about a secret, and don't tell Mama."

She stifled a moan. "Well, it doesn't matter now, does it? Mama's dead, and I have to go to the house and get clothes to bury her in."

Gordon stood up. "I thought you and Birdie already did that a week ago. You said Birdie took them to her house."

Emma wiped her hands across her face. "Oh. Yes. You're right. I'm so confused. This is a horrible time for all of us…what with Hunt coming back and all."

He frowned. "Why does it matter if your oldest brother came back for his mother's funeral? It would be weirder if he had not."

Emma was beginning to feel trapped. "Well, because he left us all so long ago, and now—"

Gordon shoved his hands in his pockets, eyeing the flush on his wife's face. He knew she was lying, but wondered why.

"Why did he leave, anyway? Every time I ask, someone always changes the subject."

"I'm not talking about it," Emma said, and got up and went into the bathroom, slamming the door behind her.

"Right! Just like you're changing the subject now," he yelled. "Just for the record, I'll be glad to meet your brother. Maybe he'll be nicer to me than Ray and Junior are."

Emma heard him and groaned, then turned on the shower and stepped in beneath the spray, wishing she could wash away the demons from her past as easily as she washed the sleep from her eyes.

―――――――――

Birdie Knox worked as a bookkeeper at Truesdale's Feed and Seed just off Main in Blessings. She'd gone to work there straight out of high school, and considering the lack of jobs there were in a place this small, she considered herself lucky she was so good with numbers.

Because it was New Year's Day, the feed store was closed, but tomorrow was payday, and since she'd taken the last two days off to be with her mother, she was behind in her work. With only four hours of sleep, she'd gotten up to a cold, quiet apartment, eaten toast and jelly, then taken her coffee with her as she headed to the store.

The building was dark, except for the night-lights, and she left it that way as she went down the hall to her office. Once inside, she turned on the overhead lights, turned up the thermostat, and got to work.

At first it was difficult to focus, because she kept thinking of her mother. There was no longer anyone to call for advice—no shoulder to cry on.

Her mother had been failing and they'd all been so wrapped up in their own lives that they hadn't noticed something was wrong until she began to lose weight, and the bottles of pills on the kitchen counter grew from two to seven, and then more. And then she'd told them she was dying, and to let her be. She'd wanted to stay in her home until she dropped.

They were all in denial and let her call the shots when there were days she was too weak even to feed herself. The house was let go. The laundry piled up. And they'd ignored the dust and pretended the situation would resolve itself.

They were stupid…and selfish, and Birdie felt horrible.

They'd taken their mother's presence for granted. They'd taken her for granted. And so her mama had sent for Hunt. It made Birdie feel sad that they'd failed their mother and their brother, and she still didn't fully understand why it had happened.

Then she glanced at the clock and got down to business. Emma would call when she was ready to go to the funeral home, but until then, Birdie had work to do.

Junior Knox was still asleep when his phone rang. He woke abruptly, thinking it was the hospital calling about their mom, and then remembered she was already gone. He rolled over and grabbed the phone.

"Hello?"

"Junior, it's me. Did I wake you?"

"Hi, Emma. Yeah, but that's okay. So what's up? Did you go by Mom's last night? Was Hunt there?"

"I went by but he wasn't there. His motorcycle was at the bed-and-breakfast," Emma said.

"Oh, well then," Junior said. "So, what do we need to do?"

"I'm not sure. But I just got a text about the reading of Mama's will. Mr. Butterman is holding it at his office tomorrow morning at nine. We're all supposed to be there."

"Yeah, okay. I guess that means Hunt, too."

"I guess."

"Are we supposed to tell him?" Junior asked.

"Butterman just asked me to let the three of you know, and that's all I'm doing. Hunt is not my responsibility."

Junior was silent a little too long. Emma knew immediately what he was thinking, and it made her mad.

"Don't go getting a conscience at this late date," she said. "You were fine with it fifteen years ago, and you will still, by God, be fine with it now. Tell Ray about the reading. I'll tell Birdie."

"Yeah, yeah, I will. Calm down," Junior muttered.

"Calm down? Really?" Emma snapped, then hung up in his ear.

She was in a mood now and didn't want to go to the funeral home in this state, so she went to the kitchen, popped a coffee pod into her coffee maker and pressed Start. She needed food in her stomach before she faced this day, so she put a couple of frozen waffles in the toaster.

Gordon had gone to Granny's Country Kitchen to hang out with the other guys who were home from work today. They had time to kill before all the football games began, and for a while, Emma had the house to herself. If she was lucky, Gordon would go to his buddy's house and watch the games on the new 65-inch HDTV they had given themselves for Christmas. It's all Gordon had talked about since he found out, and she knew he wouldn't be happy until they had one, too. Men were such babies. It didn't occur to her that women were no different. They just had a different set of wants.

Her waffles popped up. Her coffee was done. So she took them to the table and ate in silence, thinking about the upcoming funeral. Thinking about Hunt being back in their lives. She didn't know where he'd been, but it had changed him. He looked hard—even grim. All she knew was that she didn't want to stir anything up again, because this Hunt Knox wouldn't run.

Birdie had just finished payroll and hit Send, routing the money into the employees' respective bank accounts via direct deposits. It felt good to know she would not be the cause of anyone suffering a financial hardship—even if only for a day. But now she wasn't thinking of numbers anymore. She was thinking of Mama again.

She'd been the baby and was still living at home when Ray finally moved out, leaving her and Mama home alone, and she stayed until she turned twenty-one. On the morning of her twenty-first birthday, her mama had come in to wake her up with her special birthday breakfast—a jelly doughnut.

Birdie closed her eyes, still remembering that morning as if it had been yesterday, and her mama's sweet voice as she woke her up.

"Happy birthday, sugar. This morning you are an adult, and I want you to know that if you ever want to be out on your own, I do not expect you to stay here with me. I'm proud of the woman you've become, and I want you to spread your wings and fly. This home is not your forever nest. It's mine. You do what pleases you now. Find a man who will love you forever, but don't ever let him control you."

Birdie sighed. She could almost hear what Mama would be saying to her now.

It's okay to grieve, but do not bury yourself in my grave. That belongs to me.

Birdie wiped away tears. God, but she was going to miss her. Then she turned off her computer, grabbed her coat and her purse, and left, turning off the lights in her office as she went. She was just getting into her car when her cell phone rang. It was Emma.

"Hello."

"Hi, Sis, where are you?"

"Just leaving the office. I had to do payroll," Birdie said.

"I think it's time we head to the funeral home. I'll meet you at your apartment to get Mama's clothes. We can go together from there."

"Okay, I'll be on the way there now. See you soon," Birdie said.

CHAPTER 3

IT WAS HABIT THAT MADE BIRDIE TURN DOWN THE BLOCK THAT would take her past their old house. But when she saw Hunt's motorcycle there, and the van from Mills Locks, she slowed down, then on impulse braked and pulled up in the drive behind the old pickup to see what was going on.

Cecil Mills was on his knees at the front door, replacing the doorknob, when she walked up the steps.

"Hi, Cecil," she said.

"Oh, hi, Birdie. Hunt's inside."

"Thanks," she said, and slipped by him as she went inside, then paused in the living room and called out. "Hello?"

"In the kitchen," Hunt said.

She was hesitant to face the angry stranger he'd been at the hospital. She was barely ten years old when he left, so her memories of him were vague. She paused in the doorway, uncertain of what he'd say.

Hunt wouldn't have recognized this Birdie as his little sister. She'd grown up to be a pretty young woman, but she was still one of *them*, and he didn't know where he stood with any of them anymore.

"What's going on?" Birdie said.

"Getting ready to fix the place up to sell," Hunt said.

"Changing out the locks, too?" she asked.

"On advice of Mom's lawyer," Hunt said.

She blinked.

"Why?"

"I guess so people can't come and go and carry stuff off that doesn't belong to them."

"Are you talking about us?"

He shrugged.

"But it was Mama's stuff. Who else would it belong to but us?" Birdie asked.

"And now it belongs to five people. Not just one. And while we're asking questions, didn't anyone ever come in here and clean for her after she got sick? And what happened to the middle of the kitchen floor? It sags. A lot."

Birdie's cheeks reddened with anger. "We checked on her. And why do you think you have the right to criticize? You went off and left everyone fifteen years ago and never came back. What's that all about?"

Hunt's eyes narrowed. "You don't remember? Any of it?"

"Remember what? You were here when Mama left to take me to school, and when I came home that evening you were gone and everyone was acting like something bad had happened."

"Oh, something bad happened all right. Someone in this house stole my college money. Eight thousand dollars I'd worked and saved for four years, and the morning I'm leaving for college, it was gone. Someone in this house took it. They all knew who did it, but they covered up for the guilty one, and Dad told me what was done was done... to get over it and figure something else out, so I did. Mom didn't know what happened, either, but she knew where I went. She always knew. The fact that she never shared that with any of you is telling."

Birdie was stunned.

"Oh, Hunt. Oh my God. I didn't know. Where did you go?"

"To war. Now, I've got a lot to do to keep the promise I made. I'll be staying here until I've finished, and then the house will go up for sale, as stated in Mom's will."

"You've seen the will?"

"She sent me a copy, along with a key to the house and a request to get it fixed up to sell."

Birdie's eyes welled. "I'm so sorry."

Hunt shrugged. "You didn't take it. One of them did. So you don't have anything to apologize for. And just for the record, I didn't come here expecting a warm welcome. I am a bad reminder of someone else's sin."

Then he turned his back on her and went back to work measuring the kitchen floor.

Birdie's heart ached for him in a way she couldn't put into words. But she offered what she knew.

"About the floor. Blessings flooded a while back during a hurricane. Water never came into the house, but it was beneath it. That might be why it's sagging. I guess I never noticed."

Hunt sighed. Her voice was trembling. Dammit.

"It's okay, kid. I'll fix it," he said.

Birdie turned on her heel and left.

Hunt closed his eyes briefly, gathering himself and his emotions, and then went back to work. At least now they'd all know he was in the house, and why.

He got a text from his boss, expressing his sympathies, and after he answered it, noticed he also had one from Butterman, the lawyer. So the reading of the will was at nine tomorrow morning. That should be interesting.

———————

Birdie cried all the way to her apartment, then went in to gather up the things they needed to take to the funeral home. She was still in tears when Emma knocked on the door and let herself in.

"It's me!" she said, and tossed her purse on the sofa.

Birdie came out of her bedroom, red-eyed and glaring.

"Oh my God, honey! What's wrong?"

"Hunt was at Mama's house, and so was Cecil Mills. He's changing the locks on the house. Hunt's going to stay there to fix up the house before it's put up for sale."

Emma frowned. "Why does he think he has the right to change out locks and keep us out of our own mama's house?"

Birdie turned on her with a vengeance. "Maybe because Mama sent for him? Maybe because Mama sent him a copy of her will and asked him to do it? Maybe because he doesn't trust anyone not to steal things that don't belong to them? Maybe because someone in our family already stole his college money from him, and he has no reason to believe we have morals or a conscience?"

Emma froze. "He told you that?"

"Not intentionally...I challenged him about it, and he just reminded me of what had already come to pass, thinking I already knew."

"Jesus," Emma muttered.

Birdie swiped at the tears on her face. "Who did it? And why, for the love of all that's holy, would the rest of you protect a thief? I am so shocked and so hurt for him right now that I don't really even want to look at you. Mama's clothes are in a bag on the sofa. Take them and go."

Emma picked up the sack. "Just so you know, there's a reading of the will at Peanut Butterman's office tomorrow morning. Nine a.m. We're all supposed to be there," she mumbled, and started out the door.

Birdie followed her, then slammed it shut behind her.

Emma flinched, and when she heard Birdie turn the lock, she swallowed past the lump in her throat. This wasn't going to get better. Mama wasn't here anymore to be the wall between them and Hunt. He didn't have to play nice anymore.

She got back in her car and headed to the funeral home to give them the clothes. They still had to get through a funeral in some semblance of family unity—or not.

———

Ava woke up just after 3:00 p.m., trying to remember why today felt different, and then she remembered.

Hunt Knox came home, and Marjorie died.

She rolled over onto her back, snug beneath her covers, thinking about the next two days. She didn't often have two days off in a row, and she was looking forward to a little time to herself. She wondered if Hunt was staying at his old home, and then decided if he was, she was going to bake him a pecan pie. It would be a simple gesture of kindness to the family during this time, and she remembered it used to be his favorite.

She also had laundry to do, groceries to shop for, and bills to pay, so she got up and headed for the shower. As soon as she was dressed, she stripped her bed, tossed the bedding in the washer, and started her day by making a grocery list.

Later, she made herself a sandwich and a glass of sweet tea and read the local newspaper while she ate, only vaguely aware of the washer chugging away in the little alcove off the kitchen. As soon as she was finished, she grabbed her jacket and purse, stuffed the list in her pocket, and headed out the door. It wouldn't hurt to drive by Marjorie's place. She'd seen Hunt walk in with a biker helmet, so she guessed he was riding a motorcycle. If it was parked at his old home-place, then she would know he was staying there.

A few minutes later, she turned down Peach Street and saw the black truck. But when she got closer and saw a big black and silver Harley parked between the truck and the house, she knew he was there. So now she knew where to find him, and drove past without stopping, heading for the Crown to get groceries. If she hurried, she could get that pie made and over to Hunt before suppertime.

Also by Sharon Sala

Blessings, Georgia